Also by Lucy Score

KNOCKEMOUT SERIES

Things We Never Got Over

*Things We Hide
from the Light*

Things We Left Behind

BENEVOLENCE SERIES

Pretend You're Mine

Finally Mine

Protecting What's Mine

RILEY THORN SERIES

*Riley Thorn and the
Dead Guy Next Door*

*Riley Thorn and the
Corpse in the Closet*

*Riley Thorn and the
Blast from the Past*

**SINNER AND
SAINT SERIES**

Crossing the Line

Breaking the Rules

**WELCOME
HOME SERIES**

The Christmas Fix

BLUE MOON SERIES

No More Secrets

Fall into Temptation

The Last Second Chance

Not Part of the Plan

Holding on to Chaos

The Fine Art of Faking It

Where It All Began

The Mistletoe Kisser

**BOOTLEG
SPRINGS SERIES**

Whiskey Chaser

Sidecar Crush

Moonshine Kiss

Bourbon Bliss

Gin Fling

Highball Rush

STANDALONES

By a Thread

Forever Never

Rock Bottom Girl

The Worst Best Man

The Price of Scandal

Undercover Love

Heart of Hope

MR. FIXER UPPER

LUCY SCORE

Bloom books

Copyright © 2017, 2023 by Lucy Score
Cover and internal design © 2023 by Sourcebooks
Cover design and illustration by Elizabeth Turner Stokes

Sourcebooks and the colophon are registered trademarks of
Sourcebooks. Bloom Books is a trademark of Sourcebooks.

Published by Bloom Books, an imprint of Sourcebooks
P.O. Box 4410, Naperville, Illinois 60567-4410
(630) 961-3900
sourcebooks.com

Originally published in 2017 by That's What She Said, Inc.

Cataloging-in-Publication data is on file with the Library of Congress.

Printed and bound in the United States of America.
VP 10 9 8 7 6 5 4 3 2

*To Adam and Abbie, may I one day be fortunate
enough to pay for your college education.
Or at least a really nice vacation.*

SPRING

CHAPTER

1

Paige St. James crossed her long legs restlessly under the glossy wood of the conference table. She wasn't cut out for marathon meetings with multipage agendas. The longer the suit with the receding hairline and the PowerPoint presentation droned on, the antsier she felt. She had things to do, and listening to a bunch of network drones salivate over how to milk more ratings out of an already hit show didn't get her any further down her to-do list.

"What we really need is to see some emotion out of Gannon," the suit announced. The next slide appeared with Gannon King's sex god face and a bar graph. Paige was pretty sure none of the handful of women in the room were looking at the graph. "That's what the female demographic is clamoring for."

"To be clear, you're not talking about his usual emotion. Correct?" Eddie Garraza, the man on her right, was the executive producer and ringleader of the three-ring circus known as the reality show *Kings of Construction*. In a room full of designer suits and shoes that cost more than most people's first cars, Eddie was wearing his trademark khakis and rumpled button-down. His trusty moccasins tapped an incessant beat under the table.

Paige hid her snicker behind a cough.

Gannon King's usual emotion was fiery temper that singed anyone within a forty-foot radius. A builder by trade, he was an artist with woodwork, producing furniture pieces that were one-of-a-kind works of art. The female viewership worshipped Gannon's shirtless physique, but Paige saved her lust for the furniture, not the man. With that talent came a passionate, argumentative, stubborn attitude that often held up shoots and pissed Paige off.

"We want to see the human side of him. Cat plays great in the ratings, but Gannon needs to soften up a little. Viewers will eat it up."

Cat King was Gannon's equally attractive and talented twin sister. Younger by two minutes, she shared Gannon's long-lashed hazel eyes but had miles of California blond tresses where her brother had dark hair usually worn shaved short. Where he was abrasive, Cat was smooth. Where Gannon argued, she orchestrated compromise. Without their uncanny family resemblance, it would be difficult to make the familial connection by behavior alone.

"Paige." The man in the too tight Hugo Boss—Raymond? Ralph?—gestured at her with the presentation remote. "You've gotten into a few skirmishes with Gannon. We're looking to you to rile him up and catch him on camera. You know he's a softie for kids. See if you can push him over the edge there. There's a five-thousand-dollar bonus in it for you if there's tears from him."

She gave a nod, acknowledging that she'd heard the man without actually agreeing to anything. It was true. There had been more than a few on-set arguments between them in season one of the home renovation reality show. Gannon seemed to instinctively know what buttons to push to send her into an internal maelstrom. Given the instant success the show had been, the network had ordered a twelve-episode second season, which would give her plenty of time to get into it with the brash host.

If she were that kind of field producer.

But as much as she needed an extra $5,000, she wasn't going to set up Gannon and push him over the edge or stir up his emotions for fun. He might be an asshole, but he was an extremely talented asshole. And in her heart of hearts, his open hatred of "network bullshit" was something that she could respect.

Not that she'd ever tell him that.

Eddie jabbed her under the table with the capped end of his ballpoint pen. "We'll do our best," Eddie told Raymond-Ralph, his face a perfect poker mask while Paige's fingers flew over the laptop, making notes.

Behind the same wire-rimmed glasses he'd worn since the mid-1990s, Eddie never gave up what he was thinking with unnecessary facial expressions or body language. He spoke plainly and knew when a battle wasn't worth fighting. That was why, in an industry of perpetual youth chasers, Eddie rocked a head of fluffy silver hair and had never been near a Botox needle.

The presentation moved on, and Paige's gaze wandered to the view of New York through the wall of glass. They were downtown, six floors up at the production company's headquarters. Summit-Wingenroth Productions sounded like a company

3

with a long, respectable history, but it was founded five years prior by a former reality star and made its profits churning out dozens of barely unscripted shows for the networks.

Kings was the only show in the company's lengthy credits that Paige could stomach. They helped people, and that—to her—was the endgame. For Summit-Wingenroth, it was a schmaltzy hook to reel in an audience and sell advertising.

The double doors to the conference room opened, drawing everyone's attention. Gannon King, larger than life, strode into the room. Cat breezed in behind her brother, smiling warmly at everyone gathered. Smoothly, Raymond or Ralph clicked to the next slide, and Gannon's face disappeared behind another chart of audience demographics. Paige turned her attention back to the laptop screen in front of her and refused to stare.

Gannon was the kind of man who wrestled your attention from you as soon as he walked into a room. Built like a Norse god, his broad shoulders and muscled pecs gave way to a taut abdomen that had Twitter lighting up every time he took his shirt off on camera. The gray Henley he wore today stretched across his chest and molded to his impressive physique. A trio of leather cords wrapped around his left wrist.

Disheveled as usual but in the careless, confident way, his hair was a little longer on top than last season. Paige bit her lip. She was a field producer, not some lovestruck teenage fan. And he was the narcissistic bane of her professional existence.

"There are our rising stars." The suit's tone had an extra layer of phony to it that had Paige barely controlling an eye roll.

"Sorry to interrupt," Cat said without a hint of apology in her tone. "But we were in the neighborhood and thought we'd stop in."

"You're welcome to join us. We were just going over the demographics."

And ways to break your brother on camera, Paige added silently.

Gannon ignored the pleasantries and stalked to the coffee station. He poured himself a mug—black—and leaned against the counter. Cat took a seat near the head of the table and stared raptly at the presenter until he turned a bright shade of fuchsia and fumbled over the word "ratings."

Paige grinned. Cat was a master at manipulating men. What looked like a pretty smile and keen interest was actually a calculated move to disarm the enemy and get her what she wanted. The more she was underestimated, the more she was able to get away with before her victims realized they'd been victimized. Paige wondered what Cat was after this time.

Still smiling, she glanced in Gannon's direction and cursed herself when she found him watching her. He must have taken her expression as an invitation because he rounded the table to take the empty seat next to her.

The denim of his worn, ripped jeans brushed her forearm as he took his seat. Paige immediately yanked her arm off the armrest and put her hand in her lap. Once seated, he shoved his long sleeves up, revealing a hint of new tattoo on his forearm, and settled in, leaning on the arm closest to her.

She could smell sawdust and noted he was wearing his scarred work boots. He had probably spent most of the morning in his workshop in Brooklyn before Cat dragged him here for whatever scheme she was cooking up.

Why did he have to be so drop-dead gorgeous and so profoundly talented? It wasn't fair.

He leaned in closer. "What's not fair?" he whispered. His breath was warm on her neck. Paige turned to look at him, finding him entirely too close. Was he a mind reader now?

He nodded toward her screen.

It's not fair. It's not fair.

Crap. Her subconscious was trying to make itself public. Paige bit the inside of her cheek. She shrugged. "Carpal tunnel exercise." She wiggled her fingers, committing to the lie.

"Sure it is, princess."

His smirk made it clear that he wasn't fooled. And the "princess" pushed just the right buttons with her. He'd called her that ever since an unexpected downpour last season had soaked her to the bone. One of the volunteers happened to have her daughter's gym bag with her, and Paige had spent the rest of the day into the night in a pair of volleyball shorts and a bedazzled too tight T-shirt that said *Princess* across the chest. As soon as Gannon found out the nickname irked her, he became steadfast in his regular use of it.

Paige deleted the lines and tried to tune back in to the speaker, who was finally approaching the important part of the meeting. The families that would be featured on the show this season.

"Our first family for the season is the Russes." A slide showing an older couple surrounded by kids of all ages filled the screen. "Phil and Delia Russe have three kids and nine grandkids." He clicked to the next slide, which showed the exterior of a nondescript commercial building. "Twenty years ago, they opened a soup kitchen in town and have served up something like one million meals. The entire family still volunteers there." Another slide, this one showing a shabby-chic office with the Russes accepting a giant check from two men in suits. "Five years ago, they added a job placement service to the operation. So we've got formerly homeless ready to volunteer, all the kids and grandkids will be on hand, and the rest of the community is on board. It'll be a schmaltz fest. Perfect season opener."

Paige purposely left "schmaltz fest" out of her notes.

"We don't have an update on exactly how extensive the renovation will be. I'll send out a complete project scope when I have it," Paige volunteered.

Gannon cleared his throat, and every gaze turned to him.

Kicking back in his chair, he swiveled toward the screen. "My guys touched base with the local crews and the township zoning board. There's enough room in the back to add an addition for a first-floor master, and then we can reconfigure the front for an open concept. The areas of concern are the roof and the forty-year-old electric. Both are going to need to be replaced. The permits shouldn't be an issue."

Gannon King was speaking in a meeting. Willingly. And helpfully. Wonders never ceased. Of course, he was also making her look like an out-of-touch idiot.

The three women around the table were hanging on his every word. The half dozen men were nodding thoughtfully as if he had just delivered the Gettysburg Address. Paige spared a glance at Gannon, who cocked an eyebrow and opened his hands. "I can play nice, princess," he said quietly.

"I didn't say you couldn't."

"I can hear you judging me."

Ass. She bet he didn't hear that.

"I'll admit to judging you if you stop calling me princess for the season."

Gannon leaned in. Again, too close. There were flecks of gold in his eyes that caught the light. The scar through his eyebrow made him look dangerous, rakish. "Yeah, that's not gonna happen."

CHAPTER

2

B y the time the meeting was over, Paige's empty stomach was complaining, and she was dying to get away from Gannon. A glance at her watch told her she had half an hour to find something to stuff in her face before she and Eddie hooked up with the location manager to get details on the first three shows.

She rose to pack up her laptop and papers, but Gannon remained seated at her elbow. She felt his eyes on her and tried to ignore it, but the searing heat finally broke her.

"Do you need something?" she asked primly.

His mouth quirked into a crooked grin. "I've never seen you in a skirt before. It's…" His gaze skimmed her. "Nice."

Gannon had seen her in everything but professional clothing. On the road, the crew uniform was jeans, T-shirts, and any layers that could be added or removed. When they were filming, Paige considered herself lucky if she found time to swipe a coat of mascara on her lashes before heading to the set in the predawn hours. There were some benefits to being behind the camera.

The tingle on her skin told her that her legs would blush if they could under his scrutiny. She resisted the urge to tug her pencil skirt down. "So glad you approve," she said coolly. "See you on location."

She scurried out the door at a pace she hoped suggested busy but not fleeing for life even though she could feel his eyes boring into her with every step.

"Paige!" Cat caught her at the door. "Hey, wanna grab lunch?"

Paige peeked at her watch. "What can we consume in twenty-five minutes?"

Cat wrinkled her nose, and then her face lit up.

"Hot dog cart," they said in unison.

Paige laughed. "What about your brother?" The conference room door was closing behind them but not before she caught Gannon's voice rumbling over two words that gave her the chills: Meeghan Traxx.

"He's got business to take care of," Cat said with a wave of her hand. "Let's go eat terrible things and catch up."

Paige stashed her bag and papers in an empty cubicle, and they took the elevator down. They found a vendor around the corner and headed into the park, loaded hot dogs in hand. The early spring sunshine immediately lifted Paige's spirits.

"Oh sweet Jesus, this is delicious," Cat said, rolling her eyes heavenward.

Paige muttered in agreement as she worked her way through a mouthful of sauerkraut. "I don't know how you eat like that and look the way you do," Paige grumbled. Cat had two inches on Paige's five foot seven and was built like a damn ballerina.

"Please. Pot, kettle."

"Yeah, I'm going to spend an hour and a half in the gym tonight regretting this. You're probably going to go home and eat six pounds of fettuccine."

Cat patted her flat stomach. "Good genes and liposuction."

"You're such a liar," Paige accused.

"I've been assured that it will catch up with me, and when it does, I'll look like the adorable Italian meatball my noni is."

"As long as it evens out in the end," Paige waxed philosophically.

Cat shot rapid-fire questions as they walked and ate. "So how was your break? Holidays good?"

"Yep. How about yours?"

"Crazy and hectic but awesome. Are you seeing anyone yet?"

Paige rolled her eyes.

"I'll take that as a big fat no." Cat's platinum ponytail swung rhythmically. In her skinny jeans, boots, and tunic sweater, she looked as if she had just strolled away from a photo shoot.

"You know what my schedule's like. I'm too busy for men." Paige crumpled her napkin and tossed it in a trash can as they passed.

Cat shoved the last bite in her mouth. "Your priorities are out of whack."

"I can't understand you with all that meat in your mouth," Paige teased.

"Oh!" Cat high-fived her. "Nicely done. Now, back to me pressuring you to date or at least get laid. You're a beautiful young woman, Paige. It's a crime to keep all this"—she gestured at Paige's chest—"buttoned up."

"You're ridiculous. Please tell me you're not seeing anyone right now."

Cat had a history of falling head over heels for the occasional unworthy man who proceeded to break her heart or piss her off. The whole cycle usually lasted around three weeks, and when it happened during filming, havoc was wreaked.

"Nope. Mama's going through a dry spell. Want to be lesbians?"

"Well, it *would* be more convenient on the road," Paige mused. "Which side of the bed do you sleep on?"

"The middle."

"Nope. It would never work. I can't be crowded under the covers."

Cat sighed. "Fine. I'll go back to men. Distrustful and confusing though they may be."

"Speaking of confusing, what's with you and Gannon crashing the production meeting?"

"We're strong-arming for a raise for the production crew and our guys."

"My dwindling bank account thanks you," Paige said. Gannon and Cat had very strong principles about spreading the wealth. The production company had offered them both astronomical raises for the second season, and Paige wasn't surprised that they wanted to make sure everyone else was taken care of too.

"I heard Gannon mention Meeghan on our way out."

Cat mimed vomiting. "Gross. Let's not talk about that overinflated, poor excuse for a human being."

Meeghan Traxx was the network's biggest star. She had the blondest hair, the biggest breasts, and an infamously super-sized ego. A designer with two of her own shows, she was also Gannon King's girlfriend.

Crews talked. And Paige had heard enough to know that Meeghan was considered a monster on and off set. As obnoxious as Gannon could be, even he didn't deserve Meeghan.

"Does she show up at your family functions? Like, did she bring some gold-plated designer sweet potato side dish to the King Thanksgiving?" Paige pressed.

Cat snorted. "God, no! We've never met her. Gannon's never even talked about her. Which is a good thing because if he were all, 'Meeghan is so amazing,' I'd be all, 'I'm taking you to the ER to get a head scan because you obviously have a head injury.'"

Paige laughed. "I'm just now realizing how much I missed you."

Cat wrapped her in a one-armed hug. "Mutual, babe."

"Oh my gosh! It's really you!" A woman in a pink jogging suit squealed at Cat, hands fluttering. "My husband is *not* going to believe this! Cat King just walking around the park like a regular person." She started digging through her giant purse.

Cat winked at Paige. "It's always nice to meet a fan of the show. Would you like a picture?"

The woman triumphantly rescued her phone from the depths of her bag. "I would *love* one!" She shoved the phone at Paige. "Is your brother here?" The woman's head swiveled from side to side fast enough for a low-grade whiplash.

"Just me today."

The woman sighed. "It's probably a good thing. I'd faint if I met him."

Paige grinned as Cat good-naturedly accepted the bear hug turned headlock. She took a couple shots, making sure she captured the excitement and Cat's best side.

The woman unhanded Cat and immediately flipped through the pictures. "This is so exciting!" She hurried off without a backward glance.

Cat grinned. "How long before she realizes she didn't say goodbye?"

"Two blocks," Paige predicted. The star factor hadn't hit until halfway through the show's first season, making stardom still new to the Kings. "Is being recognized still fun?" Paige asked.

Cat rolled her shoulders. "I signed up for it. Might as well embrace it."

"Better than your brother has." Gannon had an offseason run-in with an aggressive photographer who wouldn't leave Cat alone at an awards show. The incident had been captured on tape, and though he was mostly heralded for acting as the protective big brother, the incident left a slight smudge that the network was eager to erase.

"Gannon just has a little trouble overcoming his protective instincts," Cat said. "He always has." She glanced at the gigantic watch on her slim wrist. "I guess it's time we get you back for the rest of your thrilling meetings."

Paige sighed. "It's going to be a good season."

———

Hours later, after three more meetings and a conference call, an exhausted Paige let herself into her apartment. She peeled off her heels and tossed them in the direction of the couch. With her roommate, Becca, out of town on a shoot, she didn't stop there. The skirt and blouse came next as she padded down the shabby hallway to her bedroom. Big enough for only a full-size bed and a dresser, it was still home.

Paige dropped facedown onto the bed and stretched out.

Shooting started next week. They would fly into Columbia, South Carolina, and spend a day laying the groundwork, verifying permits to begin shooting, and then the chaos would begin.

It was hard work with long days. But the experience was invaluable, and she'd be a damned liar if she didn't admit to getting a little teary-eyed when shooting wrapped and they turned the keys over to the family. As greedy as the production side of things felt, they were still giving a deserving family a home they could be proud of.

Of course, she made sure no one ever saw the tearful side of her. She was on set to do a job and do it well. Eddie depended on her to keep things under control and on budget. And Gannon King challenged her at every turn.

She sighed into her pillow. Soon she would be able to take that experience and apply it to something more important, more personal. And far, far away from Gannon.

CHAPTER
3

The Russes reminded Paige of a South Carolina–based Mr. and Mrs. Claus. With wispy white hair and ruddy cheeks, the two were rarely not smiling. The joy appeared to be genetic, spilling over into the second and third generations. It was a full house, and Paige was wrangling the chaos.

"So tomorrow," Paige said, handing Phil and Delia copies of the layman-friendly call sheet, "we'll be arriving around seven a.m. to set everything up with the intent to start shooting no later than eight. That means we need everyone"—she circled her finger around the crowded living room—"here by seven thirty for Gannon and Cat when they come knocking."

The "surprise" scene was a bit of not-so-real reality. The families already knew they were chosen by the show. They had already spent hours on the phone with various producers and assistants, nailing down the details of their backstory, their cause, and what issues needed to be resolved with their homes.

In the twenty-four hours before shooting, they worked with more crew to pack up items that weren't necessary to and in the way of shooting. Everything was shipped off to a local storage facility for the duration of the shoot.

The families were strictly instructed by Paige to be at the home at the predetermined time so they could all answer the door with proper enthusiasm. They protected the slim surprise factor by making sure the first time families met with the Kings was on camera and that the crowd of volunteers that appeared was full of friends and neighbors.

It was a lot of preparation for a two-minute door-knocking scene that was usually shot nearly a dozen times.

"Okay, kids," Paige said, turning her attention to the grand-kids in the room. "Tomorrow, we're going to need to see your best surprise faces." She pointed at a little girl with a skinned elbow and freckles on her nose. "Molly, let's see your surprise face."

Molly obliged with an expression of utter shock, and Paige applauded.

A little boy with eyes the color of denim tugged at her hand.

"Are you going to fix Pop-Pop's house?" The face was a killer, all big eyes and round cheeks. He was definitely going to get some screen time.

Paige knelt down. "That's the plan, Trevor. Is there anything special you think we should fix?"

He nodded, his expression earnest. "Pop-Pop likes popcorn."

Paige pursed her lips. "Okay. So popcorn for Pop-Pop."

A lithe brunette in a Gamecocks sweatshirt laughed and joined them. Paige searched her memory banks for a name. *Susan*, she recalled. Phil and Delia's middle child. "When Trevor has sleepovers at Pop-Pop and Grammy's, they make popcorn and watch movies. But Dad's air popper broke last month, so it's been nothing but microwavable stuff."

"It's gross," Trevor sighed.

Paige nodded. "Well, I'll see what we can do to solve Pop-Pop's popcorn problem. Now, what happens when you see the TV cameras?"

"I pretend they're not there," Trevor recited.

"Good job. So the only thing left—and this is really important—what kind of surprised face can you make?"

His solemn expression transformed into one of terror, eyes wide, mouth agape.

"Yeah, pretty sure that's *scared* surprised. How about *happy* surprised?"

———

Paige made it back to the motel before eleven and considered the day a success. Everyone was briefed. All the unnecessaries had been moved to Big Bob's Climate Controlled Self Storage. And the local crew was ready to start demo as soon as they were cleared to go. They were as prepared as possible, even though she knew by experience that every shoot was destined to run into disaster regardless of preparedness.

She changed out of her jeans and pulled on a pair of sleep shorts and a tank before yanking back the bedspread and settling back against the pillows with her laptop.

Paige rechecked the call sheet and returned a few nonemergency emails that had trickled in while she was on set. She checked the time and texted Cat.

Paige: Make it to the motel?

The reply was instantaneous.

17

Cat: Here and ready to party!

Paige: Maybe you should go to bed instead. Early call tomorrow.

Cat: Yes, Mom.

Paige smirked. Some looked at her job as that of a glorified babysitter. But to her, she was the details keeper. She was double-checking the releases and updating her notes when her stomach grumbled.

The chicken sandwich she'd scarfed down in two minutes flat had been hours ago. She ignored the internal rumbling and got up to inventory her set bag. Phone charger, bandages, a digital camera and charger, pens, paper, iPad and charger, fifty dollars cash, and a company credit card, all in their rightful places.

The next growl from her stomach was echoed by a dull ache. Paige sighed. A vending machine snack on her first night did not light a beacon of hope for the healthy season she had planned, but there would be no going to bed with her stomach gurgling in protest.

She grabbed her room key and change and followed the nauseating orange-and-red hallway carpet to the vending and ice nook.

It was a toss-up between peanut butter crackers and a single-serve bag of popcorn. Paige went with the popcorn in honor of Pop-Pop. She already had an email in to see if there was room in the budget for a theater-style popcorn maker.

She bent over to wrestle the bag free from the machine.

"Aren't you the one who always says those machines are filled with poison?"

Paige jumped and swiveled.

Gannon was leaning against the doorway. He wore a leather

jacket over well-fitting jeans and a T-shirt. His hair was shaved short now.

She frowned and crossed her arms over her chest, suddenly feeling very naked. "Did you *just* get here?" Gannon was notorious for arriving too close to the comfort of Paige's carefully crafted schedule.

"I'm here, aren't I? And don't change the subject." He strolled in and grabbed the popcorn out of her hand. Opening the bag, he shook out a handful and handed the rest back to her. "I catch you sneaking in here after all those lectures to everyone last year about the dangers of living off vending machines."

Paige had the good grace to look guilty. "It was a late night, and I haven't had a chance to stock up on nonpoisonous snacks."

Gannon popped a kernel into his mouth. "It's nice to know you're human, princess." He walked out of the room without a backward glance.

"You have an early call tomorrow," Paige yelled after him. "Don't be late!"

CHAPTER

4

He was late. Not late enough to hold anything up but enough that Paige shot him her ice princess look when he strolled past with two dozen doughnuts for the crew. Gannon hid his grin when she turned her back on him and stormed off, her windbreaker rustling in indignation.

He wasn't as big of an asshole as he made himself out to be, but damn if he didn't like getting a rise out of her. It made the frigid early morning calls, the long hours in downpours and drywall dust, and the general bullshit from the network more tolerable when he could see that little tic in her jaw, the blaze in her blue eyes.

She never once lost her temper, a fact that fascinated him. Gannon came from loud, passionate Italian stock that wasn't afraid to smash a plate to make a statement. Paige, on the other hand, systematically choked down any temper and, with frosty efficiency, made him dance like a fucking puppet.

He paused to check out the facade of the house they'd be essentially gutting. The weathered two-story jammed in between two other homes was just the kind of project he liked to sink his teeth into. The house was showing its age in sagging gutters, dingy siding, missing shingles, and from what he remembered from photos of the interior, decor that paid a horrendous tribute to the 1970s.

The tight lot would be an issue, he mused. But the neighbors on either side were big fans of the Russe family and had volunteered to help with the show, which usually meant no noise complaints. Plus, to be extra safe, Paige had worked her magic to get a stipend to put both families up in a hotel for the week of the shoot.

Gannon found his sister huddled under layers of coat and sweatshirt, guzzling an iced coffee on a chair. She was flipping through the day's call sheet while crew buzzed around her, laying cable and erecting pop-ups.

"Morning, Cat." He flipped the lid on a doughnut box and watched her eyes light up when they spotted the Boston cream.

"Best brother ever," she said, taking a decadent bite. She checked her watch. "You're late."

He grinned.

She gave him a bland look. "You were ready to go when I left. You could have gotten a ride with me."

He shrugged, all innocence. "I had doughnuts to pick up."

"It's the first day of shooting for the season, and you're already torturing poor Paige," Cat complained. "Why do you mess with her?"

"She's too buttoned up. One of these days, I'm going to push her over the edge, and she's going to have to scream at me and call me an asshole to my face instead of saying it in her head and pulling the ice princess routine."

"You're totally into her," Cat accused.

"I am not!" He wasn't. His gaze tracked to Paige where she had her head together with the local contractor they were using for the project and a production assistant. Her hair—a rich brown cut in a chin-length bob—was pulled back in a stubby ponytail and fed through the back of a battered ball cap. She wore jeans, work boots, and a shapeless windbreaker probably over one of the T-shirts she favored.

Cat raised an eyebrow. "Well, it's probably a good thing if you're not. Looks like the contractor's son has the hots for her, and I'd love to see her get laid."

Gannon's head whipped around on his neck as if it were possessed. He zeroed in on the lanky guy in ripped-up jeans and a Clawson Construction fleece who strutted up to Paige and the GC. He couldn't hear what he said, but the guy had Paige laughing and looking up at him as if he was a fucking comedian.

"Yep. Good thing you're not into her," Cat said, hopping off the chair and patting his shoulder.

Muttering under his breath, Gannon decided to muscle in on their little chat. He was the host of the show. He should know what was going on. He stepped over cables and around one of the two production assistants their little crew boasted.

"Hey, Mike, right?" he said, offering his hand to the burly, bearded contractor. "I'm Gannon. We talked on the phone."

Mike's ham-sized fist closed around his in a hearty handshake. "Good to finally meet you, Mr. King," Mike said with the quick grin of an actual morning person.

"It's just Gannon."

"I was just telling Paige here how excited we are to get started. The Russes are personal friends, good people."

"Well, Paige will make sure we do a good job for your

22

friends," Gannon promised, sliding an arm around Paige's shoulders and hauling her up against his side. She stiffened under his touch. "She does a great job puppet mastering chaos."

"We've certainly been impressed so far," Mike agreed. "This is my son, Brandon," he said, jerking his thumb at the guy in the fleece.

"Brandon." Gannon offered his hand. He put a little extra power into the shake. "Paige and I are looking forward to working with you both. Clawson Construction has a solid rep."

"What the hell was that?" Paige hissed, sliding out from under his arm when the Clawsons headed over to talk with their crew.

"What was what?" Gannon asked, all innocence.

She didn't answer him. Someone needing something chirped in the earpiece of her headset. Paige adjusted the microphone and told them she'd be right there. "Behave yourself," she said, pointing a warning finger at Gannon.

———

They had a preshoot meeting for the production team and both the Clawson and the King crews. Director Andy Sanders walked everyone through what they planned to accomplish that morning and then Paige took her crew aside to cover the finer points. It was a good, solid team. Traveling reality shows couldn't afford the expense or headache of large crews, which meant much of their team played two or three roles to cover all their bases.

They had three camera operators, Tony, Ricardo—Rico for short—and Louis. Felicia was the sound mixer knocking on twenty years of experience. Mel and Sam were the fresh-faced production assistants who doubled as camera assistants and generally indispensable gophers.

Paige covered all the loose ends that were left over, acting as production coordinator and assistant director. Andy liked to joke that she knew more than he did and should have been named director. It wasn't really a joke though. It was tough to break into the boys' club, not that Paige would let that stop her. She had plans to get there.

The sun was up, the Russes and their extended family had arrived on-site, and they were ready to roll. Satisfied that everyone knew what his or her job was, Paige did one last check-in with the family. They were clumped together in the Russes' living room, nerves evident on all the adult faces. Trevor was in tears. "But I wanna wear it!" His wails added to the tension.

"What the hell's going on in there, St. James? Stop pinching the kids," Andy's voice crackled in her ear.

"Gimme a minute," she murmured before cutting her mic.

Trevor slid out of his mother's arms and stomped over to Paige.

"Hey, buddy. Are you ready for the big day?" she asked.

"Mom says I can't wear dis but I hafta!" Trevor ran his little hands over the toy tool belt he wore on his hips. "I'm gonna help build Pop-Pop's house!"

"Wow, you came prepared," Paige told him.

"He hid it under his jacket," his mom sighed, running a hand through Trevor's hair. "We'll make sure he doesn't wear it on camera."

That statement started the tears again.

Paige dropped down to her knees on the orange shag carpeting that was in its last hours of existence. "This tool belt is awesome, and I think Gannon is going to be really impressed."

Trevor wiped his eyes with the back of his hand and leaned morosely against his mother's leg. "Yeah?"

Paige nodded. "Definitely. But listen, since we're supposed

to be surprising you, you have to pretend that you didn't know we were coming. So you wouldn't have your tool belt on yet."

He frowned at her, his blue eyes thoughtful.

"But when we give Gannon and Cat the tour of the house, I think it would be awesome if you put the belt on to help show them around."

Trevor's eyes lit up, and his mother muttered an "Oh dear God" under her breath.

"Does that sound good?" Paige asked.

Trevor nodded emphatically.

"Great! So why don't you give me your belt now, and as soon as we reset for the tour, I'm going to have you put it on, okay?"

His little fingers worked the belt free, and he all but threw it at her. "Woo-hoo! I get to help! Hey, Molly!" He ran off in search of his sister.

His mom sighed after him. "Thank you for that. Really, if it's a problem at all—"

"A face like that showing Gannon King his tool belt?" Paige shook her head. "What a way to kick off the season."

She moved on down the line to Phil and Delia, who perched on the faded yellow-and-brown sofa where their oldest son was comforting them. Delia held a fistful of tissues. "How are you two doing? We're just about ready to get started," Paige promised.

Delia blew her nose mightily. "It's hard to believe this is the last time we'll all be in this house as a family."

Smiling sympathetically, Paige sank down on the couch next to Delia. She'd dealt with this exact reaction from nearly every family the show had helped. It always amazed her, the connection that people could feel to a house. She'd never experienced that in her mother's sprawling Long Island Tudor.

Sure, she'd grown up there, but it had never felt like home. She put her hand on Delia's.

"I promise you that Gannon and Cat and all the people on Clawson's crew are going to make sure this stays home. We're just going to make it more functional and safer for your family. This is just the beginning of the memories you'll have in this house."

Delia squeezed her hand. "Thank you, Paige."

"Get your ass out here, St. James," Andy ordered good-naturedly in her ear. "We're ready to roll."

CHAPTER

5

There was nothing like the first "action" of the season. They all felt it: the crew, the contractors, the family. The excitement of a new beginning for all. At its heart, what they were doing was storytelling, Paige thought as she watched Gannon and Cat roll up into the driveway in the tricked-out Chevy, a stipulation of the very generous advertiser.

That storytelling, the validation of each family and their contributions, was the reason Paige had stuck it out on the show. While the network and advertisers chipped away at the basic joy of the job, the families and volunteers and contractors they worked with made it bearable.

Gannon gave his trademark honk with the horn, and the Russes poured out of the front door with the enthusiasm of an elementary school recess. Andy was grinning, and that was a good sign.

They shot five more takes, getting different angles, before Andy was satisfied and they reset for the interior tour.

Brandon broke away from where he was sequestered off camera with the rest of the Clawson team and joined her under the awning. "You ready to get started?" Paige asked him.

He grinned down at her and patted the hammer on his belt. "I was born ready."

Trevor ducked out of his mother's grip and rushed up. "Paige! Is it time?"

"Perfect timing, Trevor." Paige pulled his tool belt off her shoulder and helped him secure it around his little waist.

"Hey! Mine's just like yours," Trevor announced to Brandon.

Someone from the construction crew called Brandon's name. "Sorry, kiddo, gotta go," he said, ruffling Trevor's thick hair, and the little boy's face fell.

Paige spotted Gannon frowning over blueprints at a folding table under a pop-up tent. "Hey, how about we go tell Gannon you're going to help with the tour," she suggested.

"Yes!" Trevor grabbed Paige's hand and together they scampered over to the man. Gannon King could be an ass with most people, but hand him a kid and he was charming, sweet, and funny. It was one of his very limited redeeming qualities.

"Hey there," Gannon said when Trevor stopped just short of running full speed into him. "Are you with Clawson Construction? Because I have a question about these blueprints."

Trevor, eyes bigger than a Japanese anime character, shook his head.

Amused, Gannon raised an eyebrow at Paige. *Too bad labor laws don't allow us to cart children around on set with us all the time*, she thought.

"This is my friend Trevor," Paige said, introducing the momentarily shy kid. "He's going to help give you a tour of the inside of his grandparents' house."

Trevor found his voice and launched into an explanation of every plastic tool on his tool belt. Gannon listened intently, nodding without interrupting.

Sam's Southern baritone came through her headset. "Okay, Beast Mode, your presence is requested inside, and bring that handyman."

Paige touched her ear and nodded toward the house, telegraphing to Gannon it was time to wrap it up.

"You know, bud, I think your belt is missing something," Gannon told Trevor.

Trevor immediately twirled the belt on his little hips, looking to make sure he hadn't lost any tools.

Gannon produced a carpenter pencil from behind his ear. "You're definitely going to need one of these."

"Whoa!" Trevor accepted it with the excitement of Christmas morning. "Hey! Mom! Look! Gannon gave me a pencil!" He took off at a sprint toward his parents.

"Thank God you didn't give him something sharper like a chisel," Paige breathed.

"Come on, princess. I believe we're needed on set."

———

The first day of shooting went as smoothly as reality TV could. The Russes had been perfect on camera with their sincere combination of excitement and nerves, and Cat had glamorously made the same promises to Delia that Paige had. They would return to a family home ready to house decades' more memories. Trevor leading Gannon around by the hand with his new pencil tucked behind his ear was guaranteed to melt hearts across the country when the episode aired.

They finished filming the tour by four, and Paige handed the family over to the production assistants to send them off with final reassurances. The Russe kids and some family friends had all kicked in to send Phil and Delia on a seven-day cruise.

By six, Paige was going over the demo plans with Mike Clawson while an army of volunteers packed away the rest of the family's furnishings and belongings into storage pods.

"We can't touch these rooms because we need the light to shoot the demo, and they're usually the biggest bangs for the buck," Paige told Mike, indicating the kitchen and bathroom. "But whatever your crew can do in the two guest bedrooms and the downstairs powder room overnight will help keep us on schedule."

"I'll let you know if any of our inspectors find any bad news when we start poking around," Mike promised.

"I appreciate that. You have my cell, right?"

He did. And her email and her hotel room just in case.

Paige cut Tony and Louis, checked tomorrow's call sheet that she'd distributed after lunch, and had Sam set up the interview "booth" before sending him and Mel home for the night. Rico and Felicia would stay and help her get a couple hours of volunteer interviews. She consulted her list. She had ten interviews to do. She liked to start them on the first night when everyone's energy was high. That way, if she uncovered a story that deserved more screen time, they had the rest of the shoot to work it into the story line and expand on it. It always made for a long day, but the end results were worth it.

She set up shop under a pop-up erected outside the craft services and show sponsor tent. She found that shooting at night gave the feeling to the audience that everyone was tired and more vulnerable than in the bright light of morning. She was just getting ready to track down her first interview when Gannon stormed up.

"What the hell is this?" he demanded, shaking papers in her face.

She took them from him, perused them. "It's tomorrow's call sheet."

"Why aren't we having Clawson demo the main bath tonight?"

"Because of the magic of TV," she said calmly. It was an old argument. Gannon was an actual contractor, which meant the ass-backward timelines of shooting a TV show about home renovations were ridiculous.

"We'd be a hell of a lot further ahead in the morning if we have them demo it tonight. Do we really need to see Cat carry out another leaky toilet or me break another fucking mirror?"

"If you wouldn't do such a good job at it, the audience wouldn't want to see it. The Kings doing demo is a highlight of the show, and for continuity's sake, it looks better in the episode when we do the tour, and it looks as if we start the demo immediately after."

"It doesn't make fucking sense to shoot it this way." Gannon's contractor sensibilities were officially in a bunch, but Paige had no sympathy.

"If you would look at the call sheet when it's distributed, maybe we could do something about it, but since you can't be bothered to review it in advance, this is what happens."

"You're just a network kiss-ass. You don't care about doing things right. You just care about cutting corners and manipulating ratings. This is a waste of everyone's time."

Nose to nose now. "No, *this* is a waste of everyone's time." Paige was the epitome of calm on the outside. On the inside, she wanted to take the hammer out of his tool belt and smack him in the forehead with it. "Either shoot the scenes the way we planned, offer up a goddamn solution, or go throw your temper tantrum somewhere else so we can continue. We're all on the same team, and we all work long hours, and holding up

31

production doesn't help anyone. Now if you'll excuse me, some of us still have a couple hours of work to do."

That was as good of an exit line as she was going to have. Paige turned and stalked away from him. Rico let out a low whistle as he playfully filmed her storming off.

"Yeah, go ahead," Gannon called after her. "Walk away and find someone else to exploit, princess."

She heard a thud and knew he'd thrown his tape measure into the tent wall. For whatever reason, his tantrum made her smile. Every time he broke and she didn't, she counted it as a victory.

She busied herself with the remaining items on her to-do list and promptly forgot about Gannon and his asshole-ish tendencies. Darkness fell, and Paige blew through the interviews with a speed and efficiency honed by years of experience. She'd gotten her start as a production assistant on a dating reality show. She knew which questions to ask that would get emotional answers and build good stories. Most of it was a ratings ploy. Taking exhausted volunteers who had strong feelings for the family they were helping and pushing a few buttons guaranteed tears.

Paige's personal challenge wasn't to deliver the drama. It was to deliver the truth. It always rang differently than a Frankenbite story that postproduction cobbled together. Tonight's volunteers were more than happy to sing the praises of the Russes, and with the family's background, there was no shortage of backstory.

She sat off camera while Mariel, a woman who had been homeless for two years before the Russes coaxed her into the soup kitchen and then their job placement center, made herself comfortable on the stool. She wore her bright green *Kings of Construction* volunteer shirt over a sweatshirt to ward off the evening chill. Her dark hair was pulled back in a stylish bun—her work hair, she called it. She clutched a tissue in her hand. "For the inevitable waterworks," she told Paige.

"Well, let's start there. What about helping the Russes makes you emotional?" Paige began.

Mariel rolled her dark eyes heavenward. "What about the Russes doesn't make me emotional? I was a very young mom, and when my children's father left, he took every dime we had in our checking account. I had no savings. I was working part-time as a cashier in a drugstore. It wasn't enough to support me, let alone me and three children. We were evicted from our apartment and living in our car when one day Phil Russe saw us in the library. It was cold, and we were trying to stay warm, and the library was quiet and safe. He asked if we were hungry—"

Mariel's voice broke, and Paige gave her a moment.

"My little boy, God bless his heart, said 'Yes, sir. We're always hungry.' And my heart just shattered into a million pieces. My children were *hungry*." Tears glistened in those beautiful dark eyes. "I was failing them. They should have been happy and warm and safe, and I was failing them." Mariel took a shuddering breath. "But Mr. Russe didn't judge. He just handed me a business card and said he had a hot meal waiting for us."

Understanding the rhythm of storytelling, Paige prodded gently. "How long did it take before you went to the soup kitchen?"

Mariel smiled. "I had to make sure he was on the up and up, you see. So I used one of the library's computers to look him up. We left for the kitchen thirty minutes later. And when my kids were having cookies for dessert, Mr. Russe brought Mrs. Russe out to introduce us to her. And my kids were never hungry again."

Paige led Mariel through questions about the soup kitchen and the job center. The Russes helped Mariel find a better paying job, got her enrolled in online college courses, and gave her money to help furnish her first apartment.

"I paid them back, every dime, and started making contributions to their endeavors," Mariel said with pride. "It wasn't much at first, but I'm a vice president at a bank now. My two oldest are in college, and I fund a scholarship for teens who have been homeless."

Paige smiled and wrapped up the interview. "That's perfect, Mariel. I'm so happy for you and your family, and I know the Russes are really going to appreciate you being here and sharing your story."

"Do you know that no one I work with knows my story?" Mariel cocked her head to the side. "I used to be embarrassed about my past, but now? Now it feels like something I can be proud of. I fought my way out of poverty, and now look at me."

"Now look at you," Paige echoed. "You should be incredibly proud of yourself." She reached out and squeezed Mariel's hand. "One last question. You've been a big supporter of the soup kitchen and the job center. You've already given back to the Russes. Why are you here tonight?"

Mariel straightened her shoulders, a single tear escaping her eye. "My family owes all that we have and all that we are to Mr. and Mrs. Russe. None of us will ever forget that. And so I am proud to give back to them in any way I can for the rest of my life."

"I think that's the perfect sentiment to end on," Paige said, clearing her throat. She nodded at Rico, who gave her a wink and started tearing down. "Thank you so much for being willing to talk to us and for volunteering." Paige offered Mariel her hand but the woman reached in and hugged her instead.

"Thank you for doing this for them. I can't think of anyone who deserves something beautiful more than those two."

Paige packed up her headset and gave herself a few minutes in the shadow of the craft services tent to swipe at her damp eyes. It was real people like Mariel and the Russes who made the rest of her job worthwhile. She may be dabbling in "drivel" as her mother liked to remind her, but she was also telling the stories of the brave, vulnerable, and triumphant.

"Didn't know you were human, princess."

CHAPTER

6

Gannon's rasp of a voice came from behind her, startling her. She took her time turning around, not wanting to give him any glimpse of weakness or humanity.

He was much closer than she realized when she came face to chest with him. She stuck out her chin and forced a cool expression. "What are you still doing here? Shooting wrapped hours ago."

He reached out and swiped a tear off her cheek. Her skin burned where his thumb touched her.

"It's allergies," she said and shrugged.

"Whatever you say," he told her amicably. "I'm here because I had to fix a hole in the tent, and I'm waiting for you. I wanted to talk to you—calmly and politely—about tomorrow's call sheet."

"I can't tell if you're being a smart-ass or not."

He crossed his massive arms in front of his chest. His

stance was wide, powerful. "You may have had a point earlier," he admitted, looking down at the toes of his boots. "A small one. Minuscule really."

She raised an eyebrow. "Why, Gannon King, I didn't know you were capable of listening."

"Let's not get carried away here. I have a potential solution for my…concern about the main bath."

"I'm all ears," she sighed, not seeing a way out of listening to him try to mess with her schedule.

"We always shoot the bathroom because it's big drama, lots of smashing and glass, right?"

"Right."

"Why don't we mix it up? Let's give Clawson a GoPro or two and let them demo the bath tonight. We get the footage just in case anything ratings-worthy happens, and tomorrow, to make up for not smashing my thirteenth mirror on camera, I'll run through the back wall when we demo it to start the addition."

She laughed. She couldn't help it. "You're willingly going to run through a wall on camera?"

"Between the studs. I was thinking about challenging Cat to see who can smash through it better. But don't pass that on to Andy. He'll just tattle to the insurance company. If we let Clawson do the demo tonight, we're going to be at least an hour ahead of schedule, and we're going to need it if we're doing the addition. Cat and I will make up for the drama in some way tomorrow."

It made sense, and if Paige were completely honest, she was pretty bored with watching the Kings cart old toilets around the set. The bit had run its course.

"Okay." She glanced down at her watch. It was only nine. She could talk to Clawson's crew and make the change to the call sheet. "If it will put us ahead of schedule and you promise to deliver something the audience will love, I'm all for it."

"Deal." He offered her his hand, and she hesitated for a second. His grin teased her. "I don't bite…hard."

Reluctantly, she took his hand and shook. It was just exhaustion that had the zing of physical contact running up her arm, she told herself.

"You look beat, princess. Why don't you head back and get some sleep?"

Paige pulled her hand out of his grasp and rolled her shoulders. "I've got a call sheet to update and a trailer of supplies to unload." She nodded to the street where a box truck idled.

Gannon looked around. "Where the hell is everybody? You're not unloading a truck yourself."

Paige quelled the urge to roll her eyes. "We don't like to pull the crew off the job to unload," she explained. "So me and a handful of nice, muscly volunteers take care of whatever we can to keep things moving. You've seriously never wondered why your bathroom tile and hardwood boxes are always waiting inside every morning?"

Gannon looked over his shoulder at the truck and frowned.

"You ready, Beast Mode?" Flynn, a member of Gannon's crew and Gannon's best friend, held up his hand for a high five on the fly.

"Let's do it, Muscles." Paige winked, slapping his palm. She turned back to Gannon. "Thanks for talking to me like a person and not a 'network kiss-ass.' Now get some rest. Big day tomorrow."

She left him, mouth open and staring after her, as she and Flynn stalked toward the waiting truck. They waved over a handful of volunteers who were bravely determined to stick out the night. She mentally juggled the call sheet as she hefted a box of ceramic tile. She had to run Gannon's plan past Andy before she talked to Clawson but didn't foresee any issues there. They were always looking for ways to get a little ahead on the schedule.

She turned on the ramp and nearly ran smack into Gannon. He pulled the box out of her grip. "What are you doing?" she demanded.

"We're all on the same team, remember? Now be a good girl and put another box on top."

The volunteers worked even faster with Gannon hefting boxes of tile like they were reams of paper and unloading bulky bathroom fixtures. Paige didn't bother hiding her eye roll. He was trying to prove a point to her that didn't need proving. They had a small crew, and everyone pulled their weight. Just because Gannon and Cat didn't hang out much after the cameras stopped rolling didn't mean they weren't working their asses off while they were on.

"Must have impressed the boss," Flynn said to Paige, nodding in Gannon's direction where he and two volunteers were guiding the master bathtub out of the trailer.

"She just played ice queen on him," Rico teased, coming down the ramp with the toilet box. "Got it on camera too." He grinned.

"That footage had better never see the light of day," Paige said sternly. "Unless you also caught him chucking his tape measure through the tent wall like a baby."

"What kind of shooter would I be if I missed that? Even got a few seconds of him fixing the hole he ripped in the side."

Paige laughed. "I love you guys."

"We love you, Beast Mode."

CHAPTER

7

The sun was still up when Paige dumped her laptop on the lumpy bed in her room at the Comfy Inn in Mobile, Texas. They were on their third house of the season, and their little band of misfits was really hitting their stride. They'd scored yet another gold mine of a contractor for this house, and Paige was looking forward to working with their crew.

She flopped down in the rickety desk chair and surveyed her room. They'd checked in this morning, and Paige had lobbed her bags into the room before heading back out to the site to tackle the prep work.

The room wasn't awful. It could have been worse. The walls, once white, wore the yellowed cast of its storied past as a smoker's paradise. The carpet too wore badges of honor in the form of cigarette burns. But the bathroom was clean, and there were extra pillows in the closet.

It would do for the week.

Paige stripped out of her jeans and T-shirt and pulled on a clean pair of capris and a tank top. She texted Cat to see if she wanted to do dinner and then pulled the bedspread back before flopping down on the mattress.

She closed her eyes and reviewed the details about the new family. Joy, at twenty-seven with her sunny smile and dirty-blond pixie cut, raised enough money through 5Ks, bake sales, and silent auctions to bring an art and pet therapy program to her local nursing home after her grandfather was diagnosed with dementia. She dedicated every waking moment outside her full-time job as a social worker to caring for her beloved Poppy.

Poppy had played matchmaker and introduced Joy to the visiting physical therapist who volunteered at the home twice a week. Joy and Teagan were married in Poppy's room when he fell too sick to attend their ceremony. He passed away shortly after their ceremony, leaving Joy and Teagan the home he'd built with his own two hands when he and his bride were first married. It had fallen into disrepair since his diagnosis, but the family connection made it home.

It was a sweet, heartwarming story, and Paige was looking forward to telling it.

Her phone signaled an incoming call, and she rolled herself up. Eddie's name flashed across her screen.

"What's up, Eddie?" she asked, bypassing any pleasantries. He trusted her to do her job and only called when there was news—usually bad—to deliver.

"Bad news, kid."

Restless now, Paige dragged open the sliding glass balcony door. It squealed under protest. She stepped out onto her narrow strip of outdoor living space overlooking the cracked asphalt of the parking lot. A flimsy wall that separated her balcony from the one next door provided minimal privacy. "What's the damage?" she asked, leaning on the iron railing.

"Interiors at Home just came on board."

The show and the chain of home decor stores had been courting each other in the off-season. They were a major advertiser, which meant a big influx of cash and most likely some pretty spectacular demands.

"What do they want in return for their massive piles of money?" Paige sighed into the phone.

"Cat and Gannon now get to make a trip to the store every episode to choose pieces for the finished project." Eddie was big on ripping the Band-Aid off.

Paige slapped a hand down on the railing, making it rattle. Judging its instability, she took a step back from it and paced. "Are you kidding me, Eddie? Are they trying to strangle every ounce of sincerity out of the show? Viewers love how real Gannon and Cat are. This is going to make them look phony."

"I know. I know. But it was the keystone of the contract."

"That's bullshit, Eddie. Can't you change their minds? Gannon's going to go nuclear over this, and I don't blame him. It's a stupid idea."

"At this point, there's nothing we can do. The deal is done."

Paige shoved a hand through her hair, scraping it away from her face. "I don't like that these decisions are being made without at least consulting the Kings. It's their show. They are the show."

Eddie heaved the world-weary sigh of a man too long in the business. "I hear what you're saying, kid. I really do. But…"

"Yeah, yeah. There's nothing we can do," she finished for him. "When does this go into effect?"

"This shoot. There's a store about a hundred miles from the shoot."

42

Paige swore under her breath. "How much time per episode?"

"Three minutes, and the pieces shown in the store have to be used in the reveal."

"Who's breaking the news? You or me?"

Eddie's pause told her everything she needed to know.

"Great. Awesome."

"So how's everything else?" Eddie asked cheerfully.

———

Gannon stayed where he was leaning against the paint-chipped railing of his balcony. He hadn't realized Paige was right next door until he heard her husky voice getting pissed about something on the phone with the show's executive producer. He could have felt guilty about eavesdropping, but since Paige interested him and he'd heard his name, he felt justified in listening.

She hung up with Eddie, and he heard the squeal of her door as she slammed it behind her.

It was further confirmation that Princess Paige wasn't the "yes man" he had assumed she was. He never expected her to fight on his behalf, and listening to her dish it out to Eddie told him it wasn't the first time she'd stood up for him and Cat.

Shit.

He hated being wrong.

He'd written her off from the very first day of shooting last season when she'd coolly told him he needed to be respectful of the network's timetable.

A network shill, he'd labeled her then, he remembered. But that didn't stop him from noticing her mile-long legs when she wore shorts to the sets in the dead heat of the summer. Or her full, usually unpainted lips that parted just before she laughed at something her crew or he said.

He'd gotten an eyeful of the body that was typically hidden by her usual jeans and T-shirt uniform last season when she'd had to borrow someone's gym clothes midshoot. She wore her rich chocolate hair in a sexy short cut that allowed her to plow her hands through the layers when she was frustrated or tie it back in a stub when she was doing the heavy lifting.

Yeah, she was attractive enough that he'd frozen her out from the get-go. He'd fallen for a pretty package before and paid a steep price for it. He'd met Paige shortly after his self-imposed celibacy to get his damn head back on straight. And maybe, just maybe, he'd been unfair to put Paige St. James in the same category as his past mistake.

Anyone could see that she was strong, smart, and completely unflappable. It was the cool attitude that had thrown him, though he hadn't been exactly friendly to her either. Yet when she thought she was alone, she showed her human side with an unexpected empathy for the people they were generally exploiting on camera.

Snippets of conversations, insults he'd thrown in bad moods, accusations he'd made in jest came back to him now. She'd never bothered correcting him or defending herself, never commiserating with him that she too thought the network was a bunch of greedy assholes.

He didn't like being wrong.

Gannon grabbed two beers out of his mini fridge. He wouldn't apologize. After all, she had never defended herself or trusted him with her opinion. It made him wonder if she ever confided in Cat. Those two were thick as thieves.

Before he could change his mind, he grabbed his key card and went next door to be neighborly.

She opened the door with hardly a trace of the anger Gannon knew she was feeling. But the telltale signs were there in the clench of her jaw, the flash in her eyes.

"Here," he said, holding out a beer.

She looked down at it and then up again at him.

He wiggled the bottle, and when she took it, he brushed past her into her room.

"What are you doing?" she asked.

He ignored her question. "How do you do it?"

She followed him but left the door open. "Do what?" she asked, frowning.

"Keep all that anger locked up like that?" he asked, sinking down on the yellow paisley couch next to the cloudy balcony doors.

"Come on in. Have a seat," she muttered and took a swig of beer.

"I like seeing you pissed off. Makes me think you care."

She gave him a long, cool look. "Want to get to the point? I've got a lot of work to do tonight."

"First tell me how you keep it all inside. Don't you ever feel as if you're gonna blow?"

"I've had years of practice dealing with frustrating people," she said with ice in her tone.

"I wouldn't know any of them, would I?"

Paige arched a sexy eyebrow at him. "You may have met one or two of them." The show of amusement evaporated quickly, and she retreated behind her walls, taking another long pull on the beer. "So what can I do for you, Gannon?"

"I was studying my call sheet—"

"Don't be a smart-ass," she interrupted.

"Do you want to know what I'm doing here or not?" he asked.

She held up her hands in surrender. "Please, continue."

"I was studying my call sheet when I realized I don't know you very well."

"And that's suddenly a problem?" Paige looked skeptical.

"It is when we're spending the next few months together, depending on each other."

"Why wasn't this an issue last season when we spent three months together depending on each other?"

She was quick and showed only a suspicious interest in his presence. "Who says it wasn't?" Gannon countered.

He rose from the couch and prowled around her room. Being contrary, she took a seat on a rickety armchair when he stood. She didn't bother with any personal mementos, he noted. Neither did he. There was no use carting around pictures or knickknacks when he spent so much time on the road. Besides, he traveled with his sister, and they usually had a weekend or two that allowed them to head home between states and shoots.

"It's a problem for me now."

"Gannon," she sighed his name out, and it made him wonder how she would sound if she were naked and he was touching and tasting her. He'd never not been physically attracted to her. He'd just come into the show with a chip on his shoulder and a lesson learned about women who shouldn't be trusted. But it appeared he'd been a little hasty when he'd shoved Paige into that category.

"Did I mention where I was when I had this epiphany?" he asked.

"No. But I'm sensing a punch line."

"I was enjoying the sunset view of the parking lot from my balcony—"

She swore colorfully, and he laughed.

"How much did you overhear?"

"All of it. You've got balls, sweetheart, talking to an executive producer like that."

"Eddie's a good boss. He at least listens even if there's nothing that he can do."

She shoved out of her chair and got up to walk off her frustration. It was another tell. Whenever Paige was stressed, she had to move. She couldn't stay still.

"Why aren't you screaming and swearing at me?" she asked, stopping at the balcony door, her back to him.

He came up behind her, invading her space just a bit, letting her feel him there. She stiffened but didn't retreat.

"Honest?"

She shrugged her shoulders.

"I was more interested in hearing you saying things no network kiss-ass would ever say and getting pissed about whatever scheme they're cooking up for ratings or dollars."

"What are you saying?"

"I'm saying I may have misjudged you, Paige."

CHAPTER

8

Paige closed her eyes and rested her head against the back of her seat. The plane would be taking off and delivering her team to their next shoot in Maine, and in the interim, she'd grab a few hours of well-earned sleep.

Production for the last episode had gone perfectly—an unheard-of feat in reality television—and at the end of the week, Gannon and Cat were able to turn over the keys to a completely renovated Craftsman bungalow to a tearful Joy and Teagan.

Gannon had had a mysterious talk with some of the higher-ups at the network, and the stipulation that the Kings visit an Interiors at Home for every episode was magically lifted. As a compromise, Cat was ordered to include mentions and pictures of products in her behind-the-scenes blog, but Paige considered it a victory for the integrity of the show.

The whole crew was flying high from a good week, and

Paige considered it a blessing since the next shoot was going to be gut-wrenching.

Single mom Carina was a beauty with impossibly high cheekbones, glossy dark hair, and the kind of flawless bronze skin that made models weep. She'd raised one hundred thousand dollars through crowdfunding for the children's hospital that treated her daughter for brain cancer. Malia, now six years old, had just suffered a relapse after nurses at the children's hospital had applied to the show on the family's behalf.

The odds for remission the second time around were starker, less favorable, and Paige knew it would be tough on everyone involved. But the story was ready to be told, and she would do her best to be as sensitive to the family's needs as possible.

Sensitive wasn't exactly Gannon's middle name, and she hoped he'd behave himself as he had on the last set. But she knew better than to put money on consistency when it came to his temperament.

She felt a body ease into the seat next to her and opened her eye lazily. She usually sat with Sam or Louis because neither of them liked to talk in flight. They didn't mind a seatmate who was usually sound asleep before beverage service came through coach. But it wasn't Sam's pearly smile or Lou's bony shoulders that she recognized. It was Gannon's golden-brown eyes filled with amusement.

Paige straightened in her seat. "You're not sitting with me."

"You're grumpy when you wake up," he said, cramming his frame into the seat and settling a book in his lap. He was wearing jeans and a navy T-shirt that hugged every bulge of muscle in his chest and arms. A savvy traveler, he'd opted for flip-flops to make it through security faster.

"I'm not grumpy, and I didn't just wake up," she grumbled,

proving his point. "I meant to say, why aren't you up in first class?"

It was one luxury that Gannon didn't complain about given his tall frame. The legroom of first class was a necessity. His knees were already spread wide to accommodate the length of his legs. Gannon's left knee was unapologetically encroaching into her space.

"I thought Sam would enjoy the legroom for once."

"Sam is a good three inches shorter than you," Paige argued.

"Ah, but Sam has something I don't."

"And what's that?" Paige asked dryly.

"A crush on my sister."

Paige smirked. "So a PA has a crush on your sister, and you're magnanimous enough to give up your first-class seat to spend the next four hours crammed into coach with me?"

"What can I say? I'm a giver."

He grinned at her, and she felt her stomach do an involuntary somersault. She let her skeptical eyebrow raise do the talking for her.

"You know, I used to think you were stuck up," he began conversationally. "Then I thought you were some kind of network puppet spy."

"Oh really?" she asked, pulling her book from the seatback pocket as if she had no interest in their conversation.

"But I was wrong."

She gave him a dry look. "I'm sorry, I think I misheard you. It sounded as if Gannon King just admitted to being wrong."

He held up his hands. "Bear with me. I know it's a lot to take in."

Paige wished desperately for a pair of earbuds to drown out her unwelcome seatmate.

"I've been watching you."

50

"Just because you look the way you do"—she let her gaze travel down his body and back to his face—"doesn't make that statement not creepy." Though she was certain there were legions of women around the world who would turn into puddles of lust if Gannon King admitted to watching them.

"Not in the creepy stalker way," he corrected her. "I watched you work this week, and I came to an entirely different conclusion."

She sighed, telling herself not to bite, but she was already asking the question. "And what did you conclude?"

"You're an observer."

Paige blinked.

"See? That right there," he said, pointing his finger in her face. "I'd be asking questions and trying to dig into that statement, maybe argue. But you? You just wait to see what happens next."

She wanted to interrupt, to say something, anything, but she was dying to know where he was going with this.

"I'm the opposite. I want to dive in and make things happen, but you're wired to sit back and watch things unfold naturally. You're not disinterested. You're calm."

"And patient," she added.

He grinned, and that world-famous dimple winked into existence next to his mouth. Dear lord, he'd never smiled at her like that before. No wonder Instagram freaked every time Cat posted a picture of him. Paige fought the urge to fan herself with her book. The proximity was getting to her, and there was no way she could escape without climbing over his lap. The plane began to taxi down the runway, picking up speed.

Her whole life, Paige had been—for the most part—unfairly judged as stuck up or disinterested. Gannon was the last man on earth she'd have expected to actually get her. "So you have me all figured out then?"

"Not even close. But I'm enjoying my research," he said, his voice husky as the wheels left the ground. "Makes filming more bearable."

The lift of the plane resonated in her body. She wanted to look away from Gannon, to stare out the window as Texas vanished beneath them. But she didn't. She held his gaze, searching those warm hazel eyes for what he wasn't saying. He was interested, but she didn't understand why.

"Gannon." Her voice held a light hint of warning.

"Paige."

"I didn't think you knew my name," she told him dryly.

"I know a lot more than your name, Paige St. James. Why don't you ask me what you really want to ask? We've got a long flight ahead of us."

"That's precisely why I don't want to ask you what I want to ask you. Four hours of verbal sparring with you would be exhausting."

"How about we keep it to an hour? And then you can read your book or plot ploys to raise ratings or whatever you do on planes." He was being playful, and it was a side of him that was very hard to say no to.

"Fine. *Why* are you on TV?" It had bugged her since day one. There was nothing about Gannon King that screamed fame whore. He abhorred being on camera, hated his one-on-ones with her and the camera, and had no tolerance for delays in the work schedule that were caused by filming.

"Oh, you mean besides my brutally sexy good looks?" he asked. His tone was flippant, but he cruised a hand over his head, a nervous tic.

Paige gave him a level look.

"You're insinuating this isn't my dream job. And you're right. I've got bigger plans than TV. And you do too."

52

Paige opened her mouth and closed it again. Everyone around them had plugged into the seatback screens or were enjoying a bit of shut-eye. It almost felt like they were all alone.

He leaned in, taking over her armrest. "Go ahead and deny it, but I know."

"What gives you that idea? Maybe this is my dream job."

"If you go with that, I'm gonna call bullshit. It took me a while to see it, but you can get just as riled as I do about it all. You do this thing when you're pissed where you clench your jaw for five seconds. I think you dig your nails into your hands too. Five seconds and then you answer in this pleasant, benign tone that's a complete load of crap. But you look so sincere everyone buys it. Just once, I'd love to hear what runs through your head in those five seconds. See the real you."

She'd underestimated Gannon. He saw far more than she'd ever given him credit for. Paige wet her lips.

"See? There you go again. What's that internal dialogue saying?" Gannon demanded quietly.

"It's saying that maybe I've misjudged you. Slightly. A lot is hinging on your answer to the question that you're avoiding."

Gannon studied her carefully for a moment and then pulled his phone out of the pocket of his jeans. "This is the reason I'm on TV." He held it out to her. The picture on the screen was Gannon smiling down at the round little woman under his arm. She had a head full of silvery curls and a smile that matched his.

"Your grandmother?"

"My nonni." He said it with such affection and in perfect Italian that Paige felt her heart flutter.

"Your nonni's lifelong wish was to see you and Cat on TV?"

"More like my lifelong wish is to see her happy."

"That's very sweet," Paige said, handing him his phone.

"But it still doesn't make you trust me," he guessed.

"Why do you want me to trust you?"

He gave her another one of those long, smoldering looks, and she wondered if her toes were going to combust in her sneakers. "I don't know yet. You interest me. I like to take things apart, figure out what makes them work."

Paige nodded. She could see that about him. Gannon thrived on challenges wherever he found them.

"If I tell you something, I need to know that it won't go anywhere beyond these seats. I don't need this getting back to the network. I don't even want Eddie in on it."

"Okay." Paige nodded.

"Just like that?"

"Gannon, I don't know what it's going to take to get you to understand that my loyalty is to this team and the people on our show. Not the network and not the goddamn ratings." She heard the exasperation in her own voice and sighed.

He was smiling approvingly. "See? That's the inner dialogue I'm interested in."

The flight attendant appeared at his elbow with the beverage cart. Since she wasn't getting any sleep anytime soon, Paige ordered water and accepted the bag of pretzels Gannon handed her. The flight attendant's gaze never made it past Gannon. It could be that she recognized him from TV, but to be fair, he was attractive enough that he garnered plenty of attention based on looks alone.

Flustered, the woman nearly bobbled Paige's water and profusely apologized to Gannon. He accepted his Pepsi, thanked her, and turned his attention back to Paige. The flight attendant reluctantly wheeled the cart backward.

Gannon rubbed the bridge of his nose and settled in. "After we lost Pop, Nonni went through a rough time. His construction business was already struggling, but when we lost him, it almost went under."

He reached over and took the pretzel bag she was struggling with. He opened it easily and handed it back to her.

"We were inches from bankruptcy, this close to laying everyone off. It was heartbreaking, the idea that we'd lost him and now we were losing the family business. That's when Cat came up with the 'brilliant' plan to send a tape to a production company. And the rest is history."

"And the rest is history?" Paige prodded. "You travel with part of your grandfather's crew. What happened to the rest?"

"With salaries and endorsements, Cat and I were able to funnel most of it back into the business last year. We're on more even ground now, and my nonni still goes to the office every day to answer the phones and help with the books."

Paige dropped her head against the seat. "That explains so much. Why Cat is so much happier on camera than you—"

"You make me sound like a miserable bastard," he complained.

"Gannon, I'm going to tell you this because we're on the same team." Paige leaned in, copying his posture. "Come day three of shooting when you're running low on sleep and the project is behind schedule, you're a miserable bastard."

"Maybe I haven't embraced the whole TV thing as well as Cat," he admitted. "But I think I'm doing a damn good job."

"America obviously agrees," Paige teased. Ratings for the show skyrocketed during the first season, making the network scramble to lock down a second season.

"America agrees, but what do you think?"

Gannon King fishing for compliments. Interesting.

"I think it's refreshing to work with someone who could give a damn about ratings and looking good on camera."

"Now you're tap-dancing," he accused, stealing a pretzel from her.

"I think you're good for the show," she admitted. "And maybe not just because of your brutally sexy good looks."

CHAPTER

9

Gannon gave Paige a break. He considered her not order-ing him out of the seat next to her a small victory and was even more pleased when she actually talked to him. He'd been wrong about his princess, and he was looking forward to finding out what made her tick.

He glanced in her direction. She was huddled against the window, and he couldn't tell if she was giving him extra space for his big frame or if she was trying to avoid any accidental physical contact.

She yawned and closed the book she'd been paging through.

"A little light reading?" he asked, tapping the book in her lap.

She pinched the bridge of her nose between her eyes and held up the book. "Homework," she said by way of an explanation.

It was a thick psychology tome on the narcissism epidemic in America.

"Homework for what?" he asked, studying the cover.

Paige flipped the book around and tapped the jacket photo of the author. "My mother."

Gannon snatched the book from her and studied the picture. He could see the resemblance especially around the eyes and the jawline that Paige shared with Dr. Leslie St. James. Of course, Dr. St. James looked as though she'd never wear a pair of holey jeans like her daughter or be caught without her hair done and subtle makeup on.

"Wow."

"If you think that's impressive," Paige said, pulling her phone out of the seatback pocket and flipping through her photos. "This is my sister."

She showed him a screenshot of a younger woman, nearly a carbon-copy version of her mother, in a white coat, staring unsmilingly at the camera.

"Another Dr. St. James?"

"My sister, Lisa. She's doing a neurosurgery residency at Memorial Sloan Kettering."

"How often do you get the 'why are you wasting your time with this'—"

"Drivel, garbage, pandering," Paige filled in, and he felt immediately offended on her behalf.

"Do they have any idea how hard you work?"

"I sit around off camera getting wannabe starlets coffee. Meanwhile, my sister is saving lives, and my mother is freeing people from behavioral patterns that have afflicted them for lifetimes."

"You don't buy that crock of shit, do you?"

She smiled at him. A real one, and it warmed him from the inside out.

He'd noticed from day one that she was gorgeous in the girl-next-door way. Her big, denim-blue eyes framed by thick lashes, her high cheekbones and their light dusting of freckles highlighting the delicate hollows beneath. And he was enjoying the up-close view.

"I don't buy it entirely," she admitted.

"So why are you wasting your time with us drivellers?"

She went quiet on him, and he could feel her withdrawing on him. "Oh no, princess. No shutting me out. What you whisper in my ear on this plane stays here. Besides, I told you about my nonni."

She sighed, and he knew he was close to winning.

He pressed his luck. "How about this? You can tell me, and I will have no outward reaction whatsoever."

He had her.

"You won't ask any questions? Make any inappropriate comments?"

"When have I made any inappropriate comments?"

"I don't know? Maybe when you called me 'princess' at my job for the last year."

Gannon took her hand and traced an X over his heart. "Cross my heart."

She studied him. And Gannon watched those cool blue eyes calculate the risk as her hand held steady over the thrum of his heart. She tried to tug it away, but he held fast.

"Ugh. Okay," Paige finally agreed, yanking her hand out from under his.

Gannon leaned in, all ears.

"Stop looking at me like that," she demanded.

"Like what?"

"Like you're going to take a bite out of me."

"See how much fun it is to say what's on your mind?"

She cleared her throat, ready to deliver a lecture. "Gannon, I need you to behave. I'm not about to start flirting with the star of my show. I've worked my ass off getting here, and I'm not going to have that derailed by people starting rumors about me and…you."

"I *am* behaving," he argued. "I'm just waiting for my assistant director to stop stalling and tell me what she wants to do with her life that's not reality TV."

She dropped her head back against the seat. "No outward reaction whatsoever," she reminded him.

"None," he confirmed.

"I want to produce and direct."

Gannon didn't move a muscle. Paige met and held his gaze, but he didn't break. She looked away and primly opened her book. Her disinterest in his reaction lasted all of thirty seconds.

She slammed the book shut. "Okay. I'll allow a small reaction."

"Then that would be 'duh.'"

"Duh?"

Gannon shrugged. "You should already be a director. You had two years on Andy, and I like the guy, but the only reason he got it and you didn't is because he's got a dick and family relations. You end up doing half of his job anyway."

Paige blinked.

"Cat and I pulled for you this season, but Andy's the nephew of one of the suits, and they're grooming him for one of the bigger shows."

"Well, hell." Paige's breath whooshed out of her, tension slipping from her slim shoulders.

"It's a tough industry for women," Gannon said. "The network wanted to give Cat her own design special between seasons, and she turned it down because she didn't feel confident enough to demand to call the shots yet."

He could see Paige's wheels turning. "It's hard to imagine Cat with a confidence crisis," she mused.

"She wanted a little more experience under her belt before she said yes to anything else. She enjoys all this a lot more than I do. Eventually, I'll get back to just contracting, but I think she'll make this a long-term career."

Paige cocked her head, a smile playing on her pink lips. "You know, I'm not regretting our seating arrangement as much as I thought I would," she admitted.

Gannon laughed softly. "I'll cherish that compliment always. So what do you want to produce?"

"What makes you think it's not a reality show?"

"Ha," he snorted. "You have about as much tolerance as I do for this shit. You're just too professional to show it."

She didn't bother confirming or denying, but Gannon knew he was right.

"I'm still working on what kind of project I want," she told him.

She was lying to him. Those guileless blue eyes were looking down at the book in her lap again.

"But you have to have some idea," he wheedled. "And I trusted you."

She blew out a slow breath and stared at the seat in front of her. "My roommate and I are saving up to produce a documentary on women in the television industry. Pay gap, gender stereotypes, sexual harassment. And then we'll flip it and look at women who have broken through to pave the way for the rest of us."

"Wow."

"Yeah, you can imagine how unhappy Summit-Wingenroth would be to hear about my pet project."

"Are you quitting the show?" Gannon asked, suddenly seized by unease. He was just getting to know her. He wasn't ready to say goodbye when he hadn't figured her out yet.

She shook her head. "Not for another season yet. Becca and I are saving up so we don't need to do much if any crowdfunding for the production. I need this season and next to come up with my half."

"You make shit money."

Paige laughed, not taking offense.

It was true. For the amount of work that he saw her putting in on set, Gannon knew she should have been making almost double what she was.

"We've been saving for two years now," Paige continued. "And shit money is still money. We eat bananas and ramen and drink tap water when there's no craft services to be had."

Gannon leaned back in his seat, assimilating the information she'd just given him. So not only was she not a network puppet, but Paige St. James wanted to pull back the curtain and reveal to the world the dirty goings-on of television and the women who made it.

"Tell me more," he demanded.

———

When Paige started yawning at the end of every sentence, Gannon decided to let their conversation drop and let her rest. She got the least amount of sleep of anyone on the crew. First to arrive on set, last to leave. She set the example, and everyone else followed suit. When he looked at their little team, really looked, he realized Paige was the glue that kept them all moving, kept them all positive. And he felt like an idiot for not being more appreciative of it.

When her head lolled to the side to rest against his shoulder and she snuggled into his side in her sleep, Gannon wondered if maybe it was time to renegotiate his no women policy.

She was soft and warm against him, and that made him go

hard and hot. The sun was setting outside their window as they flew over the Midwest, bathing Paige's face in a golden glow.

He studied her at his leisure now. She had her hands tucked between her knees as if she didn't trust them to stay still while she slept. Her eyes were closed under the fringe of long inky lashes, and her hair smelled like tropical islands. The worry line that resided between her eyebrows was absent right now. He could see her freckles scattered across her nose and cheekbones. Who knew he had a thing for freckles?

"Don't you two look cozy?"

Gannon dragged his gaze away from Paige's face to his sister, who was tucking her phone away and standing in the aisle. "We get along better when one of us is asleep," Gannon joked softly, careful not to jar Paige awake.

Cat was looking at him expectantly.

"What?" he grumbled.

"I *knew* you had a thing for her," Cat whispered, looking triumphant in her statement.

"Keep your gibberish down, or you'll wake her," he threatened.

"And then cuddle time would be over." She gave him a playful pout. "Admit it. You've been into her forever."

He gave her his best "don't fuck with me" look, but Catalina King was immune to his temper.

"I'm just trying to get to know her a little better," he told her. "Some new information came to light recently—"

"That you want to take our little Paige here and make sweet, sweet love to her?" Cat interrupted.

"Shut the fuck up, Cat," he warned.

She held up her palms, the King symbol of surrender. "I'm just teasing. You know I love her. I'd do a Zumba routine right here and now if you told me you were throwing Meeghan over for Paige."

At the mention of Meeghan's name, Gannon stiffened and Paige murmured against his chest.

"I told you before. There is no me and Meeghan. Now, go back to your seat before I throw you in the overhead compartment."

"Whatever you say, big brother," Cat said, reminding him that he was indeed two minutes older than she was. "But you could do a lot worse and, in my opinion, not much better than our Paige here."

CHAPTER
10

Paige's phone had been blowing up all morning with calls and texts, but she was knee-deep in prep with their on-location general contractor and a denied permit that had to be unbotched before shooting could start the next day.

Usually they managed a few days to a week between filming episodes, but with twelve episodes to produce this season, the Texas to Maine jump was the tightest they'd ever had.

The field manager had warned her it would be a big job done on a tight lot, but it would be worth it. So Paige had worked an extra two days for filming into the schedule. And looking at the dingy two-story on a skinny swatch of lawn, they were going to need it. Carina Dufour had purchased the house with her then husband when they were pregnant. The location was ideal. It was a quiet, cozy neighborhood where backyards connected and neighbors called out greetings from front porches. The perfect place to start a family.

Unfortunately, the marriage hadn't lasted, and down to one income and facing an ongoing health crisis, the dreams of renovations and a comfortable family home were put on the back burner.

Blah beige siding and mud-brown shingles added no more curb appeal to the home than the chipped wrought-iron scroll-work holding up the crooked porch roof. Inside, it was spotless but dated. There were too many too-small rooms chopping up the layout and rendering the house practically useless. And taking a second leave of absence from her job, Carina had no hopes of beginning renovations on her own. She never stopped dreaming though. At least not according to the Pinterest board she'd been happy to share with Paige.

Cat, of course, had been thrilled with Carina's fearless design taste. The color and texture and creativity had sent Cat into her design software creating and re-creating each room until it was perfect.

We are all in on this one, Paige thought. No one complained about the tight schedule or the optimistic construction plans. Her team was just as invested in the family as the locals were. There was no way any of them were leaving Carina and Malia with anything less than the beautiful home they deserved. So nothing, not even the torrential downpour that left crater-deep mud puddles everywhere overnight, would slow them down.

Paige blew out a sigh of relief when Billie, office manager and wife of Brunelli Construction president, gave her the thumbs-up.

"Okay, great," Billie said into her cell phone. "Thank you. We'll send someone down to pick up the permit right away," she said, disconnecting the call.

"Fixed?" Paige asked hopefully.

"All set," Billie said, wiping the imaginary sweat from her brow. "Good to go for tomorrow."

"Thank God," Paige said, pulling her phone out to send an update text to Eddie and Andy and wondering again why her phone had ten missed calls and twenty-two texts. She'd just hit Send when she spotted Gannon dragging Cat her way.

"Oh wow," Billie breathed, staring at Gannon. "He's even hotter in person."

He sure is, Paige agreed silently.

He was wearing gym shorts and a faded T-shirt that looked as though it had seen a hundred washings and still had every inch of his broad chest memorized. Those golden eyes were hidden behind sunglasses, and the scowl on his face gave her a giddy rush of adrenaline up her spine. She'd been avoiding him since the plane landed last night and she woke up with her face plastered to that spectacular chest.

She wasn't one to wake quickly in the first place, and waking up to that face? To all that masculine heat? She had stared up at Gannon dazed for longer than necessary until he reached over and gently nudged her gaping mouth closed.

"Hey, guys. Have you met Billie? She's Brunelli's office manager and Mrs. Brunelli."

Gannon's frown softened marginally. He offered Billie his hand and a "nice to meet you" before introducing his sister.

Cat looked guilty, and Gannon looked furious. Paige hoped whatever it was wouldn't derail shooting.

Starstruck or, more accurately, Gannon-struck, Billie excused herself to go take care of some vague errands. Paige had a feeling the woman was going to go stick her head in a freezer to cool off from her first encounter with him.

"So what has you dragging your sister to the set a full day early?" Paige asked, addressing her question to Gannon.

"Cat has something she'd like to tell you."

Cat pouted. "I don't see what the big deal is—" she began.

But Gannon was pulling her phone out of her grasp and handing it over to Paige. "She's sorry," he said, his voice short.

Paige raised an eyebrow and looked down at the screen. "Oh shit."

Cat's Instagram account was open to a picture of Gannon and Paige on the plane, Paige's head nestled cozily on his chest. Beams of the setting sun from the window held them in a kind of spotlight. He was looking down at her, his expression soft, almost tender.

Paige's gaze flew back to his face. He wasn't soft or tender now.

"I didn't know she took it," he said quietly.

"I don't know why you're so upset," Cat began again. "Everyone loves the picture."

Paige looked back at the phone. "Oh my God, Cat." There were sixty thousand likes and a few hundred comments.

"I'd remortgage my house if I could have Gannon King look at me that way."

"Trouble in paradise for Meeghan and Gannon?"

Paige silently handed the phone back to Cat, her heart thudding in her chest. This was bad, very bad. She was behind the scenes for a reason. Gannon had been spot-on when he talked about what a boys' club the industry was. If people thought in any way that she and Gannon were having some kind of an affair, she could kiss being taken seriously goodbye.

"I posted pics of a bunch of us on the plane. But this is the one everyone got excited about." Cat chewed on her lip, finally sensing that there really was a problem. "I thought you were being oversensitive," she said to her brother.

"Paige, would you like me to explain to my asshole sister why this picture shouldn't have been shared?"

She nodded, not trusting her voice yet. The panic was clawing its way up her throat.

"This photo makes it look like there's something going on between the two of us," Gannon snapped. "If people start to believe that, Paige's ability to do her job is compromised."

"I don't see how—"

"If they think she's fucking her way to a job, no one's going to take her seriously as a producer. She's going to get passed over for good projects and forced into taking jobs for assholes who think they can score with her." His voice had risen by the end of his explanation, and while Paige was impressed that he really got the ramifications, she was mortified that they were drawing more attention.

"Oh shit! Paige, I swear I didn't think—"

"Damn right you didn't think," Gannon cut her off. He was good and pissed, and now Cat's lip was trembling.

"Okay, let's just take a breath," Paige ordered, regaining her voice and forcing down the panic. *Panic never helps*, her mother's cool voice reminded her.

"Take it down, Cat," Gannon snapped at his sister.

"The thing is, I don't think I should," Cat said, her eyes beseeching Paige. "If I take it down, it's going to look like we're trying to hide something. Regardless of whether there's anything there to hide."

Paige sighed and shoved her hand through her hair. "Cat's right. You guys don't need to worry about this. I'll deal with it."

Gannon's phone let out a shrill noise. It sounded like a security alarm. He made a grab for it, and when he nearly fumbled it, Paige spotted "Meeghan" on the screen. He hit Ignore and shoved his phone back in the pocket of his mesh shorts.

"Same team, princess," he reminded her.

Her phone rang. Eddie. She swore under her breath before walking a few paces away and answering.

"Hey, the permits are all in order," she said by way of a greeting.

"Yeah, I got your text. Good job…" He trailed off, and Paige knew, she just knew, that this wasn't a checking-in call.

"So I just got a phone call from the minion of a suit," Eddie said.

"Uh-huh." Paige didn't trust her voice to say more than that.

"They saw the picture of you and Gannon on the plane."

"Uh-huh."

"They loved it. And the footage of you reaming him out in South Carolina? It was a hit. So they want you miked."

"What?" Paige found her voice.

"They want to include you in the story line. You butting heads with Gannon played really well. They want you to be kind of a behind-the-scenes, in-front-of-the-camera part of the show."

"What?" She was shouting now and didn't give a flying fuck who heard her.

"It comes with a bump in pay. A small one. But you're part talent now."

"Eddie, there's no way in hell—"

"Oh, hey," Eddie interrupted. "Heading into another meeting. I gotta go."

He disconnected, and Paige had to fight the urge to throw her phone into the mud puddle in front of her. She won. Barely. And shoved the phone into the back pocket of her jeans. She stared down at the muddy water and counted to five. When that didn't work, she counted to twenty.

They were essentially writing her into the story as a love interest for Gannon. Her career as she knew it was officially over.

"Paige?" Cat's voice was tentative behind her.

Paige didn't turn around. "Yeah, Cat?"

"Is everything okay?"

"It's fine. I've got to go take care of some things," she told the Kings without looking at them and, much the same as Billie, wandered away, claiming vague important tasks.

CHAPTER 11

For the first time in her life, Paige cut out of work early. Granted, it was still a nine-hour day, but there was more to do before shooting started in the morning. She left detailed instructions with Andy and Mel and made sure Billie had her cell and hotel room numbers before heading back to her room. The advertising from Interiors at Home had boosted the show's budget enough that the whole crew was staying at a nicer-than-usual hotel. No cigarette burns, no bathroom ceiling mold, and the remote control wasn't sticky.

But the ambiance was lost on her morose mood as she let herself into her room.

She dumped her laptop bag and sweatshirt in a pile just inside the door and face-planted on the queen-size bed. She'd worked so fucking hard, and all of it was derailed by one picture. One fucking picture.

She let herself wallow for exactly five minutes before she

dragged her laptop out and started reviewing the damage. Cat was popular enough that the picture had caught the eye of an entertainment gossip news show. They'd posted the picture, doctored with hot-pink question marks and hearts, on their blog, wondering if Gannon King had thrown off the beautiful Meeghan Traxx for a tryst with his producer.

"Oh God," she murmured. They had her name. Thankfully, her fanatical privacy standards on social media had left them with little else.

Her mother, responsible for two of the missed calls, was going to be disappointed…and righteous in her "I told you so."

She reread the article and perused a handful of others before it started to sink in. She was worried about her career, but one innocent nap could have derailed Gannon's relationship with his girlfriend, who was, by all accounts, not commenting on the situation.

Meeghan may actually be the gigantic bitch she was rumored to be, but if Gannon cared about her, and Paige had unwittingly done damage…

She felt like a jerk. A violated one. But she hadn't even considered what this meant to Gannon. It was a hot fucking mess, and she couldn't see a way out of it. Not with the network deciding she was now part of the story. If she refused, she'd lose her job. If she complied, she'd never be taken seriously again in the industry.

All this just one season shy of actually accomplishing her dream. It was a nightmare. She didn't even want to break it to Becca that she might have just shot their plans in the face. Who the hell was going to want to be involved in a documentary about television and feminism when the director had been accused of sleeping with her show's talent?

More wallowing followed as did the desire for a good, stiff drink…or six.

It was dark now, and Paige didn't bother turning on any lights in the room. She just wanted to sit in this dark room, all alone, and pretend that all her carefully laid plans hadn't just imploded in her face.

She heard the knock at her door and ignored it. She knew exactly who it was despite the fact that he'd only knocked on her door once before.

The knock came again, followed by, "Open up, Paige."

"Go away. I'm asleep."

"Open the door, or I'll get a key from the front desk."

She could hear it in his voice, the bored determination that meant, no matter what, he was getting into her room. Paige recalled that it had been a sweet, perky brunette at the desk when she returned to the hotel. Exactly the kind of girl who would melt into a puddle of mush and do anything Gannon King asked.

In the dark, Paige dragged herself off the bed and stomped to the door. She yanked it open with more force than necessary and glared up at him.

Ignoring her lack of welcome, Gannon, juggling a paper bag and a pizza box, pushed past her into her room.

"You visiting me in my room isn't going to make the rumors go away," she snapped.

Immune to her attitude, Gannon switched on lights and dropped his supplies on the glass table in the corner. He flipped the lid on the pizza box, and Paige's stomach growled reflexively at the smell of tomato sauce and pepperoni.

"Are you going to eat, or are you going to pout?" He looked at her with expectation and freed a gooey slice from the box.

"I'm not pouting," she argued, crossing to the pizza. He handed her a paper plate and flopped down on the couch with his own plate. She wasn't pouting like some child. She was thinking about how screwed she was. There was a distinct difference.

He leaned over and flicked her lower lip. "Looks like pouting." For a second, she thought about biting his finger, and the idea must have telegraphed because Gannon abruptly pulled his hand back and grinned. His dimple flashed.

"Why are you here with pizza?" She gave in and took a bite of her slice. "Mmm." Damn, it was good. Gannon had a special talent for tracking down the best pizza place in every town they visited. Usually he didn't share.

"If you make noises like that after letting me in your room, people will talk," he warned, cocking an eyebrow her way.

"Gannon!"

"Yelling my name isn't helping."

"I'm so glad you find my situation funny."

Gannon got up and returned to the table in the corner. "I'm taking your situation seriously, but you're taking it like a death blow." He pulled out a bottle and plastic cups and poured generously. Offering one to her, he sat again.

She sniffed the liquid.

"Bourbon," he told her.

She took a small sip and let the exquisite warmth blaze a trail down her throat. "Good bourbon," she guessed.

He gave a slight shrug with his massive shoulders.

"Tell me why I shouldn't be upset." She took another sip and then switched back to the pizza.

"As a very wise woman once told me—and I seem to keep having to remind you of this—we're on the same team." He held up a finger when she started to interrupt. "As part of your team, Cat and I have a plan that will shift focus away from you."

"What kind of plan? Gannon, please don't do anything stupid that's going to draw even more attention—"

"It's better if you don't know. Then you can plead innocent if Eddie and his boss's bosses start making noise."

"I forbid you from doing anything that is going to put your own careers in jeopardy."

Gannon snorted. "Please. We're the Kings. Badass talent comes with a few perks. Namely being slightly more untouchable than our crew. Don't worry. It's a good plan, and the embarrassment will be all someone else's."

"I don't even want to know at this point," Paige muttered, going back to the bourbon. They ate in silence for a few minutes before she broke again. "God, Gannon, what am I going to do on camera? I don't think I can do both."

He laid a big hand over her knee and squeezed. "Princess, if anyone can do it all, you can. This doesn't have to be the end of the world."

"I don't see how it isn't." Great, now she really was pouting.

"Look at it this way. You're getting a chance to have a voice."

"I don't need a voice."

"That's bullshit. Everyone needs a voice. Why do you work on this show?"

"Besides getting to sleep on one of the stars?" she asked, her tone snarky. He shot her a cool look, and she rolled her eyes. "Because we get to tell the stories of people who have used their lives to make a difference, and we give back to them in a fun, flashy way."

"Bingo. So use your voice to make sure those stories are heard."

It made sense. Solid sense. "I just don't know if anyone's going to take me seriously after this."

"Make them." He said it so simply, as if it were the easiest thing in the world.

"It's not that easy. Maybe for you, a network star and a man—"

"Is it harder for a woman to be taken seriously in this industry? Hell yes. But it's even harder if you hide in the background and accept what's being doled out. Demand more. Do more. Speak up. They just gave you a voice. Make sure you use it."

She sat and stared at him. Gannon King of all people had just gotten wise on her.

He leaned in to study her face. "You're looking at me like I just impressed you."

"What?"

"Usually you only look at me like that when I finish a really sexy piece of furniture or I play nice with kids on set."

Paige dropped her gaze to the plate in her lap. After today, it wasn't safe to admit to him that there were certain aspects—both physical *and* emotional—that drew her to him.

"There are some impressive things about you," she confessed, doing her best to keep it vague.

"My ego's a fragile thing, Paige."

"Oh, I'm sure it is," she smirked. Her breath stilled in her throat when he leaned into her space. She could smell his laundry detergent, and it suddenly became the most erotic scent in the world. She dug her fingers into her knees but kept her gaze glued to his face.

"So I have to know. Was your freak-out at being linked to me only about work, or does the idea of being mine disgust you to the point of hibernating in your hotel room?"

Being his? Very few people could get away with language like that and make it sound smoldering hot. Gannon was one of them.

"Gannon—" she began but he cut her off.

"I don't want filtered, censored Paige. I want the real you. Tell me."

He wanted the real her. That wasn't what he meant, she

reminded herself. But it didn't stop her heart from thrumming faster.

"I take my job seriously. I have a responsibility to everyone in front of and behind the camera," she said, choosing her words carefully. She made the mistake of looking at his mouth. His lips looked hard, firm, and she wondered what it would be like to have them on her.

"You're filtering."

She dragged herself out of the ill-conceived fantasy. "Only the work part." The words were out of her mouth before she could second- or third-guess herself.

The slow, cocky-as-hell grin spread across his face. "Good."

"Don't get arrogant on me. I didn't say anything other than you don't disgust me."

"Coming from you, princess, that's a compliment. It could give a man hope," he teased.

Paige picked up her bourbon. "Well, let's both be thankful that you piss me off on a regular basis, so I don't think we need to worry about exploring how not disgusting I might find you."

Gannon laughed and she found herself smiling. "I like you, Paige."

She sipped and swallowed hard. "I tolerate you, Gannon."

CHAPTER

12

It was just like any other day of filming, Paige told herself, except for the fact that Felicia was attaching a microphone to the scoop neck of her T-shirt.

"This is stupid," Paige muttered.

"Don't be a whiner." Felicia gave her a motherly pat on the shoulder. "I've miked a few thousand people in my lifetime, and not one of them died from it."

She was indeed whining, and being called out for it made it even worse. She blamed Gannon. After he left her room last night, she'd spent the better part of the night tossing and turning and trying to force thoughts of him out of her head.

She'd never bothered to pretend that he wasn't built like the sexiest man in the history of the planet. That would have been stupid. She, just like every other viewer with a taste for the male form, salivated every time he took his shirt off on set. However, she'd neglected to understand that there was a human being behind his perfect pecs and stupendous shows of temper.

And now that she knew there was something good and solid and thoughtful underneath that godlike exterior, it spelled trouble. Big trouble. She could feel it lurking and prayed it would only wreak havoc on her personal life and leave filming in peace.

This is not the episode to fuck up on, she thought as she raised her hand to return the cheery wave from Malia as she and her mother approached. She was tiny for six, her body carrying the burden of its second diagnosis of cancer in as many years. Her full, dark hair that Paige imagined would look much like her mother's was gone thanks to aggressive chemotherapy. She wore a colorful scarf over her head and a sunny smile that showed a missing front tooth. The smile of a typical kindergartener.

This is going to be a tough one, Paige thought, steeling herself.

Carina, all svelte five feet ten inches of her, wrapped Paige into a warm hug. She was a stunning woman who should have been walking a runway somewhere, not picking her way over cables and around tent poles.

"We're early," she said with a smile like the rising sun, "but Malia and I have been up since five and couldn't wait a minute longer."

"This is going to be the best day ever," Malia announced, hands on her little hips, surveying the crew trickling in clutching cups of coffee. She gave each one a happy wave, and even Rico, the notorious morning grump, gave her a wink.

"I'm excited to get started," Paige told them. "Let's go get some coffee and maybe a hot chocolate, and I'll tell you what to expect today."

"Mama, can I have a doughnut?" Malia tugged on the sleeve of Carina's sweatshirt.

"Baby, you can have two doughnuts if you want," Carina said indulgently. "As long as you don't throw them back up."

Malia punched her little fist into the air. "Yes!"

Paige directed them to the tent where craft service was already setting up.

"Any time she has an appetite for anything, I'm happy," Carina sighed.

"If there's anything we can do today to make Malia more comfortable, please let me know, and we'll make it happen."

"You're already doing it," Carina told her, stepping into the tent. "She's been talking for weeks about her new pink bedroom and unicorn pillow."

Paige grinned. "Cat's designing Malia's room, and I can't tell you anything specific, but I will say it's spectacular."

Carina squeezed her shoulders. "I have a really good feeling about all this for all of us."

Paige felt her eyes inexplicably dampen. There was so much riding on this and not just for her.

"Mama, that's the handsome man you like," Malia said, a doughnut in each hand, goggling at the tent entrance.

Gannon, dressed in jeans and a Henley, walked in with Andy. They were laughing about something.

"Oh boy," Carina sighed in a sublime state of male appreciation.

Paige wet her own lips and wondered if she was imagining it or if Gannon had gotten even more attractive since he brought her pizza and booze last night. He looked up, his gaze raking her, and she felt her toes curl in her boots while something fluttered in her stomach.

Shit. A crush on a coworker was generally inconvenient, but one on Gannon in their current predicament would be disastrous.

They were coming over. Paige wished she had something to do with her hands.

"Oh my God. He's coming toward us. How's my hair?" Carina hissed, her hands frantically combing through her perfect short Afro.

"You look like you just walked off the set of a photo shoot," Paige told her. She, on the other hand, looked like she just walked out of a thrift store on senior discount day. Why hadn't she at least put on some eye shadow? Because she worked behind the scenes, and any makeup would disappear with the sweat that inevitably exploded out of her pores, she reminded herself. Besides, she didn't want to actually encourage Gannon to keep looking at her like anything other than his field producer.

"Good morning, ladies," Andy said with enthusiasm. "Who's ready for a new house?"

Malia's hand clutching the chocolate sprinkle doughnut shot into the air.

Carina pulled her daughter in front of her like a human shield. "We're both very excited," she said shyly.

"Gannon wanted to come in early and introduce himself before it's loud and busy," Andy explained mostly to Malia.

Paige mentally smacked herself in the head. It was a good idea. Gannon's size could be intimidating to some kids, and it was just Carina and Malia. There was no extended family to cover up nerves or hesitation during the opening surprise scene. But meeting him beforehand would give Malia time to get comfortable with him.

Paige should have thought of it herself.

Andy's phone rang, and he excused himself, nodding at Paige to take over. "Carina, Malia, I'd like you to meet my friend Gannon. Gannon, this is Malia and her mom, Carina."

Gannon shook hands with Carina and grinned when

she squeaked out a greeting. He solemnly offered his hand to Malia, who handed Paige her doughnut and wiped her hand on her purple sweater so she could shake.

"Are you ready for today, pipsqueak?" he asked Malia.

She grinned up at him. "I'm getting a pink room," she announced. "Do you have a fever?"

Gannon slapped a hand to his forehead and frowned. "No. I don't think so."

"My mama says you're hot, hot, hot."

Paige couldn't stifle her laughter. Carina looked like she wanted to die on the spot. Malia, on the other hand, was waiting for an answer from Gannon.

His bark of laughter turned heads around the tent, but he recovered quickly. "I promise I don't have a fever."

"Oh good." Malia breathed a sigh of relief. "'Cause then you would have to go home and rest, and you couldn't help build our house."

"It was really nice meeting you," Carina said, sounding as though she was being strangled. "We're just going to go…over here." She dragged Malia across the tent, and Paige's laughter let loose.

"I love when kids sell out their parents." Gannon grinned.

Paige recovered enough to reach for a cup of coffee. "That was really nice of you to come in early and make sure Malia would be comfortable with you."

"I'm a nice guy," he insisted.

"You look like one now, but you'll have to remind me when you're throwing a hissy fit and flipping a worktable."

He looked offended. "I have never once flipped a worktable."

"Maybe not, but you've thrown plenty of hissy fits," she argued.

"Hey, you're talking to the guy who brought you the best pizza that Portland, Maine, has to offer last night."

"And I thank you for your generosity, but I don't think last night should happen again." Paige looked pointedly around them, keeping her voice low.

Gannon's eyes skimmed over her face to the neckline of her T-shirt and widened. He hooked a finger into the scoop neck, a deliberately intimate move. "You're miked."

Paige felt the color drain from her face. The last line of their conversation rang in her head. *I don't think last night should happen again.* They hadn't even begun filming, and she'd already added fuel to the fire. She tried to push past him, but he caught her and spun her around to face away from him.

"Relax," he ordered.

He tugged at the hem of her shirt. And Paige nearly screamed. Why was he taking her clothes off? What the hell was happening?

"Mic's not hot," he said, pulling her shirt back down.

The microphone's power pack was clipped on the back of her jeans and apparently not on. Relief had her forgetting to mind her words. "Jesus, I thought you were undressing me," she gasped out and then clapped a hand over her mouth. One plane ride with him had her spilling her guts, filter-free.

Gannon's expression changed subtly, going from amused to something…darker, edgier. "Princess, when I'm undressing you, you'll know it."

CHAPTER
13

True to their word, the Kings had cooked up a scheme to detract from the rampant speculation about Gannon and Paige getting naked. #NapsWithGannon was trending on Twitter thanks to Cat and the rest of the crew sharing photos with people napping on Gannon.

Paige's personal favorite was the one of grumpy-looking Gannon cradling the two-hundred-and-fifty-pound Louis in his arms while Louis pretended to sleep. The rest of Twitter began to respond with photoshopped versions of the pictures, some of which ended up on the gossip blogs and a late-night talk show or two, fueling the fun.

Paige felt as though she'd dodged a bullet when requests for comments stopped piling up in her Facebook inbox. The network was still hell-bent on her being part of the show, but at least the world wasn't still questioning whether she'd played a role in destroying reality TV's hottest couple.

"One more season," Paige chanted to herself until she remembered she was miked. She continued to set up the interview booth in silence. She'd set up under a pop-up in the front yard so the house would provide the backdrop. The action in the background of swarming construction teams and volunteers combined with the interview should keep viewers interested.

Paige waved Carina over and ran through the questions for the interview with her. She didn't want to risk upsetting her or Malia with an insensitive question or assume that Malia knew more about her condition than she did.

"These are all fine," Carina assured her. "Honestly, Mal knows as much about her cancer as I do. She wants to be a cancer doctor when she grows up."

Carina hadn't said it, but Paige heard it all the same. The "when" in her statement was a conscious choice.

"Great. Just think of this as a platform for awareness," Paige suggested. "We'll go over the questions a couple of different times just to make sure we get the best answers possible."

Carina nodded and called her daughter over. Paige got them settled on two backless stools, their backs to their house as it would be for only a few more hours. Felicia scooted in with the boom, and when Tony was satisfied with the lighting, they began.

Paige started with questions on how Malia was diagnosed, making sure Carina hit on the early symptoms. This episode was as much a public service announcement for pediatric brain cancer as it was one family's story, and Carina was happy to treat it as such.

She was eloquent and sincere in her answers, and Paige knew Carina would connect with mothers everywhere. When Malia started to fidget, Paige knew it was time to get her involved in the conversation.

"Malia, can you tell me about your cancer?"

The little girl nodded proudly. "I have medulloblastoma cancer. I had it before, an' it came back, so I've had two surgeries, radiation, and now I'm going through my last round of chee-mo-therapy." She ticked off the treatments on her tiny fingers as blasé as if she were describing a field trip to the zoo.

"You're very brave," Paige told her. "Do you ever get scared?"

Malia nodded, her brown eyes wide. "I don't like it when my mom cries. It makes me feel bad. An' I don't like the dark very much, so I sleep with a Ninja Turtle nightlight." She wiggled her little butt on the stool and grinned at her mom.

Carina stroked her daughter's head. "One of the nurses at the hospital got it for you, didn't she?"

Malia nodded again. "Miss Jayne. Hey! Do you think Miss Jayne will see this?" she asked Paige.

"I think all your doctors and nurses are going to see it."

Malia launched into a personal greeting for each and every one of her medical team. It would never air, Paige knew, but she could get Cat to use the outtake on her blog. As far as she was concerned, men and women who worked with kids with cancer deserved all the shout-outs and thank-yous they could get.

Bringing Malia back to show-worthy sound bites, Paige asked her about how the cancer treatments made her feel.

"Sometimes barfy," Malia said, her pert nose wrinkling. "'An' sleepy, too. I hafta take more naps. Oh, and I don't have any hair again. But it makes it easier to see my scars. I showed 'em to Gannon, and he showed me some of his scars. He said scars mean you're tough." Malia flexed her tiny biceps at the camera, and Paige melted inside. "Do you wanna see my scars?"

"Do you want to show me?" Paige directed the question to Malia but looked at Carina. Carina gave her a wink and a nod.

"Sure!" Malia shrugged. "I only wear the scarf or a hat so no one thinks I'm in a zombie Halloween costume or something like that. I don't wanna to scare someone when they're 'spectin' to see hair." She whipped off the purple scarf and spun around backward on the stool. "See?"

The scars were red and ragged, a violation of her otherwise perfect mocha skin. Paige quietly blew out a breath. "Wow. Those are some scars. You really are tough."

"That's what Gannon said. He's got scars too, but none as cool as mine."

Swallowing hard, Paige shuffled through her notes and scratched out another one to find out if there was footage of Gannon and Malia trading scar stories. She couldn't imagine the inner strength that Carina had, dealing with this on a daily basis. Watching her perfect little angel of a daughter ravaged by a disease and suffering through harsh treatments? They deserved a hell of a lot more than a nice house.

They talked more about treatments and what Malia wanted to do when—always when—her cancer was gone.

"Let's talk about what you and your mom are doing this week while we're working on your house," Paige said. "Usually our families go on vacation for the week, but you wanted to do something different."

"We're going to Washington, DC, to talk to some people about more funding for cancer research. Mama thinks it'll be hard for them to say no to this face," Malia said, pointing at herself. "And *then* we're going to go visit a children's hospital and play with some kids!"

"That sounds like a really important trip."

Malia gave her an exaggerated nod. "Uh-huh."

"Do you know what you're going to say to the people about cancer?"

"I'm going to tell them that we need better treatments, and even if they can't give us money that will save me now, we have a responsibility to other kids who might be sick in the future."

Paige had to swallow hard to dislodge the lump in her throat. Carina looked surprised by her daughter's response. "Baby, where did you… We're going to beat this."

"Mooom, I know numbers. The doctors told you when it came back, I didn't have as good a chance. If I don't get cured, I still want other kids to hopefully get cured."

Carina grabbed her daughter in a tight hug, and Paige could see her willing away the tears that threatened to fall.

Paige wanted to look away. It was too raw, too personal. But it was also something that would make someone care and care deeply. She scrawled a note on her pad to identify pediatric cancer charities to highlight on the episode and blog.

Tony swiped the back of his hand under his eye, and Paige heard Felicia sniffle.

"Keep it together, guys," Paige murmured into her headset as she fished a tissue out of the box she kept on hand for interviews and blew her nose.

A movement off to the side caught her eye and she spotted Andy, arms crossed with one hand covering his mouth. He stood next to Louis, who was pointing his camera in her direction. "They wanted more behind-the-scenes," Andy's voice said in her ear. "Wrap it up, and we'll do a quick one-on-one with you, and then we can move on."

Damn it. I am not interested in or willing to be part of the story, Paige wanted to rail at Andy. The focus should be on Malia, not cooking up some fake behind-the-scenes romance for ratings.

And, of course, they were going to get her on camera when her own eyes were glassy with unshed tears and the fresh pain of watching a hopeful six-year-old consider her own mortality.

Paige ended the interview on a high note, letting Malia talk about the pink bedroom Cat promised her and what she thought of being on TV. Sweet answers that would remind viewers that Malia could be any six-year-old from any family.

It was the last they were needed on camera, and Paige was surprised to find the production and construction crews as well as Gannon and Cat lined up to say their goodbyes. Seeing the little girl pull Gannon down for a hug didn't do anything to calm Paige's emotional state. Wouldn't the network love it if she bawled her way through her first interview? That thought was enough to have her tightening the reins on her emotions.

"Let's get this over with," she growled at Andy and flopped down on the stool.

CHAPTER 14

Catalina King was generally a sane, stable human being. Sure, sometimes she was flighty and irresponsible. But between managing her or Gannon into a productive, helpful mood, Paige would take Cat every damn time.

However, on the birthday Cat shared with her brother, the tables turned, and *she* became the unmanageable one. The whole crew took the opportunity to call it a night a little early on set and hit whatever hole-in-the-wall bar chosen by the network's location manager who scouted families and towns prior to shooting. Massive quantities of beer, tequila, and nachos were consumed. It was a good midseason break, provided no one got too shit-faced or too hungover, which Cat always did.

Paige never let loose like the rest of them. She considered herself to be Cat's unofficial babysitter, and knowing that his sister was looked after, Gannon never went. Probably because Cat might use the drunken binge to pick up guys. And while

Cat enjoyed the birthday spectacle, Gannon preferred to celebrate in private…alone.

"You need to try this on," Cat said, thrusting a filmy white button-down shirt into Paige's hand. They'd just wrapped up an off-set shoot involving Cat shopping for the perfect princess bedding for Malia and, with everything under control on the set, hit a department store for some impromptu shopping.

"What would I wear this with?" Paige asked, wrinkling her nose.

"Black bra underneath, your cutie-cute denim shorts that show off your perfect legs, and those brown leather sandals. Guys love it when things wrap up girls' legs," Cat insisted knowledgeably.

"You're not trying to get me laid, are you?" Paige asked with suspicion, holding the shirt up in front of her.

"And what exactly is wrong with that?" Cat countered.

Paige thought about it a beat. It had been a longer-than-usual dry spell. But she wasn't into the whole one- or two-night stand on the road thing. It was just awkward, weird.

Before she could craft her answer, Cat continued. "Look, this isn't necessarily about sex. You're nearing end-of-season exhaustion already and we're only halfway through filming. I just want you to have a night off where you can slap on some makeup and a smile and enjoy yourself. Is that too much to ask?"

Paige sighed mightily. "No, I suppose not."

"Good. Now bring the shirt. We've got bras to shop for."

―――――

Cat and her design sensibilities were right as usual, Paige thought, studying herself from the waist up in her hotel room's bathroom mirror. She'd done a half tuck with the button-down that she wore over the fancy bralette that had caught her eye with its lace back. Cat had talked her into a chunky belt and a layered necklace with a crescent moon and stars.

Paige had put some effort into her hair, giving some lift and texture to her short bob with strategic messy waves. She kept her makeup simple but pretty, and damn if she didn't feel good about her reflection. Maybe, just maybe, with #NapsWithGannon trending and her first on-camera one-on-ones behind her, things would start looking up.

Paige gave her hair a final fluff with her fingers and grabbed her bag. Checking that her phone was charged, she stuffed her hotel key in her back pocket and headed for Cat's room.

Shaney's Pub was exactly the kind of local watering hole that the crew favored. It had a menu full of deep-fried delicacies and forty beers on tap. And it was packed.

Cat's entrance brought with it the usual stir in the crowd, but as they most often found, locals of smaller towns were more respectful of her time and space. This suburb of Portland was no different. After a handful of polite autograph requests, everyone settled back into their Friday night routine.

Paige perched at a high-top table in the bar with the members of her team rotating in and out of the other seat. *It's fun to see everyone cut a little loose*, she thought, nursing her beer. And it said a lot about them that even midseason, they still chose to spend their downtime together.

Felicia, in jeans and a Steely Dan T-shirt, plunked down across from Paige and fished a cheese stick off the appetizer plate. "So how's it feel to be talent?" she asked, biting into the melted cheese.

Paige groaned. "How long do you think they'll play this out until they give up on it? I'm not bringing anything to the table with my scripted behind-the-scenes observations." Yesterday she'd muddled through it, avoiding any emotional hotspots in her answers to Andy's questions, and guessed that she came across as more hostile than anything else.

"It's all part of the game." Felicia had been in the game for a good number of years more than Paige. She'd seen it all as reality TV evolved. "You know, just because the network is hoping for some crazy affair with you and Gannon doesn't mean it's a terrible idea."

Paige gaped at her friend.

Felicia shrugged her broad shoulders. "All I'm saying is don't let them pull your strings, and don't let them scare you off something that might be great. Just because they want it for ratings doesn't mean that it wouldn't be a good thing for you personally."

"Me and Gannon?" Paige was still stunned.

"The way you two rub each other the wrong way? That's all spark. You just might combust someday." Felicia glanced over her shoulder at her name being called. "Looks like I'm up in darts." And with that, she left Paige gaping after her.

She didn't have much time to be shocked. The Friday night entertainment, a five-piece country cover band, was pumping out an enthusiastic beat. Cat spotted her and towed her out onto the crowded dance floor.

"Let's see if your feet remember how to do anything besides stand all day," Cat yelled over the music.

Paige gave up on trying to think or maintain her wallow and matched Cat's footwork. Cat loved to dance when she was sober, and she became much more aggressive about her love when she drank. It was Paige's job to keep her entertained and hydrated so she didn't try to disappear with a stranger or drink so much that she'd be suffering the next day.

It wasn't necessarily a hardship. Paige appreciated the chance to kick back during the back-to-back shoots. There was something about letting go of everything else and just following a beat with her body that felt good. It helped that she'd taken a ton of hip-hop dance classes with her girlfriends in college. Together, she and Cat were drawing attention, and since it had nothing to do with Gannon or her job, Paige embraced it.

Cat whirled off with a guy in a checkered shirt and cowboy boots, waving over his broad shoulder. Paige turned to head to the bar on a quest for water when she found herself making eye contact with warm brown eyes and a cute smile. The man wore a golf shirt and cargo shorts. Preppy without going too far into the country club direction, he had short blondish hair and no wedding ring.

"Hi," he said, almost shyly.

Paige smiled in response. "Hi."

"Can I buy you a drink?" He wiggled the empty beer bottle in his hand.

"I'm on a quest for water," Paige told him. It was as much the truth as a test. There was always the guy at the bar who "jokingly" tried to ply a single woman with alcohol even when she said she was just drinking water.

"I'd be happy to accompany you on your quest," he offered.

Passed the test. Paige's smile was even warmer now. "Sure."

They made their way to the bar, a dark, sticky slab of wood similar to every other bar in every other town. There, Cute Blond Guy flagged down the bartender. He ordered "a water for the lady" and introduced himself as Marcus.

"It's nice to meet you, Marcus of Hydration. I'm Paige."

"So come here often, Paige?" he grinned.

She laughed. "First time ever. I'm only in town for the week. Do *you* come here often?"

He shook his head and handed over the water the bartender passed to him. "I'm not a regular. I just met a client for a drink, and then I saw you."

Sweet and honest. She liked that.

Paige felt a change in the atmosphere as if the temperature in the bar suddenly rose a dozen degrees. And there was Gannon. Wearing clean jeans, flip-flops, and a T-shirt that molded to his spectacular chest, he stood in the doorway surveying the lay of the land.

Her heart limped unevenly in her chest.

When the hell did that happen? When did a distant and completely understandable appreciation for his fine form transfer into an actual crush? She had Marcus standing in front of her, an actual nice guy who was interested in her, and she was drooling over a man who had proven himself to be too temperamental to be trusted.

As if he'd locked on to her thoughts, Gannon met her gaze from across the space. The corner of his mouth tugged up.

A loud whoop originated from the dance floor. "Paigey!"

"Does she belong to you?" Marcus asked, pointing in the opposite direction with his bottle. Cat was now riding the shoulders of the hulking plaid shirt cowboy and waving like she was on a bull.

Paige sighed. "She's going to knock herself out before she passes out."

"She looks familiar." Marcus's thought trailed off, and Paige could see him trying to tease out where he knew Cat from.

"Do you watch the Welcome Home Network?"

He frowned, still looking at Cat. "Occasionally." And then the dawning realization crept over his face. "She's one of the twins, right?"

"Catalina King," Paige sighed. This was usually where the guy tried to casually ask for an introduction, as if anyone needed a formal invitation to go meet Cat.

"Huh," Marcus said, turning his attention back to her. "I'd

heard the show was coming to town. So do you work on the show? What's it called?"

Paige found herself pleasantly surprised when the drunken, beautiful blond blur of Cat King did nothing to sway Marcus's focus. "*Kings of Construction*. I'm a field producer for the show."

"And what does a field producer do?"

"Well, tonight, the field producer is babysitting Cat on her birthday."

"Ah, one of those never-off-the-clock positions?" Marcus said with wry amusement.

"You sound familiar with the concept," Paige laughed. She had the cutest guy in all of Portland, Maine, flirting with her, and all she could focus on was the weight of Gannon's gaze on her.

"I work for an IT company that serves small businesses, so everything is always an emergency."

"You have a lot of people depending on you," Paige guessed, toying with the straw in her drink.

Marcus leaned in a little closer. She could smell a hint of his cologne, something subtle and spicy.

"It sounds like you do too." The band shifted gears into a slow number. "Do you want to talk about work, or would you like to dance?"

Paige bit her lip. He was so cute. What the hell. "Let's dance. Just watch out for TV stars falling out of the sky."

He laughed and took her hand, leading her toward the dance floor. Her eyes met Gannon's as she skirted a table of middle-aged ladies drinking a pitcher of margaritas. There was heat in those hazel eyes, and she could feel it as he looked her up and down. On the dance floor, other couples parted and closed ranks around them, and Paige felt a sense of relief, as if the human barrier could protect her from those steamy glances.

Whatever her relationship had been with Gannon, something had shifted for them both, and she only hoped it wasn't too late to go back to the way it was. It was safer that way. Easier.

Marcus pulled her gently into his arms, still respectful of her space, and she forced herself to give him her full attention. He made her laugh and asked her about her life. He was smart and sweet and confident. And Paige couldn't figure for the life of her how he was single. When she voiced just that—damn Gannon and his encouragement to say what was on her mind—Marcus gave a heavy sigh.

"Just got out of a long-term relationship."

"How long?" Paige asked in sympathy.

"We started dating when we were seventeen."

"Ouch."

"It's for the best," he told her. "You know, you're the first girl I've hit on since the breakup."

"Really?" Paige was unreasonably delighted.

Marcus nodded. "You should feel very flattered," he teased.

"Oh, I do," she promised.

"In fact, if I weren't heading out of here to catch up with some family that's only in town tonight, I'd ask if you wanted to go someplace quieter. Maybe have a piece of pie?"

He brushed a curl back from her face, and Paige felt a sweet warmth at his touch. *Finally*, her body was reacting appropriately. Sure, it wasn't the internal inferno she felt when Gannon had dug under her T-shirt to find her mic pack, but still, it was something.

"A girl would have a hard time saying no to pie."

He grinned. "I'm glad I met you, Paige."

"I'm glad you did too."

She felt a frisson of heat spark across her skin and found Gannon at the bar, beer in hand, staring at her.

The song ended, and she and Marcus broke apart. He reached into his pocket and pulled out a business card. "I really do have to go. But if you have any time while you're in town, call me for pie."

She took the card. "I really don't get any downtime during shoots, but if I did, I'd be calling you."

He smiled and offered his hand. "It was great to meet you."

She took it, enjoying the gentle squeeze. "It was really nice meeting you, Marcus."

He tapped the card in her hand. "Don't forget me."

She watched him leave, a goofy smile on her face.

Marcus's card was snatched out of her hand. "He's not your type," Gannon said, appearing at her side.

CHAPTER

15

"Give me that," she ordered, reaching for the card. "You don't know what my type is." She wondered why it was that the scent of Gannon's deodorant and laundry detergent was so sexy to her.

"Do you?" Gannon countered. "I've never seen you date."

"You only see me four months out of the year," Paige reminded him.

The band slowed it down again, and Gannon, with the practiced smoothness of a highly skilled ladies' man, encircled her waist and guided her back onto the dance floor. His palms burned into her skin through the thin layer of her silky shirt. She didn't feel protected anymore. Not with Gannon pulling her in too close. He wasn't interested in keeping a friendly space between them. He wanted to feel her body against his, and the part of Paige's brain that didn't give a damn about consequences agreed.

She put her hands on his shoulders in part not to cause a scene and to also control the infinitesimal space between them.

"Your hair smells like piña coladas," Gannon said, his voice raspy in her ear.

"This isn't a good idea with everything that's happened this week," Paige warned. He was so tall and broad, she couldn't see the rest of the dance floor behind him. He'd skillfully led her to the darkest corner, and she'd gone along unknowingly or, worse, willingly.

"Sometimes bad ideas are the best ideas."

"Why did you take Marcus's card?" Paige asked suddenly.

Gannon's lips quirked. "Because I'm interested."

"In Marcus?"

"In you, Paige. I'm interested in you."

"I'm not interested in being interested in you," she said, feeling panic slick through her stomach.

"That's different from not being interested," Gannon observed.

She didn't know how to respond to that. She could tell him she wasn't interested, but Paige got the distinct impression he'd call bullshit on her. For someone who hadn't known her long, he'd figured her out quickly.

"You're not boyfriend material."

"I'm not?"

Paige shook her head. "You're a fixer-upper. I don't have the time to take on a project man right now."

When he simply squeezed her harder, she sighed.

"Do you want me to go into all the reasons we would be a terrible idea?" Paige asked.

He shook his head. "I'm only interested in one reason why we'd work."

"I'm not risking my career for a night in your bed."

"We can use your bed then."

"I love how you take my concerns so seriously." Paige scowled up at him.

"What concerns you most about having sex with me?"

"Jesus, Gannon!" There was such a thing as being too unfiltered.

"See? You already have the vocabulary down."

She stomped on his foot, which had no effect on him whatsoever. "I don't want to deal with the fallout of having my private life become public interest."

"It doesn't have to happen that way."

"What? You mean sneaking in and out of each other's hotel rooms and hoping no one notices?"

"Think about it," he said, sliding his hands lower on her hips, his long fingers digging into the denim of her shorts, and Paige felt herself go wet. "No one would have to know."

His breath was warm against her face. She couldn't stop staring at his mouth, and when her body brushed up against his, she could feel the hard length of him through his jeans. Her nipples pebbled against the lace of her bralette.

"There's also the matter of your girlfriend," she said, trying to remind him as well as her body that what they were discussing was off-limits.

Gannon looked genuinely confused. "What are you talking about?"

"Meeghan Traxx. Your girlfriend."

His expression darkened. "Meeghan and I are not involved. And you're pissing me off suggesting that I'd be propositioning you if I were with someone."

"But the news…"

"Gossip. Rumors. We never dated. Do you really think that's my type?" He looked pissed off for a whole different reason now.

"This is…intense. I think I need a drink." The words came out in a rush.

"That makes two of us." He held her still with one arm and used his free hand to subtly adjust his erection before turning around and leading the way back to the bar. Gannon kept her hand clamped in his, and Paige had to jog to keep up with him.

He ordered for them both, and she was surprised that he knew the beer she preferred.

She took a long swig, trying to cool her body down from the inside out.

"Look," Gannon began. "I'm not thrilled about this either. We work together in an intense environment. It's a terrible idea to hook up. But I'm starting to think it's an inevitable, terrible idea. I keep waiting to stop thinking about you, and it only makes me think about you more."

Raw. Honest. Unfiltered. That was Gannon King.

"Paige!" Cat's squeal was the only warning Paige had before Cat barreled into her, knocking her into Gannon's solid chest and still-hard cock.

She shoved herself away from Gannon and turned to study her friend. "Oh boy. Let's get a water and chicken fingers in you," Paige assessed.

"That sounds awesome! Gann, you order. I'm gonna take my best friend Paige here out to shake her ass."

She didn't wait for Gannon's consent, just clamped a hand on Paige's wrist and started dragging. Paige gave herself a second to think about how many Kings had dragged her all over the bar that night. She really needed to look into shoes with better traction.

"My brother looked like he was going to devour you," Cat shouted in Paige's face.

"We were just…arguing."

Cat ignored her lie. "I had a feeling about you two from the very first time I saw you put him in his place. Gannon needs someone who's not going to kiss his ass. He really likes you."

"Cat, I don't want to talk about your brother!"

Cat did a little spin on the floor. "Okay, then tell me about cute polo shirt guy."

"Why don't you tell me about tall plaid shirt man?"

Cat lasted two songs on the dance floor before she finally let Paige drag her back to the bar. "It's my birthday," she announced at the top of her lungs, and the crowd around them cheered.

Drink tokens started lining up in front of her as if they sprouted out of the bar. Paige slapped one out of her hand. "Uh-uh. Grease and water first."

Cat picked up a chicken finger and bit into it. "Paige is my babysitter," she explained to Gannon.

"I can see that," her brother said, enjoying drunk Cat.

Cat stopped chewing abruptly, her face going serious. "Did you know it's *your* birthday too?"

Gannon looked at Paige over his sister's head. "How much did you let her drink?"

"Hell if I know. I was distracted. Rico?" Paige waved the cameraman down. "Did you see how much Cat drank?"

He shrugged his shoulders under his purple bowling shirt. "Saw her do a couple of shots with that table of college kids. You see Cat drinking anything, Mel?"

Mel cruised up with a gin and tonic in one hand and a fistful of phone numbers in the other. "Cat? I saw that plaid shirt cowboy buy her a couple of rounds. Oh, and then the bartender gave her some pink frothy drink."

"Crap," Paige muttered. Between Marcus and Gannon, she'd shirked her duties. There was no way Cat was coming out of this unscathed. And a hungover Cat during shooting was worse than a sober Gannon.

They lasted another hour at the bar before Paige recognized Cat's puke face and dragged her out. The bushes in the parking lot took the brunt of it, but Cat promised she felt good enough to not throw up in the van. They all piled inside in varying stages of sobriety and inebriation, and Gannon—sober on his birthday—drove them back to the hotel. Cat made good on her word and waited to throw up again in the hotel parking lot. She waved enthusiastically to the desk worker, slurring out something about birthdays.

Gannon and Paige helped Cat to her room. Paige forced her friend to wash off her makeup and brush her teeth before tucking her into bed. She found Cat's stash of Gatorade in the mini fridge and left a bottle of it on the nightstand next to a bottle of aspirin. Cat was snoring by the time Paige let herself out.

Gannon was waiting in the hallway.

"She's passed out," Paige reported. "But we'd better send Mel or Sam for breakfast sandwiches in the morning. She's going to need the grease."

Gannon nodded but said nothing.

"I guess I'll turn in too," Paige said, her nerves making her chatty.

"I'll walk you to your room."

She shot him a warning look.

"I said I'll walk you to your room, not peel your shorts off you."

The image he planted in her mind taunted her enough to trip over her own feet as they walked side by side down the hall without touching. He grabbed her arm, righting her, and she pulled away.

She stopped in front of her door and fished the key out of her pocket. "Good night, Gannon."

"Good night, Paige. Dream good dreams." That sexy smirk told her exactly what he knew she'd be dreaming about.

She let herself in and shut the door before she could lose her mind and invite him inside. They both knew it was a terrible idea. She had no interest in being publicly linked to him. It would be career suicide for her, and she needed one more season before she could move on from this life.

But it was still tempting. He was tempting.

She looked down at the bakery box on the table. "Crap," she muttered.

CHAPTER
16

Gannon wasn't sure who was more surprised to find Paige at his door, him or her.

"Is everything okay?" he asked, certain only a disaster or emergency could have brought her knocking on his door after the brush-off she'd given him.

She took a deep breath. "You know, Cat makes such a big deal of her birthday that sometimes I forget it's yours too."

He gave her a half smile. "It's been that way my whole life. I don't want the fuss, and she thrives on it."

"Still. It *is* your birthday." She produced a cupcake with a lit candle from behind her back.

She'd brought him a chocolate cupcake with a candle for his birthday. The lust he'd been tangling with for weeks ratcheted up another notch, and something else, something warm and sweet, rolled through him.

He leaned in and, closing his eyes, blew out the candle with a puff.

"Did you make a wish?" Paige asked. She sounded a little breathless. He liked it.

"This." He moved before she could, taking the cupcake from her and yanking her by the shirtfront into him. He laid his lips on hers and felt his body light up. Her soft mouth parted, in shock, in invitation. It didn't matter. He used the opening to sweep his tongue into her mouth, tasting her leisurely, deliberately.

She fisted her hands in his T-shirt and kissed him back. There was no slow thaw here. There was a spark that started a wildfire. The kiss was a battleground, each fighting for the upper hand. Gannon won, barely, kissing her senseless. Slowly he gentled his lips, brushing them lightly over hers before eventually pulling back.

He was hard as granite for her, and Paige looked as if she'd melt to her knees if he let go of her. Her blue eyes were glassy as they stared into his, searching for answers to unknown questions.

"That doesn't taste like not interested to me."

The dazed look vanished and was replaced with a mutinous one. Paige whirled around and stormed down the hall, temper snapping off her like lightning.

Oh yeah. It was a terrible idea, but it was happening whether they both liked it or not.

———

It was exactly the kind of day that made Gannon hate his job. Cat was hungover as hell. They were shooting around her as much as possible, which forced him into more camera time, which he resented. The weather didn't help. Late spring in Maine was a clusterfuck. The high winds and spontaneous downpours were wreaking havoc with the tents they'd set up

108

on the family's uneven front yard and driveway. He was soaking wet and pissed off, and it wasn't even nine in the morning yet.

The GC, Brunelli, was a decent enough guy and had things under control inside, freeing Gannon up to spend an hour or two on his project. When he saw Cat's designs for Malia's bedroom, he knew exactly what his contribution would be. He'd sat down and sketched out a canopy bed fit for a princess that had Cat crumpling her plans for a store-bought one. And now he was stuck actually making it.

They were stealing space from an oddly shaped spare bedroom on the second floor to enlarge Malia's room, giving them the space for a queen-size. Carina had mentioned that after chemo treatments, she usually slept in Malia's room on the floor to make sure the little girl didn't need anything in the middle of the night. A queen-size would give them both a comfortable place to rest, and Malia would—hopefully—grow into the bed and still be able to use it as an adult.

He ran his gloved hand over the cherry two-by-ten and clenched his jaw. In his opinion, kids shouldn't get cancer. No one should, but especially not fucking kids.

"Gannon, you're glaring at that piece of wood like you're going to break another piece of wood over it," Paige called from off camera, her tone mild.

He raised his gaze to hers, shoving his pencil behind his ear, and got a little kick out of seeing her blush. That was another reason he was annoyed. He'd kissed her last night with the intention of doing some structural damage to her walls. Instead, she'd greeted him with a cool "good morning" when he arrived on set pissed off and tired from spending the night trying to will away a never-ending hard-on.

Somehow it was her fault. He was sure of it, and he was going to make sure Paige knew it too.

"If you've got a problem with how I look when I work, you should point the camera in someone else's face for the next hour," he snapped, stalking over to the table closest to the camera in search of the damn tape measure he kept misplacing.

She raised her eyebrows at him, not in surprise but in frosty judgment. Usually he enjoyed riling her, but this time he was the one getting riled.

Building furniture was an artistic process to him, and doing it in front of a camera felt like making porn. He was taking something satisfying and exciting and turning it into a shitty facsimile that gave the audience unrealistic expectations. It was bullshit. He gave her a look that transmitted that message loud and clear.

"We're going to need you to walk us through the cuts for the headboard," Paige called out again. This time, there was an edge to her voice.

Good. It was about fucking time.

"Well, guess what? I'm not ready to move on to the goddamn headboard. I'm cutting for the frame."

She crossed her arms, and he bet money she was digging her nails into her palms. "I know it doesn't make sense to you to shoot out of sequence—"

"No, no, it doesn't make sense to me. I'm making a bed here for a six-year-old with cancer. Why don't you let me do my job and just shoot *reality* for once?"

There was a blaze in her eyes, and he wanted to know what was going through her head.

Paige held two fingers to her ear and murmured something into her headset. She paused, listening. "Why don't you take five, Gannon?" she suggested calmly.

"I don't need to take five. I need to get moving on this project."

"Yeah? And we need to wrap up filming this scene so we can stay on schedule," she snapped back. "Everyone take five."

No one argued with her order given like the crack of a whip.

Gannon chucked his pencil to the ground and stalked up to her. "Let's talk," he said, grabbing her by the wrist and hauling her up the driveway into the house. The place was crawling with contractors and workers. But there was one place no one would interrupt them.

Yanking open the basement door, which squealed in protest, he pulled Paige down the stairs after him. It was a musty, dingy space with a concrete floor and a ceiling so low he couldn't stand straight.

Paige wrinkled her nose and started to speak, but he pressed a finger against her lips. Reaching around her, he yanked the power pack out of the waistband of her shorts and turned it off. Then he did the same to his, tossing them both on top of a large plastic tub filled with wrapping paper.

"What the hell are you doing?" she hissed. There was fire in those blue eyes, and it only served to fan his own flames.

"I'm doing what I've been thinking about since last night." He grabbed her by the front of her windbreaker and closed his mouth over hers with something close to violence. She fought him for half a second before digging her fingers into his shoulders and doing some ravaging of her own.

It was like tasting the sun. An inferno ignited between them and bloomed hotter yet with every stroke and slide of their tongues. He wasn't sure they weren't in danger of spontaneously combusting. He let his hands slide over her, over her shoulders and down her back where he cupped her tight ass, holding her against the hard-on that was back with a vengeance. She moaned and cuddled her hips closer to his dick.

This wasn't supposed to happen. She wasn't supposed to make him feel like this, out of control and needy. But that didn't change the fact that that was exactly how she made him feel.

Then she was pulling back and slapping a hand to his chest.

"You can't just drag me away from work because you're turned on or pissed off. I'm not into this caveman shit. Got it?" She was mad *and* turned on, and it was a potent combination. Those blue eyes were glassy with desire, her mouth swollen from his assault, but the rest of her body practically crackled with anger, passion, *need*.

"Got it." He nodded, grinning. "God, I'm so into you."

She growled in frustration and pulled his head down for another kiss. He cupped her ass and lifted her, wrapping her long legs around his hips. She fit against his cock like a key sliding into a lock, and he had to fight the urge to drag her shorts off right here and now.

With the aid of his hands, she ground against him, sighing into his mouth. Pulling back again, she looked into his eyes. "I am not going to be some kind of red-carpet groupie for you."

His laugh was pained. "Of course not."

"My personal life is private, and being with you is way too public. I'm wearing a mic at work, for God's sake."

"That's understandable." He slanted his lips over hers. The sexy little whimper she made had him frantic. He didn't bother breaking the kiss to say her name. "Paige?"

"Mmph?"

"I need to fuck you."

She pulled back as if he'd told her he wanted to shave her head. "Jesus, Gannon. Not here."

"I know not here!" Although his dick clearly had no qualms about the location. "Tonight?"

She went rigid and then relaxed slowly, muscle by muscle,

in his arms. He looked into her eyes, willing her to say yes, needing her to say yes.

When Paige started nodding, he gripped her ass harder. "Tonight?" he said again.

"Tonight," she whispered.

CHAPTER 17

Paige did her best to compartmentalize her feelings on set that afternoon, but holy hell. She'd climbed Gannon like a tree and ground on him with a desperation that scared the ever-living crap out of her. Now, she was counting down the hours until she could go back to the hotel and at least shower before she let Gannon ravage her. Or she ravaged him.

All her very logical doubts about her job, his absolute wrongness for her, were still there. But they were much quieter since they'd kissed…and nearly gotten naked.

She wanted him. He wanted her. They were two single, consenting adults who could keep a secret. So what if the network wanted this to happen? So what if it would be career suicide?

Okay, that one still bothered her. Which was exactly why she wasn't going to think about it. She had a whole host of other things to think about, and thankfully Gannon wasn't here on set to further distract her. He was shooting an hour and a half away on location at a metal shop where they were creating a custom canopy for Malia's princess bed. Lou and Mel were with him.

Here at the Dufour house, Paige was in charge of wrangling Malia's class from school in helping Cat with a giant mural for the little girl's bedroom. Twenty-three six- and seven-year-olds were currently running amok on set.

Rico and Tony were shooting the chaos while Cat snapped selfie after selfie with the kids.

The late afternoon sky was darkening ominously with swollen clouds that Paige willed to pass. The last thing they needed was to juggle filming, children, and a storm.

"Okay, let's get this circus under a tent," Paige said into her headset. She flagged down Sam and enlisted his help herding the kids into the second tent they'd set up in the Dufour driveway. The parents were all ushered into the craft services tent where plenty of coffee and snacks awaited. It didn't leave a lot of room for the shooters to maneuver, but if it was going to rain, they needed to be under some kind of roof.

Paige wished Cat would have had this brilliant brainstorm before shooting commenced because she could have arranged to do it at the local elementary school rather than having an entire class running around a construction site. But it was a lesson learned for future shows.

Paige stood in the tent entrance, subtly blocking the way out so none of the kids could wander without her seeing them. Cat stood in the center with Billie Brunelli, whose son, a bespectacled little guy with freckles and a Brunelli Construction shirt, was in Malia's class.

There was no point in blocking the scene. Cat would go where she needed to go, and Rico and Tony would follow as best they could. They were hoping for a few minutes of cute kid footage and an end product that could be used in the reveal.

Cat handed out blank canvases to groups of three and explained the hand-printing process. The parents had been warned in advance to send their kids to the set in clothing that could be destroyed. The show had coughed up an additional hundred bucks in the budget for kid-sized volunteer shirts that would soon be unrecognizable under shades of pink and purple paint.

It was chaos, but cute chaos. It sounded like a cafeteria with all the chatter under the tent. It was so loud that Paige almost mistook the long rumble of thunder for a truck on the street. Her phone vibrated silently but insistently in her pocket. She pulled it out, expecting to see a call from Mel, but was greeted instead with a weather alert.

Severe thunderstorm warning for their location.

As if to punctuate the alert, the wind gusted behind her, rippling the tent walls and drawing squeals from the kids. A bolt of lightning forked across the darkened sky behind her and a long roll of thunder echoed on its heels.

"Shit." Paige muttered into her headset. "Andy, I think we're gonna need to get everyone inside in the basement."

She saw him nod across the tent before he called cut. Cat looked up from where she was immersed in a painting with two kids.

"Okay, everyone." Paige clapped her hands. "We're going to take a little break and go inside."

The thunder crashed outside and a handful of kids screamed. Cat and Andy sprang into action, marshaling the kids into a line.

Paige got back on her headset and yelled for Sam. "Sam, I need you to get all the adults in the house. Storms coming in fast."

Rico headed outside first with his camera to get the kids as they hustled out of the tent behind Cat. "Everyone keep going!" Cat yelled into the wind. The clouds burst open, sending the first fat drops falling to earth. Andy ducked out of the tents, waving parents over and directing them into the house.

"Basement, everyone! Go!"

Paige stood by the tent entrance with Tony, counting little heads as they ran by.

"Twenty-one," she said as the last little boy jogged past. "Shit. We're missing two, unless I miscounted." She ducked her head out into the yard. Andy and Cat were rushing everyone inside.

Lightning struck again, this time close enough that the hair on her arms stood up.

"I need a head count," Paige shouted into her headset. She heard garbled voices coming through on the other end and knew it would be impossible to get a definitive number with everyone crammed into the house. "Goddamn it," she muttered. "Tony, go inside, I need to make sure no one else is still out here."

She didn't wait for his response but ran toward the back of the tent. There were tall studio lights set up against one wall of the tent, which was billowing like a jet was taking off outside. Back in the corner, there were two tables stacked with art supplies and boxes. Paige spotted a little sneaker with ducks on it and then another one. She jumped over still wet canvases on the ground and ducked down.

Two tear-stained faces greeted her. The little boy was holding his hands over his ears, and the little girl was stroking his leg and telling him everything would be okay.

"Found them!" Paige said into her headset. "Hi, guys, I'm Paige. I'm going to take you inside so we don't get wet from the rain, okay?"

The little girl nodded. "Dis is Ashton. I'm Regina. He's a little scared." She pronounced her own name with a *w* instead of an *r*, and it was freaking adorable.

"Okay, Regina and Ashton. I'm going to hold your hands, and we're going to run real fast and catch up with everyone else inside, okay?"

Regina nodded earnestly and held one hand out to Paige. Reluctantly, Ashton took a hand off his ear and held it out to her.

Paige tried not to let her urgency show and carefully led them toward the front of the tent. Tony had ignored her orders to seek shelter and was waiting for them, holding the flap open.

Paige looked beyond Tony to the downpour that obscured the front of the house. "I think we're going to get a little wet," she warned the kids. "But it will still be better inside."

"Where are you, St. James?" Andy yelled in her ear. "We've got everyone in the basement."

"We're coming in," Paige said, keeping her voice calm. She squeezed the kids' hands reassuringly. "Everybody ready? We're going to run real fast."

Regina nodded and Ashton looked like he wanted to throw up.

"Okay, on three. One, two, three."

They took off, Paige keeping her strides short so the kids could keep up with her. Tony trotted along behind her. The gust of wind caught them all by surprise, and she almost didn't hear the snapping sound. Ashton's hand slipped from hers, and he started to run toward the craft service tent. One of the lines securing the tent whipped up, slicing through electrified air.

God, the tent was going to collapse, and Ashton was running right for it.

"Mommy!" he yelled, his voice fearful.

"Regina, you go with Tony to the house," Paige yelled over

the sound of the wind and thunder. She took off at a dead sprint. It happened so fast she didn't have time to think. Another tent stake broke loose, and with one slow-motion flutter, the front half of the tent lifted off the ground. Ashton froze in place, and Paige threw herself over him. She caught something heavy across her back, and had she been standing, the blow would have felled her.

Canvas covered them, blocking out the light but also the rain. The pain was shocking, but she didn't want to scare Ashton any more than he already was by crying like a baby.

"Paige!"

It sounded like Tony's voice, but she couldn't tell over the wind. Her headset was gone, and all she was conscious of was Ashton shivering under her and the weight of something crushing down on top of her. There was a moaning shudder, and something sliced over her bare leg. It hurt like a hundred bee stings. Something solid smacked her in the side of the face, and she saw a flash of light before her head fell limply to the ground.

She wasn't unconscious. She was floating on pain and confusion. She could smell blood, taste it too. Or was that tears?

Ashton was sobbing. The poor kid had already been afraid of thunder. Now he was going to be scarred for life. She hoped to God everyone had gotten out of the craft services tent, hoped everyone on-site had made it inside.

Somewhere, over the whip of wind and the crack of thunder, she heard sirens. She felt a trickling warmth over her skin and hoped it wasn't as much blood as it felt like. Nothing hurt too badly right now, but the fog that was closing in on her could be shock. Hopefully it wasn't anything that would interfere with her plans with Gannon tonight.

"Hey, Ashton? Buddy? Are you okay?" she asked. She was surprised at how weak her voice sounded.

"I'm s-s-scared," he howled in the throes of tears.

"It's okay to be scared, but I promise we're going to be okay."

His next wail was a little quieter.

"Do you know your ABCs?"

"Uh-huh," he sobbed.

"Let's sing the ABCs until our friends come find us," she suggested.

"I want my mommy," he sniffled.

At this moment, I wouldn't say no to my own mother, Paige thought.

"Well, let's sing until your mommy and my friends come help us."

He smelled like bubble gum shampoo, and Paige found it oddly comforting. She tried to shift her weight off him, but something was pressing her into the earth from above.

"A, B, C..." he started off with a shaky voice, and Paige joined him. She wondered why she could see colors behind her closed eyes and was glad that she didn't feel cold anymore.

CHAPTER
18

Gannon adjusted his welding goggles and watched as Rocco, a skinny man in his midfifties with a bushy mustache, finished off a clean weld. They were shooting in a tiny rural town an hour and a half west of Portland in a custom welding shop.

He didn't mind shooting scenes like this, giving other artisans some camera time while he looked on or tried his own hand at it.

It was, to him, one of the better parts of the show. Showcasing local artisans was a good karma kind of thing to do. Not only did viewers love the custom stuff they were able to do for families, but the artisans got a boost in business after the episodes aired.

Of course, Gannon would never let Paige know he liked doing these segments. He preferred to keep everyone thinking that he hated everything about filming. It was better if there were some things no one else knew. Though after tonight, he and Paige would know each other a whole lot better.

He felt his blood immediately leave his brain. *Tonight.*

His impatience was probably translating to the camera loud and clear, and if he chose to watch this episode when it aired, he'd remember exactly what he'd been thinking in this moment. *Paige.*

Rocco shut off the torch and flipped his visor up to admire the weld.

"That looks great, man," Gannon said, clapping the man on his back.

Rocco's lips twitched under his mustache in a shy grin, his earlier nervousness about the camera long forgotten. "Not too shabby," he agreed.

"Can we take a look at the final design?" Gannon asked.

"Sure, sure."

Rocco led the way over to a workstation designed purely for function with no regard for form. Three flat-screen monitors squatted on a heavy, paint-splattered worktable. He pulled the design program up, and Louis sidled up behind them to get a look at the screen.

"I took the sketch you sent me and then put some finishing touches on it here and here," Rocco said, pointing to the corners of the canopy. Gannon listened as Rocco walked him through the finer points of the design until Mel laid a hand on Gannon's shoulder.

He took one look at her unusually pale face and knew something was wrong. Gannon rose, his stomach sinking as the wheeled stool under him skidded out from under him. "What? What is it?"

She took a shaky breath. "There was an accident on set. Paige—"

He grabbed Mel by the shoulders. "Is she okay?"

Her eyes watered, and his heart stuttered.

"I don't know." Mel shook her head, a tear slipping out from the corner of her eye. "Andy texted, and he's not answering his phone. 'It's bad' is all he said."

Gannon didn't wait for anything else. "Keys!" he yelled and caught the van's keys out of midair when Louis chucked them. "I'll send a ride for you," he called over his shoulder.

He was peeling out of the lot and dialing Andy's number and then Cat's. Neither of them answered. He slammed his palm down on the steering wheel. "Fuck, fuck, fuck." Gannon tossed his phone on the passenger seat and floored the gas pedal. The van sluggishly lumbered up to speed.

She had to be okay. Had to be. What if she wasn't? What if "bad" was the worst that could happen? Goddamn it.

He let the fear plague him until he felt like he could crawl out of his own skin and then picked up his phone and started dialing again.

———

Paige let the water drum against her skin, trying to feel something other than pain. Every inch of her hurt. She wasn't supposed to get her dressings wet, but she sure as hell wasn't going to bed still wearing blood and grit.

She had promised the well-meaning, helicoptering Cat that she was heading straight to bed to get rid of her friend so she could blatantly ignore doctor's orders alone. The hospital had been an exhausting blur. Ashton was fine, thank God. He'd sustained a scraped elbow and lost a ducky shoe but had been otherwise unscathed. Tony, hero cameraman and child saver, had needed stitches in his arm. The details were still foggy, but Paige thought she'd heard he'd tucked Regina under his arm like a football and sprinted for the house where one of Brunelli's crew grabbed her. Tony had dumped his camera on the porch and ran back, trying to dig her out of the tent that had fallen on her.

Both her phone and mic had been destroyed. The phone cracked when a falling tent pole landed on her like a piñata, and water damage had taken care of the rest. She'd been pissed about the phone and not the least bit upset about the mic. But now she was just tired. Exhausted. Everything hurt. It felt as though a truck, not a tent, had leveled her. Thank God she hadn't been under one of the woodworking pop-ups with two-by-fours and sharp tools.

No one would tell her anything about the set or the shooting schedule. She could only imagine that it was a chaotic mess. Andy had just repeatedly assured her via Cat's phone that there was nothing to worry about and to get some rest.

It was bullshit. She hadn't broken anything, although her face still felt a little wonky where one of the camera equipment cases had smashed into it. She'd hardly needed any stitches, yet they were treating her like an invalid. Cat had shot alternating dirty and then worried looks at her the whole way back to the hotel from the hospital where Paige had refused to stay for observation.

She just needed a shower and some sleep. Maybe a solid eight hours of sleep. Then she'd be back on her feet and everything could go back to normal. Thank God she'd scheduled an extra two days for this shoot. The cleanup alone would probably take a full day.

The warm water soothed her aching muscles, and she rested her forehead against the cool tile. The only thing she hadn't anticipated was her inability to lift her arms. She couldn't seem to get them past shoulder height, which left her hair a damp, dirty tangle of dried blood and who knows what else. Paige shifted her feet and winced as pain shot like electricity through her system.

How was she going to get out of the tub?

Great. She was going to drown in the shower. This was the way her life would end. Not with a peaceful passing in her sleep at age ninety-seven. No, she'd just slide down this ivory tile and drown.

The door to the bathroom flew open and bounced off the wall.

"Jeez, Cat!" Paige groaned pitifully. "What the hell?" Annoyed that her friend had ignored her wish for privacy, she was a little relieved that Cat could help her out of the tub.

But it wasn't Cat ripping open the shower curtain and glaring at her.

It was Gannon.

CHAPTER

19

She stood with her hands braced against the tile, water cascading down her bruised and bandaged body. But she was alive. The part of him that had clenched into panic with Mel's announcement finally released.

When she didn't attempt to yell at him or shield herself from his gaze, a new worry bloomed. She was every color of purple across most of her back, and he cringed at the patches of gauze and tape that looked as though they were holding her together. Steam billowed around his head.

"I can't wash my hair," she said finally. Paige's voice had none of its usual authority, just exhaustion and that jagged edge of pain that hurt him to hear.

He wanted to scoop her up and lecture her on set safety. But that wasn't what she needed. She needed comfort.

Gannon studied her, hands on hips, for almost a full minute and then sighed. He started to work the laces of his boots loose. Toeing them off, he tugged his T-shirt over his head.

"Oh my God. What are you doing?" Paige's voice barely rose above the spray from the shower head.

"I'm washing your damn hair."

His jeans came next, and as his thumbs hooked into the waistband of his boxer briefs, Gannon noted that Paige's head spun back to face the shower wall. The last thing she needed was to add whiplash to her ailments.

He stepped in behind her and pulled the shower curtain back in place.

"Gannon—"

"Save it. We'll argue about this later." He guided her head under the spray and brushed her hair back from her face.

"This isn't happening." She murmured it so faintly he wasn't sure if she knew she said it out loud.

Gannon squirted a puddle of her shampoo into his callused hand. It smelled like coconuts. No wonder he always had visions of her on a beach in a tiny bikini—

He derailed that train of thought as soon as he felt the blood start to leave his head. Now was not the time.

He lowered the spray away from her face and worked his fingers through her hair in slow, gentle circles. A sigh escaped her lips and brought a lift to his.

The crown of suds grew with his ministrations until bubbles floated down between their bodies. He assumed that meant her hair was clean and adjusted the shower head to rinse it clean.

The warm water swept the lather from her hair, sending it streaming down her bare back and lower still over the round curves of her—

Gannon clenched his jaw. She was hurt. A damn tent had clobbered her. This wasn't the time to let his flag fly. Since he was in there with her, he sudsed up his own hair with her shampoo and quickly rinsed.

"Now what?" he said quietly in her ear.

"Conditioner." She pointed weakly toward the skinny blue bottle perched in the corner. He reached around her, wet skin skimming wet skin, and went instantly hard.

"Fuck," he muttered and grabbed the bottle. So much for self-control.

He knew she felt him against her. Goddamn it. When had he lost complete control of his body? Suddenly he was fourteen again and getting hard-ons with a slight breeze.

She cleared her throat, and Gannon gritted his teeth. He poured the conditioner into his hand and put the bottle down behind him where he wouldn't risk contact with her. But now she had goose bumps on her skin. Again, he reached around her, this time to adjust the hot water. And again his cock brushed the smooth, wet curves of her ass.

"Sorry." He gritted out the word. *The woman is in no condition to be poked and prodded with an erection that has a mind of its own*, he chastised himself.

Gannon began to work the conditioner through her hair. He had to force himself to slow down, to be more gentle.

"This isn't how I thought tonight would go...or how I thought I'd see you naked for the first time," she admitted.

Gannon's fingers paused in her hair. "So you *have* thought of it before today?"

He could hear her roll her eyes.

"Shut up. I'm delirious and don't know what I'm saying."

Gannon made a tail with her hair and worked the conditioner through it to the ends. "Just so you know, I'm choosing to be a gentleman now. But eventually you're going to have to face the music and tell me how you did think you'd see me naked."

Before she could answer, he pushed her face under the stream of water.

"Stop trying to drown me," she sputtered.

"Princess, drowning you is not what I have on my mind right now. What's next?"

"I'm not having you shave my legs."

"Agreed." His cock wouldn't be able to take it. "Soap?"

"Body wash," she corrected. Paige pointed to yet another bottle and the weird fluffy loofa on a string that all women seemed to own.

Gannon squeezed the thankfully unscented wash onto the ball. "Tell me if I hurt you," he said gruffly.

And since she was already aware that he was hard, Gannon wrapped an arm around her slim waist from behind to hold her steady and worked his way down from her shoulders, avoiding bandages.

Her goose bumps reappeared when he got to her lower back. "Are you cold?" he asked, slowing his circles.

She shook her head but didn't answer.

"Keep your hands on the wall, okay?" He knelt down to focus on the lower half of her body. She had a bruise blooming from her hip all the way around to cover most of her right ass cheek. But even with the contusion, he could see the perfection in her curves. He swirled a soapy path over it gently and worked his way down the backs of her thighs and her shapely calves, skipping the one that was bandaged with already blood-soaked gauze. He took a deep breath. "Okay, turn around."

Paige paused, and Gannon thought that she might be working up a refusal. But she gingerly shifted her weight and carefully turned to face him. Her knees buckled slightly, and she instinctively reached out and held on to his shoulders.

"You okay?" Gannon's voice felt like sandpaper in his throat.

She nodded, eyes closed tight.

He started with her feet and ankles and worked his way up. The iodine used by the doctors had stained parts of her sexy as hell bronze skin orange. Her fingers clenched reflexively on his shoulders when he swept the soapy ball higher, skimming over knees and thighs. Those mile-long legs guided his hands up and up.

She gave a little gasp when his hand skimmed over the flat of her stomach and her ribs. Gannon got to his feet. He was surprised when Paige kept her hands on his shoulders. To keep her steady, he slid an arm back around her waist. When he ran the soapy sponge over her breasts, he tried not to notice how full they were or how her nipples hardened under the glide of his hand.

Tried and failed. His throbbing dick noticed and jerked against her slick stomach in response. "Almost done," he whispered, streaking a soapy swath around the borders of bandages on her arm and ribs.

She was watching him now, her eyes heavy, lips parted. The steam from the shower slowly fogged the room. He wanted to lean in. To taste that mouth. To learn all the secrets her body had to tell. But more than that, he wanted to take her pain.

Gannon reached behind her and turned off the water. He swept open the curtain and watched the flush on Paige's cheeks spread. "Can you get out?"

She nodded but didn't move. He gave her three seconds, and when she still hadn't made the attempt, he scooped her up and stepped out. He had her sitting on the lid of the toilet and was wrapping her in a towel before she could even bluster at him. The way she was eyeing his monster hard-on had him yanking a second towel off the metal shelf and putting a terry-cloth barrier between them.

Working quickly, he dried her skin as gently as he could

and dragged his T-shirt over her head. Okay, not staring at her gorgeous, bare breasts helped him relax a little.

"What's next?" he asked, his voice gruffer than he intended. He could tell she was running through her postshower ritual in her head and trying to figure out if there was anything she'd allow him to do. He hoped to God she didn't need lotion applied to every inch. There was no way he'd survive that.

She looked up at the top of his head. "I don't suppose you know how to use a hair dryer?"

He searched the bathroom and found the hotel dryer stashed in a vanity drawer.

"I was just kidding. You don't have to do that," Paige said, eyes wide as he plugged the cord into the outlet.

"You're just afraid I'm going to fuck it up."

"You can probably catch hair on fire with one of those if used incorrectly," Paige predicted, eyeing the dryer in his hand with apprehension.

"Relax. I grew up with Cat. She made me help her with her hair sometimes, and if you ever repeat that to anyone," he said, wielding the dryer like a weapon, "I will have you dismembered."

"My lips are sealed," she said, a hint of a smile playing around the corners of her mouth. "Can you French braid?"

"Better than Cat can," he snorted. "She made me learn to French braid. I made her a paintball warrior."

"You are a man of many talents."

He had talents he was looking forward to her discovering.

"Do you have any…" He mimed squirting something into his hands.

"Product?" Paige asked.

"Yeah, like mousse stuff?"

She pointed at a silver can on the corner of the vanity. "Do you know how to use that?"

"I build fine furniture and houses and host a TV show for a living. I think I can handle squirting shit out of a can." Still, he paused long enough to read the directions before squeezing a dollop into his palm. He rubbed his hands together and worked them through her hair.

She closed her eyes, and he used the opportunity to study the bruising on her face. Purple and mottled, the goose egg rose proudly just under her temple. She winced when he got too close to the bump, and he gentled his hands.

Paige sighed as he worked the white stuff into her roots, rubbing gently with the pads of his fingers. He felt the tension in her begin to give and loosen. It physically hurt him to see her like this.

"Concussion?" he asked.

She shook her head slowly. "Hard head."

He turned the dryer on low and worked his hand through her hair, holding up strands, and when he was done, Paige shoved her hands through the roots and sighed.

"Do I want to know how I look?"

"Princess, you've got bigger problems than a hairdo," Gannon said glibly.

Paige groaned. "I was trying to forget about that. How bad is my face?" she asked, prodding the bruising with her fingers.

Gannon pulled her hand away from her face. "I've seen worse," he promised. He'd seen a few mixed martial arts matches that outdid Paige's damage, but damn if those injuries had affected him in the slightest. It was seeing Paige scraped, bloodied, and bruised that wrecked him.

He tugged at the hem of the T-shirt she wore. "We're going to have to get you naked again."

She slapped his hand away weakly. "We're not having sex tonight, Gannon!"

"You are a piece of work, you know that, Paige? I'm changing your damn dressings that you probably weren't supposed to get wet."

She looked guilty. "You don't have to do that."

"You must really be looking forward to sleeping in wet bandages all night?" She was already shivering though the steam from their shower still hung heavy in the thick air.

Paige shook her head.

"Good girl."

"But I'm not comfortable with you—"

"I'm your only option right now. So let's get this over with and get you to bed."

CHAPTER
20

Her resistance faded as quickly as it had risen. "The stuff's out on the table," she said, her teeth starting to chatter.

"Okay, come on. We'll do this on the bed so you can lie down." It was brief, but he saw the look of gratitude cross her face. Exhaustion was setting in, and he needed to get her comfortable. He helped her out of the bathroom, taking most of her weight and guiding her onto the bed.

He scooped up the gauze and tape along with a photo-copied sheet of doctor's instructions for wound care and carried it to the bed. He read as he dumped everything on the mattress next to her before getting to work. She had bandages every-where, and it just wasn't feasible to leave the T-shirt on, so Gannon stripped it off.

"Damn it, Gannon!" Paige reached for the bedsheet to cover herself.

"Honey, I've already seen it all, and I'm really looking

forward to seeing it all again when you're healed up. So let's hurry the process along." He tore a piece of tape into fours with his teeth and adhered them to the sheet.

She muttered something about being ridiculous under her breath while he worked as quickly as he could, moving from bandage to bandage. She'd needed stitches in two places and had the equivalent of road rash in several spots. The slice across her calf was the worst of it, deep and angry looking. Nearly a dozen stitches held the wound shut.

"They said it would probably scar," Paige said into her pillow.

"Scars just mean you're tough," Gannon told her, gently securing a fresh strip of gauze to the wound.

"Malia said you told her that."

"That is one tough kid." He sealed the tape around the gauze.

"The bed you're making for her is amazing."

Gannon raised his hand, intending to smack Paige on the ass to have her roll over, and then thought better of it. "Back's all done. Roll for me."

She started to roll and let out a muffled yelp before slowly complying.

"Almost done, honey," he promised softly.

He worked quickly, trading out old gauze for fresh on her arm, hip, and thigh before helping her back into his T-shirt. She was still shivering, so he pulled the covers up to her neck.

He found the bottle of pain meds in the pharmacy bag. "How many of these are you supposed to take?"

She shook her head. "I don't like that stuff. Makes my head fuzzy."

"You've got to be in pain."

She attempted a sad one-shoulder shrug. "It's not so bad. I'm fine."

Stubborn to the point of idiocy, Gannon thought. He could respect that. He found a bottle of ibuprofen in the bag and dumped three into his hand and prodded her arm on a square inch of unbruised skin. "Over the counter," he promised.

She tossed them back and washed them down with an open bottle of water. Once she started drinking, she couldn't seem to stop.

"Are you hungry?"

She shook her head and handed the empty bottle back to him. Paige was as pale as the pillows beneath her.

"When did you eat last?" he prompted.

"Ugh. I don't know," she said, closing her eyes. "Breakfast?"

"You don't eat breakfast," he reminded her.

"I forgot. Then it was dinner last night. I was going to have lunch after the kids…" She trailed off as if the effort to speak was too much for her.

He swore quietly. "You need a damn babysitter," he muttered, reaching for the phone on the nightstand and fishing out the room service menu from the drawer. He dialed the front desk and ordered for both of them.

She didn't even attempt to argue with him, and that worried Gannon. He went back in the bathroom and pulled on his underwear and jeans. By the time he came back out, Paige was dozing. He sat on the mattress next to her and pulled out his phone and texted Cat. He'd finally connected with his sister after showing up at the hospital and being told that thanks to HIPAA, the ER desk couldn't confirm if Paige St. James was a patient. Thankfully Cat had finally answered her damn phone before Gannon had deemed it necessary to yank the doors off their hinges and go looking for Paige himself. She was in the pharmacy picking up the newly discharged Paige's prescription and had given him what details there were to be had.

Paige had saved the little boy's life. That part was clear. The kid would probably be scared shitless of thunderstorms for the rest of his life, but he was going to have a rest of his life thanks to the woman next to him who wiggled a little closer to his heat.

For the first time since he'd nearly ripped her shower curtain down, Gannon let himself take a deep breath. Paige was alive, and after a carefully monitored recovery, she was going to be fine. He rubbed a hand over his chest. He hoped to God his heart would recover too. He'd thought the worst, had fought those demons on the drive back, holding on to that terror until he saw her with his own eyes.

He distracted himself by perusing the doctor's instructions on recovery and wound care.

His phone vibrated against his leg.

Cat: Tony's got footage of it if you want to see it. Pretty messed up.

Before he could fire off a pissed-off reply about what the hell Tony was doing standing around filming the disaster rather than helping Paige, Cat texted again.

Cat: Calm down, Lover Boy. It's not what you think. Tony ended up playing hero. Saved a little girl and dug Paige out. But the second the network heard about the accident, they demanded the footage. No way it's not making it into the show.

Paige would be pissed and humiliated. Gannon had no doubt about that. And it would also mean Paige sitting through some lengthy, invasive interviews to milk it for every ratings point possible. That pissed him off.

There was a knock at the door, and Paige stirred next to him.

He levered himself off the mattress and answered the door. Room service consisted of a scarecrow of a kid with a shock of white-blond hair and a face full of freckles.

Gannon cut the small talk short and took the tray from the kid before sending him on his way with a ten-spot.

"Oh, hell. Did you answer the door like that?" Paige demanded from the bed.

He looked down at his bare chest and unbuttoned jeans, shrugged. "Princess, again, you've got bigger problems. Besides, the kid's more likely to be a fan of Cat than me."

She sniffed the air. "What smells so good?"

"My burger and onion rings. I got you chicken noodle soup."

"Aww."

"Serves you right for being a health food snob."

They ate side by side against the upholstered headboard, and she shot longing looks at him until he finally ripped off part of his burger and gave it to her.

"Happy now?"

"Mmm," she sighed, eyes closed to savor every bite. "Okay, chewing made me tired." Energy gone, Paige slumped back against the pillows.

"Bedtime," Gannon agreed. He cleaned up the dishes and left the tray in the hallway. Tomorrow was going to be a long-ass day, starting with a conversation he was going to have with Andy during which he would make it crystal clear that no one was going to turn Paige's accident into ratings.

He turned off the lights in the room and secured the locks before shucking off his pants and climbing under the covers next to Paige. She felt like an ice cube under the sheet, and he shifted closer, offering her his heat.

"What do you think you're doing?" She yawned. She had no energy to fight him, and Gannon sure as hell wasn't leaving her to sleep by herself.

"I'm sleeping here. Don't bother trying to argue."

"This is also not how I pictured our first time in bed together."

He could hear the smile in her voice. "That makes two of us," he admitted and immediately tried to stop thinking about how he *had* pictured their first time in bed together.

Paige went quiet, and after a minute or two, he thought she'd fallen asleep. But she tried to roll to her side and muffled a yelp of pain.

"What are you trying to do?" he asked gruffly.

"Get comfortable." Pain and exhaustion laced her tone, yet still no complaints from her.

Gannon slid an arm under her and carefully pulled her against him, her back to his chest, her ass nestled against his thighs. "Better?" he asked.

He thought she nodded.

"Gannon?"

"Hmm?"

"Thanks for taking care of me."

"Even though you don't need anyone to take care of you?"

"Yeah. It was still nice."

"You know, princess, you didn't have to go to these lengths to get out of having sex with me tonight."

"Har har, ass."

CHAPTER

21

Paige woke slowly, advancing into different stages of awareness. She was warm and safe. But she froze when the soft snore reached her ear and she became aware of strong arms wrapped around her.

Gannon.

He'd helped her shower, dried her hair, changed her dressings, and fed her. And then he'd climbed into bed next to her as if it were the most natural thing in the world. She let that soak in, ready to feel the humiliation of him seeing her at her most vulnerable. But that thought was derailed by the twitch of what promised to be an exceptional erection prodding her back.

She'd witnessed it with her own eyes last night. It was official. There wasn't an inch of Gannon King that wasn't impressive. And what should have been a night of mind-blowing pleasure for the two of them—because Gannon didn't half-ass anything—had been downgraded to an unfulfilling evening of nursemaid and patient.

That sucked.

So did the cacophony of aches and pains that began to plague her as they settled into her consciousness like a cloud of rabid locusts. There were so many of them she couldn't identify or isolate them all. Paige felt like she had the flu times a million.

She lifted her head ever so slightly and could tell that the world beyond her room was still dark outside. She should wake Gannon, send him back to his room. But she was so comfortable. The steadiness of his breathing, the slow thrum of his heartbeat, soothed her. She wasn't alone.

He stirred, burying his face in her hair. "Go back to sleep, honey," he murmured. And for once in her life, she did what she was told.

———

Gannon woke to the incessant ringing of a phone and cracked open a bleary eye. Paige was cradled in his arms, and he could just make out a lightening in the sky around the edges of the curtains.

Blindly, he reached for the phone and sat up, easing his arm out from under Paige.

"'Lo?" he rasped quietly into the phone.

"I'd like to speak to my daughter who didn't bother telling me she'd been in an accident yesterday." The voice had more than enough ice to refreeze a melting iceberg.

"You must be, Dr. St. James," Gannon said and yawned.

"And who are you?"

"Gannon King, your daughter's"—he glanced back at the silhouette of Paige's sleeping form next to him—"friend."

"I'd appreciate it if you would put Paige on the phone,"

the woman said icily. Gannon imagined it was the tone she reserved for slow valets or dimwitted servers.

"She's sleeping—"

"I never should have let her take that ridiculous job. Reality television." Dr. St. James gave an inelegant snort. "She could have gone into medicine like her sister or—"

"Look, Dr. St. James. I understand that you're pissed off and worried, but you're a psychologist, right?"

There was a slight pause. "That's correct."

"Then I imagine you can hypothesize how berating your daughter after a physical trauma might not be the right call."

Dr. St. James sputtered on the other end of the line. He could hear it. The anger, the worry in her tone. She cared. She just didn't know how to show it. Sometimes his own mother, a tough Italian broad as she liked to tell everyone, was the same way.

"Paige is going to be okay, by the way. Pretty banged up, but she'll live and so will the boy whose life she saved."

"I didn't realize—"

"Look, Paige needs more sleep. Why don't you call back this afternoon, and I'd suggest leading with 'Are you okay?'"

"Mr. King," she began.

"Gannon."

"Gannon, I appreciate that you're looking out for my daughter, but I find your tone disrespectful and entirely uncalled for."

"I was just about to say the same to you." He yawned again. "I'll tell her you called and asked about her. I'm sure she'll appreciate it." Gannon hung up the phone.

He swiped his hand over his face. It looked as though he was officially awake for the day. As much as he wanted to stay in this bed with Paige, he needed to get back to his room before anyone saw him sneaking shirtless out of hers. Gannon didn't care much about appearances, but it would upset Paige if people knew he'd spent the night with her.

He'd play ball. For now.

He switched on the bedside lamp and gave himself a moment to study her. The bruising on her face and the bump looked even worse now, mottled purple and blue. The violent evidence of her injuries still managed to work him up. He could have lost her without ever really having had her. This was no potential fling. These feelings were real and deserved to be explored, for both their sakes.

They were officially dating whether Paige liked it or not, whether she acknowledged it or not. And he wasn't leaving her side.

"Paige," he whispered her name. She murmured something in her sleep, and he took the opportunity to lean closer, his lips brushing her ear. "Princess."

"Mmph."

"Paige, I'm going back to my room."

"You're leaving?" she croaked.

"It's almost morning." He brushed her hair back from her face, avoiding the bump on her head.

"I'm getting up," she murmured, but her body looked like it was refusing to acknowledge her words.

"Why don't you get some r—"

Paige rocketed into a sitting position and tried to cover her yelp of pain with a yawn.

"You're going to hurt yourself all over again."

She gingerly scooted herself to the edge of the bed but seemed in no hurry to attempt standing. She had to be hurting. Every visible inch of her was black and blue. He could only imagine what her muscles were screaming at her right now.

"I have to get to the set," she said, refusing to look at him.

Gannon rolled his eyes and walked around the bed, stopping in front of her. He nudged her chin up. Or at least tried to. Her gaze seemed to get stuck somewhere around his crotch, and then he remembered he was wearing only his underwear.

"Eyes up here, princess."

The grumpy look she gave him did his heart good. She was going to be okay. If she took her recovery seriously, but he'd help her with that.

"About this going to the set—"

"I'm not staying in bed all day while everyone else works and worries," she said defiantly.

Gannon had already anticipated there'd be no keeping her from the set. He preferred to have her there anyway so he could keep an eye on her. Besides, the rest of the crew was most likely still torn up over seeing her being carted away unconscious and bleeding. It would do them all some good to pretend that everything was normal today.

"You can go to work on the following conditions."

She was trying to work up a mutinous expression, but it took too much energy. "Ugh. What?"

"You sit your ass in a chair and don't lift a damn finger. You eat breakfast *and* lunch. And you come back to rest in the afternoon. We'll see how you feel after a legitimate nap and then we decide if you can come back to the set tonight."

She argued weakly. "Gannon, there are a million things to do. I can't just sit around and—"

"It's either that or you're banned from the set for the next two days. And Andy will back me up there." He held firm and stared her down. In her weakened state, he was confident in a win.

"You're really bossy."

144

"Yeah? How's it feel to be on the receiving end?" he asked cheerfully as he helped her to her feet.

Paige kept her face impassive, but he sensed her body tensing with pain.

"Paige."

She shook her head. "I'm fine. Just a little stiff and sore."

"Do you need anything before I leave?"

"You should probably put your pants on before you go."

"I should probably check out all your bumps and bruises before I go," he countered, reaching for the hem of his T-shirt that she wore, but Paige slapped his hand away. "Be ready to go in thirty," he said, dropping a soft kiss to the top of her head. He stepped into his jeans and boots and, on the way out, grabbed Paige's oversize windbreaker and put it on. His biceps strained the seams. He pointed at her. "Thirty minutes."

"Don't hulk out of my jacket," she called after him as he let himself out.

———

He'd snuck into his own room like a teenager after curfew and changed into fresh clothes before having a text conversation with Andy about exactly what Paige would and wouldn't be asked to do today. Andy was on his side, but there was no way they were going to get her out of an invasive one-on-one about the accident and its aftereffects.

Gannon didn't bother with a soft knock on Cat's door. His sister could sleep through an earthquake that sent a six-lane highway into collapse. He gave the door a good three or four pounds before it opened. Cat looked as if she hadn't slept all night, dark circles hovering under her bloodshot eyes.

"Why are you punching my door in the face at six in the morning?" she demanded, her voice a sleepy rasp.

"You and I are taking Paige to the set."

"I knew she'd talk you into it." Cat yawned, leaving the door open and fishing through dresser drawers for clean clothes.

"How do you know she talked me into anything?"

Cat shot him a look over her shoulder. "You're the only one on the team who can talk her out of anything. If she's going, it's because you said it was okay."

"I didn't bother having the argument with her. I'd rather keep her where we can see her, make sure no other disasters befall her."

"Gannon King walking away from an argument?" Cat arched an eyebrow at him and yanked one of a dozen pairs of shorts out of her drawer. "You must be rattled."

"You're the one who looks like she didn't sleep a wink last night."

"It was bad, Gan." Cat shook her head as if trying to dislodge the memories. "Tony and some of the other guys literally had to dig her out of the debris, and she was just huddled there on the ground over that boy. I thought she was dead. I thought they both were. Everything was dead silent, and then we hear the kid singing his ABCs."

"Fuck." Gannon sat down on his sister's unmade bed.

"My sentiments," Cat said, heading into the bathroom to change. "So you saw her this morning? I wanted to check on her again last night, but I figured she needed rest."

"She's gonna be hurting today," Gannon said, sidestepping the question. "But I think everyone will feel better having her on set."

"Agreed. Think we're gonna see some trouble today?" she called through the door.

He knew exactly what she was thinking. The network or at least Summit-Wingenroth would smell blood in the water

146

and demand a gory retelling. The network wouldn't sweep this under the rug. Either they'd exploit Paige's pain, or someone would be facing some serious trouble over the accident.

"I'm sure the network will poke their asshole noses in to it," he said.

Cat strolled out of the bathroom, her hair tucked through the back of a Kings Construction cap. She yawned mightily. "Well, those assholes are going to have to get through us to get to her," she said.

Gannon felt his spirits lift and stood up. He could always count on nothing less than the fiercest loyalty from his sister.

He put his hands on her shoulders and shoved her toward the door before she could decide to spend another half an hour on makeup. "I hope they put up a fight," he said.

Cat snickered and then tossed over her shoulder, "By the way, when were you going to feel like telling me you spent the night with Paige?"

"What are you talking about?" he hedged.

"You smell like Paige's coconut shampoo."

CHAPTER

22

Gannon half shoved her into a folding camp chair.

"Do not under any circumstances move your ass," he told her.

Paige argued with him for posterity's sake but wasn't fooling anyone. Cat had taken one look at her bruised and battered form and burst into tears in the doorway of her hotel room. Gannon had to pry her off Paige.

But it reminded Paige that everyone was going to feel a little traumatized today, and she might as well get used to it.

Gannon tucked a blanket around her knees and handed her a coffee.

"If I see you out of this chair for any reason," he said, his finger in her face, "I'm going to interrupt filming and embarrass the shit out of you."

Paige glowered at him until Felicia barged in to mike her. "Sorry, Paige. Network's orders," she muttered, but her hands trembled when she reached for the body pack.

"Felicia, I'm fine," Paige promised her.

The woman's lower lip trembled. "It was real scary yesterday."

"You can say that again," Paige joked and then found herself wrapped in Felicia's sturdy arms.

"Your hair looks real nice," Felicia said, sniffling and patting Paige awkwardly on the shoulder before pulling back.

Paige caught Gannon's smirk over the woman's shoulder. "How did everything get cleaned up so fast?" she asked, trying to distract Felicia.

"Honey, we had volunteers here all night helping us clean up the mess and set up new tents."

Paige worked her mouth into a smile. "Nothing's gonna stop us from giving the Dufours the house of their dreams."

"Not if we have anything to say about it," Felicia agreed.

She took her leave, but Paige wasn't left alone for more than a few seconds at a time. Andy walked her through the call sheet he'd done for the day, and Paige walked him through the changes that would make the most of shooting. Tony, her hero, brought her a dish of oatmeal and an awkward hug. Mel and Sam hovered around her until she had to make up tasks to get them both out of her hair, Mel to send out an updated call sheet and Sam to get Paige a new phone.

Every member of the Brunelli crew took time out to come over and welcome her back to set.

To everyone, herself included, it felt as though she'd been gone forever instead of a few hours, and they were just now starting to get back in the groove. She surveyed what she could see of the front yard. The craft services tent was gone and replaced with a series of mismatched pop-ups that had been secured to the ground with what looked like a thousand ropes and stakes. The tent the kids had been in was gone as well. She wasn't sure if it too had been destroyed or just damaged.

It must have been more than a couple of kindhearted volunteers, she thought, noting the tired eyes of her crew and Brunelli's. They may have been making reality TV, but they were all pretty damn good people, she decided, taking a bite of the oatmeal and ignoring the twinge in her shoulder.

"Well, well. You look like shit."

"Eddie?" Paige craned her neck to see her executive producer pulling up a chair next to her. "What are you doing here?" Eddie Garraza didn't set foot on set unless something big was happening.

He pushed his glasses up the bridge of his nose. "Checking up on you, kiddo. I hear you had an eventful day." Eddie crossed his right leg over his left, flashing her a shot of his fawn-brown moccasins.

"The weather got a little unpredictable, but we're back on track," Paige said. She knew she was being flippant, but she had a hollow in her belly. If Eddie was here, he had bad news. She ordered herself to relax. Eddie wasn't the bad guy. Whatever it was, they could work through it.

"You look like you got hit by a dump truck," he said, leaning his elbows on his knees.

"I kind of feel that way too."

"Anything broken?"

She shook her head. "Nothing serious. Should be back to normal in no time."

He nodded and stared out at the front of the Dufours' house, which was currently being re-sided while Louis shot some footage. "House is looking good," he ventured.

"Eddie. You might as well get to it."

"I'm here primarily to head off any legal issues that might arise from 'the incident,'" he said, tossing up lazy air quotes. "Got some worker's comp stuff to fill out. And the suits want you to sit down with me or Andy and walk through the 'incident' step-by-step. Talk about how harrowing it was to almost die on camera. Maybe work up a few tears. You know the drill."

She did and had anticipated as much.

"But there's more, isn't there?" she prodded.

Eddie yanked off his Orioles ball cap and shoved a hand through his curling gray hair. "They want Tony out."

"What?" Paige gasped. The sharp breath hurt her ribs and pretty much everything else. "That's not going to happen," she argued. "He pulled us out of there. He carried that little girl into the house and then came back and dug me out from under two fucking circus tents."

"Well, see, the network feels that he should have continued to film instead of getting involved."

"That is bullshit, and you know it, Eddie."

"Have you watched the footage?"

"No, I've been busy being in the hospital," she snapped.

"Now, look, kid. I don't like this either. So I need your help."

He wasn't asking her to fire Tony, Paige realized. He was asking her to come up with a way out of it. "I'll quit, and I'll sue if they fire him," she told him.

Eddie was shaking his head. "Not big enough." He wasn't saying it to be mean. It was just a fact that field producers were about as plentiful as production assistants. If she quit, they'd fly in some other idiot to replace her the same day.

Well, if she wasn't big enough, she knew who was.

"Andy, can you send Gannon and Cat out here as soon as you wrap that scene?" Paige said into her headset.

"You've got an idea?" Eddie asked.

"Tony's not going anywhere," Paige promised.

"We're resetting for a new shot," Andy reported in her ear. "You can have them for ten minutes."

"Works for me."

They came out of the garage, both covered in dust and dirt, Gannon with his powerful strides and Cat with her dancer-like stroll, their long legs eating up the driveway as if it were a catwalk. Paige saw the tightening around Gannon's jaw, knew he was expecting a fight.

"Eddie," Gannon said, offering his hand.

Eddie shook it enthusiastically. "Good to see you both. This season's shaping up to be pretty great."

Gannon said nothing, but Cat gave Eddie her for-the-cameras smile.

"So to what do we owe the honor?" Cat asked. Her tone was friendly, but Paige knew better than to be fooled by that.

"Eddie has some news," Paige told them. "Go ahead, Eddie."

"Well, I was just telling Paige here that the network has instructed me to fire Tony—"

"The fuck you are," Gannon cut him off. He was scary when he was pissed, and hell if he wasn't furious right now.

Cat stepped between her ticking time bomb of a brother and the messenger. "Eddie, Eddie, Eddie. I don't think that's a good idea. See if you fire Tony, Gannon and I are going to quit right here, right now. And then we're going to spend the next year doing interviews talking about what dipshits run the network and put footage above human life. Right, Gan?"

Gannon nodded. "Yeah, that sounds about right. Did we mention that we got an offer from Netflix? For an original show where we call the shots?"

Cat crossed her arms over her chest. "So what's it gonna be, Eddie?"

Paige looked at Eddie. "Does that work for you?" she asked him.

He took off his hat and mopped his brow. "Oh yeah. They'll be pissing their pants." He took out his phone and wandered a few paces away.

Paige grinned. "Nicely done, Kings."

"You diabolical little puppet master," Gannon said, glaring at her.

"Eddie wanted a reason to keep Tony. You guys gave him a big one."

"Good to see the head injury didn't screw with your manipulation capabilities," Cat said, looking impressed.

Eddie returned, shoving his phone back into the pocket of his jeans. "Good news. Tony's staying, and I think it would be better if we didn't let him know how close he came to the chopping block."

"Agreed," Paige said.

Gannon and Cat nodded.

"Now for the bad news," Eddie said, stuffing his hands in his pockets. "In addition to your in-depth interview, they'd like to see shots of your injuries."

Gannon stepped in on Eddie, and Paige put her hand on his arm. "Don't roundhouse the messenger," she told him. She turned to Eddie. "If it puts this whole stupid thing behind us, then fine. I'll bawl for the camera, give you a close-up of the stitches, and that's the end of it."

"Taking one for the team." Gannon scowled.

"The guy pulled me out of a ton of rubble. I think I owe him."

Eddie, sensing an argument brewing, slapped Gannon on the back heartily. "While I'm here, why don't you show me around?" he suggested.

They started to walk off toward the house when Paige saw Eddie sniff the air.

"Do you smell piña coladas?"

Between filming scenes, Gannon stayed glued to Paige's side. He dumped an entire kitchen scene on Cat and Brunelli so he could stand sentinel off camera while Eddie interviewed Paige on camera.

She had every right to be miserable and whiny with the amount of pain she had to be feeling. But he'd yet to hear a complaint. It was impossible not to admire her for that. And now, watching her walk through what had to have been an incredibly traumatic moment without bursting into tears, he was impressed.

Paige was toughing it out, answering the intrusive questions with humor and sincerity and giving a shout-out to the brave little girl, Regina, who hadn't left her scared friend behind. He caught a wince every now and then when she shifted in her seat. She had to be in pain, lots of it, judging by the bruises she revealed to the camera. But she was a consummate professional through the entire thing.

Gannon, on the other hand, wanted to grab the camera out of Rico's hands and smash it over Eddie's head. It wasn't either of their faults, but he couldn't help lumping them in with the network assholes demanding Paige's humiliating recount of "the incident" as Eddie called it.

"You're doing great," Eddie said, peering at his notes through his glasses. "Couple more, and we're done."

Gannon shook his head as Eddie asked her what her biggest relief was. *What the fuck did they think she'd say? That she got a few hours off work? Assholes.* He'd meant to say the words in his head, not actually mutter it under his breath, but Paige caught it and gave him a nearly imperceptible shake of her head.

"My biggest relief is that Ashton is okay. He was a tough little kid." She kept her face neutral, her voice steady. She wasn't about to parade around some emotions just so the network could exploit her, and Gannon had never respected anyone more than Paige St. James in that moment.

"Do you feel lucky to be alive?" Eddie asked.

"I feel lucky to be alive every day," she countered. "Maybe a little extra today though."

"Okay, kid. One more," Eddie said, shuffling papers. "Who's taking care of you?"

That one almost tripped her up, Gannon noted. Of course Eddie was fishing—under orders, probably. But there was no way she was admitting that Gannon King had stormed her shower, bathed her, changed her dressings, and spent the night in her bed.

"We're a family here on *Kings*," she answered primly. "We take care of each other."

Gannon had heard enough. He stepped in, blocking Rico's shot. "Okay, that's enough," he announced. "Come on, Paige. I'll take you back to the hotel."

She looked relieved and immediately slipped the mic off her shirt. She put up a fuss about leaving, but it was all for show. Gannon got as far as having Cat stuff Paige's bag in the truck when she slipped away from him. He found Paige back at the interview tent where Tony was in the hot seat while Eddie led him through his questions.

"Fuck," Gannon muttered and stormed over. But Paige stopped him. So he forced a bottle of water on her and stood with her while she showed her silent support for Tony.

Tony was a big lug of a guy who bore a striking resemblance to Billy Joel. He was quick to laugh and slow to take offense, and he was very, very good at his job. He was a little awkward on camera, Gannon noted, but Eddie smoothed him, out easing him into the questions. He walked him through the whole thing a couple of times, and just when Gannon was getting anxious enough to pick Paige up and carry her to the truck, Eddie asked the big question.

"Some camera guys would question why you stopped shooting and got involved."

"Some camera guys are assholes," Tony said without missing a beat. He glanced over to where Paige stood and winked. "There's a difference between ratings and life and death. We're not saving the Amazon here. We're making a TV show. No ratings are worth losing Beast Mode over."

Paige ignored protocol and gingerly stepped around Felicia and her boom to hug Tony.

The corner of Eddie's mouth quirked up, and when Paige and Tony took a second to wipe their eyes, Gannon saw he'd managed to get exactly what the network wanted without violating them too much.

CHAPTER
23

Paige woke in the early dredges of dawn to the now familiar feel of Gannon's heat enveloping her. She breathed in his scent. He'd slept in her bed for the past three nights, and every morning, she'd wake with the weight of his arms around her, his scent and heat comforting her.

They'd never discussed it.

It felt too…intimate.

And Paige hated to admit it, but she thought if they did talk about it, he'd stop coming to her bed. As bad an idea as she knew it was, she still wanted him there.

She was healing, slowly but surely. The throbbing pains were fading to dull aches, her bruises and scrapes changing colors and becoming less tender. The stitches would dissolve on their own, and provided she wasn't leveled by another tent, she'd be just fine in another week.

There was just one issue she'd yet to deal with. She wanted Gannon King fiercely.

Seeing him naked had only tweaked her curiosity at what it would feel like to touch him. And when she woke up every morning, feeling him hard and throbbing against her back, well, it was getting harder to focus on maintaining a strictly professional relationship with him.

She'd never felt this *enamored*. She supposed that was the right word. When they were on set, she found herself keeping tabs on him. And the long looks they'd shared were enough to send her blood humming. He hadn't tried to kiss her again. Not since the day of the accident, and she worried that playing doctor had pushed him out of attraction mode and into the friend zone.

It should be a relief. She didn't need a complication like Gannon. What she needed was to heal and to focus, and in another year, she'd finally be on the path she'd set for herself.

But.

There was something so right about being wrapped in his arms. She'd never been a cuddler. She liked her space in bed to sprawl as it suited her. But Paige had also never slept better in her life than she had these past three nights. Gannon's warm body next to her was a comfort…and a torture.

She felt the steely length of his erection nestled against her lower back and shifted her hips back into him. God, she could *feel* him throbbing against her, she thought, clenching her jaw. She wanted to roll over, to throw her leg over him and pin him down. Strip him of the useless boxer briefs he wore to bed, notch his cock in place, and ride.

She was starting to want that more than she wanted to steer clear of any kind of personal relationship with him. *Entering the danger zone*, she thought and wrinkled her nose in the dark. But Gannon was in full-on nurse mode, making sure she wasn't overdoing it, keeping track of her eating, her sleeping. It was annoying but sweet.

Her mother hadn't been impressed with Gannon during the phone call Paige had been both horrified—and maybe a little gleeful—to hear about. Paige had gotten an earful of her mother's criticism for her "friend's attitude," though that did come after Leslie had made sure her daughter was physically okay.

Her mother viewed Paige's entire adult life as a rebellion of sorts. She was convinced Paige would eventually give all this up and go to grad school for a respectable career. It wasn't that her mother looked down on her, Paige thought. It was more that the St. James women had responsibilities to be respectable, contributing women in the world. A psychologist and a neuro-surgeon, yes, were perfectly respectable. A field producer of a reality show just a handful of steps up from the all-out brawls of the housewife spin-offs? Not so much.

In fact, Paige was fairly certain her mother wouldn't be any more thrilled with her documentary dreams than she was with the stint in reality TV. Unfortunately for Dr. Leslie St. James, she'd raised two independent, headstrong daughters, and Paige was going to shape her own life in the way she saw fit.

Gannon's alarm sounded, and he stirred next to her. And for just a moment, Paige let herself pretend that it was a lazy Sunday morning in the off-season, and she'd have the luxury of rolling over and waking Gannon up in her own way.

He slapped at his phone on the nightstand and then flopped back down on the pillow, his arm anchoring her against him again.

"Uh-uh." Paige yawned. "You've gotta get out of here before someone busts in here and jumps to the wrong conclusions."

He yawned mightily, stretching his body until she could feel his tensile strength against her. "It'd be a lot more fun if they were the right conclusions, but someone had to go and get the shit beat out of her."

"Har. Har. Now get out of here."

To antagonize her, he dropped a peck on her shoulder. "See you on set, princess."

———

Day five of shooting dawned bright and warm enough that Paige went with shorts instead of the jeans she'd been wearing to cover the bruises and cuts on her legs. It was going to be too hot to be vain, and she'd be able to stay on set longer if she were comfortable.

The house was transforming quickly. Slate-blue siding had replaced the dingy white, and a crew of masons worked to finish the brick on the expanded front porch. New dormers broke up the expanse of new roof that had been reshingled.

The yard, on the other hand, had been destroyed by production tents and an army of people tromping over grass and plants and bore none of the signs of early summer that the neighboring lots did.

Paige called up the contractor's schedule on her iPad and checked the landscaping timeline. They were definitely going to need an extra day for construction and filming, and she was glad she'd squeezed two in. Everyone had been staying on set much later than usual, busting their asses to help Brunelli's crew and lending hands wherever they were needed.

There was usually a family or two that the crew really connected with, and for this season, that family was the Dufours. The handful of hours they'd all spent with Carina and Malia had cemented everyone's resolve to do the best job possible.

Satisfied that the schedule was intact, Paige opened Facebook to check the show's page. Cat's blog posts were shared there as well as behind-the-scenes footage and pictures of jobs in progress.

Meeghan Traxx's name jumped off the screen at her. She didn't want to tap on the link, Paige told herself, but that damn index finger betrayed her and opened the article.

The article led with a splashy picture of the busty blond in a skintight red dress, wearing safety glasses and wielding a sledgehammer. Her bloody-murder red lipstick matched her glossy, talon-like fingernails.

Meeghan Traxx doesn't let rumors about her boyfriend bother her. "Things with Gannon and I?" she laughs. "What's better than perfect? He's the kind of guy who holds my purse while I try clothes on because he doesn't want to be too far away from me."

Paige felt twin urges to vomit and smash the iPad over Gannon's head. But since he would be wearing a damn hard hat to help with drywall, it wouldn't be nearly as satisfying. Compelled by righteous anger and a sick sense of masochism, she couldn't stop herself from reading on.

Recently Traxx's relationship with rising star Gannon King hit a public rough patch when rumors linked him to his show's production assistant, Paige St. James.

"I'm a field producer, not a production assistant," Paige muttered to herself.

Traxx laughs off the idea that King's eyes would wander. "Believe me. There's nothing some starstruck coffee fetcher could do to tempt Gannon away from me. He's incredibly loyal to me…"

Paige dumped the tablet on a worktable rather than giving in to the urge to toss it over the fence into the neighbor's koi pond. Cognizant of the microphone that suddenly seemed to weigh a thousand pounds, she kept her string of four-letter words to herself and buried herself in work.

Paige kept her head down and slogged through the morning, avoiding eye contact with Gannon and focusing on the job at hand. Drywall was a pain in the ass without filming, but throw in a camera crew, and things got even more hectic. Thankfully no viewer wanted to watch drywall be sanded so that stage of the operation usually afforded her crew a little time off.

Unfortunately, in order to get to *that* step, they needed to have the plumbing and electrical inspected, which was why an entire reality TV crew was waiting around with nothing to do while a middle-aged, bespectacled Tim Conway look-alike poked his way through two floors of chaos.

Paige paced through the Dufours' now open living space and tried not to look at Gannon, who was deep in discussion with Tim Conway Jr. Andy caught her eye and jerked his head toward the door. She followed him outside, and he handed her his phone. "They just sent me the teaser for this season," he told her.

"The way you're looking at me makes me think I'm not going to be happy," Paige guessed.

Andy scratched behind his ear and moved the claw hammer someone had left on the railing out of her reach.

Oh boy.

She hit Play and kept her face expressionless as clips rolled to the show's theme song. There was Gannon looking sexy and broody, Cat mugging for the camera, then the action picked up with Cat throwing a volunteer's axe through drywall and Flynn, Gannon's foreman, chucking a toilet through a plate glass window. Both toilet and glass rained down in slow motion into a dumpster.

The announcer's voice, a favorite talent for the network, came on.

"You never know what disasters you'll find in a renovation…"

Clips of termite damage and plumbing leaks escalated into a heated argument between Gannon and Paige. The next shot showed stone-faced Paige storming away from Gannon while he watched appreciatively. They wrapped with footage Rico had captured of the storm and Tony running toward the house with the little girl under his arm, the tent collapsing behind him. The shot went dark, and Gannon's voice shouted her name.

The announcer wrapped with "Sparks are flying on *Kings of Construction*."

"Gimme the hammer," she demanded.

"Uh-uh." Andy shook his head and pried his phone out of her hand.

She stood rooted to the spot, shaking her head back and forth as if she could dislodge the visual from her mind.

She wanted to yell, to throw something, to do anything to let this buildup of anger out. She wanted to pull a Gannon and throw a hissy fit that someone else would have to clean up. They'd pasted together a relationship and deliberately waited to release it until Meeghan had made her statement, guaranteeing huge views. It was diabolical. She kicked at the freshly painted newel post, winced.

Everything she had hoped had blown over was going to roar back to life. Her name would once again be appearing at the top of internet searches relating to the show, and the higher-ups would eat it up like the asshole vultures they were. And no #NapsWithGannon would deflect it this time.

"I thought you should see it now rather than…" Andy

trailed off, either unsure how to finish the sentence or unsure of his personal safety in her vicinity.

Mel stuck her head out the door. "Hey, Paige—"

Andy jumped in front of Mel before she could finish whatever she'd wanted or needed. "Now's not a great time."

Yeah, now was not a great time. Now was a clusterfuck, the fuckiest clusterfuck in the history of clusterfuckery. And her career, her reputation, were at the center.

Paige inhaled slowly and with great effort and, deciding it still wasn't safe to talk, yanked off her mic and body pack and stalked down the porch steps. She'd take five, try not to give herself some kind of brain aneurysm, and then get through the rest of the day. Then tonight, she'd lie on her bed *alone* and try to figure out a way to salvage this disaster.

She made it halfway down the block when she heard him. "Paige!"

She hunched her shoulders and wished she was healed enough to run. He caught her easily, his big hand grabbing her by her good shoulder. Even through her fog of anger, she realized he did it on purpose. He'd kept track of her injuries to make sure he didn't accidentally hurt her.

But he sure as hell had hurt her on purpose.

"What do you want, King?"

He raised his eyebrows in surprise. "I thought you were upset, *St. James*. My mistake."

She stabbed a finger at his mic.

He rolled his eyes and yanked the power pack out of the back of his shorts and shut it down. "Better?"

She wanted to let it out. But if she started, she wasn't going to stop, and it would just be an indecipherable load of verbal vomit.

"I'm fine. I just needed some air."

"You know there's only so much bullshit a man can take in a day, and when he works in reality TV, he reaches that level pretty quickly." His tone was so amicable she wanted to slap him across his sexy face. "So why don't you just cut to the chase and tell me why you're limping down the block away from your job."

"Why would I be upset? What could I possibly have to be upset about?" And she'd snapped. Oh well, might as well embrace it. She stepped into him and jabbed a finger into his chest. "Could it be the fact that your girlfriend just proclaimed to the world what a loyal, loving boyfriend you are when you've spent the last three nights in my bed? Or that she calls me a production assistant? Nah. That's just par for the course in Gannon's world. Maybe it's the trailer the network is wheeling out as we speak that paints a nice little love story between you and me."

Her voice had risen so high that dogs were barking in the neighborhood.

"Whoa." Gannon grinned. "So that's what goes on in there."

Paige had to restrain herself from stomping her foot. "You said you weren't dating Meeghan."

"Not this again." Gannon made a fatal mistake and rolled his eyes heavenward as if asking for patience.

Paige gritted her teeth. "Look, Gannon. I appreciate every-thing you've done for me, but I'm not interested in any kind of relationship with you beyond professional."

"Paige, you're back to lying again. I don't like it." His tone held a warning in it, one that she was happy to ignore.

"I'm not getting involved with you. You're the 'rising network star.' Another network star seems to be convinced that you're in a serious relationship with her. There's too much attention. I don't want to be a part of it."

"What are you so afraid of?"

"Everything that has happened!" Her hands were fisted at

her sides. "You're like kryptonite to my career. Besides, I don't think your *girlfriend* would like it," she retorted.

This time, it was Gannon fighting for control. "She's not my fucking girlfriend. She never has been. The network paired us up for ratings. That's it. And I told them at the beginning of the season that I was done with that. The show can carry itself now. It doesn't need to drum up ratings from a fake relationship."

"I guess you haven't seen the teaser yet then," Paige quipped. "God, you're ruining my career, and it's like you don't even care!"

"You're so ready to roll over and play dead. Why don't you fight for it?" Gannon snapped back.

Paige's phone vibrated in the pocket of her shorts, and she yanked it out. Reading the text, she felt her blood pressure rocket up into the danger zone. "Oh, great. Just fabulous. Eddie says the network wants you and I giving on-camera interviews together."

"Well, that should be fun," he drawled.

It should have been the last straw, but somehow there was no more anger left to feel. She just felt a dark numbness sweeping over her, an acceptance of defeat.

"Sleep in your own room tonight, Gannon, and leave me alone."

CHAPTER

24

Paige spent the next two nights tossing and turning on the lonely expanse of mattress and cursing Gannon King and his somniferous body. Her only joy came from seeing him exhausted and pissed off on set. At least she wasn't the only one suffering.

The show's teaser had been viewed over one million times, cementing to the network that the subplot of a rocky romance between Gannon and Paige was ratings gold.

She spent an inordinate amount of time thinking about what he'd said about Meeghan. Was it true? Was there really no relationship there? Why was Meeghan so committed to pretending?

Tensions were already running high on set. It was the last day before the family came home, and there were fifty million things to do and zero time to do them. Adding Paige's and Gannon's shitty moods to the mix didn't help. People were avoiding them both like they were stomach flu carriers.

Gannon was a roiling temper tantrum waiting to happen while Paige played ice queen. Their first interview together for the show was so awkward and full of eye rolls that it took nearly half an hour until Andy let them go back to their separate corners. And then he called in the big guns.

"Can I talk to you for a sec?" Cat approached Paige in the replacement craft services tent where Paige was debating between an apple or a pack of jelly beans for a midafternoon snack. "It's important, and I don't know who else I can talk to."

"Of course," Paige said, dropping the jelly beans and running through all the possibilities of things that could worry Cat. Sometimes the things that threw her were…unexpected. They ran the gamut from seeing a stray cat that she thought was too skinny to men problems.

Cat yanked open the sliding door of the production van and ushered Paige inside in front of her.

"You're not pregnant, are you?" Paige asked over her shoulder.

"Pregnant?" Gannon's voice cracked like a whip.

"What's he doing in here?" Paige demanded, trying to turn around but finding her exit blocked by Cat. Cat yanked the door closed behind her.

"What's your problem with me being here? My sister asked me to be here. What are you doing here?" Gannon snapped.

Cat clapped her hands. "Enough! Guys, I've been elected by the entire freaking crew to sit you both down and talk to you about how your preschool behavior is affecting our team."

Paige closed her mouth with a snap. Gannon, the picture of apathy, kicked back in the one and only chair at the crowded workstation.

"Now, I say this with love, but you two need to get your heads out of your asses," Cat said, hands on hips. "You're driving us all nuts during what's already been the toughest shoot we've ever had. You got hurt," she said, pointing to Paige, "in front of all of us. And there were a few seconds when we thought we might have lost you."

"I'm sorry—" Paige began, but Cat cut her off.

"We're working on a house for a little girl who might not be here much longer to enjoy it if her treatment doesn't take a turn for the better. Walking on eggshells around you two idiots is hurting our abilities to do our jobs." Gannon started to argue, but Cat pinned him down with a stare. "Uh-uh. I talk. You listen. I don't know what's going on between you two, but I need you to fix it. We need you both on top of your game if we're going to deliver the house that little girl deserves. So play nicely, work it out, and get your heads out of your asses!"

"Sorry," Paige said in a sulky tone.

Looking uncomfortable, Gannon avoided eye contact with both of them.

"Now, on a personal note. I know you two have feelings for each other. Shut up," Cat ordered when they both opened their mouths. "I think you'd be idiots if you let that go just to rebel against the network and the gossip sites. Figure out what you want, go after it, and forget about the rest of it. Understand?"

Paige and Gannon nodded.

"Good. Now get your asses back to work so we can finish this house." Cat wrenched open the door and stormed outside.

———

They managed a tremulous truce for the rest of the afternoon, and the work pressed on despite the steady rain that began to fall. Paige pushed them all to get as much footage of the finishes as possible. Gannon installed the hardware to the new kitchen cabinetry while Cat jumped in to help with the tile backsplash. They shot Flynn connecting overhead light fixtures and Brunelli's crew attaching the custom-built bookcases to the living room wall around the TV. Everyone else was painting every vertical surface in the house.

Furniture move-in needed to be shot in daylight, not downpour, so Paige and Andy juggled the schedule, which was, at this point, broken down into hour intervals. It was the final sprint when everyone was already tired and the amount of work to be completed seemed never-ending. The pizza shop in town sent over three dozen pies to feed their army of crew and volunteers, and the delivery girl was welcomed like a hero. Paige gritted her teeth when Gannon obliged the girl with a smiling selfie before handing her a paintbrush.

By the time there was nothing left for her crew to do, it was after midnight the morning of reveal day. Paige surveyed the nearly finished house with tired pride. They'd pulled it off again. Provided move-in went well in the morning, they'd be filming the reveal and tour by early afternoon, and Carina and Malia would spend the night in their brand-new home.

And Paige and her crew would sleep like the dead before catching a flight out the next afternoon.

Upstairs, the carpet installers worked to finish the bedrooms while the tile guys wrapped up in Carina's paradise of a master bathroom. Malia's room had blush-pink walls and a deep window seat filled with pink and purple cushions. Paige had gotten a peek at the bed that Gannon would assemble in the room tomorrow, and it was indeed fit for a princess.

She touched base one more time with the overnight Brunelli foreman, who assured her she had everything under control, and called it a night.

Soaked to the bone with not an ounce of energy left, Paige left a trail of wet clothes from the door of her hotel room to the bed. She didn't bother turning on any of the lights except the one on the nightstand. There was no energy for a prolonged bedtime ritual. She triple-checked her alarm. It was one in the morning now, and she had to be back on set no later than six thirty. *Ugh.*

Paige flopped down on the mattress, assured that tonight she was too tired to lie awake thinking, missing, yearning. She wouldn't think about Cat's lecture, wouldn't think about Gannon's claims that he and Meeghan had been a publicity stunt. Nope. Wouldn't think about that at all.

She waited for sleep to come. And waited. But she was still wide awake minutes later when she heard the knock at her door. She debated ignoring it.

"Paige, open up." Gannon's voice, tired and annoyed, came from the other side of her door.

Grumbling under her breath, Paige yanked a tank top on over her head and stumbled out of bed.

"What?" she demanded, opening the door a crack.

He pushed past her into the room, his wet T-shirt molded to his chest, his sneakers squishing with every step. Without bothering to look at her, he peeled off his shirt and let it land in a wet heap on the floor.

"What are you doing?" She was too tired to work her way up to anything other than mild irritation. He toed off his shoes and peeled off the damp, dirty socks.

He shoved his thumbs in the waistband of his shorts and looked at her, annoyed. "Do you want to sleep? I do. I'm not in the mood to spend one more night staring at the fucking ceiling wondering why I sleep so much better with you next to me." He shucked off the shorts and stood defiantly before her in gray boxer briefs.

His body hypnotized her. It was Paige's only explanation

171

for why she didn't stop him when he yanked the covers down and flopped onto the mattress.

What the hell was she supposed to do? He'd just charged in here and taken over her bed. If she climbed in, she'd be surrendering. But did she really have the energy to fight him?

Gannon held the covers up, and after a second of internal debate, Paige gave in. She climbed in, settling her back against his delicious warmth. His hard thighs and broad chest cradled her body, and she bit back a sigh. Whatever the reason, she slept better with Gannon King's spectacular body wrapped around hers, and tonight she was too tired to question it.

Gannon slapped at the nightstand lamp until it turned off. Darkness settled once again, but this time, Paige knew sleep would come. He shifted behind her just enough to nuzzle against the top of her head.

"I can hear you smirking." She yawned. "Don't think we won't discuss this tomorrow."

"Shut up, princess."

CHAPTER 25

Paige's eyes fluttered open to the still dark of her room. She'd slept and slept deeply. The nightstand clock read 5:30, yet she felt as though she'd gotten a full eight hours. Her breast felt heavy, aroused, and then she realized Gannon was cupping it with one big hand. His rough palm had teased the nipple into a hard bud.

He stirred in his sleep behind her, his hips shifting against her. The thick length of his erection prodded her to a new level of awareness.

Warm and safe in his arms, her body came to life as a raw need began to bloom between her thighs. She bit her lip and tried to will herself back to sleep, but her body wasn't having it. There was only one thing it wanted, and it was so close. Testing, she wiggled her hips against him and was rewarded with the throb of his cock where it nestled against her.

The ache within her intensified, pulsing with an emptiness

that demanded to be filled. The room was so quiet and so dark, it felt...apart from the rest of the world. As if whatever happened within these walls could stay here while everything else moved forward. Whatever occurred on this bed in this room could stay here, in its shrine of solitude, while outside day broke and work began.

She was talking herself into it. The neediness of her body was providing too sharp a temptation to fight. Did he want her? *Really* want her the way she craved him? And was she ready to find out, ready to stop fighting everything but what she wanted?

His fingers flexed restlessly against the flesh of her breast, and Paige bit her lip. She rolled in his arms to face him in the dark and trailed a palm down his chest and over each ridge of abs. Her breast burned where his hand had been. She hadn't realized he was awake, but without a word, his hand came to hers, guiding it lower and lower over the V of muscle, down the light trail of hair leading her onward.

Wordlessly, he shoved her hand under the waistband of his underwear. His breath caught when her fingers closed around his shaft. He was thick and hot beneath her touch as if he were molten steel encased in smooth, veined flesh. She paused, just gripping him in her greedy fist. Paige felt his breath, one slow exhale, on her face.

Still gripping him, she tugged the waistband down until she'd freed his cock, until she could palm his balls freely. His intake of breath was sharp, almost pained, and when she began to work his cock with her hand, he groaned between gritted teeth.

She stroked up, her closed fingers catching on the ridge of the crown before gliding back down to the thick root. Touching him like this turned the needy pulse inside her into a steady, aching throb.

"Paige. Are you sure?" His voice was gravelly with sleep and need.

Was she? In this second, she was more sure of this than anything else in her life. Would she be sure after? Did it matter?

"Paige. Answer me. I need to know."

"Yes."

That one word seemed to set him free. He reached over her and smacked on the light.

"I need to see you," he breathed.

She stroked up his length, squeezing at the top, and felt the moisture beginning to gather at his tip. His eyes were glassy.

"Do you want me?" she whispered the words, not wanting to break any spell.

He reached down between their bodies and swiped at the moisture that leaked from his cock. Bringing those fingers to her mouth, he pressed them against her lips. "What do you think?" he rasped.

She licked at the pads of his fingers, tasting the salty moisture, and he groaned, low and guttural. She could feel the pulse of his blood throbbing beneath her grip.

"We don't have much time," he murmured to her.

"I don't care. I want you, Gannon."

Reaching for her, he shifted onto his back, pulling her over him to straddle his hips.

"Don't let me hurt you," he warned.

She couldn't help but wonder if he was talking about her injuries or her heart. But the second the wide crest of his penis grazed her swollen clit, she forgot any such worries.

"Whoa, honey. I don't have a condom." His entire body was rigid beneath hers, his big hands flexing into the flesh of her hips.

She did. In her emergency kit she carted around with her.

Though now wasn't the time to mention to him that the reason she carried condoms was because Cat once forgot her own and came knocking in the middle of the night. A brother didn't need to know *everything* about his sister.

"Wait here," she murmured, reluctantly sliding off his body and rummaging through the bag she'd dumped just inside the door. She found them in an inner pocket and returned triumphantly to the bed.

Paige paused, caught up in the hedonistic picture he made, sprawled naked across her white sheets, the heavy length of his erection lying across his stomach.

"Honey, if you stare much longer, I'm not going to have enough time to make you come more than once," he warned.

It was all the encouragement Paige needed. She slid her underwear down her legs and enjoyed his groan. Gannon palmed his cock, fisting it around the root and stroking up as he watched her crawl across the mattress to him.

Careful of her bruises, she slid one leg over him and perched on his concrete thighs.

"You are so goddamn beautiful, Paige," he whispered, slowing his strokes to a lazy pace.

He hissed out a breath when she rolled the condom onto his column of flesh. With his eyes closed tight, Paige slid up and over him, notching the head of his cock against her wet center. His hands busied themselves by tugging her tank top up to expose both breasts. And as he palmed her heavy, round flesh, Paige slowly lowered herself onto him. The angle, the girth of him, forced her to take it slow, relaxing carefully to accommodate him. He abandoned her breasts for a moment to grip her hips and slide home, fully sheathed in her.

Paige rocked her hips side to side, trying to get a little room. He was so damn huge, and she was so full of him. They stayed like that for a moment, joined as deeply as two souls could be, their breath ragged.

"Okay?" he gritted out.

So much better than okay. So much better than perfect. She wanted to tell him, but there were no words. So Paige showed him instead. Tentatively, she rose up on her knees, feeling him withdraw inch by inch before she glided back down, taking him back inside her. When he was buried in her again, he groaned, a sound of exquisite pain. Gannon reached up to grip her hair and pulled her down for a kiss. His tongue mimicked the aggressive thrust of his cock in and out of her wet mouth until Paige felt weak with the all-consuming need that grew between them.

This was what she'd wanted, what she'd tried to fight. This was what she had no intention of living without now.

She was on top, and she should have been the aggressor, but it was Gannon who set the pace. Rearing up, he broke the kiss and found an aching nipple to ply with attention. She gasped at the rough stroke of tongue, the gentle suction and tug of his lips. She felt…heavenly. As if, for the first time in her life, she was using her body as it had been designed, to give and receive pleasure.

She accepted his shallow thrusts, rocking her hips into him.

"Gannon," she gasped. "I'm going to—"

There was no other warning as the climax ripped through her. She felt it everywhere, in the nipple he licked at, in the muscles that clenched his shaft as he thrust deeper into her, in her toes that curled as the heat shot through her body like lightning. It built and broke, built and broke, and each wave made Gannon wilder beneath her.

She sobbed out a gasp, throwing her head back to surrender gloriously to him.

"Again," he demanded. With more care than she would have thought possible, he rolled them, pressing her back into the mattress while he loomed above her. He knelt between her thighs, the broad head of his erection heavy against her slit. "Tell me if I hurt you," he growled.

She nodded, willing to agree to anything at this moment.

"I'm going to try to be careful, but I can't guarantee I won't lose it," he breathed, adjusting himself against her entrance. He skimmed his palms over her inner thighs, gently pressing them open. "Are you ready?"

She nodded, her eyes wide, lips parted. She was ready for anything Gannon had to give her. He drove into her with one swift thrust. Paige's hips levered up to meet him as if they had a mind of their own. The biological need to chase down that next orgasm took over. She opened herself to him. He pressed her knees up against her shoulders and held them there, draping her thighs over his upper arms.

She was folded up and completely at his mercy. But rather than feeling terrified, Paige felt hungry for more. Her first orgasm was still echoing within her, but all she wanted was another.

"This isn't enough," he muttered, echoing her thoughts. "I need more time with you. I need to taste you." He slammed into her, his intention to be gentle fading beneath the bloom of desire. "I need to explore every fucking inch of you."

His thrusts were becoming wilder and wilder. Paige's breasts bounced with the ferocity of his pace.

Words failed them both, but their gazes locked, and she knew what he was thinking and feeling. They were racing together, chasing down their release. She knew he was ready just by the way his hazel eyes seemed to sharpen on her.

"Yes." She got the word out, and it was as if it had set them free.

He slammed into her up to the hilt and grunted. She felt the slow-motion pulse of his first ejaculation, and it set off her release, closing her muscles around him and gripping him as everything exploded around them. He poured himself into her, and she wrung him dry with her own climax. Still echoing in and around each other, Gannon collapsed on top of her, their breath coming in pants, sweat-soaked chests sliding over each other.

He was kissing her, pressing chaste pecks to her face and hair as the last of the waves began to recede.

"I need more," she confessed, wide-eyed at the magnitude of what lay between them now.

"I promise you, princess, this is just the beginning."

Before she could tell him to prove it, a frantic knock at the door had Paige wiggling out from under him.

CHAPTER
26

P aige?" Mel's voice carried through the door.

"I'm going to murder her," Gannon muttered. "She's a dead woman."

Paige slapped a hand over his mouth. "What's going on, Mel?" she called. She shot Gannon a warning look and jumped out of bed.

"Billie just called from the site," Mel yelled through the door. "Said she couldn't get through to you. The furniture truck just showed up and is blocking the street. It's gotta be unloaded ASAP, or we'll get cited for obstructing traffic."

"Shit, shit, shit," Paige muttered, yanking on a pair of shorts. "I'll be out in a minute," she called through the door.

"Meet you in the parking lot," Mel said.

"Goddamn it." Paige pulled a tank top over her head. "I hate this job."

"For the love of God, woman, please put on a bra," Gannon

begged. "If I know you're braless under there all day, they're going to have to pixelate my crotch in postproduction."

Paige paused, glancing down his body and raising an eyebrow. "I don't know if they have enough pixels."

He grabbed her by the waistband of her gym shorts and kissed her hard. "This isn't over," he promised.

"It better not be."

———

It was chaos, but they managed to get the damn truck unloaded and moved before traffic control came in with their stupid pink ticket and fat fines. Of course, they had to drive the truck around the block, reload some of the furniture, and then unload it again for the stupid cameras, but Gannon was in a good enough mood that he didn't bitch about it…much.

Four hours of sleep and one hell of an orgasm left him feeling pretty much on top of the world. And getting to spend his day staring at Paige in those little blue gym shorts and her #BeastMode tank top while she managed eight thousand details? That wasn't so bad either.

There were a lot of things that surprised him about Paige, none of which disappointed him. She was tough as nails, limping around the set without letting her injuries slow her down. She was a goddess in bed. Independent and smart-mouthed, she could handle him no matter what his mood. She never made any demands of him, at least not beyond work. And there? Paige challenged him to be better.

His only regret was waiting an entire year before really getting to know her.

When *Kings of Construction* started, he'd deliberately kept himself out of the production side of things, preferring to focus on his sister and his guys instead. They'd been through it all with him, had stood by him, and had earned his loyalty. He needed to make sure they came first.

But trying to ignore Paige, and any other network or production company drones, for the entire first season had been a mistake. He'd missed out on too much time with her, and he could have nipped the whole Meeghan Traxx debacle in the bud long ago. That grated on him. He'd been lazy there, avoiding and ignoring the situation, and now it was a volcano ready to blow.

He'd fix it. But first, he had plans for Paige.

They had a few days off coming up, and he was planning on spending them in bed with her. That thought kept him obnoxiously amiable on set.

He didn't even put up a fuss when Paige made him reassemble the canopy of Malia's bed after she found out cameras hadn't caught him putting it together. He was in too good of a mood to bother. It appeared the mood was contagious.

Mother Nature showed her sense of humor by replacing yesterday's rainstorms with brilliant sunshine and drenching humidity. His crew busted their asses through the final hours before the reveal, whistling off-key pop songs and ribbing each other.

The air was filled with the scents of fresh paint and carpet, of newness.

The production crew, for the most part, let his guys do their thing and recorded load-in. By this point in filming, the focus was on Cat and her design crap. Cat could swing a hammer as well as he could, but because she had "lady parts," she'd been labeled the show's designer.

There was very little to do in the house. Brunelli's crew had done such a good job, Andy had them undo a few of the things they'd done to get shots of Gannon and Cat furiously working up to the deadline to finish the house. Another little lie that added to the story. *Hurry up and finish Cancer Kid's house*, he imagined the show's teaser would hint.

Paige's mantra ran through his mind. *One more season.*

Unlike his sister, who was mugging for the camera while she frantically reattached vanity drawer pulls in the master bath, he was not cut out for TV. With one more season's paycheck, he could keep his grandfather's company out of the red and finally get back to his own life, his own dreams.

His gaze traveled to Paige, hovering in the doorway just behind Louis as he filmed. She was beautiful. Not punch-in-the-gut fashion model beautiful. She was no Meeghan Traxx, thank God. That was a mistake he'd never make again. That kind of beautiful came at a very steep price with very little return.

Paige, on the other hand, was the kind of girl you wanted to take home to bed and would have no qualms inviting to Sunday dinner at the parents'. She was real. Irony of ironies, he'd gotten into reality TV—the fakest thing in existence—and met someone he had real feelings for.

He scrubbed his hand over his head and looked away. One night with the woman, and she apparently called a monopoly on his every waking thought. Would she try to bail on him after shooting wrapped for the season? Would he let her?

———

Reveal day was a different kind of chaos than all the construction shooting. They weren't rushing to complete. They were frantic to capture every tear, every shocked expression, every delighted "thank you." And when things weren't accomplished in the first take, it was Paige's job to keep the energy and excitement up so that subsequent takes rang true to viewers.

Carina and Malia were en route according to Mel's text. So they had twenty minutes of nail-biting tension on set, keeping the volunteer army cordoned off across the street with their handmade signs and exuberant enthusiasm. Paige had learned in the past that it was best to keep Gannon and Cat in the production truck or craft services tent until right before the family rolled up. Otherwise the crowd sometimes got a little too enthusiastic. Last season, two middle-aged women had jumped the barrier and tried to take Gannon's T-shirt...while he was wearing it.

Security on reveal day had beefed up since then, and Paige did her best to keep the energy high and the talent safe.

She was checking her watch for the eighth time when her phone rang. It was the third call from her sister. She'd avoided the first two, sure that Lisa was just reaching out to give her a follow-up grilling on how her injuries were healing.

She debated briefly and answered. "Hey, Lisa, now's not a great time," she said over the sound of an anxious crowd.

"Do *not* hang up on me," Lisa snapped. Her sister didn't sound like her usual dispassionate self. She sounded...human. And excited.

"What's going on?" Paige asked, pressing the phone tighter to her ear to hear over the noise of the crowd.

"Listen, you know how Mother and I feel about your career choices." Lisa sighed as if she carried the weight of her sister's disappointment every day. "But maybe there is something to it."

"Your approval means so much," Paige said dryly.

"Don't be a brat. I'm trying to tell you something important."

"Then stop putting it in a thesis and cut to the chase. I swear medical school has ruined your ability to communicate."

"Memorial Sloan Kettering is starting a pediatric cancer trial, and I think Malia could be an ideal candidate."

"What?" Paige hadn't meant to yell the word, but she wasn't sure she'd heard her sister right.

"Look, I follow Cat King's blog—"

"Why?" Paige interrupted.

"Because you're my sister, and I like knowing what you're up to," Lisa huffed. "*Anyway*, I saw the outtakes of Malia talking about her cancer. I passed it on to a colleague, Dr. Singh. He's young but brilliant, and he's got this trial that's getting started here in New York. Anyway, long story short, the trial starts in three weeks, and we need to talk to Malia's mother and doctors, like, five minutes ago."

Paige's world blurred into a whirl of paint fumes and power tools. Words like *stem cells* and *remission* floated to her from far away.

"Lis, this would be…incredible."

"Yeah. No kidding. Now give me the mother's number."

"Geez, okay. Look, we're getting ready to shoot right now, so Carina's going to be pretty busy."

"Just get me ten minutes with her. Today, okay?"

"Today. Yeah. Keep your phone on you."

"So are you sleeping with him?" Lisa asked, changing subjects as abruptly as a senior citizen changed lanes in Miami.

"What? Who?"

"Gannon King."

"I didn't think TV gossip reached your bubble," Paige muttered.

"That's definitely not a no."

"I'm kinda busy here."

"Mom's certainly not thrilled with the idea, but if you're going to date in that world, you could do worse," Lisa said drolly.

"I've gotta go, Lisa. I'll call you later with Carina."

"Talk soon," her sister signed off.

Paige disconnected and hugged the phone to her chest. She deliberately ignored her sister's interest in her sex life and chose to focus on the good news. If anyone deserved a miracle, it was the Dufours. This could be so much bigger than a nice place to call home. She felt like she was going to explode with excitement.

A tug on the hem of her tank top had her jumping out of her skin.

"Ashton!" Paige was delighted to see the little boy grinning up at her. Flanked by his parents, he was dwarfed by the huge bouquet of flowers he held.

"Miss Paige, we brought you these," he said, holding the bouquet up to her.

"For me?" Paige buried her face in the lovely blooms.

"We can never thank you enough for keeping Ashton safe," his mother, a lovely brunette with a shy smile, told her. "If it weren't for you…" She trailed off, and her husband slid an arm around her shoulders, squeezing gently.

Ashton's father, tall and lanky with his son's blue eyes, smiled. "We're indebted to you. If there's anything you ever need in Portland, all you have to do is ask."

"Thank you. I'm…speechless," Paige admitted.

"You got a lot of boo-boos," Ashton announced, studying the visible bandages on her arms and legs. Paige wished she'd worn jeans.

"Just some bumps and bruises," she assured him.

"Was I brave, Miss Paige? Mama says I was." Ashton danced from foot to foot in new dinosaur sneakers.

She crouched down in front of him. "You were very brave," Paige agreed. "You stayed calm, and that made me feel calm too."

He grinned and threw his arms around her neck, squishing the flowers between them. Paige laughed and returned the tight squeeze.

"Five minutes out," Andy announced over the headset.

Paige released Ashton and stood up. "The Dufours are on their way. Are you staying for the reveal?"

"We wouldn't miss it," Ashton's dad promised. "Come on, buddy. Let's get the signs for Malia ready."

They hustled off, leaving Paige with an armful of flowers and damp eyes.

"If you go get the Kings, I'll find some water for these," Sam volunteered, appearing at her side.

"You're the best, Sam. You can never leave this show." It was a threat she made weekly and interchangeably.

He grinned, his Colgate smile blinding. "You say that to all the PAs."

She headed off to the craft service tent and found Gannon and Cat tossing popcorn into each other's mouths across a table.

"We're ready for you guys," Paige called.

Cat caught a kernel with her mouth and shot her fists in the air. "Popcorn Mouth Catcher Champion!"

Gannon tossed a handful at his sister. "I demand a rematch."

"The rematch can wait for a few hours," Paige said with mock sternness, picking kernels out of Cat's hair. "Meanwhile there's a crowd of two hundred waiting to be dazzled by you two."

"Tough job," Cat said, applying a shiny pink layer of lip gloss with a handheld mirror. "You ready, big brother?"

"Let's get this over with," Gannon sighed. It was his trademark reveal day rally cry, and Paige had often joked she was going to get T-shirts made with the saying on it.

He followed his sister out and gave Paige a smoldering look promising naked, sweaty things to come as he sauntered past.

It was going to be a really good day.

CHAPTER

27

The reveal went down in Gannon's book as one of his favorites. Carina was in tears before he and Cat dropped the sheet unveiling the house. Malia was so excited she ran in circles until Paige had to catch her and coax her back into frame.

When she saw her bedroom, Malia was rendered completely speechless, which according to Carina had never happened in all her six years on the planet.

They deserved it, in his opinion. The show always did a decent job of vetting the families, but the Dufours were a home run. He watched Carina and Malia thank every single crew member personally and knew they all felt the same way. That little girl and her strong-as-hell mom were the reason they'd come to the set early and stayed late, the reason they'd had more volunteers this week than on any other job. And he felt proud to be a part of it.

He ducked out of the chaos inside the house. He wasn't

exactly a people person to begin with, and spending an entire week surrounded by bodies and questions and people needing things from him was draining…and annoying. He was looking forward to a few days of peace and quiet. But for now, he'd take the pockets of it where he could find it. And he could find it in the craft service tent. No one wanted cold coffee or stale breakfast pastries, so he helped himself and enjoyed the solitude, kicking back in an uncomfortable folding chair.

His solitude was short-lived.

"Gannon!" Malia poked her bald head covered by a pink ball cap into the tent. She was still carrying the Disney princess backpack she'd worn when Sam had delivered her to the set for the reveal.

Gannon held up a doughnut. "Want some? What are you doing out here?"

She skipped over to him cheerfully, and he sent up a silent "fuck you" to cancer. Malia grabbed the doughnut and took a healthy bite. "I came to say thank you."

Gannon laughed. "I think you already thanked me about a hundred times."

"Yeah, but that was around everybody, and there were cameras, and I didn't know if you really heard me."

Smart kid, Gannon sighed to himself. "Well, I hear you just fine now."

She took another bite of doughnut and climbed into his lap. She was still at the age where adults were as much furniture as they were people. "I wanted to say thank you, 'specially for my bed!"

He riffed the bill of her hat. "You like it?" he asked. He'd wanted to get it just right for her.

"It is seriously awesome," she said, nodding fiercely. "The most coolest bed ever!"

"What do you think of the rest of the house?" he asked.

"It's so different." Her brown eyes widened. "Mama cried when she saw the kitchen. But she said it was a good cry this time."

"You two deserve it," Gannon assured her. "You've done a lot of good for a lot of people."

"Mama says if we raise enough money, some day little kids won't get sick anymore."

Gannon felt his throat tighten. "Yeah. That will be a good day."

"I made you somethin'," she said, sliding off his lap and shrugging out of the little backpack. "When we were in Washington, DC, I worked on this."

She handed over a rolled-up piece of paper tied with a pink ribbon. He unrolled it and felt his throat get tighter still. She'd drawn him, or what he assumed was him, flying above a crayon-sketched mansion with smiling stick figures representing Malia and her mother on the purple front lawn.

"What's that?" he asked, pointing.

"That's your cape. 'Cause you're a superhero, and you saved our house." Malia danced in place. In painstaking capital letters, she'd written "HERO" across the top. She pointed to it. "See that? H-E-R-O. That's for hero because you're mine."

Well, shit. His vision blurred, and he couldn't do anything to dislodge the lump in his throat.

"You're mine, kid," he said, his voice gruff and strained.

"I haven't even done anything yet. I'm just six," she said, frowning. "You saved our whole entire house."

"You're a hero by example," he explained.

She shrugged. "Are you happy crying?" she asked, touching his arm, her eyes warm with concern.

He nodded and gave her another hug.

"Thank you for my house, Gannon."

"You're welcome, pipsqueak."

———

Paige's throat tightened, and she pressed her fingers to her lips. She'd come looking for Gannon for a couple of quick photos and found him sharing a sweet moment with Malia inside the craft service tent.

"You want me to…" Tony hefted his camera and jerked his chin in Gannon's direction.

Paige shook her head. "Nah. Why don't you go get one last pan of the master now that it's cleared out," she said quietly.

"You got it, boss." Tony winked and wandered off.

Paige felt the prickle on her skin and knew Gannon was watching her. Busted. She turned in the doorway of the tent and met his warm gaze.

Malia released Gannon from the hug and skipped toward Paige. "Hi, Paige! I'm gonna go find Mama!" she announced cheerily.

"I think she's upstairs," Paige told her with a wink.

Gannon yanked the ever-present red bandanna from his back pocket and swiped it over his eyes.

"Could have pocketed five K for catching that on camera," he said, shoving the bandanna back in his pocket and leaning back against the scarred folding table.

"How did you know about that?" Paige demanded, recalling the "bonus" she'd been offered.

"Eventually Cat finds out everything everyone ever said or did and she blabs to me about it, whether I want to hear it or not," Gannon complained.

"I wasn't ever going to do it," Paige said defensively.

He shook his head. "Didn't say you were." He paused,

working his way through the lingering emotions. "Why didn't you?"

She gave him a small smile. "Because on the off chance that you did prove to be human, I didn't think it would be nice to exploit that."

"It's not that I don't care," he said, searching for the right words. "It's that it's hard to connect with people through all the layers of production. I'm supposed to feel something for people who I meet very briefly and have coached, sometimes scripted, interactions with. That's not how I work. That's not how life works."

"You need a more authentic environment to make a connection."

"Yeah." He nodded. He stretched his arm out to encompass the site. "We're putting on a show. At the end of the day, that's what we're doing. Maybe we're helping someone, but what it all boils down to is we're selling some advertiser's product. It's hard to drill down from that and find actual human beings."

"I know," she said and nodded, crossing to him. They'd both turned in their mics to Felicia an hour ago, and with no audience, Paige felt safe sliding her arms around his waist.

She felt him tense against her and then relax. He rested his chin on top of her head. His arms banded around her, holding her tight.

"I wasn't ever going to try to collect on the bounty," Paige told him again. She needed him to know that.

"I know. You're not like the rest of the suits." He pressed a kiss to the top of her head. "What are you doing with your days off?"

"Laundry and sleeping," she smirked. "You?"

"I was thinking maybe you'd like to do your laundry and sleeping at my place."

CHAPTER

28

Gannon's place was a one-bedroom, fourth-floor walk-up in a squat brick building two blocks away from the factory his family had renovated into Kings Construction headquarters and three from his beloved nonni's house.

"This is *not* what I expected," Paige announced when Gannon shoved the key in the lock of the heavy wood door. She was nervous, which embarrassed her.

"Don't knock it," Gannon smirked. "It has a bed and laundry facilities."

"I don't mean that. I mean why don't you live in some concrete and glass loft somewhere downtown?"

"My family's here," he said, giving the door a shove.

The apartment was small, but Paige could see touches of Gannon everywhere. He made much better use of the space than she and Becca did in their crappy little apartment. A battered leather couch faced the massive flat-screen mounted to the wall. It was flanked by custom built-ins that housed a sparse collection of books. The coffee table was obviously a King original with its thick wooden top and hefty metal legs.

The kitchen was no bigger than a medium-sized closet with a skinny L of countertop. Pocket doors painted a glossy black led to the only bedroom. There were no plants, no homey touches or pictures.

"Are you a minimalist?" Paige teased, crossing her arms and studying the view through the three windows in the living room.

He gave the pocket doors a shove and dumped her bag on the serviceable navy spread on the bed.

"Smart-ass," he said without any heat. "I don't like to have to worry about a bunch of crap when I'm on the road so much of the year," he said and shrugged.

Paige crossed to him and slid her arms around his neck. "I'm just teasing. I'll show you my place, and you'll get the joke. It's just a dumping ground between shoots. We don't even have a coffee table. My bed is my desk."

"You're nervous," he accused, running his hands down her back to rest on the curves of her hips.

She nodded. "We've never not been working. I don't know how not to work," she confessed.

He blew out a breath. "I hadn't thought about that. Consider this though. If we can get along on set with deadlines and drama and bullshit, don't you think we can enjoy a few days of peace and quiet together?"

She bit her lip. "I want to say yes, but it's us. We thrive on deadlines and drama and, yes, bullshit."

He laughed, squeezing her hips. "Maybe this will help with the nerves."

Gannon kissed her, softly, sweetly, and Paige felt the tension melt from her shoulders.

"How about some wine?" he offered, pulling back and rubbing his thumb over the lips he'd just kissed.

She nodded again. He left her to explore the bedroom and connecting bath and returned to the bedroom moments later with two glasses of red wine.

She accepted the one he offered and sipped.

"I like seeing you off-center," Gannon admitted with a sly look. "It's nice to know that you're human."

"I'd like to point out the fact that you're the one the network wanted proof of humanity from. Not me."

Gannon moved her bag from the bed to the floor and then took her wineglass from her, setting both glasses on the nightstand.

"Let's see who's more human," he insisted, cupping her face in his hands. This time when his mouth closed over hers, there was nothing gentle or sweet about it. The kiss was raw and possessive, his lips bruised and battered hers as his tongue invaded her mouth, stealing her breath.

Grateful to have something to cling to, Paige poured herself into the kiss and gripped Gannon's T-shirt in white-knuckled fists. Here she could hold her own with him, matching fire with fire.

"I've thought about taking you here a thousand times," he murmured against her mouth.

"But we just started—"

He didn't let her finish. "This started a while ago for me." His hands slipped under the hem of her raspberry sleeveless shell, drawing it up and over her head. He focused his attention on the front clasp of her capris. Catching up quickly, Paige shoved her hands under Gannon's T-shirt and yanked it over his head.

"God, you are so gorgeous," she murmured.

"That's my line, princess."

He stripped her and tossed her on the bed. She bounced once before his body covered hers, and they rolled. Paige found herself on top and took advantage, straddling his narrow hips and sliding flesh against flesh. The cords on his neck stood out as Gannon closed hands over her hips and worked her against him.

"I can't believe I've been missing out on this," Paige murmured, not entirely conscious of the words slipping through her lips.

"We've got a lot of time to make up for," Gannon agreed. He rolled them again, pressing Paige's back into the mattress. "When you look at me like that…" He shook his head, losing the words.

"Like what?" She was breathless with need.

"Heavy eyes, full lips, like you're begging me to be inside you. It makes me lose my mind." As if to prove his point, he levered his hips, bringing the swollen head of his cock to her entrance.

She bucked against him. The hand he pressed to her shoulder and then her breast held her in place. "Not yet, honey. Not yet," he said.

Paige thought he was reaching for a condom, but Gannon slid down her body, biting and teasing his way across her stomach to the inside of her hip bone and lower still. He bit her inner thigh, and she gasped.

"Open for me, princess." His voice was rough, thick.

She forced her legs open, bent at the knee, and quivered when she felt his hot breath tease her. "Gannon."

"I love hearing my name from your mouth," he said darkly. "Say it again."

His tongue flicked over the swollen lips of her sex.

"Gannon!" she hissed.

"Fuck," he whispered, pressing his mouth to her.

Paige arched up, fighting the pleasure that such vulnerability brought. He pinned her legs with his big, rough palms and sampled her flesh. His tongue blazed through the slickness, the proof of her desperation for him. When he brushed over her clit, Paige gasped.

"That's what I want, honey. Give it to me," he murmured against her, his lips and tongue working her.

Her blood heated, her breasts ached, lonely and full. Paige wanted, no, needed more. And when Gannon pressed two rough fingers against her opening, she stopped breathing.

Sliding them home into her tight, wet channel, Gannon began a relentless assault with his tongue.

"Gannon!" He'd taken over her body, and now all that mattered was the climax shimmering on the horizon. His fingers flexed inside her, grazing that secret spot, and Paige bowed back against the pillows, levering her hips up, greedy for more.

He growled against her, and she sobbed out another breath. He was all-consuming, ruthlessly driving her toward the peak. His fingers and mouth worked in concert, tempting her higher and higher.

She felt the first tremor, and her legs fought to close on him, but he forced her open, devouring every sweet drop of her climax. Fighting it made it harsher, more jagged, and the orgasm ripped through her without regard for anything other than its own brilliant existence.

Gannon groaned his pleasure into her, tasting her and driving her harder into it. Paige's hands knotted in the comforter beneath them as her body shook with ripples of pleasure.

"That's what I've been dreaming about," Gannon whispered on a ragged breath, kissing her inner thighs with his sinful mouth.

"More," Paige sighed.

"Oh, baby, you have no idea."

He moved away from her, leaving her body loose and used on the bed. She opened a lazy eye and saw him frantically pawing his discarded shorts for his wallet.

"Bag," she murmured.

"What, honey?"

She pointed at her bag on the floor. "Condoms. Whole box."

He pounced on her bag and triumphantly pulled out the box she'd stashed inside. "Have I ever told you you're the smartest woman I know?"

"No, but I'm going to expect it regularly now," she teased, rolling to her side. She enjoyed the view as Gannon rolled the condom on his impressive erection.

She felt her pulse kick up a notch. There was something about knowing that she did that to him, that she made him that hard…

"Roll over," he said, his voice a dark rasp.

She complied and felt adrenaline surge through her as he shoved her shoulders down. She pressed her face down into the comforter still warm from her own body heat.

"I want to take you in every way I've thought about for the past year," he rasped.

"Then take me."

He drove home, sheathing his thick cock inside her. The force of his invasion caught her breath, and it took her a moment to relax around his thick length.

He growled deep in his throat, and her sex rippled around him, her body begging without shame for more.

"Is this okay?" he asked, flexing into her.

"God, yes," she gasped. Paige pressed up on her hands and tossed her hair back, meeting his gaze over her shoulder.

He swore and began to move in her. When she looked away, Gannon gripped her hair with one hand and her hip with the other. He began to ride relentlessly. She was so full of him, so dominated by him. He thrust into her with a restrained desperation that was an aphrodisiac to Paige.

The angle pulled him deeper than he'd ever been. And Paige gasped at the fullness. Her body burned for him. There was no way a fire like this could last. Something this hot, this bright, had to extinguish itself.

But that didn't matter right now. What did was the man behind her shuddering into her and making her burn.

On a long, guttural groan, Gannon pushed her down flat, slapping at her ass to have her roll over. "Need to see you," he murmured.

She opened for him, accepting his weight with a greed she'd never known. She wanted him on her, in her.

"Please," she whispered.

And he sank into her again. That beautiful stretch of her muscles to accommodate him was easier this time. "Anything you want, Paige. I'll give it to you," he promised, his lips searching her neck, her jaw, until they found her mouth.

She kissed him with a terrifying need. His hips levered into her, powerful thrusts that had her muscles clutching and clenching.

He brought a hand to her breast. "I need everything from you." He dragged his mouth away from hers and latched on to her straining nipple. He stroked over it once, twice, with his greedy tongue, and she was panting under him.

"Gannon, please!"

He released her nipple and moved to the other that was begging for his attention. He was buried in her, and she felt the incessant desire grow. She bucked her hips against him, demanding a faster pace. He let out a laugh, a deep rumble in his chest.

"Greedy," he accused.

But she was so close. The next orgasm loomed over her, and it was all she could think of, all she wanted.

He withdrew, lapping at her nipple before giving her a shallow thrust. She gasped out a litany of incoherent words. Paige released the sheets and dug her hands into his perfect, round ass, begging him with her body to fuck her. To fulfill her. To *own* her. The muscular chest that had hypnotized millions of women across the country flattened her to the mattress. The hazel eyes that had enthralled strangers bored into hers.

"Now, Paige," he ordered, slamming into her with the relentless force of a piston.

He rammed into her again and again, forcing her body to accept him. She could only cling to him, digging nails into that bronze, beautiful flesh.

"Now," he repeated, and she heard the desperation.

She obeyed with early, teasing tremors that shoved him over the edge. And when his body stiffened to unleash his first load into her, Paige was tensed to receive his pleasure as well as her own.

He groaned and grunted his way through his release, never ceasing in his attention to her, dragging her orgasm out until she was a puddle beneath him, used and wrung out, swamped with pleasure.

Gannon collapsed on top of her, his hard chest and rippled abs pressing into her, melting her into the mattress.

"Paige?"

"Mmm?"

"That's only a small sampling of the things I want to do to you in this bed."

CHAPTER
29

The princess shirt," Gannon said, digging into the to-go container between Paige's legs, helping himself to the pad thai. "You come out in these tiny shorts and this tight, white T-shirt. I went hard so fast I thought I was going to pass out."

Paige laughed, covering her mouth, and leaned back against the headboard of his bed. "You're such a guy!"

"Honey, with a body like that, there was no way I was going to not want you."

Paige rolled her eyes. "Well, you're going to feel like a shallow asshole when I tell you that the first time I had nonprofessional feelings for you was when you finished that dining room table." She wrinkled up her nose, pulling the information from her mental files. "Episode four, the Ratakowski family."

"Right, right. The brick bungalow."

"You worked on that table for hours, and when you were done, I thought it was the sexiest piece of furniture I'd ever seen, and you'd created it with those two very talented hands." She tapped one of those hands with her foot. "I wanted that table bad and would have taken you too to get it."

"Do you even have space for a dining table?" he teased.

"God no. Becca and I would have to give up our couch… and probably take down a wall. But someday, I'll have a home with a dining room worthy of a Gannon King original."

"What kind of home?" Gannon asked, biting into an egg roll. She shrugged and he nudged her with his bare foot. "Uh-uh, princess. You don't do anything without a crystal clear plan in your head."

Paige chewed, debating. "It's way out of my league, but I've always wanted one of those big three-story brownstones. The kind with a fireplace in every room and all these crazy nooks and crannies, sky-high ceilings, space for an incredible kitchen, which would force me to learn to cook. And some kind of backyard space, an oasis with trees and grass and a patio."

"Big dreams," Gannon commented.

"What about you? I know this place isn't your style."

He lifted a shoulder. "I haven't given it much thought. With my grandfather's business tanking, it's been a frantic couple of years."

"And now that you're coming out on the other side?" Paige prodded.

"It's probably time to start thinking long-term. Something with history, character. Something close to my family and the office because I do not plan to do TV forever."

"Will you go back to building full-time?" She dug into the sweet and sour chicken.

"Probably." He paused. "I'd actually like to do custom furniture."

The way he said it, without meeting her gaze and focusing

intently on the cardboard container in his hand, told Paige this was the first time he'd put it into words.

"Want to know what I think?" she asked.

He raised his gaze, arched an eyebrow. "Sure."

"You'd be insane not to. I don't know if you've noticed, but you're kinda talented."

"Oh, I've noticed," he said, smirking.

"Good thing your bedroom has pocket doors. Otherwise, you might not fit that noggin through the opening," Paige quipped.

"No one likes a field producer with a sense of humor," Gannon said, pinching her with his chopsticks.

She yelped.

"Bruises are fading," he commented, reaching for another little packet of soy sauce.

Paige nodded through a mouthful of noodles. "Feeling more normal every day."

"I saw the footage," Gannon said, watching her carefully.

"Mmm." She hadn't, except for what was in the season teaser, and didn't care to. Not only did she not want to relive it, she wasn't part of the show and had no desire to be. She hated knowing that she'd be crossing the line from behind the camera to talent this season.

"You were very brave. Maybe a little stupid, but definitely brave. It's amazing you weren't hurt worse."

She frowned, focusing on the food. "It was the perfect storm—ha—of unforeseen circumstances."

"Something you deal *so* well with," he smirked.

She rolled her eyes. "I like being organized and planning ahead," Paige reminded him primly. "It's smart to know what's next."

"And what's next for you is one more season."

She nodded, fiddling with her chopsticks. "I'd hoped to

pick up a special or something between seasons, you know, pad the bank account. But I'm afraid I'm going to be untouchable after this season. No one's going to want an on-screen field producer who slept with her talent."

"Paige, stop being so hard on yourself. Hell, you make it sound like this"—he pointed between them with his chopsticks—"ruined your career."

"I guess we'll see," she said morosely. "I just hate feeling like a puppet."

"Join the club," he said, raising his beer. "Now stop pouting. Just because something isn't going to plan doesn't mean it's a disaster."

"Look who's Mr. Pollyanna all of the sudden."

"It's hard to be pissed off about anything from where I sit."

Paige cocked her head. "Hmm, well, maybe I should sit where you are." She slid one long leg across his lap and straddled him. She shuffled food containers to the nightstand and put her hands on his bare chest, enjoying the thud of his heart as it sped up.

"I do like the view from here."

———

They took a break from bed and laundry and takeout. While Gannon had dinner with his grandmother and a couple of cousins, Paige went to her apartment to make sure it was still standing and stock up on fresh clothes for shooting in the heat of summer. He'd invited her, even enticed her with meeting his nonni, but she'd declined. Whatever they were together was so fresh, so new, she wasn't prepared to open their circle. And she didn't want to do anything that would fuel the rumors that had spread again since *Kings of Construction* released the season teaser.

It was the first time they'd been apart for more than a few

hours since spring. Even now, she had a low-grade urge to text him, which she brushed off.

She let herself into the apartment, wrinkling her nose at the stale air. Becca was on a movie shoot in Vancouver and hadn't been home in three weeks.

Paige lugged her suitcase over the threshold and down the narrow hallway to her tiny bedroom. *Home.* Yeah, right. This tiny, crappy apartment had never been home. Just as her childhood home had never laid claim to that title either. Had it been home to anyone within its walls?

She wondered briefly about her father. About the kind of man who had allowed Leslie St. James to cut him out of the family home and the lives of his daughters. An astrophysicist, he'd been given the opportunity to teach in Germany. Her mother hadn't deemed Germany good for her own career, and neither wanted to sacrifice, so they quietly divorced. Paige had been five and Lisa three.

St. James women weren't supposed to become dependent on men. It was a lesson drilled into their heads from childhood. A lesson that had actually stuck with Paige, unlike the dozens of others she'd ignored, such as dinner party etiquette and dressing to impress.

Her mother was deeply disappointed in her career choice, and Paige could only hope that Leslie St. James would see a sliver more worth in documentary filmmaking. Though she wasn't holding her breath over it. It would probably be regarded as yet another rebellion, a topic that would have her mother clucking into her wineglass in disbelief that a child she raised could be such a disappointment.

Well, the disappointment was mutual as far as Paige could see. Who raised children to be further extensions of a parent's own success?

Her phone buzzed, and she saw the text from Carina with a picture of Malia sound asleep under pink covers and pillows in her princess bed.

Carina: A few more nights in our perfect house before heading to New York for the drug trial! Dr. Singh is almost as excited as we are!

Paige grinned and texted back before she shoved her phone back in her pocket. She had a good feeling about the trial and Dr. Singh.

Enough stalling, she decided and opened her bag on the bed that hadn't been slept in for two months. She swapped out coats and sweaters for tanks and tees and, thinking of Cat and—okay—Gannon, added two sleeveless sundresses.

Repacked in less than ten minutes, Paige flopped back on the mattress and stared up at the ceiling. On a whim, she took out her phone and dialed Becca's number. Her roommate answered on the second ring, surprising and delighting Paige.

"Holy shit, do we have so much to talk about," Becca announced.

"Are you busy? Can you talk?" Paige asked, enjoying the energy she heard in Becca's voice.

"I've got ten, probably more. We're resetting for a big action sequence that is sucking the life out of all of us," Becca said, not sounding the least bit discouraged. "How are you feeling? Healing well?"

"Yeah, I'm fine," Paige said, glancing down at the yellow, mottled bruises on her legs.

"You sure? I saw the teaser. It looked pretty rough."

"You know how TV works. Gotta make it look worse than it really is," Paige said glibly.

"I can tell you don't want to talk about it, so I'll be an awesome friend and change the subject. Are you really dating Gannon King?"

"Can we go back to the injuries? I'd rather talk about that."

Becca squealed. "I knew it. I just knew it. When you took me to the wrap party last season, didn't I *tell* you he looked at you like he was into you?"

Becca had indeed insisted to Paige that Gannon looked far more interested than disinterested. "Yes, you told me, and if there is something going on there, I'm not ready to talk about it yet."

"Fine, fine. I'll pretend to respect your boundaries, but I'm dying to know where Boobalicious Traxx fits into all this."

"From what Gannon says, they were never a thing."

"You believe him?" Becca asked.

"Yeah. I do. He's got no reason to lie, and it does sound like something the network would do to drum up attention for a new series."

"And now they're drumming up more attention by making it a love triangle," Becca hypothesized.

"Yeah. Okay, enough on that topic. Where are you and what are you up to?"

"No time for that. Let me get to the good stuff. We've got Sarah Holden."

"For what? The movie?" Paige asked, flexing her feet at the ankles and wondering if she should pack another pair of sandals.

"Nope, the doc."

Paige sat up, her feet hitting the floor with a thump. "Our doc? The documentary you and I will be producing?"

"One and the same. She's on set doing a cameo, and I told her I read the piece she wrote in the *New Yorker* on pay standards. I may have gushed a little and then told her what we're working on."

"And what? You tied her to a chair and threatened her until she agreed to be a part of it?"

"No! I didn't have to. She was all over it. Gave me her email and her agent's number so we can stay in touch. And get this—"

"There can't be more."

"Oh, there is. Our pal Sarah is friends with several of TV's most acclaimed stars, and she hinted that she may have a few more ladies willing to chat with our cameras."

"I am totally in love with you right now, Becca."

"I know, right?" Becca laughed. "This is going to be bigger than we hoped, babe. I can't wait to start."

"One more season," Paige sighed. It would be like waiting for Christmas morning.

SUMMER

CHAPTER
30

Paige wondered whose asinine idea it had been to shoot in New Mexico in July. As far as she could tell, the dry heat of the southwest was just as damn hot as the sweltering humidity of the south. It was a special kind of misery that had their entire crew working in the bare minimum of clothing, a sure boon to ratings she predicted as she watched Gannon swipe his arm over his forehead, droplets of sweat collecting on his broad, bare chest.

It was their last episode. Unfortunately one hundred and six degrees had a way of dampening spirits, and no one was feeling particularly enthusiastic about wrapping. They had two days left on the shoot after today, and Paige was ready for it to be over. What she wasn't ready for was not waking up to Gannon every day.

He still snuck out of her bed every morning before the rest of the crew stirred to life. The rumors were still circling, and now that the first episode had aired—with a few after-the-fact interviews with Paige and Gannon they'd filmed on a different location—there was probably no hope that the gossip mill would run dry on its own. She dreaded when she had to come face-to-face with the fallout. Right now, the network and production company were singing her and the show's praises.

But sooner or later, shooting would end and it would be time to find more work before next season. And she had the distinct feeling that this season was going to hold her back. However, she at least had the pleasure of being guilty of what the network had suggested…having an affair with Gannon.

There were times when Paige wondered if they were fooling anyone at all with the subterfuge. She could tell by Andy's smug smiles behind his monitors that their chemistry was translating loud and clear, but what could she do?

She was happy. Really happy.

And Gannon seemed to be pretty pleased with life too.

As if she'd called his name, he glanced up at her over the bookcase he was sanding and winked.

She knew he was remembering the very enjoyable shower they'd shared last night when she'd slid down that gorgeous wet body of his and teased him with her mouth until he'd fisted her hair in his hand, demanding a knee-buckling release.

The water had gone cold before they'd finished with each other.

Yeah, things were good, and Paige wondered what the off-season would hold for them. They'd crisscrossed the country together, working on impossibly tight deadlines. Could they survive real life? Not yet. As far as she could tell, they were just having sex…and working together. Was a relationship something either of them was capable of? Was it even something Gannon would be interested in exploring? They hadn't discussed it.

Now, battered under the breezeless oven of New Mexico sky, was probably not the best time to have a "where do you see this thing going" conversation, she decided.

Andy guzzled water behind the screen, studying Gannon as Tony followed his every move. Felicia wiped her forehead on her raised arm and moved the boom pole in closer to catch whatever Gannon was muttering under his breath.

A white Escalade rolled up to the curb behind them, and Paige squinted through the mirages shimmering over the white concrete. Without being ordered to, Rico broke away from shooting Gannon and focused on the SUV. The driver, in suit and tie, hustled out and around to open the back door. One tanned, shapely leg ending in a bloodred stiletto appeared and then another.

What. The. Hell.

Meeghan Traxx slid out of the back seat in a fitted red pencil skirt and nearly sheer white sleeveless top. The cowl neck lay atop her spectacular breasts, calling even more attention to their excessive volume.

Her blond hair was salon fresh, set in perfect beachy waves. Movie star sunglasses obscured most of her face, drawing more attention to her perfect painted red lips.

She brought a finger to those lips and wiggled her fingers, tipped with fresh fake nails, at Rico's camera. Andy's mouth fell open, surprise written all over his sweaty face. Paige glared at him, willing him to yell cut, but he kept rolling.

Meeghan waited until Rico moved into view and then pranced over cables and around fans that were doing nothing but stirring the heat. She came up behind Gannon and put her hands over his eyes. Paige clapped a hand over her mouth as Gannon nearly fumbled the electric sander. Worksite safety be damned.

"What the—" What was sure to be a colorful question was cut off when Gannon spun around and Meeghan attacked.

She launched herself at him, and the kiss she laid on him was enough to suck the oxygen out of his lungs. The kiss that he didn't exactly fight his way out of, Paige couldn't help noticing. It wasn't until she'd dragged in a sharp breath that Paige realized she'd stopped breathing.

That lying sack of—

"Kitty Cat!" Meeghan squealed, spotting Cat approach. She released the dumbfounded Gannon and grabbed Cat in a choke hold. "It's so good to see you!"

Cat shot poison dart eyes at Gannon, who stared back blankly at them. Cat wiggled out of Meeghan's hold and moved to stand next to her brother.

"Surprise!" Meeghan said, spinning back to flash her million-wattage smile at Tony and Rico.

"Uh, cut?" Andy called weakly. He glanced in Paige's direction, confusion and embarrassment evident in his eyes.

Meeghan's driver, eager as a golden retriever, tottered over to hand his mistress her giant Michael Kors tote.

"Here, sweetie," Meeghan said, tossing the giant tote into Paige's arms. "Do something with that for me, and get me an iced skinny soy vanilla latte, extra whip."

Paige's breath left her in a silent whoosh. She glanced down at the bag in her arms and dumped it on a chair as if she'd accidentally accepted fresh roadkill. She wouldn't look at Gannon or Cat.

Meeghan pranced over to Andy, shaking her hair over her shoulder. "Mind if I watch the playback?"

"Uh, why don't we all take an hour?" Paige heard Andy's voice in stereo through her headset and her uncovered ear. She didn't wait for anyone else to move. She yanked off her headset and mic and bolted.

"Paige," Gannon began.

But she held up her hand and cut him off. He had nothing to say that she wanted to hear. Not with Meeghan Traxx's lipstick smeared over his mouth.

———

Paige felt bad about taking the production van back to the hotel, but she couldn't deal with being around anyone else. She needed to be alone.

She stopped at a drive-thru and got herself her forbidden comfort, an ice-cold Coke, and numbly stabbed the elevator button for her floor. The doors closed, and finally sure she was alone, Paige slumped against the back wall. And began the internal debate that had wanted to rage for the last ten minutes.

What the hell happened?

Gannon lied. That's what happened. He'd lied to her repeatedly about his involvement with that…that…person. Did she hate Meeghan because she was Gannon's whatever? Or did she have a legitimate reason?

The doors slid open silently, and she shuffled out onto the red-and-gold carpet that reminded her of a casino.

They didn't see her, she realized as her heart thudded in her chest. Gannon, with Meeghan wrapped around him like a weed, was fighting with his key card to open the door.

"I like it when a man is impatient," Meeghan all but purred. Paige nearly vomited.

"Get inside," Gannon ordered, dragging Meeghan over the threshold and slamming the door behind them.

Hot tears burned Paige's eyes. She turned and ran to her room at the opposite end of the hallway. Forcing her way through the door, she threw herself on the bed and pulled a pillow over her head.

What were you thinking? her mother's voice demanded smugly inside her head. *What did you expect, getting involved with Gannon? You should have known better.*

She felt dizzy and sick. Crushed. She hadn't noticed her feelings for Gannon growing so strong. They had snuck up on her. What a fool she'd been. And he let her be a fool. She couldn't understand it, couldn't reconcile the Gannon who held her in his arms and shared childhood stories with her with the Gannon who just dragged Network Barbie into his hotel room.

She wanted to rage at him, to pound her fists into his chest until he felt as bad as she did.

But that wasn't how she handled problems. She had a job to do, and she wouldn't be chased off by a lying, cheating asshole. No, she would go ice queen and freeze his ass in the New Mexican summer heat.

Five minutes. It was all she'd give herself to feel this horrible, broken ache in her chest. And then it was back to business.

Before Paige returned to the set, she went down to the front desk and asked to change rooms. She moved up a floor, away from Gannon, and made the clerk promise that he wouldn't give out her room number to anyone. She wasn't sure if any of the female clerks would be able to hold out against Gannon's charm, but it was better than nothing.

Stomach churning, she took a moment to sit on the edge of the bed. She let out a shuddery breath and immediately regretted it.

"Crap," she murmured weakly. She made the dash to the bathroom just in time to lose her lunch. *The sobs are from being sick*, Paige told herself as she cried, *not from hurt. Not from loving Gannon.*

She stretched out, resting her face on the cool tile floor. It smelled vaguely and comfortingly of cleaner.

Her phone vibrated again. It had started in the middle of her move, but she had no desire to answer it. Especially not when she saw who was calling. A dozen missed calls from Gannon King and another ten text messages. She was surprised he'd have time to call or text while he was banging Meeghan into oblivion.

Her stomach rolled again at the thought, but there was nothing left to cleanse. Just raw emptiness.

Gannon: Paige please answer. I can explain.

Explain? What was there to explain? She didn't need an explanation that the man she'd been sleeping with was a lying sack of shit. God, the whole season was one big lie. And she'd bought it hook, line, and sinker.

Gannon: Are you okay? Please talk to me. Please.
Gannon: Goddamn it, Paige. Answer your fucking phone and tell me if you're okay.

The many shades of Gannon King, she thought sadly as she turned off her phone and stowed it back in her pocket. God, she hurt. Her chest felt like there was a weight pressing on it, crushing her. Her head ached at the base of her neck, the pain promising to only worsen. There was nothing she could take, nothing she could do to dull it. It was the price she had to pay for falling for a liar.

She made herself stand up and look in the mirror. She looked pale and sick. Sweat covered her ghostly pallor, so she washed her face. She grabbed her makeup bag. If any situation called for armor, it was this one. Carefully, she applied a tinted sunscreen and brushed on waterproof mascara. She still didn't have much color in her cheeks, but nature would take care of that quickly enough. Her hair was a curling mess, so she did the best she could, parting it on one side and leaving it wild. She changed into fresh shorts and her favorite tank top that read BeastMode across the chest, a gift from Kings Construction foreman Flynn.

She could do this. She nodded at her reflection.

She wasn't going to let some huge, colossal, gut-wrenching mistake chase her away from her job. Even if said huge mistake's big-deal girlfriend hung around set. She swallowed hard.

Christ on a cracker. Paige St. James was the *other* woman.

CHAPTER

31

Paige stared into the dredges of her glass of bourbon and felt absolutely nothing. The numbness that set in was a welcome relief from the burning agony she'd felt on set for the last four hours of shooting.

He'd pounced on her the second she stepped foot on-site. And she'd held him off with the iciest look she could muster.

"Now is not the time or place. Let's be professionals," she'd said coldly.

He'd tried to argue, had been ready for a throwdown in front of everyone, but Cat had stepped in, dragging him off. Paige didn't know what Cat said to him, but the sisterly advice had kept him away from her, and by the time Andy called cut on the last take, Paige was halfway to the van.

But once in her room, she felt the walls closing in on her, and she knew sooner or later he'd find her here. Or he wouldn't. He could be too busy *entertaining* Meeghan.

The woman hadn't returned to the set, and not a word was said about her by anyone. So Paige could only assume Meeghan was waiting on her shapely ass in the hotel's air-conditioning for Gannon to wrap for the day.

She kept her phone off, even left it in her room so she wouldn't be tempted to listen to the voicemails or read the texts, and then walked until she found a crappy bar. The bar top was sticky, and her barstool cushion was ripped, but at least no one knew who she was and what she'd lost today.

The bartender, a straight-faced beauty with an expertly drawn cat eye in black liner, pointed to her nearly empty glass. "Another?"

"Sure," Paige said, neither enthusiastic about nor opposed to the idea of drowning her troubles. She'd started with a beer and found it lacking before switching to the brand of bourbon Gannon had brought her once in a different hotel room in a different state.

The bartender poured. "Penis?" she asked.

"I beg your pardon?" Paige blinked.

"Usually the only thing that makes a woman look the way you look is a penis that turns into an asshole."

Paige snorted despite herself. How apt. "That's a pretty accurate assessment," she nodded.

The woman put the bottle back on the top shelf. "Eventually you learn they're all assholes in their own special snowflake kind of way."

She wasn't wearing a wedding ring, Paige noted without surprise. "So what are we supposed to do?"

The bartender shrugged strong, lean shoulders. "Love 'em anyway or switch teams."

Paige drank to that.

"I don't suppose your guy is ripped and tatted and looks

as if he wants to murder anyone who gets in his way?" the bartender asked, her tone conversational.

Paige's gaze flew to the doorway where Gannon, his hard jaw set and his fists clenched at his sides, stared at her. "Fuck."

"Is this a cop matter?" the bartender asked blandly.

Paige shook her head. "No, just a temper tantrum waiting to happen."

"There's a back door through the kitchen if you need it."

Gannon strode to her and then seemed to battle with himself when he got within striking distance. "What the hell is wrong with you?" he snapped.

Paige could have iced him out if he led with a half-assed apology. She could have ignored him if he pleaded with her to listen to his side. But jumping on her as if she was the one who did something wrong?

The fuse was lit, and detonation was imminent.

"How dare you!" Paige hissed at him. The bartender eyed them from arm's reach of the greasy phone mounted on the wall. "What the hell is wrong with me? I'll tell you what's wrong with me. The guy I've been sleeping with has been cheating on me with his girlfriend, who showed up at my job and humiliated me today. That's what's wrong with me, you imbecilic asshole!"

"You get pissed off over a misunderstanding, freeze me out, and then I have to come looking for you, and I find you drinking alone in a bar in a city you don't know!" Gannon plowed down his list of Paige's offenses.

"A misunderstanding?" Her voice had reached dog whistle heights. She knocked back the rest of her drink, threw some bills on the bar, and rose. She wobbled a little and then righted herself, turning on him. "You want a fight? You got one. Let's go." She threw a little salute to the bartender and stormed out the front door.

He didn't let her go far. She'd barely made it to the curb when he gripped her upper arm with surprising force. "Stop it." He gave her a little shake that rattled her teeth, and she rounded on him.

"You're giving me every reason in the book to break that pretty face of yours," she warned him, enjoying the slow burn of alcohol and anger mixed in her gut.

He hauled her down the sidewalk, ignoring the looks they got from the handful of late-night wanderers. Paige noted none of them seemed remotely interested in intervening.

"Let go of me!" She tried yanking her arm free, but he only tightened his grip. In an impressive show of immaturity, Paige tried to kick him in the shin. She missed, catching him instead in his muscled calf. He solved the problem by slinging her over his shoulder and carrying her the half block to his pickup truck.

He put her down and caged her against the door with his arms. "Now, I'm going to put you in this truck, and you're going to stay put and listen."

She glared at him, her hair disagreeably falling over one eye.

He brushed it back for her. "Please." The word sounded like it pained him.

She didn't agree, and he didn't wait for it. He opened the passenger door, manhandled her inside, and strapped her into the seat. When he slammed the door, he locked the truck with the key fob to slow her down if she tried to make a break for it before he could get behind the wheel.

Paige didn't want to run. For once in her life, she wanted to fight.

Gannon climbed in and relocked the doors but didn't make any moves to start the truck. "What in the hell were you thinking?"

Paige waded in with every ounce of hurt and rage that

222

her body held. "I'd ask you the same thing, but judging from Meeghan's rack, I can take a wild guess."

Gannon slapped the steering wheel. "There is nothing between me and Meeghan!"

Her gasp fogged up the windshield. "Do you think I'm an idiot? Do you think I have no mental faculties whatsoever, and I'll just decide that I'm fine being the other woman?"

"I expect you to trust me! Do you honestly believe that I'd put you in that position? How can you think that?" Volcano Gannon had just erupted. But this time, it wasn't Paige's job to calm him down and refocus him.

"Trust you? Your *girlfriend*—who I asked you about repeatedly—showed up on set to surprise you and suck your face off, and then I saw you dragging her into your hotel room!"

That shut him up for a second. "Ah, Christ. That wasn't what it looked like, Paige."

The look she shot him would have felled a lesser man.

He clenched and relaxed his fists, took a deep breath and then another. "Look, I know exactly how it looked and how that sounded. I'm sorry. Okay? I'm sorry you were ever put in that position. But I thought you knew me. I thought you trusted me."

"You aren't making any arguments about the facts, Gannon."

"What the fuck do you want me to say? That that"—he gestured in the direction of the hotel—"could never on its best day be real? That it never was anything and that it kills me that you don't believe me or that she thought she could come in here and stir up trouble for you so she could get attention and ratings? She's a fucking piranha, and she's nothing to me. It was the network, and I told you that."

She felt it, that unwelcome spark of hope burst to life inside her aching heart. But she shook her head, trying to ward

223

it off. He lied. He made her look and feel like a fool. Her job, her reputation, was at risk because he'd played games with her.

"Don't shake your head, Paige. That was never real. But what I feel for you and what I think you feel for me? That's fucking real. I need you, Paige. I…" He trailed off, fighting the words.

"Just say it," Paige murmured, staring woodenly at the dashboard.

"I love you."

She took the words like a hit, crumpling in on herself. Nothing he could have said could have produced more pain than those words.

"I had my suspicions," he continued. "But when you walked off set today, I felt like I was watching my life walk away. And I knew. I love you, Paige, and you're killing me by not trusting me."

"Don't you dare say that! Not now, not because of this. That's cruel, and that's one thing I never thought you were," Paige said with a sob. No, she didn't want the hurt. She didn't want those words as an apology. She wanted to get back to the anger. It was safer, meaner.

She reached for the door handle, but Gannon was grabbing for her over the console. "Don't go."

She heard the desperation, the pain, and hated how her skin heated at his touch.

"You can't go," he said as if he'd made the decision for her and that was that. She shoved at his hands, but he was pulling her back. When she turned to tell him exactly how much she hated him in that moment, his mouth was so close.

Looking back, she couldn't remember which one of them made the move, but in one heartbeat, they were fighting each other, and in the next, their mouths were fused together. There was so much heat, so much anger, in the kiss.

It felt mean and desperate and needy. His hands were everywhere, and it vaguely registered to Paige that hers were greedily trying to drag him across the console to her. She *needed* him like oxygen.

His lips bruised hers, teeth dragging over her, tongue delving into her. "I love you, Paige. I love you so fucking much."

She barely heard the words over the racket of her heart pumping thickened blood through her veins. She tasted something salty but didn't care. She poured herself into the kiss. But it was Gannon pulling back.

"Honey," he breathed, his voice ragged with pain. Gannon dragged his thumbs over her cheeks, and it was only then that Paige realized she was crying. "Please don't cry. You're killing me, Paige."

He pulled her to him again, but this time it was to cradle her against his chest. He kissed the top of her head, and her heart broke just a little bit more. This was the Gannon she knew, the Gannon she wanted. But who was the man who dragged Meeghan Traxx into his hotel room?

He couldn't be both.

"Take me back to the hotel, please," she said, her voice flat as she looked away from him and leaned against her door.

"Paige—"

"I can't do this, Gannon. You obviously have things that need to be worked out, and I can't risk my reputation on a mess like this. Not when I'm so close to really doing something."

Without his warmth, she felt cold, empty. Alone.

"This isn't over."

"It is for tonight."

CHAPTER
32

She wasn't a coward, Paige told herself as she dragged her
suitcase down the hallway to her apartment. She had just
avoided an unnecessarily messy scene.

Filming the morning of reveal day had been so tense that
when Andy took her aside, she actually thought he was going to
fire her. But in a shining moment of heroics, Andy had offered
her an out.

"I'm not going to pretend to know what's going on. The
network didn't tell me they were sending Meeghan here, and
I don't want to know what they hoped to accomplish. But I
think you could use a break. So Mel's got a plane ticket with
your name on it. I told her you had a family emergency. Go
home and promise me you'll be back next season," he'd told
her.

She'd hugged him hard and pretended she didn't see
Gannon watching them. Under normal circumstances, she

would never have left the set. Not on reveal day and certainly not when the family was a sweetheart of a military couple who was finalizing the adoption of two kids out of foster care.

But it was impossible for her to be around *him*. He hadn't explained anything. Certainly not why, if he wasn't dating Meeghan, she felt so comfortable just showing up on a shoot across the country to lay a kiss on him. A kiss that he hadn't exactly fought off. And then he had taken her back to his hotel room. That couldn't be misconstrued. But then why had she spent the entire flight from Albuquerque to New York trying to come up with alternatives to the facts?

Was she that desperate to be with him that she was willing to sweep all his lies under the rug?

Pathetic.

Her mother would be horrified.

She let herself into the apartment and was immediately accosted by five feet of Latina fire.

"What are you doing home so early?" Becca launched herself off the couch and covered the eight feet to the door in record time, wrapping Paige in a suffocating hug. "Oh my God, you didn't get fired, did you?"

She almost wished. Home now, Paige just stood in the doorway. She didn't want to go back out into the world, but she didn't want to face her sad mattress in her sad room either.

"Okaaaaay," Becca said, picking up on the cues loud and clear. "I'm just going to take this bag from you, and you're going to go sit on the couch, and we don't have to talk." Becca hefted the suitcase with one hand and shoved Paige toward the couch with her other. "Go. Sit."

Paige did as she was told, slumping down on the worn cushions that Becca had hidden under a gold slipcover. She pressed the heels of her palms to her eyes.

When she dropped her hands and opened her eyes, a glass of red wine floated before her.

"Take your medicine, babe," Becca said, wiggling the glass.

"Thanks, Bec."

"Okay, I know I said you didn't have to talk about it, but I'm revising. Does this have anything to do with Gannon?"

Paige shot Becca a look over the rim of her wineglass. "Maybe."

"Does it also have anything to do with a vapid vampire blond named Meeghan?"

Paige thumped her head back against the low cushion of the couch. "Ugh. Does the entire world know?"

"Of course not. I, being your caring and protective roommate, have been stalking Meeghan—stupid fucking name, by the way—on social media since you and Gannon started…"

"Having incredible, mind-blowing, cheater-y sex?" Paige suggested.

Becca patted her on the shoulder. "We've all been there through the divorce that was never finalized or the long-distance relationship that 'just ended.'"

"I asked him straight up on multiple occasions, and he said they weren't together. He said it had been a publicity thing set up by the network to help launch *Kings*."

"I saw her post on Instagram. 'Surprising my man at work!'" Becca mimicked in her very best Valley girl voice. "Does she get her lips injected with car tires? Because that's some serious perma duck face going on there."

"She showed up on set, after I had decided to talk to Gannon about maybe continuing things in the off-season, and laid a porn star kiss on him."

"What did he do?"

"He didn't exactly fight her off."

"Did he kiss her back? Bend her over a sawhorse and start going to town?"

"Gross. No to the second. I don't know about the first."

"Is it possible that she's just psycho and trying to make it look like they're together?"

"Well, that could have been a possibility if I hadn't seen Gannon physically dragging her into his hotel room like he couldn't wait to get her naked."

"Hard to misconstrue that one," Becca mused.

"Exactly what I said."

"So you had it out with him?" Becca leaned forward. "You didn't just go all frosty-Leslie-St.-James on him?"

"I may have had a few drinks and defrosted my ice queen all over him."

"You didn't."

"I tried to kick him in the shins."

Becca nodded in approval. "Classy and not at all over the top."

"I kept it classy until he accused me of not trusting him and then told me he loved me."

Becca, for once, was speechless.

Paige wished she'd kept her mouth shut. Talking about it didn't make her feel any better.

"Does he?" Becca ventured.

Paige shook her head. "If he loved me, he wouldn't have kept me as a side piece and humiliated me at work."

"Does everyone know?"

Paige slumped, sipped. "I don't know. We were pretty careful, but Andy obviously knew something was going on and felt bad enough about the whole thing that he told my PA that I had a family emergency and sent me home halfway through reveal day."

"Ouch."

Paige buried her face in the crook of her elbow. "I let it get in the way of my job. A job I need."

"Babe, we'll figure this all out. I promise."

"I've got to get attached to another show, like, now. I can't do another season with him, with them."

Becca shook her head in understanding. "No, you can't." She gripped Paige's hand in hers. "We're going to figure this out, I promise you, and one day, we're going to look back at this night and laugh about how we didn't know how awesome things were going to turn out."

Paige hoped so, but it sounded too optimistic thinking about a time when she wouldn't feel so damaged.

———

Paige wasn't sleeping when her phone vibrated on the sad, pressboard box she used as a nightstand. She'd held firm and ignored the calls and texts from Gannon after he finished filming, but she was looking at the screen when the text popped up.

Gannon: We wrapped. Everyone's out at the bar and I'm lying here thinking about you. You didn't have to leave.

Maybe it was because it was two in the morning her time. Maybe it was because she still felt like he didn't get why she was so hurt. Whatever the reason, she picked up her phone.

Gannon: I wish things hadn't ended this way. Or that we'd never started.

It was the truth. The painful, honest truth.

Her phone signaled an incoming call. Gannon. She debated, nearly sending it to voicemail, and then relented.

"Hey." Her voice was flat, tired.

"Paige." Her name was a rush of relief from Gannon's lips.

She squeezed her eyes closed tight. "I don't know why I answered the phone."

"Don't hang up." He made the demand abruptly before adding, "Please."

She sighed but didn't disconnect.

"Did you get my messages?" His voice was low and husky.

"I didn't listen to them or read them."

He blew out a breath. "I can't believe how fucked up everything got."

Her laugh was bitter. "Tell me about it."

"You didn't give me a chance to explain. You just packed up and left like I didn't even matter to you."

"What's there to explain?"

"Paige."

"Did you know she was coming? Was I some kind of joke to you?"

"Jesus. Is that what you think?"

"I'd like to think you're not that good of an actor," Paige admitted.

"I'm not. You know I'm not. Paige, you know me." He sounded frustrated. "I hate this. I'm not good at communicating when I'm pissed off."

"*You're* pissed off?"

"She's trying to ruin everything because I didn't play ball," Gannon said. "And you're going to let her. So yeah, I'm pissed."

"Meeghan?"

"I told you it was for publicity, but I told the network I

231

wasn't doing it anymore. The show was good. We didn't need any of that bullshit to pull in an audience."

"Obviously, she didn't get the message." Paige rubbed a hand over her forehead in the dark.

"I didn't pay any attention to the press she was giving about us still being together. She's the network's problem now. So when she showed up on set and laid one on me and treated you like…like a fucking lackey…" He broke off.

"Did you ever sleep with her?"

His pause was damning. "Yeah, but—"

"Maybe that's okay in your world. Sleep with some girl, let her think you're together until you find someone else, but it's not okay in mine. I never would have slept with you if I thought you were with someone. Even if it is *her*."

"Goddamn it, Paige. I'm not with her. I never was."

"You slept with her." There was no point arguing. He'd never seen it from her point of view. "Look, I'm sorry for leaving like I did. I should have at least stuck around to have this conversation in person. Whatever happened, it doesn't really matter. What matters is how this relationship is making me feel, and it's not good. I'm out, Gannon."

"You can't just—"

"Thank you for respecting my decision. Good night, Gannon."

She hung up and shut down her phone. She wasn't going to waste any more sleep on him.

She finally fell asleep just after dawn, missing the feel of his arms around her.

CHAPTER

33

He was fucking crazy. That was the only explanation for him acting like a damn stalker. She'd made it clear—crystal clear—that she didn't want to know the truth. Yet here he was on her damn doorstep.

He had to make her understand…and then he would let her have it for not trusting him.

Cat had tried to talk to him out of it on the flight home, but he'd shut her down and taken a cab from the airport to Paige's apartment.

He should have his head examined.

Fuck it. He knocked and looked up and down the hall. They'd been "together" for roughly two months, and this was the first time he was seeing her place. Was that weird? He shook the thought out of his head. Everything about them was weird.

He was just raising his fist to knock again when the door opened.

The woman had wild black hair shoved back from her face

with a wide purple headband and scraped in at five feet even. She was definitely not Paige.

She eyed him skeptically. "You must be Cheater Magee."

He bit back a defensive retort. "Is Paige here?"

She shook her head, and her thick hoop earrings jiggled. "Nope, she got a text from an anonymous source that a jackass of a carpenter was headed her way."

He was going to have to kill his sister.

"You might as well come in." She walked away from the open door, and Gannon followed her in, dropping his bag and slipping his backpack off his shoulders.

The woman reappeared with two beers and jerked her chin toward the couch, the only place available to sit besides a pair of rickety-looking barstools tucked under the two feet of kitchen counter. He sat, accepted a beer, and stared at it.

"Why are you letting me in and giving me beer if you think I cheated on Paige?"

"I'm Becca, by the way." She offered a small hand, which he took in a perfunctory shake.

"Gannon. Not a cheater."

"I figured."

"So she didn't tell you?" Gannon ventured.

"Oh, she told me. I've just been in and around the industry long enough to recognize a narcissistic, loose cannon who doesn't care who she hurts to get what she wants."

"Meeghan." Gannon spat out the name. "She's psychotic."

"So you were not dating Meeghan."

"No," he said emphatically.

"But Paige doesn't believe you, or she's just humiliated enough that it doesn't matter that you weren't dating her. A woman still showed up at her place of work, laid claim to you, and then treated her like garbage."

"Yep."

"And what did you do immediately after the claiming and the garbage treating?"

Gannon's hand cruised the back of his head. "Not enough," he admitted.

"Why not?" Becca pulled her feet up on the cushion, looking comfortable and relaxed.

"Paige and I were trying to hide our…"

"Go ahead and say it. Relationship," Becca said with a royal flourish of her hand.

"Relationship. She didn't want anyone to think she was sleeping with the talent for…perks."

"Sounds like Paige."

"I had no idea what was happening. One second, I'm working with power tools, and the next, someone's kissing me. When I pulled back, I saw Paige's face…" He shook his head. "And then Meeghan's strutting over to her, throwing her purse in her face, and giving her a coffee order."

"Bitch," Becca said with enthusiasm.

"This is after the network miked Paige and made her start doing on-screen interviews to feed the interest in a potential relationship between us. I couldn't say anything. Or if I started, I wouldn't be able to stop, and everyone would know."

"Well, clearly you're screwed," Becca announced, taking a swig from her beer.

"I love her."

"Which you should *not* have told her in the middle of a fight when it looked like you had cheated on her."

"Shit." He took a long pull from his beer and looked around. "She wasn't kidding. You guys really don't even have a coffee table," Gannon said, eyeing the apartment. His childhood bedroom had been bigger than this living space.

"Want to make us one?"

"Will that get her back?"

Becca grimaced. "Look, man, I hate to be blunt like this, but Paige is a 'fool me twice' kind of girl. In her book, you're a mistake, and she won't be inclined to repeat you."

"That can't be the end of it," Gannon argued. He wanted to get up and pace, but there was nowhere to go.

"It doesn't have to be, but it's not like sending some other girl flowers and she instantly forgives all your transgressions. Totally works on me," she said, jerking a thumb at her chest, "but not so much on Paige. If you're serious about getting her back, and you're not going to give up after a quick fix attempt, there's hope."

"What do I have to do?"

Becca leaned forward, looked him dead in the eye. "Whatever it takes. Go big or go home *alone*."

———

Gannon left Becca feeling marginally more hopeful. She'd made him promise that if the topic ever came up, Becca had slammed the door in his face, not fed him beer, and definitely did not conspire with him against Paige.

She'd given him a few guidelines:

1. Stop blowing up Paige's phone.

2. But don't go cold turkey on the contact either. Stay in her head.

3. Identify Paige's life priorities and find a way to become part of them.

4. Be patient.

5. Build them a damn coffee table.

He hated the fourth and was pretty sure the fifth was just Becca's fee for her "free advice."

Paige's priorities were easy. She had one: work. Unfortunately for him, their season had just wrapped, and if he'd been picking up on Becca's hints correctly, Paige was looking for a way out of working with him again.

He stared down the hallway with its threadbare carpet toward the paint-chipped stairwell and hefted his backpack over one shoulder. This was not the last time he'd see Paige St. James's place, he vowed. She was his, and she was just going to have to get used to it.

CHAPTER
34

The walls in Leslie St. James's dining room were covered in a lovely linen paper in delicate blues and greens that gave dinner guests the impression they were dining underwater. The conversation around the dining table had a similar effect on Paige.

Her mother, cool and beautiful as always in a sleeveless ivory sheath, continued her well-reasoned and methodical dissection of where Paige had gone so wrong as to end up on reality television.

"Honestly, Paige." Her mother dabbed her napkin delicately at the corner of her mouth. "I don't see why you won't take some time off to recover from your mishap and reconsider your path in life."

Paige, used to the criticism, slid her fork through the pepper tuna steak her mother's cook had prepared.

"I like what I do," she reminded her mother. She wasn't

about to tell her mother and her sister that she was desperately trying to find a new job. Something, anything, that meant she didn't have to go back for another season of *Kings*. She couldn't stand the thought of working with Gannon side by side again, and the further she distanced herself from the situation, the more clearly she saw the role that the production company had played in her humiliation.

The interviews, the suggestive show teasers? There was no way Meeghan Traxx just *happened* to show up on set that day.

Leslie rolled her eyes in dramatic fashion. "I don't see what there is to like about it," she insisted.

Frankly, the only thing Paige liked about her job in this moment was the fact that it irritated her mother.

Her sister, Lisa, her long, dark hair worn in a sleek French braid over her shoulder, smirked over the rim of her wineglass. "I take it you haven't gotten a good look at her costar, Mom."

Paige shot her sister a warning look, but everyone was a target around the St. James dining table. Potshots were taken with abandon until someone surrendered.

"I assume you mean that Gannon King." The disdain in their mother's voice rang out clearly.

"Rumor has it our Paige is involved with him," Lisa said, topping off her glass with the very nice Spanish rosé and handing the bottle to Paige.

Paige dumped a generous portion into her own glass before handing the bottle to her mother.

"Involved?" Leslie arched a well-manicured eyebrow at her wayward daughter. "I certainly hope that a rumor is just a rumor in this case."

Paige stabbed a steamed green bean with more force than necessary. "We were having sex, and now we're not. Happy?"

Lisa sputtered in her wineglass. Paige had said it for the

reaction, but Leslie was too experienced to let anything like surprise show.

"Sex is one thing, but a relationship with someone like that? Ill-advised. At least you're smart enough to not tie yourself down to that kind of man," Leslie said primly.

"What is it exactly that you have against Gannon, Mom? Besides the fact that he called you out for being rude on the phone?" Lisa asked.

"He *accused* me of being rude. I wasn't actually being rude," Leslie clarified the semantics. Their mother thrived on semantics. "I was having a very natural response to learning that my daughter had been injured."

Wait for it. Paige counted down.

"The fact that she didn't see fit to call her own mother to tell her what had happened and that she was all right, well, I feel that's more of a reflection on Paige's attitude than my own."

Paige hid her sigh. Her mother was nothing if not consistent. "So he *accused* you of being rude, and that's why you don't like him?" Paige asked. It shouldn't matter that her mother didn't like the man who Paige herself couldn't stand now, except for the fact that it made him the tiniest bit less horrible in her mind. But that was the rebellion talking. And she should be old enough to know that just because she and her mother agreed on *something* didn't mean she was wrong.

Leslie jabbed her fork in her direction. "That's not the only reason. In my profession, one must have a sense about people, and my sense about Gannon is he's a loose cannon. And before you even say it, it's not that he's a tradesman and works with his hands. Lots of respectable men work with their hands."

"Mm-hmm," Paige intoned. She had accused her mother on a handful of occasions of being an insufferable snob. It was one insult that seemed to have stuck.

"For god's sake, Paige. Sit up straight when you're being passive-aggressive," Leslie snapped.

Paige straightened her shoulders, a reaction as rooted as Pavlov's drooling dog.

"I don't know, Mom. He comes across as more than just a loose cannon on the show," Lisa insisted.

"You watch my show?" Paige asked, eyebrows winging up.

"Of course I do. I don't love it, but it's yours. You read my journal articles," her sister pointed out.

"And I don't love them, but they're yours." Paige tilted her wineglass in Lisa's direction in a silent toast.

"I can't believe both my daughters waste their time on that show." Leslie shook her head in disappointment.

"We read your books," Paige and Lisa said in unison.

"Well, of course you do," Leslie sniffed.

Once the subject changed to Leslie's new book that she was working on, Paige breathed easier. She was used to being a target for her own work. The criticism usually didn't do any lasting damage. But with that area of her life as sensitive as an open wound now, she didn't think she could survive too many hits tonight.

And if her mother caught even a whiff of her dejection, Leslie would have her scheduled for six grad school interviews by noon tomorrow.

———

By the time dessert was over, all sniping was brushed under the rug as Lisa spoke in broad terms about a paper on epileptic seizures she was researching for a medical journal. Paige did her best to grill her about Malia's cancer trial but got the patent and expected answer citing HIPAA and patient confidentiality.

They went their separate ways at a respectable nine o'clock,

241

Leslie upstairs to her study to transcribe her case notes and Lisa home to grab a few hours of sleep before her early-morning shift at the hospital.

Paige stood on the sidewalk outside her mother's lovely home, debating what she wanted to do. Finding there was nothing, absolutely nothing, she headed east toward the metro station. Her phone rang in her bag, saving her from the monotonous six-block walk to the Great River train station.

The picture of Cat mugging for the camera glowed on her screen. Paige debated for a second. She'd been avoiding Cat since shooting wrapped, mainly because she didn't want to put Cat in an awkward position with her brother…and also so Paige could pretend that Gannon didn't exist.

It was petty and stupid. She sighed.

"Hey, Cat. What's up?" she asked in what she hoped was an upbeat tone.

"You sound terrible. Where are you?" Cat demanded.

"I just had dinner with my mother and sister in Great River."

"Well, that explains the sounding terrible," Cat joked. She was aware of and fascinated by Paige's family dynamics. In the King household, everyone yelled at everyone else and then sat down for a meal. That was their normal.

"You're not calling on behalf of He Who Better Not Be Named, are you?" Paige asked.

Cat snorted. "I know better than to stick my nose in my brother's love life," she promised. "Now yours on the other hand…"

"Ha. Ha. How's your off-season? What are you up to?"

"So we're just going to pretend that you and my brother didn't have a steaming hot affair before some asshat at the network sent that shithead inflatable doll on set to make you look like an idiot?"

"Pretty much, yeah," Paige sighed.

"Okay. Just checking. So I landed this women's work wear endorsement deal—super cute flannels, jeans that won't show your crack or rip if you actually move in them, tank tops that don't ride up to your armpits. My parents were in town visiting for the week. They flew back to Florida wondering what the hell is wrong with their son, who's basically locked himself in his workshop and refuses to come out unless it's for beer or red meat. How about you?"

"I just had dinner with my mother and sister, who think I'm a disappointment in the family because of my job in reality television. A job I can't go back to after being puppeteered into said scorching hot affair based on lies for a network that made it its goal this season to humiliate me for the sake of ratings at every turn. So now, my only option is to start looking outside the network, which means I'm probably going to end up as a PA on some vapid, disgusting dating show."

"Oh, so everything's normal then?" Cat said blandly.

"Pretty much."

"Then this will just make your day," Cat announced. "Invites for the network's real estate hottie guy's party just went out. You, Gannon, and Meeghan are on the guest list."

Paige wanted to throw up her tuna steak. "Guess who out of that cozy threesome isn't freaking going?"

"Guess who isn't going to have a choice? Rumor has it you are going to be 'compelled' to attend."

"What are they going to do? Fire me?" *Great.* Then she really would have zero options.

"Probably. Or maybe they'll threaten to get rid of the rest of the production crew if you don't play ball."

Paige growled in frustration, scaring a guy in gym shorts and a tank top walking a fluffy dog that couldn't have weighed more than five pounds. "That's not fair! And yes, I know that life isn't fair, but when I signed up to be a field producer, I wasn't signing up to be talent and a puppet!"

"Wanna meet for a drink?"

CHAPTER
35

Paige scowled at her reflection and stood on her tiptoes, trying to see more of the dress. The tiny bathroom vanity mirror only afforded a boobs-up view. "We need to move," she announced.

Becca stuck her head in from the hallway. "Damn, you look amazing. Why are we moving?"

"We need a bigger mirror. And a dining room table. And I sleep on a twin mattress. I'm twenty-eight, and I don't have any real furniture. My life is sad, and we should move right now so I don't have to go to this thing."

Unperturbed, Becca twirled her finger in the air. "Spin, babe."

Paige complied, not feeling any excitement at all when Becca applauded.

"It's perfect."

The dress was the color of crushed cranberries. The skirt

was a short A-line that hit at midthigh. The top was fitted with a modest scoop neck. But the modesty disappeared when she turned around and the back was almost completely open, framed from the neck to the waist with a scalloped opening. It was gorgeous, but Paige wished that she was wearing it anywhere but where she had to go tonight.

"I don't want to go."

Becca crossed her arms and tapped her fingernails on her arm. "Okay. It's time whether you want to hear it or not."

"No. It's not time. I definitely don't want to hear it. I want to wallow."

"You've wallowed for twenty-five days. Time's up. You are going to this party. You are going to smile for the cameras. You are not going to burst into tears when you see Gannon King. And you are not going to shrivel up and die when you see Meeghan Traxx. You are going to go be your fabulous, professional, strong, independent, hot-as-hell self."

"But I don't wanna."

Becca jabbed a finger in her face. "Uh-uh. Does that sound like something the director of a society-changing, award-winning documentary would say?"

"No," Paige grumbled.

"What would a director of a society-changing, award-winning documentary say?"

Paige pasted on a brilliant, phony smile. "Fuck off."

"That's what your eyes say to Meeghan, to the camera," Becca told her.

Paige noted she didn't mention Gannon. It was probably because her roommate was enamored with the custom King coffee table he'd had delivered to their place. Sure, it was beautiful, sexy, stunning. All Gannon's furniture fell under that label. But it fit so perfectly into their space that Paige had wondered just how quickly Becca had booted Gannon from the apartment. It looked as though he'd had ample time to take measurements.

"I can do this," Paige gritted out.

"Reputation is everything, and tonight is the night you cement yours as a professional," Becca reminded her.

"I'm a damn professional," Paige announced to the mirror.

"That's my girl. Don't be anyone's doormat tonight. Who knows? Maybe you'll walk out of there with a job offer."

———

Paige got out of the cab and studied the twenty-story building where she would meet her worst enemies. Normally, she didn't go to these kinds of things. This was a party thrown by the network to showcase the Manhattan apartment recently renovated by Drake Mackenrowe, the network's real estate flip darling. When she received the invitation, she'd politely declined knowing that (a) it would be filmed for the show's finale, (b) both Meeghan and Gannon would be there, and (c) it was futile to say no. They'd find a way to coerce her.

The network had stood firm, insisting that her presence was required. After all, now that this season's episodes of *Kings of Construction* were running, she'd become quite popular, they reminded her. When she'd declined again, they'd called out the big guns, and Eddie had invited her to lunch to explain that if she didn't show her pretty face at what was sure to be a staged humiliation, her services would no longer be required by any show.

With her yes confirmed, Gannon had texted her twice to make sure she was coming. His calls and texts had slowed down to a point where she assumed he'd moved on. But tonight was the first time they'd see each other since New Mexico. And she'd give her left kidney to not have to walk into that building.

Paige clenched her jaw so hard it had reminded her to schedule a long overdue dentist appointment.

It wasn't that she was a coward, she reminded herself as she straightened her shoulders and headed for the doorman. She just didn't like drama.

She could do this, damn it. She was a St. James, after all.

"Hi, I'm here for the Welcome Home Network thing," she said.

The doorman in a smart black suit tipped his hat to her in perfect Manhattan fashion and held the door for her. "Enjoy your evening, miss."

In the swank lobby, she discovered a red carpet of sorts set up with a photo station and a network reporter doing live interviews. Fully intent on skipping the fuss, Paige started toward the wall of elevators only to be stopped by a fresh-faced intern with a headset and a clipboard.

"You must be Paige," he said, smiling with teeth whiter than nature allowed.

"It appears I am," she said.

"Great. Now you're just going to have your picture taken there on the WHN backdrop, and then Esme will do a quick thirty second on-camera chat, and then you can go upstairs."

"I'm not talent," Paige reminded Toothy. He was adorable and friendly. Just the sort of person she'd want as a PA on a project.

He smiled, unperturbed. "You're on my photo and interview list, and you look fabulous."

She certainly did in this dress. And if the network wanted her to play the heartbroken whatever to Meeghan's heroine, they could admire both of her metaphorical middle fingers.

"What's your name?" she asked Toothy.

"Bradley."

"Bradley, you get me through this without looking like an ass, and I may have a use for you in a few months."

"If you can get me out of carpet arrivals, I will kiss your feet."

She fished through her clutch for a card. "Email me. I have a project coming up next year that's going to need a lot of underpaid but enthusiastic people."

"You're a goddess. And just so you know, they're planning to ambush you in the video interview."

"Bradley, you're hired."

Riding the high and ready for battle, she strode over to the photographer and flashed her the power smile, one that vibrated in her bones. A harried-looking assistant with a headset then escorted her over to the camera crew. She was in line behind one show host, a popular designer, and the network's online editor. The host she recognized as a vlogger for the Welcome Home Network's website. Esme was in full on-camera makeup, and her hair had the look and sweep of a fresh blowout. The assistant snuck behind the camera and whispered something to the host, and the woman's gaze flew to Paige.

Esme waved her forward, and Paige shot an uneasy look behind her. "Sorry. Excuse me," she said, slipping past those ahead of her.

"Paige!" Esme greeted her as if they were long-lost friends, and Paige took a moment to desperately miss being behind the camera. "It's so wonderful to have you here today. Now, you just stand right there exactly like that, and we'll have you on your way in no time."

Esme beamed at the camera, and Paige followed suit, feeling like her jaw would freeze from the effort.

"I'm here with Paige St. James, field producer and assistant director of everyone's favorite surprise reno show, *Kings of*

Construction!" Esme announced to the glass lens. "I heard you had some excitement this season."

Of course she'd heard that. "We had a fantastic season," Paige said, not taking the bait. "We were fortunate enough to work with some really wonderful families and very talented local contractors. I can't wait for everyone to see their stories and experience the renovations."

"You look like you're all healed up after your on-set accident," Esme said, flashing her a faux pouty look.

"Some bumps and bruises from a windstorm. No permanent damage." Inspired, Paige did a slow turn for the camera as if to show she was injury free.

"That dress is stunning," Esme gushed.

"Thank—"

She was nudged hard from behind into Esme. Turning, she saw Meeghan Traxx, arms akimbo, cleavage erupting from the tight white bodice of her lace-up dress. She looked like a prostitute pretending to be a virgin.

"Why don't you ask her about her *supposed* relationship with Gannon?" Meeghan said, drumming her fingernails on her hips.

When Bradley said ambush, he hadn't been kidding.

"I'm sure everyone is curious to know if you and Gannon—" Esme began.

But Meeghan was running the interview now. She tossed those heavy blond curls over her shoulder, her extensions slapping Paige in the shoulder. "It's not true," Meeghan announced, looking into the camera. "Our little Paige here had a crush on my man, and who could blame her? I mean, look at him."

Paige thought about defending herself and then decided she might as well see where this idiot was going.

"So you and Gannon were never together?" Esme attempted the clarification, but Meeghan pulled the mic away from Paige.

"Never. In fact, it's kind of sad that she thinks some worthless little production assistant could tempt Gannon King away from this." She smoothed her hand down her side.

"Meeghan, I feel like we should get a few things straight," Paige said, smiling sweetly. "First of all, production assistants are not worthless. Without them, you wouldn't have anyone picking up your iced skinny soy vanilla latte with extra whip. Second, I used to be a production assistant, and I'm now a field producer, and I don't recall asking for your opinion on me or my life."

"You're just jealous that *he* wants *me*." Meeghan tossed her hair again, and Paige felt the breeze.

"I couldn't care less who you do or don't date. I'm here to do a job, and I take my responsibilities very seriously," Paige said coolly.

"Listen, you pathetic little nobody. Someone like you," Meeghan said, swiping her finger down the front of Paige's dress, "could never come between me and Gannon. No hard feelings, sweetie."

Paige's hand balled into a fist as all her calm-down techniques flew out the window.

She felt an arm slip around her waist. "I leave you alone for five seconds, and trouble just finds you."

Paige looked up, way up, at the newcomer. He was tall and lean, blond and built, with bright blue eyes and a crooked grin. Drake Mackenrowe was even more attractive, in a polished preppy way, off-screen than he was on.

If Gannon was the rough-around-the-edges bad boy of TV, Drake was the elegant knight in shining armor.

"I'm not sure what your problem with Paige is, but I don't

think she's spared you a second thought, Megan," Drake said smoothly without looking away from Paige.

"It's *Meeghan*."

"Of course it is," Drake sighed. He finally spared Meeghan a look. "Your eyelashes are coming unglued."

Meeghan gasped and reached for both eyes.

"Come on, gorgeous," Drake said, aiming that crooked grin at Paige. "Let's get you some champagne."

CHAPTER
36

I'm Drake, by the way," he said, gallantly offering his hand as the elevator doors closed on the lobby. He wore a sleek gray suit and no tie. His gleaming loafers were the color of rich caramel.

Paige bent at the waist to catch her breath. Anger was rolling through her system like a thunderstorm, and she didn't want to take it out on the man who'd saved her from further on-camera humiliation.

She straightened up and accepted his hand.

"I know who you are." She shook his hand, noting that though it wasn't callused like Gannon's, there was still strength in his grip. "Network dream boat and New York realty king. I'm Paige."

"Paige, welcome to the seventh circle of hell."

She laughed and was surprised that she was able to with rage coursing through her blood. She leaned against the back wall of the elevator and took a deep breath. "Thanks for your help back there."

"I've worked with Meeghan before. I know the warning signs of cat and mouse."

Paige shook her head. "I'm a producer. I didn't sign up for this."

"No one signs up for that. She's a narcissistic, unhinged nuclear explosion waiting to happen. Her show cycles through PAs faster than John Mayer cycles through girlfriends."

"Do you make it a habit to swoop in and rescue damsels in distress?"

The elevator doors opened directly into the penthouse, an airy space of light and concrete and stainless steel. The quintessential Manhattan billionaire's bachelor pad.

A waiter wandered by with a tray of champagne, and Drake snagged two glasses.

"The only thing I saved you from was a very public civil suit that she would have filed against you for breaking her nose. It would ruin the nose job she got last year."

Paige lifted her glass. "Meeghan's plastic surgeon thanks you." He mirrored her toast, and she drank deeply. If Drake hadn't stepped in, she very well could have done something epically stupid. One season of too much exposure to Gannon King, and he'd turned her into a reactive, temperamental woman.

"Can I offer you a piece of unsolicited advice?" Drake asked.

"I feel that I owe you. Advise away."

"Don't take it personally. Yeah, the network's pulling strings to make you dance, but they're not doing it to hurt you or humiliate you. They're just doing it to drum up ratings and sell more advertising. They use everyone as they see fit. It's nothing personal."

She knew it. Just as she knew not to take her mother's

constant judgment personally. But knowing it and not letting it eat away at her? Two entirely different things.

"I appreciate the advice," she said, not willing to delve further into it.

There were photographers and cameramen mingling in the crowd, and Paige felt exposed. There was no sign of Gannon or Meeghan, but she didn't want to look too hard.

"So what do you think of the place?" Drake asked, sweeping his hand toward the glass and metal staircase that led to a second floor.

"It's impressive," Paige said diplomatically. Her tastes didn't run to industrial formal. She preferred warmth, character.

He leaned in conspiratorially. "You can tell me it looks like a James Bond villain's lair. It won't hurt my feelings."

She bit her lip. "That's exactly what it looks like."

"I'll tell you a secret. This place belongs to the network president. He bought it and decided he wanted it gutted, and what better way to save a buck or two than have your own network handle the labor?"

"Angus Pearson made you renovate his place?" Paige gasped.

Drake looked around them and suppressed a shudder. "I tried to guide him in a more human direction, but he was insistent, and he has horrific taste. So I went with it with a dose of irony. There's a concrete urinal trough in the master."

"There isn't!" She laughed and then covered her mouth when she noticed a photographer turn in her direction.

"Oh, there is," Drake insisted. "I'll show it to you." He guided her toward the monstrosity of a staircase, a warm hand resting lightly at the small of her back. She felt it, that tingle, that awareness, that crept up her spine and *knew*.

He was there at the foot of the stairs, hazel eyes boring into her with heat and frustration. A day or two's worth of stubble graced his excellent jaw. Gannon's broad shoulders gave shape to the navy-blue blazer he wore. The white oxford shirt was tucked into jeans tight enough to display his muscular thighs to their full advantage. He was so raw, so male, that even dressed in business casual, there was a predatory air about him.

She felt like he sucked all the air out of the room, and she was left struggling for oxygen.

"Paige," he said, leaning in and brushing a kiss over her cheek. His lips singed her skin.

"Hi, Gannon," she said weakly. Cameras clicked away in the background.

Drake offered his hand. "Gannon King. I don't think we've officially met at any of these things. I'm Drake Mackenrowe."

"I try to get out of these things whenever possible," Gannon said. His tone was light, but Paige felt like the weight of his gaze was crushing her.

"Do you ever do any commission pieces? I've got this idea for a buffet and no knowhow," Drake said, raising his flawless hands.

"It depends on the customer."

"It's for my grandparents. Fiftieth wedding anniversary's coming up."

"Gannon has a soft spot for grandmothers," Paige said quietly.

"I've got a soft spot for a lot of people," he countered, eyes boring into her.

"Liar." Cat shimmied up in a designer dress worn with her typical careless perfection. "My brother doesn't like most people," she told Drake with a wink before she wrapped Paige in a warm hug. "Miss you, Paige. When are we going shopping?"

"When you start shopping at Target," Paige said, returning the hug.

"Lunch then. I hate not seeing you every day. Paige is not just a brilliant field producer. She's also a wonderful human being," Cat told Drake.

With Cat joining them, even more photographers began to circle, and Paige felt her skin flush.

"Cat, do you know Drake?" Paige began the introductions, and the two began to chat animatedly. Her entire system was on fire with Gannon standing so close, staring at her. His eyes telegraphed messages to her.

I'm sorry. I miss you. We need to talk.

She needed to escape. She'd shown her face, let the network have its little fun, even given the photographers shots of her with Gannon and Drake. No one could ask her for more, and if they did, she had two middle fingers itching to be used.

"Would you two excuse us for a minute? I'd like to talk to Paige alone," Gannon interjected.

Cat and Drake shared a look, and Paige started to shake her head, but his hand was closing around her wrist, and if she resisted, it would be one more scene for the cameras.

———

Gannon felt her working up the urge to fight free as he tugged her up the ugliest staircase he'd ever seen in his life. It looked like the result of a drunken one-night stand between an escalator and a glass elevator.

"Keep it together, princess." He nodded at the photographers shooting from below. Cat, his favorite sister in the world, had blocked them from climbing the stairs after them.

Beyond the glass railing, an acre of nearly black carpet stretched out in some useless open gallery area that housed a few pieces of ugly art. There were two bedrooms and a handful of people touring both. Gannon tried a door at the far end of the loft and, finding it empty, dragged Paige inside.

"Are you kidnapping me?" Paige yanked free and tried to get away from him in the cramped space.

"It's a linen closet, not a secret passage," Gannon argued. "You look incredible, by the way." She did. He'd spotted her the second she'd walked in, taking in the view like a fist to the solar plexus. She was gorgeous in everyday shorts and tank tops with no makeup and sloppy hair. Now, she was downright stunning.

"What the hell are you doing?"

There'd been a time when he'd teased her just to see a flash of anger, curious to see what was below that calm, frosty surface. And now he needed to put the beast back in the cage.

"I'm explaining."

"What's there to explain? You lied to me, and I fell for it. Lesson learned."

He grabbed her, gripping her arms. He couldn't keep his damn hands off her. "No, you're listening, and I'm talking. Meeghan and I were never in a relationship—"

"But you still had sex."

"Paige." The deep breath he took wasn't helping his blood pressure out of the stratosphere, and when she lunged to get around him, he moved first and thought later.

He spun her around, wrapping her in a bear hug from behind and pinning her against the empty shelves. "Goddamn it. Listen to me. I went on one date with her. The network set us up and sent us to some stupid party just like this one."

She stopped struggling in his arms.

"It was a publicity thing. The show was getting ready to film, and they were trying to build the hype. I went from googling bankruptcy to taking my first ride in a limo and standing on a red carpet. The booze was flowing, and when she put the moves on me, I didn't stop her. I thought…" He shook his head, embarrassed at the memory. "I thought my big break had finally come. I could save my grandfather's business and enjoy a piece of the good life. But I didn't know."

He released his hold on Paige and let her turn around.

"I left immediately after. She's fucking terrifying. Needy and mean and—it never happened again. But the press, the viewers, they ate up the idea of some kind of relationship. We showed up at a couple of events together and kept the 'relationship' alive. But the whole thing was a fucking lie. And I never touched her again."

Paige bit her lip and clasped her hands in front of her.

"Meeghan knew it was fake, but she's used to getting her way. She'd come at me every time we went somewhere together, expecting me to go home with her. She'd threaten, beg, try to seduce me. But once you know what's under all that shit on the outside? You don't ever have the desire to go back. I felt…ashamed of myself."

She reached toward him and then pulled her hand back, but he saw the gesture, took comfort in it.

"Gannon, why didn't you tell me this before?"

"Honey, I tried. I was stirred up when it all happened. I was so fucking pissed at Meeghan for coming at you like that. For trying to lay this fake claim on me, for trying to humiliate you in front of your friends and coworkers. I was livid. I freaked on her on set, and Andy told me to get her out of there and get it sorted. So I took her back to the hotel away from cameras and attention and told her to get out of my life and yours."

Those beautiful blue eyes welled with tears. "Why didn't you tell me this?" she asked again.

"I tried," Gannon insisted. "But you went all *me* on me and wouldn't listen!"

She gave a sad little laugh. "You taught me well. I almost

took a swing at Meeghan downstairs when they ambushed me with her on camera."

Gannon's fingers closed in a fist. His jaw tightened. "They did what?"

She shook her head. "It doesn't matter. It's over. It's all over. I can't keep working for people who think humiliating me is worth ratings."

He felt the panic well in his gut. "What about one more season?"

She crossed her arms in front of her as if she were cold. "I can't do it. Not here. Not with them. Not with you."

"Why not with me? Why can't we start over?"

She was already shaking her head. "I was never looking for a relationship. I just fell, you know? Let's just chalk it up to working in the industry we work in. There are casualties every day. This time, it was us. We were a mistake."

"Fuck that, Paige. You're not a mistake to me. You're my future." He cupped her face in his hand, and for a second, she closed those beautiful eyes. "Give me a chance, honey."

Her eyes opened, and in them, he saw only sadness. "I can't trust you, Gannon."

"I'm sorry I didn't tell you the whole story earlier. I just didn't want to put that experience into words. It was such a low point for me. It made me reevaluate everything. I didn't date anyone before you—"

She put a hand on his chest. "I understand. I really do. And I'm sorry that you had that experience."

He covered her hand with his.

She looked heavenward, her eyes still brimming with tears. "Why is this so hard?"

"Because we have something worth fighting for. I can't lose you."

She looked down at her sexy gold sandals that wrapped up her calves. "You hurt me. And I just keep getting humiliated over and over again."

Her voice broke, and Gannon couldn't take it anymore. He pulled her into his arms and pressed her face against his chest. He'd hurt her deeply, and the truth combined with a simple apology wasn't going to be enough. He needed time to convince her.

She sniffled against him, and he pressed his cheek to the top of her head, breathing in her scent.

"I'm not looking for this kind of attention. Cameras, interviews, strangers thinking that they know my business. I have things I want to do, need to do, and this might cost me my chance at that."

He pulled her in tighter, held her there, and wished she'd admit that this felt real and right. "I'm not going to let that happen," he whispered against her hair. "Meeghan is never going to get her claws into you again. I'll make sure of it."

Paige was shaking her head again. "There are other reasons I can't be with you, Gannon. Reasons that aren't your fault."

"Make me a list, and I will fix or remove every single obstacle."

She sighed, pulling back, and ran a finger under each eye. She straightened her shoulders, pulling herself back together again.

"You're too much. Too overwhelming. Too consuming. How can I focus on my dreams and work if the only place I want to be is your bed?"

"Honey, that doesn't have to be a bad thing. You *know* me. You know how I feel about you. I love you. I want to be there to watch you accomplish your dreams, and I sure as hell want to be there for everything else."

"Gannon, we just don't work. Maybe we would if we both

were willing to put in the time, the effort. But right now, I need to find a new job. If I can find something now, a special or a short series, Becca and I can start our project early next year, and I feel like I can finally start my life. No more 'one more season,' no more humiliation by the network. I can call the shots. I can tell the stories I want to tell."

"I want all that for you. I can help you, or I can just stand on the sidelines and cheer you on. Whatever you want." He was begging, but this *mattered*. Paige mattered. Her hopes and dreams were his.

"I'm so sorry, Gannon. I know this isn't all your fault. I know it. But we're just never going to work."

Fuck. She wasn't going to budge. She wasn't ready.

"Friends then." He was desperate. He wasn't going to let her close this door.

"I don't know," she said, looking at her feet again. "I don't know if that's a good idea."

"You're friends with Cat. We're bound to see each other from time to time." And he wasn't willing to let her cut him out of her life completely. It wasn't happening.

"It doesn't seem fair to you," she argued. "You have feelings for me."

She fucking had feelings for him too. She was just too damn stubborn to admit it.

"It would be more unfair to me if you just disappeared from my life," he countered.

She paused, and he could see the debate rage in her eyes.

"Fine. We'll try friends. But not 'go out to dinner and have sex' friends," she warned him.

"We'll try platonic and see how that goes," he promised.

She gave him a sad smile. "Thank you for wanting to be my friend, Gannon."

He pulled her in for another hug. "Anything you want, princess, it's yours. That's what friends do."

"I'm sorry you can't have what you want."

"There is one thing…"

"I'm not giving you a blow job in a linen closet."

"You're hilarious. You should be in comedy," Gannon shot back. "No. The last time we kissed, you were crying. I don't want to remember us that way. Give me something to remember, Paige."

She cocked her head and gave him *the* look. She knew exactly what he was up to. But she wasn't saying no.

"One kiss?"

"One kiss," he promised.

"Nothing else?"

"No hands, no blow jobs, no orgasms," he teased.

Paige put her hands on his shoulders and rose up on her tiptoes. She brought those rosy lips to his, laying them over his mouth and kissing him softly, sweetly.

The spark that lit in him reignited embers in a slow burn. He brought his hands to her slim waist and forced himself to keep them there. Gently, he opened her mouth and tasted her. Slowly savoring, he teased and tasted as the heat between them built. She was losing herself to the kiss, letting go and just feeling. And he had to end it now before he broke a promise.

Carefully, as if she were fine crystal, he brought his hands to her face, gentling the kiss and then finally pulling back.

She looked dazed and dazzled. Satisfied he'd gotten his message across, Gannon ran his thumb across her lower lip. "Now that's a memory worth having."

"Friends," she reminded him, taking a shaky breath.

"Friends," he repeated.

She looked down pointedly. "Do you have this reaction to your other friends?"

He looked down at his very evident erection and adjusted himself. "Oh yeah. When Flynn kisses me, it happens every other time."

She gave him a light shove and, even better, a husky laugh. "Thanks for telling me the truth, Gannon."

"I was lying about Flynn."

AUTUMN

CHAPTER
37

The air was finally starting to cool, fading from the roiling simmer of summer that had hugged the pavement to the crispness of fall. New Yorkers embraced the coming of autumn with thigh-high boots and pumpkin spice everything. For Paige, fall had never lost that anticipation, that excitement, of the promise of new beginnings. It stemmed from childhood with the beginning of a new school year, a chance to be someone new, learn something new.

However, her new beginning was refusing to present itself.

It had been a month since her on-camera run-in with Meeghan. She was done being a pawn and had said as much to Eddie. She'd find another network, another show, and produce her ass off for eight months. She didn't care what it was. Unfortunately, it was becoming painfully evident to Paige that job pickings were not merely slim but anorexic.

While she scoured New York for jobs, she entertained

herself by sticking a toe into the very early stages of planning and research for the documentary. She'd gotten an official and enthusiastic commitment from the actress Sarah Holden for the documentary and had begun reaching out to other actresses, production crew, directors, and producers and then expanding her web into women's rights advocates, politicians, professors, authors. She'd tapped her mother for her suggestions on who to interview and had been shocked when Leslie emailed her a detailed list of five women in specialized fields with a brief synopsis and contact information for each one.

Of course the resources had come with the caveat that Paige not embarrass the family name.

It gave her a buzz every time Paige found she'd spent an entire afternoon buried in work and loving every second of it. And that buzz evaporated every time she checked her bank balance or got a "sorry, not hiring" email.

She'd just received another one, her eighth, and put her head down on the absolutely stunning coffee table that Gannon had made. The heavy reclaimed pine top served as her desk and—more currently—her pillow of misery. She rested her forehead, inhaling the faint scents of stain and wood. It was thick, beefy, with two supporting pedestals for legs, and Paige loved it. It was exactly her. And, unfortunately, exactly Gannon.

The man had embraced their "friendly" relationship and run with it. She'd turned down all his invitations for coffee, for lunch. The episodes of *Kings of Construction* that aired did plenty to further the rumors of a relationship between them. She had zero interest in being seen in public with him and adding fuel to the fire.

She missed him, which surprised her. So Paige did find herself responding to his texts and occasionally his calls. She was just used to him, she told herself. And now that they'd cleared the air between them, she figured she was allowed to miss pieces of what they'd shared.

The truth behind his "relationship" with Meeghan? It made her hurt for Gannon. She could see it, had seen it. Getting swept up in the glitz and shine of TV was easy. Getting hurt by the darker side of it was even easier. Gannon's pride had been damaged, his faith in himself tested.

In many ways, Gannon's situation mirrored that of women in the industry. Women whose stories she would be telling. The overzealous appreciation of looks, being tempted into a bad choice, and then being forced into conforming to a role that had no appeal. She could empathize with that. But it still didn't change the fact that she couldn't be in a relationship with him without fear of losing something of herself.

Her phone buzzed at her elbow, and she glanced at the screen. *Gannon.*

The bump in her pulse, the flutter in her belly, those were good reasons to ignore the call. Just because he had reasons for not being entirely truthful didn't wipe away his transgressions. And nothing seemed to dull her physical reaction to him. That alone spelled danger.

She should ignore the call, ignore the man. Move on with her life. *Decision made.*

"Hello."

"Hey, princess." That gravelly rasp hit her at the apex of her thighs. Her body clearly wasn't interested in holding anything against the man...unless it was her body.

"What's up?" she asked lightly.

"Are you busy tonight?"

No! Yes!

"Gannon, I—"

He cut off her early denial. "Hang on. Listen to my proposal first before you shoot me down."

She was already regretting picking up the phone. She was having a weak moment, a weak week, and he would know and pick apart her defenses. "Go on."

"I have a lead on a job for you, one that starts now and should carry through to the end of December."

"What is it? Where is it?" Who cared? She'd take anything at this point.

"Have dinner with me tonight, and I'll tell you."

"You can't blackmail a *friend* into having dinner with you," she reminded him.

"This is worthy of a face-to-face conversation. I have details, numbers, even a timeline. I'm not doing that over the phone. Besides, we'll be chaperoned."

She laughed. "By who—and don't say Cat."

"Nonni. She's cooking, and she's wanted to meet you since I started telling her about this stubborn woman who wouldn't let me have my way last season."

The infamous Nonni. Paige had been dying to meet the woman even before Gannon confessed her role in his decision to be on television.

"I can hear you biting your lip," Gannon said, his voice getting huskier.

She stopped gnawing on her lower lip. "I come to dinner with you and your grandmother, and you tell me about a job?" She wanted clarification. Gannon King was nothing if not sneaky.

"Dinner at my grandmother's. You can listen to Nonni berate me in the kitchen. I'll tell you about the job, we'll eat something amazing and carb-laden, and then you can send me home to my sad, empty bed."

"Gannon." It was a warning to them both. Paige didn't fully trust herself around the man. He made her feel too impulsive, and one too many glasses of wine or a particularly low day and she didn't trust herself not to crawl into his lap.

"Just one friend confiding in another. I miss you. I want to see you, and I hate that I had to go out and find a job just so I can do that."

She missed him too. And she desperately needed gainful employment. And damn it, she was an adult. She didn't need to touch the stove a second time to know she'd get burned. She was a St. James. St. James women learned fast and preferred independence.

"What time?" she asked.

"Seven. Six," he corrected. "Then you can watch Nonni in action in the kitchen. I'll send a car for you."

———

The car Gannon sent for her was actually a truck. And he was behind the wheel.

Paige drummed her fingers where they rested on her hips. She'd gone with a short-sleeve sweater the color of ripe plums, jeans, and, in homage to the fall, a pair of soft suede boots that ended above the knee. "You didn't say you'd be picking me up," she accused.

Gannon flashed her that badass grin from behind the wheel. "You didn't ask. Had to make sure you were actually coming."

She glared at him, an effect that was ruined by her sunglasses, and climbed in. It was a work truck, she noted, with the Kings insignia on the doors and one of those shiny metal toolboxes mounted in the bed of the truck. It was tall, manly, and completely impractical for city living. But it was far more

271

comfortable than any production van or compact car rental she'd experienced.

Gannon smoothly pulled away from the curb, heading toward Brooklyn. He looked at home behind the wheel, relaxed in worn jeans and a faded T-shirt dressed up by the army-green cotton blazer he wore. He steered with his left hand, a Band-Aid riding low on the knuckle of his index finger. His right arm rested on the seatback behind her.

He looked *good*, really good. Paige felt that familiar flutter in her belly and immediately quelled it. They'd had their chance. It hadn't worked out.

"So tell me about this job."

He shook his head, grinned. "Nope. Not till we get to Nonni's."

Her eyes narrowed. "What kind of job is this? Is it something that you think would make me jump from a moving vehicle?"

"You have such a trusting nature, Paige."

"I work in reality TV. What do you expect?"

"I expect you to be nice and make small talk with me until you meet my grandmother and then we get down to business."

It was a small request, easily granted, and worse still, it was the polite thing to do. She grimaced. "Sorry. My desperation is showing. What have you been doing since we're not shooting?"

"That's my girl," he said cheerily. "I've been clearing my head with a few pieces, a dining set, and I'm getting back up to speed at Kings. Got our hands on this four-story in Cobble Hill, two retail shops on the bottom and six units above."

"A lot of work?"

"Gut job. Some asshole slumlord owned it, and the bank foreclosed. Good bones, but everything else has to go."

She nodded, bit her lip. "Can I see the furniture?" Paige asked. No matter what transpired between them, nothing would ruin her appreciation for Gannon King's artistic abilities.

"Not satisfied with your coffee table?" he teased.

"About that," she said, shooting him an accusatory look. "It's not exactly a standard size. Seems weird to me that you were able to build something that fit so perfectly in our space. It's almost like you took measurements."

He made a humming sound, and she knew she wasn't getting anything out of him.

"Have you seen Cat lately?" he asked.

Paige nodded. "We had drinks last week. She told me about the Duluth deal."

Gannon shook his head. "My sister the model for women's work clothes."

"The collection is going to be huge," Paige predicted. "She showed me a couple pictures of the samples."

"Of the two of us, she's cut out for this crap," Gannon said.

"And you'd rather be on a job site or in your shop," Paige said, understanding.

"And you'd rather be telling stories that matter."

She bit back a sigh, and they rode in silence for several minutes, until Gannon turned down an alley.

"This isn't your place," she said, peering at the squat brick building before them.

He pressed a button, and one of the three industrial-sized garage doors rolled up, groaning in protest.

"I thought you wanted to see what I was working on?"

"This is your shop? Your secret lair?" Paige was delighted. It felt like she'd just received an invitation to tour Batman's cave.

"This is the back of our offices. Used to be storage. Now it's my shop." He pulled into the bay, closed the door behind them, and shut off the engine.

They climbed down, and Gannon unlocked the door on the back of the garage wall. She smelled sawdust and stain, scents that always reminded her of him. Paige stepped inside while he flipped a row of dusty light switches, flooding the space with illumination.

"Holy crap," she breathed. The perimeter of the room was ringed with shelves and tables stacked high with every kind of wood imaginable. A metal shelving system looked like it would almost buckle under the weight of polyurethanes, stains, paints, and bins of hardware.

He had several worktables and benches, most of which bore projects in varying stages of doneness. The dining table was front and center.

"Wow, Gannon." Paige wandered up to the table, all eight feet of it, her heels muffled by neat piles of sawdust. It reminded her of the coffee table. He'd used the same reclaimed wood, distressed by decades of use, and the same design. Two fat pedestals on either end of the table acted as thick legs joined by a long board down the center.

"Like it?" He stood with his thumbs hooked into the front pockets of his jeans.

"Like is not the word," she said, running a hand lovingly over the satin-smooth wood.

"That's the buffet," he said, jerking his chin toward the next table over.

It matched the length of the table and the style of wood. A combination of yet-to-be-finished drawers and cabinets made up the base of the buffet. Its top was a long expanse of that aged and battered wood.

"Thinking about doing open shelves above it," Gannon said.

Yes. She could see it. Rustic wood shelves with the metal piping for brackets.

"Are these for you?" she asked, eyeing him.

He shrugged.

"Because I've seen your apartment. You add an eight-foot table, and you'd have to get rid of your couch."

He glanced at his watch. "We'd better go before Nonni gets antsy."

"Oh God. There really is a nonni, isn't there? This isn't just some ploy to get me to your place?"

CHAPTER
38

There really was a nonni, and she lived in a sweet little two-story home tucked away on a tree-lined street three blocks over from Gannon's apartment. Short and soft around the middle, she had snowy white hair that framed her lined face like a cloud. Her eyes, a tawny brown, held a sharpness that didn't miss much.

"It's about time," she said, frowning fiercely at Gannon as she looked up from the sauce that clouded the room with the mouthwatering scents of garlic and basil. "The canapés have been ready for hours."

Gannon was unaffected by her bluster. "I left you fifty minutes ago," he said, dropping a kiss on her papery cheek and sneaking a crispy piece of bruschetta off the silver tray.

She slapped at his hand in mock anger. "Where my daughter went wrong with this one, I'll never know," she sighed, feigning disbelief.

Gannon grinned down at her with affection. Paige caught the teasing wink Noni sent him before she reached for Paige.

"Since my grandson has never had any manners, I am Francesca Bianchi, Gannon's mama's mama." She drew Paige into a fierce hug and released her just as quickly.

"It's lovely to meet you, Mrs. Bianchi."

"Francesca, please, or Nonni," she tut-tutted. "Dinner will be ready in half an hour. You both will take the wine and canapés outside and get out of my way."

Gannon took the decanter of cabernet that Francesca left breathing on the counter and poured a healthy portion into a glass for his grandmother before scooping up the other two glasses. He nudged the tray of bruschetta at Paige and led the way out the back door onto a covered porch overlooking a garden-like oasis of a backyard.

"I love your grandmother's house," Paige confessed as Gannon set the glasses down on a pine table between two cushioned chairs. It looked like every grandmother's house should. Lived in for decades, the house had aged well, every room looking comfortable with the kind of dated furniture and rugs that held more memories than style. "When did you redo her kitchen?"

Unlike the rest of the home, the kitchen gleamed in its modernity. A six-burner gas stove dominated one wall under a copper hood and pot filler. The countertops, acres of them, were creamy, speckled granite. A mixture of glass-fronted and traditional cabinetry in warm cherry offered huge amounts of storage.

It had Gannon's fingerprints all over it.

"Last year. She'd had a rough two years with Pop passing and the trouble with the business. As soon as we had a commitment for a second season, Cat and I conned her with a ten-day cruise with my parents and my aunt and uncle."

"The network would have loved that as a special," Paige said, lifting the glass and tasting the very nice wine.

"Which is exactly why we didn't tell them about it," Gannon said. "She cried when she saw it. We all did."

She could see it. The gratitude, the pride, the overwhelming love. And wished she'd been there to witness it.

"That must have been a memorable reveal."

"Speaking of." Gannon leaned against the railing, his back to the riot of foliage spilling from raised beds and containers. "Let's talk about your new opportunity."

Back to business, she thought. It was probably wise. Being around him like this stirred up feelings, ones she didn't have an interest in feeling anymore.

"Okay, let's talk."

"How would you feel about directing a special?"

"Directing?" Paige gripped her wineglass. "I wouldn't be a field producer or an assistant director?"

Gannon shook his head. "Nope. Director. About three or four months of shooting."

"Where? For who?"

"Here in the city for Welcome Home. But you'd be calling the shots," he said when he saw her face fall. "They wouldn't be able to mess with you on this one."

"Why not?"

"Because it's my show."

She was already shaking her head.

"Don't say no yet. Just listen."

She raised a judgmental eyebrow. "Gannon—"

"Shut up and listen." He said it without any heat. "I bought a place—a house. I'll be renovating it anyway, and the network was salivating about turning it into a special to air this summer. Probably five or six episodes."

"I don't have any experience directing," she reminded him. Which was bullshit. She could do it. She just didn't know if her heart could take being around him day after day again. How could she not fall for him all over again?

"Bullshit," Gannon said as if reading her mind. He picked up another slice of bruschetta, popping it in his mouth. "Just because you haven't held the title doesn't mean you don't have the experience."

She sipped, considered.

"You'd pick the crew."

"Why me?" she asked. If he said it was because he wanted her back in his life, she would put down this very nice wine, say a polite goodbye to Francesca, and be on her way.

"This is going to be my home. I want someone I trust behind the camera. I don't want to turn this into some dog and pony show. This is what I've been working toward for a long time, and I'm not letting anyone come in and fuck up the process, the feel of it for me. I want you."

She blew out a breath. "I don't think it's a good idea for us to work together. It didn't exactly go well last time."

He ran a hand impatiently through his hair. "Princess, this is a big deal to me. I trust you to put something together that doesn't violate me in the process, and this keeps you off the streets begging for shit jobs."

"I don't want a pity job."

"Don't be an idiot. It's not your style."

She didn't bother taking offense to his brusqueness. She was used to it. She was used to him…well, working with him. But working together again? Memories of the past few months rolled through her like a cresting wave. Dark hotel rooms, longing glances, breathless kisses. She wouldn't survive that again.

"It pays a little better than what you were making before." Gannon gave her the number, and Paige gave herself credit when she didn't bobble her glass. With that money, the documentary would be a go. She wouldn't need *Kings* for another season. Another season of torture. Shirtless Gannon, on-camera interviews, toeing the line of humiliation.

Her thoughts swirled. "Gannon—"

"Don't say no now. Think about it. Have dinner, listen to Nonni tell embarrassing stories about me, and sleep on it."

The subject was closed. For now.

Paige looked out over the darkening garden. "I owe you an apology."

His eyes gleamed in the dusk. "Why?" The question was quiet, husky.

"I didn't believe that Nonni existed."

———

They ate in the dining room off Francesca's wedding china. Between forkfuls of the best chicken cacciatore that Paige had ever had, they talked. Gannon and Francesca fired stories and memories back and forth at each other while Paige laughed and drank wine and listened.

Francesca daintily wiped tears of laughter from the corners of her eyes with her cloth napkin. "What about you, Paige? Do you have memories of your grandmamas like this one does?"

"I never knew any of my grandparents," Paige confessed. "They all died before or shortly after I was born. It was just my mother and sister and me."

"That sounds like a house that is too quiet," Francesca said, eyeing her.

"My mother valued peace and quiet for our…educational pursuits," Paige said, remembering endless hours of private piano lessons, French classes. She'd counted down the hours until she was sprung free of endless instruction, preferring to sneak off to the movies or hide with paperbacks in the back of her closet where she could read without interruption. Meanwhile, her sister, Lisa, had embraced the barrage of education.

"Family is important," Francesca lectured. "Do you like children?" The hawkish look she sent Paige had her covering a laugh with her napkin.

"Uh, I suppose?"

Gannon frowned at his grandmother. "Nonni," he said, his tone carrying a warning.

Francesca smiled innocently. "I'm only asking a question."

"Why aren't you asking her where she likes to vacation or what books she likes to read?" He stabbed at a piece of chicken.

"Bah! I like to ask questions that get to the heart of a person," Francesca insisted. "What would I know about Paige's heart if she says she likes the beach or autobiographies? I want to know who she is in here." She pointed a gnarled finger at her own heart.

Paige smiled. Francesca Bianchi was a woman she could understand.

———

Paige felt nerves vibrate over her skin. It was dark and the air cool by the time Gannon pulled up in front of her apartment building. It wasn't the end of a date, but to her anxiety level, it felt like one. Only she knew exactly what it would feel like if he leaned over and laid those warm, hard lips on her, spread those calloused hands over her.

That awareness of memory, of anticipation, crawled through her veins until she was desperate for air, for space.

She wanted to speak. To thank him for dinner and

introducing her to his grandmother and then slide out of the truck and forget about the evening. Or did she want those lips and hands cruising over her until she was desperate for more?

Finally, it was Gannon who spoke. "Promise me you'll think about the offer."

Still she was silent, weighing words and consequences.

"Paige. Promise me."

"I promise." The words left her mouth on a reluctant sigh.

He was watching her, and the cab of the truck felt small, confined. The air was too warm inside. There wasn't much protecting her from his raw appeal. Nothing but the console that divided the front seat.

"Thank you for dinner. I loved Francesca," Paige breathed out, keeping her tone light.

"She's the center of our entire family," Gannon said, a half smile on his shadowed face.

"It must have been very hard to lose your grandfather."

His hand skimmed over hers where it rested on her leg, squeezed. "It was a nightmare," he admitted. "No one's ever ready to say goodbye, but especially not us Kings."

"I imagine he'd be very proud of you, Gannon."

He squeezed her hand again and then released it. "Thanks. That means…a lot."

She took a deep breath. "Listen. Whether or not I take this job, thank you for the opportunity."

He looked like he wanted to say something, was fighting the urge to say it.

"Now who's censoring themselves," she teased lightly.

"Take the job, Paige. I won't hurt you again."

CHAPTER

39

The ruffled red throw pillow hit Paige squarely in the face.

"You'll think about it?" Becca shrieked.

"Ouch! Geez, Becca." Paige tossed the pillow on the floor out of her roommate's reach.

"Let me get this straight in my addled brain," Becca insisted. "Gannon offers you a promotion and a raise that will not only give you directorial experience and enough cash to launch the doc early, giving you the opportunity to say 'fuck off' to *Kings* next season, and you tell him you have to think about it?"

"In a nutshell."

"Why wouldn't you say yes and then jump him in gratitude?"

"Uh, I don't know. Maybe because he lied, ripped my heart out and stomped on it, and let me be humiliated on TV *twice* by his fake girlfriend?"

Becca scrubbed her hands over her face. Her earrings, tiny bells on thin silver wire, jingled in frustration.

"Babe, I *know* you don't blame Gannon for the production company amping up the drama quotient."

"No, of course not. But I could have been better prepared for it if he'd been honest," Paige pointed out.

"I'm going to say this because you need to hear it. The bad guy here is not Gannon King. It's those assholes at Summit-Wingenroth and the damn Welcome Home Network. From where I sit, they played Gannon by setting him up with that shitbag blow-up doll, and they played you. All you two did was have real feelings for each other."

Paige squeezed her eyes shut. "Okay. Maybe it's more because I can't trust myself around him. You ever think about that?" She opened her eyes, her confession stretching out the silence.

Becca crossed her arms, tapped her fingers on her upper arms.

"I just spent thirty minutes in the car with him, and all I wanted to do was climb over the console. How am I supposed to work with him for months on a very personal project for him and not get sucked back into that world?"

Becca raised a questioning finger. "Would it be so bad if you got sucked back in?"

"Bec! I wouldn't survive that again. He's so...intense and raw and overwhelming. How can I concentrate on *anything* when I'm being consumed like that?"

"You think a relationship with Gannon would keep you from pursuing your dreams?"

"I don't know." Paige heaved herself off the couch and stormed into the kitchen for a bottle of water. "I don't feel steady when I'm with him. He's so...much." She shook her head. "No. There's no way I could go back to him and start everything up again."

She'd be too vulnerable, too scared about losing him again. She'd make decisions based on him, his plans, his goals. Arrange her life around him and do it all gladly. And then one day, she'd wake up and see that she wasn't her own person.

She was a St. James, and St. James women didn't organize their lives around a man.

Her mother hadn't let a relationship stand in the way of her career. She'd known what was important to her, what would get her there, and what would take her further away from it.

But is Leslie St. James happy? A little voice inside Paige asked the question. *Is happiness the same as success?*

Becca took a deep breath. "Look, I didn't want to go here, but now I have to. Paige, this documentary thing? It's not just you in it. It's me too. And if you don't take this job, when are we ever going to start it? You can't wait this out and go back to a show that's humiliating you for sport. A show that, according to a friend of mine in postproduction at Welcome Home, is blackballing you."

"What?" Paige's knees went weak.

"Don't you think it's weird that no one is willing to even talk to you about a job? They're making noise about your noncompete. They want another season of you and Gannon sparking it up on-screen."

He'd known. Gannon had to have heard about the blackballing and offered the job out of pity, out of guilt. And she'd thought it was because he wanted her back. She'd embarrassed herself and slapped at him over his generosity. Beggars didn't have the luxury of being choosers.

But they could take the opportunity offered and work their asses off.

No matter what it cost her personally.

Paige looked down at the water bottle in her hand and, as

if from a distance, watched herself hurl it against the front door before calmly walking down the hall and closing herself in her bedroom.

———

The brownstone rose four stories out of a tiny brick courtyard within a low wall that butted up against the sidewalk. The front of the building boasted a trio of arched windows on each floor except for the lower level, which lost one window to the tall front stairs in the same milk-chocolate tone as the rest of the facade.

If Paige's dream home had stepped off her secret Pinterest board, it had landed right here on Seventh Street. The building faced the greens and golds of a park just across the street, and cheerful noise rose from the playground at the opposite end of the block.

"Well? What do you think?" Gannon ranged against the waist-high brick wall, ankles crossed. His jeans rode low on his hips, and his green Henley had a rip in one wrist.

"I think if the inside looks anything like the outside, it's going to be a quick shoot," Paige said.

He smirked. "You may reconsider that when you see the interior."

She followed him through the rusted iron gate and up the ten stairs of stoop. The front door, two doors really, were tall and arched to match the windows.

"I'm going in first because I want to see your face."

"I always wanted my own reveal," Paige joked.

"Not like this." Gannon grinned. He gave the doors a shove with his shoulder, and they reluctantly screeched open on their hinges.

"Sounds like a horror movie."

"Yeah, it's about to look like one too."

She stepped across the uneven threshold behind him and gaped while Gannon found the light switch. It smelled like a horror movie too. Dusty, musty air that she could taste, not just smell.

"You're insane," she decided.

He leaned against the newel post of what had once been a grand staircase. It was missing more spindles than it still had. Cabbage-rose wallpaper peeled off the wall of the front room and looked like it continued into the next. There were holes, gaping, jagged sections, where floor had once been.

"Just watch your step," Gannon warned, grabbing her arm when she made a move. The hardwood, she noted, was unsalvageable. Water damage, stains, too many holes to patch. It creaked beneath their feet.

"Is it safe for us to be in here?"

"Mostly," he said, his cheerful tone full of uncharacteristic optimism.

There were two fireplaces on this floor with white marble surrounds and cracked-out slate hearths. Someone had converted one to a gas fireplace with an ugly brass insert.

"Well, at least your table and buffet will fit," Paige commented, eyeing the space.

"That's what I'm thinking. Living room up front, dining here, but I want to bust out the rest of this wall to open it to the kitchen. Which is—or was—back here."

He kept her hand in his and led the way, weaving between holes and ducking under plaster that hung from the ceiling. The linoleum, green and white fleur-de-lis, peeled up from all corners. There was a faded red countertop with a metal edge, a yellow refrigerator that screamed seventies, and nothing else. The tall, skinny door in the back right corner led out to what looked like a jungle of a backyard. Windows lined the rest of the back wall.

"Well, at least you got a fridge in the deal," Paige said.

"That's the spirit. I might move it to my office downstairs for beer."

He took her downstairs, which was worse. Here, a previous owner had put down thick brown carpet that now smelled like cat pee. The walls were paneled a dark, knotty brown. The footprint was the same as above, and despite herself, Paige started to see potential. There was another door all the way at the back that Gannon wrestled open onto a shabby patio with a rusted-out wheelbarrow and an old water heater. Above them, the remains of a definitely not-to-code deck wobbled with the breeze.

Gannon pointed out architectural details and talked repointing brick and running new wiring. Paige remained silent and took it all in. He led the way back to the main level and then up the rickety staircase, avoiding the missing treads.

"Easy fixes," he insisted, holding her hand as she scrambled over two steps. He flipped light switches and towed her through the space. "I think the master would go on this floor, maybe with a sitting room or some kind of den," he said.

More brown carpet, more cabbage roses, and cobwebs so thick she couldn't see through them. There was a sagging mattress covered in dubious stains propped up against the wall.

"The bath's here now, but obviously it needs to be bigger."

The black-and-white checkerboard tile looked to be original. As did the plumbing that led to the cast iron claw-foot tub. "Oh, Gannon," she breathed. "You have to keep this."

"I'm sure as hell not hauling it down that staircase," he snorted.

"Plumbing, electrical, drywall or whatever." Paige started ticking items off.

"I can fix it," he said amicably.

They pushed to the rear of the third floor, finding more windows and another door. "A balcony?" Paige asked, swiping a hand over the dirty glass to peer outside.

"Careful. You might get tetanus or diphtheria touching shit around here," Gannon warned.

"Can we see the backyard…safely?"

"If we don't breathe too hard on the kitchen deck, we should be able to get an idea of the forest for the trees."

Back down the long flight of stairs to the main floor, Gannon twisted the loose brass knob and wrestled the door open wide enough they could slip out one at a time. The knob fell off and hit the floor with a clang.

"I'll fix that."

They carefully moved to the railing, white paint flaking into piles beneath.

"Try not to inhale any of that," he said, running a hand over the flaking paint. "Probably lead-based."

"Gannon, the entire house is probably dripping in asbestos and mold. You'll have to bring the electrical and the plumbing up to code, which will be astronomical and a huge pain in the ass with four floors. You can't keep anything except the tub."

"What about the mattress upstairs? It's practically brand new."

She shook her head, closed her eyes. "Are you sure you're up for this?"

"The question is, are you up for this?"

She looked out over the weeds and tumbling paver walls. The overgrown backyard was more impassible jungle than forest. But Gannon King had vision. Ambitious vision, but if he could pull this off, he'd have a showcase home that he could be proud of.

"What do you see back here?" Paige asked, nodding toward the foliage disaster.

Gannon stepped up behind her, his arms caging her in against the railing. "Down there, a flagstone patio, curved edge into yard," he said, pointing beneath them. "I've always wanted a big-ass outdoor fireplace, and that would go there."

"And back there in the corner?" She pointed.

"What do you see?" he countered.

A slow smile worked its way across her face. "A hammock right next to a water feature. Something that makes some noise. Your own oasis in the middle of the city."

"You're hired."

She turned carefully in his arms, and the decking groaned under her feet. She could *see* it, all of it. If there was anyone in this world who could bring the lovely brownstone back to life, it was Gannon. And she wanted in.

"When do we start?"

The victorious grin she expected from him didn't come. Instead, he looked serious, intent. "There's something else you need to know before you officially accept."

She wet her lips, nervous now because she wanted it so badly. She wanted this job, this house. "What's that?"

"First, are you dating that Mackenrowe guy?"

Paige blinked. "Who? Drake?"

"You two looked pretty cozy at that thing last month."

Gannon looked like he felt aggravated that he had to ask the question.

"Not that it's any of your business, but no. He kept me from flattening your fake girlfriend's new nose on camera."

Gannon, looking relived, ignored the jibe. "I need you to know that I don't want to be just friends with you. I have every intention of wearing you down and getting back in your bed."

Her pulse kicked up, thudding away under her skin until she was sure Gannon could hear it.

"I'm not interested in revisiting us," she said firmly. Except that her voice wavered just slightly. "This is business."

He shook his head. "It's never just business with us, Paige. I'm giving you the heads-up, but understand I'm not going to be harassing you, chasing you around set. I'm going to seduce you."

"Gannon—"

"You want honest, and I want to give you what you want. I need you to take this job because you're the only one I trust with something this important to me. But I also want to be near you, to see you, touch you." His rough palm caressed the side of her face with a gentleness she didn't know he possessed.

"Business and personal don't mix," she reminded him. "We already tried that."

"For you and me, business is personal. Work is our lives. Everything we do is tangled up like that. And I just want you to understand that while I'm going to depend on your professional skills to make this project happen, to make this shithole a home, I'm going to be working my way back into your life."

"What if I tell you no?"

"To the job or me?"

"Is there a difference?"

"I would never hold a job over your head just to get you back in bed, and if you actually think that I would—"

His flash of anger comforted her.

"I don't," she promised. "You're not that guy."

"Damn fucking right I'm not that guy."

"Slow your roll, King. I'm saying yes to the job, and I'm saying I'm not interested to the relationship."

"I accept your yes, and we'll see about your not interested."

"What's the name of the show?"

"*King's Castle.*"

CHAPTER

40

Shooting started on a crisp fall morning that had the edges of gold and ruby leaves tipped with frost. Gannon wiped his palms on his jeans. It wasn't nerves. It was excitement. He always loved the first full-court press on a project. And this one was the most important one he'd ever tackled.

This was a new beginning for him, one he finally felt ready to embrace.

The shooting schedule was more forgiving than *Kings of Construction*, and at the end of the day, he got to grab a beer from his own fridge and put his feet up on his own couch. He was a producer this time around, and Eddie Garraza handled the executive producer duties. Both were stipulations Gannon had insisted on. He wasn't about to let the production company play fast and loose with the drama like they did with *Kings*, but he could use some guidance from a pro.

Eddie fit the bill.

The man was currently poking around the soaring wreck of a staircase, ball cap fitted over frizzed gray hair that needed a trim, glasses sliding down his nose.

Paige looked up from her tablet in what would someday be the dining room, caught his eye, and flashed a grin.

As expected, she'd thrown herself into the work, and with her careful scheduling and handpicked crew, they were ready to roll. She'd gone with mostly women, he noted, including Felicia for sound mixing. Well, women and Tony, who'd jumped at the chance to pick up some local work for a change.

He knew what Paige was doing, giving a hand up to crew members who probably got passed over due to gender. She was giving them experience that would jump off their résumés when it came time for them to move on to their next project.

It was part of what he loved about her. Paige was never just out for Paige. She was a team captain ready to drag the rest of her team into the end zone for a victory. He could count on her, and he hoped she'd learn that she could count on him too.

He picked his way through cables, tools, piles of production and construction paraphernalia to Paige's side. "You ready?"

"The question is, are you ready? This is your baby."

If she only knew, Gannon thought.

She must have read the change in him because she took a small step back and slid back into business mode. "Since we've got the light and the weather, we might as well start with your intro on the stoop. Then once we move inside, I'll have Chantay shoot some B-roll outside. Facade, park, etc. Now, with the walk-through…"

It had been Paige's idea for Gannon to give Cat and Nonni the grand tour before demo. That way, they could bring them back for the finale for an actual reveal. And while part of him wanted to protect his little Italian grandmother from the public eye, he knew Francesca Bianchi would get a huge kick out of it.

Paige finished briefing him on the timeline, and he nodded as if he'd been listening raptly. She'd keep him on course, on schedule. She always did.

"If we can wrap up the shooting of the walk-through by five, I think we can do an hour or two of demo before wrapping," he predicted.

"Lighting's going to be a pain, especially on the first floor. It's like a dungeon down there, so we're going to need extra setup time."

"No problem. We can run out, pick up lunch for everyone while they set up, eat when we come back, and then start there."

She eyed him. "Look at you being accommodating."

"I can be accommodating. Charming too. Handsome, strong, fairly intelligent, high tolerance for pain, I can hold my liquor, and I make a decent red sauce." He counted off his attributes. He saw her lips quirk, knew she was fighting to stay cool, and he pressed his luck. "I don't know if you know this about me, but I can also burp the alphabet. Maybe I'll show you sometime."

She made a strangled sound that she tried to cover with a cough. "Damn it, Gannon."

"Princess, all's fair in love and war."

"If that isn't the biggest misstatement ever, I don't know what is."

"Biggest demo bang for this floor is the kitchen and that horrible fridge. Then we can hit the master bath," Gannon said, switching gears to throw her off-balance.

"Don't destroy that tub," Paige warned him.

He held up three fingers. "Scout's honor."

"Let's rally the crews," she said with a curt nod.

He listened in as she talked her crew through the day, answering questions, delegating. She knew what she was doing. Giving everyone specific roles, detailed instructions. Paige wasn't big on ambiguity. He'd learned that a little late.

"Tony's first unit this morning, and we've got Chantay and Nina on second unit. We'll switch up this afternoon. Felicia's our sound wizard for the duration, and Bradley is our very energetic production assistant. He's also going to be equipped with a GoPro so he can pick up any behind-the-scenes stuff we might miss with the first or second unit." Paige consulted her tablet. "Everyone set?"

They nodded, glancing around their little circle.

"Good. Let's do the best job we can, be safe, learn something good, and try not to piss off Gannon. He can be temperamental." She winked at him.

"If I'm temperamental," Gannon interrupted, stepping into their circle, "it's because it's warranted...mostly."

They grinned at him.

He motioned his crew over and made the introductions. "And for those of you who don't know, this is Eddie. Eddie's our EP and money man, so definitely don't piss him off."

Eddie doffed his cap affably.

"And just so we're on the same page," Gannon continued, "we're all going to get to know each other real well over the next few months. It'll be hard work but worth it. At least for me, since I get to move in here in the end."

There were a few smiles, snickers.

"Paige and I are going to treat you like family, and we expect you to return the courtesy. That means what happens on set is family business, and it stays here. Got me?"

Everyone nodded, and he caught Paige shooting him a warning look.

"Here's your first bit of family business. I'm in love with Paige here, but she won't give me the time of day. So I'm going to be wearing her down during the course of this shoot, and I'd appreciate you all singing my praises to her."

"He isn't totally hideous-looking, Paige," Flynn called from the fringe of the circle.

The crews chuckled, and Paige shot poisoned darts at him from icy blue eyes.

"Try a little harder than Flynn," Gannon suggested. "Now, let me apologize to Paige for bringing up personal business, and then we can get our day started. Everyone can move out. I don't know if this floor can hold all of us for much longer."

They dispersed, and Paige scowled at him. She yanked her headset off. "What the hell was that, Gannon?"

"I'm putting everyone on the same field."

"I'm directing. I'm the boss." She drilled a finger into his chest. "How am I going to be the boss when everyone has just been given permission to stick their noses into my private life?"

"Honey, I don't want to sneak around. I didn't say you were panting after me, begging me for a quick bang."

She slapped a hand over his mouth. "Just. Stop. Talking. Or I'm going to use a nail gun to shut your mouth."

"We don't have the air compressor hooked up yet," he murmured against her palm.

"I hope you fall through all four floors of this hellhole," Paige snapped and started to walk away. But she spun around, stomped back. "You've told me that you love me twice. Once when I found out you'd lied, and again making a joke in front of my crew. For future reference, that's not the best way to do it."

She whirled around, snapped her headset back in place, and strode out the front door.

"Got your work cut out for you," Eddie said, clapping a hand on his back.

"I don't mind getting dirty."

———————

Gannon's sledgehammer bit through the plaster, sending dust and chunks flying. He yanked it back out of the ragged hole he'd created and swung again. Flynn was muscling away on the other side of the opening to the kitchen. They had a bet. Whoever busted out their side first won. Loser had to strip down and sit in the claw-foot tub upstairs on camera.

Gannon struck again and heard the unfortunate clang of metal. "Shit."

The clang was followed immediately by a different noise. An explosive gushing. Water—thankfully not sewage—spewed forth from the broken pipe, soaking Gannon and spraying in all directions.

Chantay, in cargo pants and work boots, danced sideways out of the blast zone and continued to roll.

"Who the fuck didn't turn the water off?" Gannon yelled, stripping off his shirt and wrapping it around the busted pipe. His job, his house—it was his responsibility to double-check that the water was off. At least it wasn't a gas line.

Flynn, a shit-eating grin on his face, continued hammering away at his portion of pipe-less wall. Mickey, a scrawny high school dropout with piercings all over, hustled down the basement stairs in search of the shut-off valve.

The water mushrooming out of Gannon's shirt slowed to a trickle and then a seep.

"Done!" Flynn flipped his sledgehammer in the air, caught it one-handed. "And you're already halfway to the bet."

Gannon flipped him the bird and caught Paige's smirk from

where she watched the footage on a little monitor. It would end up on the show, pixelated of course, but Gannon found she seemed more interested in letting him be himself on this set than any *Kings* episode.

He winked at her, and she rolled her eyes, but Chantay grinned behind her camera. He was winning them over, one by one. They'd all be Team Gannon by the time they wrapped, he predicted. And he was going to need all the help he could get.

So far, Paige was proving to be resistant to his irresistibility. But he'd win. He had no intention of losing now. Not with so much at stake.

While his guys cleaned up the mess, Gannon trudged upstairs to pay up. Chantay followed with Paige, and the women didn't bother hiding their laughter as he stripped out of his soggy jeans. He kept his safety glasses on and did a slow turn in his boxer briefs. He saw the spark in Paige's eyes as her gaze skimmed him head to toe and back again before she tamped it down.

Yeah, she wasn't quite as walled off as she pretended to be.

Gannon climbed into the stained tub. "There. Happy, asshole?" he asked Flynn.

"Pretty roomy," Flynn mused.

"Bet you both could fit in there," Paige said innocently.

Flynn, still wearing his tool belt and work boots, obliged. He climbed in the opposite end, sending Gannon scrambling up the back of the tub to get out of his way.

"I think we can fit more in here," Flynn said, slapping the side of the tub.

The abandoned claw-foot was a clown car for construction workers. In the end, they fit six of them in the tub doing an off-key rendition of "Rubber Duckie." Paige laughed so hard off camera she was crying, and Gannon's gut did that slow roll into happiness watching her.

They were making so much noise they all almost missed the warning creak of the floor under the tub.

"Abandon ship," Gannon ordered, sending bodies scrambling for safety.

"Better shore that up," Flynn said.

"Add it to the list," Paige said, wiping her eyes.

"That list gets any longer, we're gonna be here for the next twenty years," Flynn predicted.

That's the plan, Gannon thought.

CHAPTER

41

Paige watched Gannon as he speared a piece of bulgogi with his chopsticks. He was always finding reasons to see her off set and off hours. Tonight, he'd demanded a dinner meeting with her, and she'd offered to have it at her place. There'd be no public speculation that could get stirred up if they met at a restaurant, and she had a roommate, so they wouldn't end up in bed.

Not that she wanted to go to bed with Gannon, Paige reminded herself. It was more a precautionary measure in case she had a weak moment and too much wine. It was harder to be weak when Becca might storm in at any moment.

So they settled on her couch, eating good Korean food off an excellent coffee table and juggling timelines.

Gannon was so *big*, so *male*. His presence made her apartment feel even smaller than it was.

"Okay, so your voice work is scheduled for when?" Paige

asked, scrawling notes on paper and trying to ignore how close his knee was to hers.

"Tuesday into Wednesday. Why they need two days for me to say 'initial quality award' is beyond me," Gannon complained. "Sounds like a bullshit award anyway."

Paige scooped up some kimchi and eyed him. "I'm sure it will sound impressive the way you say it."

"Yeah, right."

He'd gotten two endorsements since season two began airing, and Paige thought he seemed more uncomfortable with those than the filming of the show. "You didn't have to say yes to these deals," she reminded him.

He shrugged. "Pays the bills. Especially since I'm dealing with a money pit of a house now."

"Well, you could cut back on what you deemed the necessities." She pointed at him with her chopsticks.

"That's an asinine idea," Gannon countered. "We're already in, doing the work. There's no point in leaving it for later."

"Because every bachelor in Brooklyn absolutely needs a six-foot walk-in steam shower." *Great.* Now she was picturing him in the shower. She was going to have to take a nerve pill or show up drunk to work the day he finished the shower. It would remind her too much of the first time she'd seen him in all his naked splendor.

"You're just jealous because you live in a walk-in closet." He spun a finger over his head, encompassing the cramped apartment.

"Ha. Okay. Maybe a little," she admitted.

"Speaking of your tiny, ridiculous cabinet of an apartment," Gannon said, reaching for his beer. "How the hell are you going to produce a documentary out of this space?"

She'd cleaned up most of her research before he came

over—and changed into a nicer sweater and fussed with her makeup a little too. But there was still a stack of binders and papers shoved into the corner under the TV. Her laptop perched precariously on top. Color-coded sticky notes littered the wall in an organized flow.

There wasn't enough room to spread out and really dig in to anything. She'd hung up one of those portable whiteboards in their hallway, jammed in between a light switch and a bedroom door, but it wasn't big enough to storyboard more than thirty minutes of film.

She shrugged. "We'll make it work somehow."

"If only you knew a generous, friendly, accommodating, handy friend who was about to have more square footage than he needs," Gannon said, stroking his chin in mock contemplation.

"Work in your house?"

"Don't look at me like I just came out of a lobotomy. You'd have to wait until it was done first. So don't even think about moving in now."

"You don't even have any bathrooms right now." They'd gutted the one and only bathroom two days ago, and everyone was making do with the permitted porta potty in the courtyard.

"That's why I said wait until it's done. You and Becca could use the fourth floor."

"You're insane." She shook her head and made a grab for her wine. Why couldn't she stop looking at his hands? "You're just trying to find a way to keep me around after the show."

"Has anyone ever told you that you're beautiful, talented, *and* astute?"

"Literally no one ever. And I'm not running my documentary out of your house, Gannon."

"Why not? We're friends."

"You don't want to be friends," she pointed out.

302

"I don't want to be *just* friends," he corrected.

"Then it wouldn't be fair of me to take advantage of your addled condition and take you up on your offer. The kindest thing I can do is keep my distance from you until you get over your crush."

"Paige." The teasing left his tone. "Don't downplay what we have."

"Had," she corrected automatically.

He stared her down, heat flashing behind those deep hazel eyes. "Don't downplay my feelings for you."

That little shot hit home nicely, just as he'd probably intended. She was in the business of telling people's stories, and to do that, she had to have a healthy interest and respect for their lives, their feelings. Gannon didn't deserve the potshot.

"I'm sorry. That was uncalled for."

He went back to his food. "Don't make me take my Korean food and go home." Playful again.

"I'm sincerely sorry. You didn't deserve that. I'm just..." She wasn't about to confess to him that his mere presence on her couch robbed her of her faculties. She could smell him, for God's sake. The laundry detergent from his clean shirt combined with the spice of his soap was enough to drive her nuts. Smell-triggered memories for everyone. Unfortunately for her, Gannon's scent triggered an endless marathon of X-rated scenes in her head that made sitting platonically next to him almost physically painful.

"I'm going to ask you something," he announced. "Something you're probably not going to like. But I'm asking it anyway."

"I can hardly wait."

"Do you honestly believe you have to choose between your career and a relationship?"

"In this case? Yes."

"Why?"

"Gannon," Paige sighed out his name.

He put down his plate and leaned back, his arm on the couch behind her. "Why do you have to choose when I don't? We work for the same company in the same industry on the same show. We were interested in each other. We're in the same, exact situation."

"Except you have a cock." One that she remembered in vivid, muscle-clenching detail.

"Explain it. Same people, same situation, yet you're saying you'd be punished for the relationship."

"This is kind of the premise of the documentary," she began. "There are double standards, some of them so subconscious we don't even know we're all behaving according to the double standards until someone points it out. When I'm having a shit day, or even if I'm concentrating, there's gonna be a guy out there who thinks it's okay to tell me to smile."

Gannon said nothing.

"Think about it. Say you're having a rough day on set, and Andy walks up to you and says, 'You should smile more often.'"

"I'd punch him in his smug-ass face."

"Because it's a stupid thing to say, right? Someone thinks he can tell you how to feel. It's condescending. But you know what happens when some guy thinks he can say that to a woman? Most of us smile."

"Instead of punching him in his smug-ass face."

She nodded. "Double standard. It's not okay to tell a guy how to feel or to not be pissed." She was warming to the topic now. "So let's move on to a specific example involving the two of us. When rumors about us started on social media, you were the stud with two women, and I was the slut breaking up a relationship. Same people, same relationship, but one of us is applauded for it, and the other's slapped down. It's the difference between penis and vagina."

He nodded. "I get what you're saying, but isn't there another layer in play here? What about your responsibility for your reaction? If you smile when someone tells you to smile or you back out of a relationship that you want to be in because of the public opinion, isn't that on you?"

She grinned. "Very good, Gannon. Feminism, sexism, misogyny, and confidence are beyond complicated. Yes, we do have a responsibility for our reactions. But some women aren't in the position or don't have the confidence to demand better treatment. Those of us who are in that position need to be willing to pay the price for standing up."

"And you want to bring everyone up together," he supplied.

"Something like that. Yeah. What's the fun of being on top when there's no one up there with you? Who wants to be the only woman in the men's club?"

"Did you like being with me?" The change of subject muddled her. "Did you see a future with me...at least before?" he amended.

Paige debated. She was walking a very fine line here. One misstep, and she could find herself either pissing Gannon her boss off or hurting Gannon her friend. But she owed him an honest answer.

She took a deep breath. "Before Meeghan showed up on set that day, I'd been planning on asking you where we stood and if you'd be interested in seeing me in the off-season."

He looked incredulous. "Did you think we were having some kind of fling?"

"Uh, yeah."

"We were in a relationship."

"What?" Paige gaped at him. "We never talked about it."

"Why do we have to talk about it for it to be a relationship?"

"That's what relationships are! Talking to each other about stuff."

"We talked all day long, every day," Gannon argued.

"We worked together all day long, and then at night we… did other things," Paige clarified.

"Relationship things."

She snorted. "Are you telling me you've been in a relationship with every woman you've had sex with?"

"Of course not. I'm telling you we were in a relationship."

"Well, it couldn't have been a very good one if I had no idea about it."

"How could you not know when my dick was in you every night?" He seemed more incredulous than mad. "I brought you coffee. I spent nights sleeping with you—not fucking you—because I wanted you safe. I let you slobber all over me on planes."

Paige blinked. Gannon King had been in a relationship with her, and she'd had no idea.

He pressed on. "So to you it was a fling, but you still wanted to see if I'd be interested in something more?"

She shrugged miserably. "I don't know. It was a thousand humiliating moments ago. It's hard to remember exactly what I was thinking."

"You wanted to continue things, and then fucking Meeghan shows up, acting like an asshole, and shames you, and then you're just done."

Shit.

"You're a strong, capable, smart woman, Paige. Yet you let someone run you off what you wanted because you weren't willing to stand up for yourself."

"And now I'm making a fucking documentary about it. It's relevant to me, okay? Happy now?"

"No! I'm not happy! I'm fucking miserable, Paige. I want to be with you, and the only way I can do that is through work because you don't want to pay the price or accept the consequences. You don't want to have to fight for it."

"People are going to think I have this job because I slept with you," she argued.

"So the fuck what? Every person? Every person in the industry who does hiring is going to think that? Do you want to work for people who don't bother looking at your work and only listen to bullshit rumors?"

"The bullshit rumors were true in this case," she reminded him.

"And did me being in your bed every night lessen your ability to do your job?"

"No, of course not. But again, if I were a man, no one would think twice about hiring me despite my sexual past."

"I get that. And you're right. It's asinine. There's definitely a double standard there. But what can you do about it? Roll over, walk away from someone who cares about you, so you can stay marketable to assholes who will judge you by who you slept with?" He grabbed his beer, violence in the movement. "Look, I get it. I do. But who exactly are you helping by backing down from the fight? What do you gain from staying away from me? You're in the position to be fighting shit like this, not bowing down to it and accepting it as law.

"Are you just going to do a documentary pointing out all the double standard shit? Or are you going to show women how to stand up to that garbage? From this penis-wielding guy, I think you'd be doing a disservice to your audience if you only show them how to identify a problem, not solve it."

Paige flopped back against the couch and covered her face with her hands. "Part of me wants to argue with you, and

307

another part of me wishes I was recording this so I could use it in the film."

The silence dragged on, both of them wallowing in their own thoughts.

"Want more wine?" he offered.

"God, yes."

CHAPTER

42

P aige!" Gannon's voice bellowed in her headset.

"Geez! What? You don't have to scream. You're wearing a damn microphone." She regretted ever giving him the headset when he wasn't shooting scenes.

"Can you come down here? I need you to look at something."

"I'm sure the rash is perfectly normal, Gannon. But if it would make you feel better, you should think about getting it looked at by a medical professional." Paige joked for the benefit of the others listening in to their conversation.

"The kitchen tile, princess. Not my impressive and rash-free anatomy," he shot back.

Paige smothered her laughter and signaled for Bradley to keep an eye on the B-roll they were shooting for the backyard landscaping. A crew of subcontractors was out there whacking away like it was untamed jungle.

"Oh, that Gannon." Nina, one of Paige's camera crew,

shook her head, her shock of platinum-blond hair with purple streaks falling across her forehead. "He's quite the character."

Paige pointed a stern finger at Nina. "As your boss, I forbid you from being on his side."

Nina shrugged. "It's kinda hard not to like the guy, you know?"

Yeah, she knew. Paige was well aware of Gannon's appeal. She just wished she only had her inner conflict to deal with, not everyone else's opinions.

She made her way down a floor on the in-progress staircase to the main living level. She'd done her best to stick to her guns since their conversation two weeks ago, but Gannon's words echoed in her head on repeat. And damn if she didn't feel just the tiniest sliver of doubt creeping in.

Had she walked away from him because it was easier than standing up for what she wanted? What kind of a feminist was she if she only wanted to call attention to double standards and unfair treatment rather than actually fight them? Or was she just too far under Gannon's sexy spell to see things clearly? That was a possibility that deserved examining.

She'd tried to explain the conversation to Becca, but when Becca announced they should interview him for the doc, she'd given up. It was a complicated situation that she seemed to be intent on complicating.

"You roared?" Paige said, picking her way around sawhorses holding two-by-fours and piles of discarded copper pipes.

"What do you think?" he asked, pointing at the spread of cabinet, countertop, and tile samples. He stood in the middle of the gutted space that would be the new state-of-the-art kitchen.

"What do I think of what?"

"What would look good in here?" He was impatient, hands on hips, shoulders tense.

"It's your house," Paige reminded him.

He closed his eyes, blew out a breath. "Just humor me."

He'd asked her opinion here and there on other things in the house. Flooring, paint colors, light fixtures. She studied Gannon and the space. White cabinets were the trend, but this space and Gannon King didn't need trendy. They required substantial, solid, masculine.

"Cabinets," she said, pointing at the black walnut sample in an espresso stain two steps down from black. "Countertops, light and clean. Probably quartz so you don't have to seal it every year. One of these," she said, waving her hand over two nearly identical samples of white quartz with gray veining.

He crossed his arms, brought a hand to his mouth, and watched her thoughtfully. "Backsplash?" he asked, giving nothing away.

She examined the samples, weighing and rejecting each one. Too feminine, too contemporary, too boring. Paige shook her head. "If you want my opinion, none of these. You need something with texture that fits with the rest of the building. Brick. But in a rough finish, nothing too smooth. Something that plays off the exterior. It would be a pain to clean, but it would look really good."

Really, really good, Paige decided. Not that she really cooked, but with a kitchen like this, she might learn to make a few dishes here and there. Gannon would probably just use it to store beer and pizza boxes. *Lucky bastard.*

He nodded. "Okay, thanks."

"That's it?"

His massive shoulders lifted. "Yep. That's all I needed. You can go on back to whatever directorial crap you were doing."

"Gee, thanks."

She headed out but Gannon stopped her. "Paige?"

She turned. "Yeah?"

She saw the twinkle in his eyes, the dimple next to his mouth. "You're doing a great job."

Flustered, she gave him a brisk nod and escaped.

"A pleasure working with you," he called after her, an odd emphasis on the word *pleasure*.

Paige shook her head and headed for the stairs but was flagged down by her associate producer poking her head in the front door.

"Hey, Tina. Welcome to *King's Castle*." Paige offered her hand.

Tina, a compact woman in a red hoodie and sneakers, gripped and shook. "After running through last week's footage with the editors, I had to come in and poke around myself. Hope you don't mind." She cracked her gum as her eyes took in the half-finished framing, the new HVAC ducts that a crew was wrestling into place.

"Not at all," Paige said. "It's a mess right now but an organized one."

"The footage of the guys in the tub," Tina began, taking a look at the view out the front windows. "It was freakin' hilarious. We get more of that? Gannon King acting like a human being? We're looking at a solid hit...provided this shithole miraculously transforms into a castle."

"Leave it to Gannon," Paige told her.

"I've got a couple pages of notes—some one-on-ones we need for episode one, some B-roll ideas," Tina said. "If I can run through those with you and Gannon at the same time, it would save me some repetition."

"No problem. I'll go wrangle him. Fifteen minutes enough?" Paige asked, consulting the call sheet. They needed to start setting up for the window installation, and delivery was scheduled in half an hour. She needed to talk to Gannon about where he wanted to start and then dole out shooting assignments.

"Should be plenty," Tina cracked.

"I need to make a quick call, and then I'll drag him away from whatever mess he's in the middle of. Poke around if you want," Paige offered. "The upstairs looks just as bad as down here."

She left Tina to it and went out on the stoop where the construction noise and the chatter of crews were at least muffled by the thick wood of the front doors. Gannon had chosen a quiet street so traffic was minimal. Things were moving along inside as if the work was a dusty, noisy purging of the demons of the past, leaving behind a fresh, new start. Today especially was a day for considering fresh starts or recommitting to old choices, Paige thought. It was her birthday, not that she'd be sharing that information with anyone else.

Birthdays in the St. James family weren't for celebration. They were mile markers of successes, moments of pause to appreciate the journey, and hers hadn't started yet.

But instead of her journey, her future success, she found herself thinking about Gannon and fresh starts.

He'd warned her flat out that he'd be seducing her. And with each morning cup of coffee that he presented her with on set, each time he'd asked her opinion or listened to her direction, he was doing just that. He brought her chopped salads for lunch and bought Paige her own pair of work gloves as she was always borrowing someone else's for lending a hand.

And anytime Gannon wasn't hanging around, he had his crew and her own singing his praises.

Chantay had taken one look at the playback of the bathtub scene and fanned herself. "That is one fine-looking man. I would not be kicking that out of my bed," she'd said pointedly to Paige.

If she wasn't very careful, she'd end up exactly where she'd been…on her back under the powerful thrusts of Gannon King.

The image hit her so hard that Paige thought she might be hallucinating. Impulsively, her fingers clenched and released. Her phone tumbled onto the concrete step. "Crap."

She shook herself out, stretching to rid her body and mind of the demons of Gannon. Satisfied she wasn't about to enjoy a spontaneous orgasm, she dialed Eddie for their daily check-in.

"Hey, kid," he said cheerily. Someone in the background yelled.

"Golf course today?" she asked.

"It's a tough job, but someone's gotta babysit the network VPs. How are things in Brooklyn?"

"Moving right along. It's the mess before the order. But I think this is going to be a showstopper when the house is done."

"Good, good," Eddie said in that distracted way of his. "You don't need to check in every day, you know. I trust you. You know what you're doing. You don't need me to hold your hand."

"Just trying to do a good job," Paige said.

"According to Gannon, you're doing better than good," Eddie told her. "And postproduction is thrilled with what you're feeding them. You and Gannon really work well together."

"Not you too, Eddie," Paige groaned.

Eddie chuckled. "Sorry, kid. He got to me. That's a man who cares a hell of a lot about you."

"I'm not having this conversation with you or anyone else for the fiftieth time today," Paige announced. "We've got the replacement windows coming on the truck, and I've got to go find the permit so I can wave it in the meter maid's face when she shows up to yell at us again."

"Have a good one," Eddie signed off.

"Yeah, yeah."

Paige made another call to an in-house production

assistant who was assisting Gannon's team by organizing orders and deliveries to the house and then took a minute for herself. The autumn sunshine was warm, and there was a thick door between her and Gannon.

He was slipping through cracks in her defenses right and left. She'd always been impressed by his talent, enough to mostly overlook his cockiness and attitude. But seeing him working with his whole crew, guys he'd known for years, some of whom had worked with his grandfather, was like getting to know his family.

They all had a genuine respect and affection for the man, and as far as Paige could tell, the feeling was mutual. More often than not, after a long day of filming, beers would be cracked open, and wives and children would appear.

It was so different from *Kings of Construction*. There they were constantly surrounded by strangers before picking up and moving on to a new group of strangers. Here was a community, a family, and Paige's own crew was welcomed as such into the fold.

She spotted a familiar woman, tall and impeccably dressed, approaching. Her dark hair was coiled in a sedate yet classy chignon. The navy-blue suit hinted at the fit figure beneath. But the stride, in nude heels precisely two inches in height, spoke of confidence and no nonsense. The walk, purposeful without being hurried, was as familiar to Paige as her own.

"Hello, Paige," her mother offered, standing hands folded over her stylish leather bag just outside the gate.

"Mom, what are you doing here?" Paige rose from the stoop, brushing off the seat of her jeans and hurrying down the stairs. Had her mother really taken time out of her day to come wish her a happy birthday? That would be a birthday miracle. Usually her mother sent her a perfunctory email, and Leslie's assistant mailed her some shiny, expensive gift.

"It's lovely to see you as well, dear," Leslie said, subtly correcting what she felt was a rudeness. "I was at a symposium down the block at the hospital, and I thought I might come visit my daughter at work."

"No special occasion?" Paige prodded.

"Must there be one for a mother to see her own daughter?" Leslie asked pointedly.

CHAPTER

43

Her own mother hadn't remembered her birthday, Paige thought dryly. She could get some serious mileage out of this around the dinner table.

"Would you like to come in and see the house?" she offered, hoping her mother would say no.

"I certainly wouldn't want to end up on camera," Leslie sniffed, her disdain evident.

"We're not shooting for another thirty minutes," Paige promised. She could do half an hour with her mother without wine. Couldn't she?

"All right then."

Crap.

Paige flipped the latch on the gate and swung it open for her mother. Leslie St. James didn't open her own doors. "Just promise not to say anything condescending to anyone inside. They've been working their ass—They've been working nonstop. So put on your cocktail reception face," Paige ordered.

Her mother rolled her eyes. "I'm not going to be rude to your…coworkers. This is your work, such as it is, and should be respected," she said, eyeing the plywood floor of the foyer with a dubious expression.

Paige smiled through gritted teeth and led her mother through the main floor, praying that Gannon would stay wherever the hell he was and away from here. Her mother had indeed slapped on her professionally cool smile and politely greeted Gannon's crew and Paige's.

Leslie listened intently as Paige gave Tony feedback on the B-roll he'd just shot and sent Bradley downstairs to help Chantay set up the lighting to shoot.

"I'd show you upstairs, but it's even more of a mess than down here," Paige told her mother, hoping that the brief tour would count as family quality time and they could be done.

Leslie arched an eyebrow as she glanced at the construction materials and inches of dirt and dust surrounding them. "I find that hard to imagine."

"Paige!"

She heard the rumble of Gannon's voice coming from the staircase. Oh, hell.

"She's in here," Flynn the traitor yelled, winking at Paige and her mother as he breezed by carrying sawhorses.

Gannon appeared and zeroed in on her. "Princess, I want to talk to you about some off-site shoots."

"Princess?" Leslie's voice took on the icy qualities of Antarctica.

Gannon stopped and looked back and forth between Paige and her mother, a slow grin sliding over his face.

"Mom, I'd like you to meet Gannon. Gannon, this is my mother, Leslie."

"Dr. St. James," Leslie corrected. "And we've met."

"Who could forget a voice like yours, Dr. St. James?" Gannon asked.

"I'll assume that is a rhetorical question."

"Mom," Paige said in a warning whisper.

"Assume whatever you like, Dr. St. James," Gannon told her with a magnanimous wave of his arm. "Of course, you know what happens when you assume."

"I see you're consistently antagonistic," Leslie announced. "Have you ever seen a therapist for that flaw?"

Paige blinked in horror. But Gannon simply laughed, which was always the wrong thing to do in front of Leslie St. James.

"Have you lost your damn mind?" Paige hissed at her mother, but Leslie wouldn't be cowed.

"I *assume* since you're working with my daughter, you must be sleeping with her again. What a shame. I'd thought she had better taste," Leslie announced.

Paige let out a breath that sounded like air leaving an accordion. "Okay. Enough," she finally snapped.

"Thank you for the tour, Paige. I can show myself out. I'm getting a headache being surrounded by all this…filth."

"I'd be happy to show you out, Leslie," Gannon offered, pushing yet another button. "It's such a shame you can't stay longer."

"I wouldn't want to inconvenience you. I'm sure you have a lot of work to do for the cameras." She glanced around the empty dining room with its stripped floors and bare walls. "I suppose some find it gratifying to make their fortunes by debasing themselves on television."

Gannon's grin bared his teeth.

"Mother!" Paige snapped. "Enough. You've overstayed your welcome."

"So nice to finally meet you in person, Gannon," Leslie said, the picture of phony pleasantries.

"I was just thinking the same thing," Gannon said, offering his hand.

Leslie shook it disdainfully and then wiped her palm on her skirt as Paige dragged her toward the front door.

"Just what have you done that earns you the right to be an asshole?" Paige demanded as she slammed the doors behind them.

"Your language leaves quite a bit to be desired." Leslie's voice carried enough frost to curdle the leaves of the pin oak above them.

"Your *attitude* leaves quite a bit to be desired. Gannon happens to be a loyal, hard-working, generous man. He beats anyone that you sneak home from your symposiums and your fundraisers for a tasteful fuck."

It was a cheap shot, but hey, she was a St. James, and they never backed down from going for the jugular.

Her mother sputtered in indignation.

"Gannon could be building custom furniture worthy of your snobbish friends and making millions, but he puts his family first. He 'debased' himself on TV to save his grandfather's construction company so his grandmother wouldn't have to sell the only home she's known and so he could keep the crew that he grew up with and their families on the payroll. What have you done? Decorated a house and written a few books? If I were you, I'd watch what insults I'm throwing in other people's faces."

Paige had worked up a full head of steam, and it wasn't just going to fizzle out. No, she was going out with a bang.

"Are you insinuating that I've done things I should be ashamed of?" Leslie demanded.

"I'm insinuating that there is nothing in your life that comes before your career. Not your marriage, not your children, and certainly not your generosity of spirit!"

"I have never been so disappointed in you, Paige."

"Yeah, well, right back at you, Mother. I find your disregard for humanity to be damned disappointing."

Leslie's ice-blue eyes chilled Paige to the bone. "Someday, Daughter, you'll understand how to prioritize your life. Men will come and go, but success that you've earned can never be taken from you. I just pray that whenever you do learn, it won't be too late."

"So noted, thanks," Paige snapped.

Her mother, head high, strode down the stairs and across the uneven courtyard to the gate. She turned and raised a sculpted eyebrow. "I'll still expect to see you at Thanksgiving."

"I'll bring the stuffing."

Paige watched her mother hail a cab and then disappear around the corner.

"I'll bring the stuffing?" Gannon sounded amused.

"Ugh." Paige threw her head back to curse the gods. "How long have you been standing there?"

"Long enough to realize you should be way more screwed up than you are."

Paige turned to face him. "It's nothing personal, so please don't take it that way. It's never personal. My mother and I just baffle each other. She was out of line and then embarrassed about being out of line."

"And then disappointed in you for calling her out."

Paige winced. "My, what big ears you have."

"Come here." He reeled her in, giving her no option other than to slip her arms around his waist and rest her face on that broad expanse of chest. Gannon placed a kiss to the top of her head. "You're an exceptional woman who is living a life you designed. If you feel one second of guilt for not doing what's expected of you, you're really going to piss me off."

"Why are you so nice to me?" Paige murmured, inhaling his scent.

"I'm a glutton for punishment, and you just defended me to the dragon lady."

Paige smiled against his chest. "She'd love that nickname."

"I'll be sure to use it at Thanksgiving."

CHAPTER

44

Preying on her reluctance to go back to her apartment and wallow, Gannon talked Paige into checking out a furniture boutique after shooting wrapped for the day.

He had shrugged off her mother's insults like they were nothing more than raindrops. Paige, on the other hand, let them burn into her skin and fester. Her mother was more intent on scaring Paige away from Gannon than remembering her daughter's birthday.

But the lesson wasn't received as intended. As Paige had learned to do in childhood when faced with the Leslie St. Jameses of the world, sometimes it was better to head in the exact opposite direction.

Gannon led her through the heavy glass doors on the first level of a two-story, repurposed warehouse in Brooklyn, and she was immediately overwhelmed by the colors and textures of the cacophony of home decor and furniture that sat in organized chaos within.

"What exactly are we looking for?" Paige asked.

"I want your thoughts on shooting here. My mom's ordered furniture from them before. Small business, family-owned, kick-ass stuff. I wouldn't mind tapping them for some furniture." Gannon cocked his head and studied a gilded birdcage.

"You don't need a birdcage," Paige insisted. "Why aren't you dragging Cat around? She's got the designer brain."

"I don't want my sister designing my house. It's weird. I want stuff I like, not stuff that someone else thinks 'works.'"

"So are we looking for anything in particular?" Paige asked, running her hand over a cherry armoire with sinuous curves.

"A bed," Gannon said, shoving his hands in his back pockets and scanning the store.

"You took me shopping for a bed? Seriously?"

"What? You know what I like."

"I know what you like *in* bed, not in a bed. Difference."

He slung an arm around her shoulders. "Close enough. Besides, there's this pizza place around the corner, and once you give the okay for shooting here, we can go grab a superior pepperoni pie and even some stupid salads if you insist on the green stuff."

"This is work, Gannon. Not a date." Her reiteration of their professional relationship felt more like an ingrained habit than an actual denial at this point.

He ignored her reluctance and dragged her farther into the belly of the warehouse. He was right. It would be a great place to shoot, she decided. Tall, industrial shelving created makeshift aisles and housed everything from rewired light fixtures to fireplace screens. The furniture section was organized without rhyme or reason, overstuffed leather couches sitting nestled next to delicate writing desks and wire-framed baker's racks in an array of colors.

Gannon flopped down on a four-poster with dizzying scrollwork.

Paige shook her head. "Nope."

He opened one eye. "Why?"

"Too feminine," she insisted.

He rolled to his side. "Okay, smarty-pants. Let's see what you'd pick."

Paige browsed the selection while Gannon yawned from his mattress. She knew he wasn't really interested in furniture shopping now. He was looking to distract her from her run-in with her mother. And she needed it.

He knew her whether Paige wanted to admit it or not. Gannon had taken the time to get to know her, and that knowledge hadn't evaporated with her ending things or their breakup or whatever the hell it had been. He cared for her. Otherwise, why would he be here dragging her from store to pizza shop to keep her from wallowing?

He was a good man, a solid one.

He'd made a mistake, but Gannon King wasn't the kind of guy to make a mistake more than once.

He'd ended up in bed with Meeghan and never let it happen again. He hadn't been entirely truthful with Paige, and when faced with those consequences, he had been nothing but honest since. He learned and adapted, and he *still* wanted her.

She saw it then. Dark wood, the slight curve of the headboard, sinuous leather inserts. The frame of the bed sat up high enough to accommodate drawers on either side. It was big, solid, and—she tested the mattress—just right for Gannon's muscular frame. Soft enough to comfort at the end of a long day yet firm enough to offer support. She relaxed against the pillows and closed her eyes, trying to imagine the bed in the space that would become Gannon's master bedroom.

Against the brick wall, she decided. Two heavy nightstands with those sexy gray-washed wooden lamps. Navy drapery and linens. *Yeah, this fit him.*

She felt the mattress dip, sensed his weight on the bed next to her.

"Okay, you win," he sighed.

"I know."

She opened an eye and turned her head to look at him. He lay on his side, one hand under his head, studying her with those serious greenish-brown eyes. Those eyes said it all. Want, need, tenderness…and something stronger, sharper. Yet he held it all back, waiting for her to be ready, for her to make the decision.

When she let everything else drop away, it was the easiest decision she'd ever made in her life.

"The pizza's going to have to wait," she breathed.

———

"Why here?" she murmured against Gannon's busy mouth as it worked hers into a frenzy. Her back was pressed against the front door of the brownstone as he blindly fumbled with the keys.

"Home," he growled. "I want you here. I want us both to remember the very first time here."

It was good enough for her. The door tripped open behind her and they stumbled inside, refusing to break apart long enough to walk across the threshold. It was dark, but Gannon knew the way. He half carried her up the stairs, avoiding the rickety banister that was somewhere further down the fix list.

The door to what would be the bedroom hadn't been rehung yet, so Gannon dragged her through the opening. "Sure? Are you sure?" he asked her, his hands busy pulling her sweater over her head.

Her lips broke with his. "Positive. I want you, Gannon. Here. Now. Fast."

"Thank God." He stripped off his own shirt and threw it on the floor, spreading it out with his foot. "It's going to be here, Paige."

She didn't question him, didn't wonder why he wanted her in the gutted, empty bedroom of his new home when he had a perfectly good bed a few blocks away.

Nothing mattered but his naked torso, his callused hands caressing her smooth curves. Not expectations, not rumors, not even truth. She wanted this, and she would take it.

She busied herself with the fly of his jeans, and Gannon flicked open the clasp of her bra. His sigh was relief, admiration, adoration, when her breasts fell into his palms. Rough against smooth, soft against heat.

She moaned when his thumbs brushed across her aching nipples.

Before she could shove at his jeans to free him, he reached into his pocket for his wallet, and she heard the crinkle of foil.

"Awfully confident, aren't you?" It was only half a joke. He'd known she'd come back to him even though she'd never let herself consider the possibility.

Just another example of Gannon knowing her better than she was comfortable with.

"Consider it a lucky charm." His voice was rough as concrete block and sent a delicious shiver up her spine. "I thought they'd expire before you were mine."

Nothing he could have said would have made her more frantic. She pressed herself against him, her breasts flattened against his stone chest.

He took her down to the floor, bracing their impact with his arm and lowering her onto his shirt. She felt the grit of the dirty hardwood under her and thought it was sexier than any mattress in any bedroom.

"Honey, this time it's going to be fast because I need you that way. I'll make up for it later."

God, yes. Her body sang with need, pulse thundering, muscles quivering. She wanted him fast and hard and a little desperate. It was how she felt right now. She needed him to remind her exactly why their bodies craved each other so fiercely.

"Make up for it after pizza," she whispered.

He laughed, sounding pained. And without another word, his mouth closed over the peak of her breast with a desperation that had Paige arching under him and crying out in pleasure. She used her feet to wrestle his jeans down his legs and reveled when one less layer separated them.

"Your body, princess, deserves to be worshipped." He groaned, licking at her nipple before switching to the other one, which strained for his attention.

"Worship later," she murmured. Her body couldn't take a slow, purposeful seduction.

"Tell me you didn't put up the time-lapse cameras in here yet." The thought wasn't enough to stop him from sucking at her peak, but it was enough for her to freeze for a millisecond before relaxing.

"Not yet. They go up for drywall and painting," she panted. She glanced around the shadows in the room for good measure but was distracted by his mouth back on her breast while his fingers peeled her jeans from her hips.

She couldn't quite catch her breath. There was too much dark and not enough oxygen in the room. There was a danger here, a danger of being consumed and never coming back to herself.

But it was a price to pay, and in this second, it wasn't even a choice.

"You are the sexiest woman in the world," he murmured, stripping the denim from her. He slid up between her legs, his teeth teasing a trail up her inner thigh. Paige drew in a sharp breath when she felt his hot breath at the apex of her thighs.

"You said fast," she accused.

"I have time for a pit stop," he promised, dipping down between her legs. His tongue slicked between her folds, and Paige levered her hips up against his mouth.

"Gannon," she hissed.

"Baby, if you only knew what hearing my name like that from your mouth did to me." He licked her again, the rough texture of his tongue triggering the nerves in her clit to dance and contract.

"Show me," she demanded.

He did just that, leading a frontal assault that left her quivering under him. He slid two fingers into her as his tongue worked her over. Paige gripped at his hair and, when she couldn't get purchase, the floor.

"I need you to come for me right now because I can't hold off being inside you, Paige."

Her body and Gannon had a special relationship, one where he gave the orders and her body jumped to obey.

He used his tongue to lave her trembling nub, fingers driving into her and curling ever so slightly.

She cried out, every muscle tight as a bow as a climax, unexpectedly violent, ripped through her.

Gannon groaned against her as she came around his fingers. His hips pistoned against the floor as if priming himself for what came next. She'd barely stopped coming when he was pulling back just far enough to slide the condom over his purple-headed erection.

He wanted her as badly as she needed him. That gave her comfort as soul-shattering aftershocks continued to rack her body.

Gannon settled himself between her thighs, and just the weight of his body, the position of his cock, sent her up again. She went from satiated to needy and desperate in less than a second.

She bucked against him, insisting with her body.

But he held her still, her face framed between those big palms.

"One thing," he said, eyes boring into her. "We're in a relationship."

"Gannon!" She was aching for him. She needed him buried inside her. They didn't have time to have a talk about expectations. She needed him to *fill* her.

"Say it, Paige. No misunderstandings this time." He cheated, probing her greedy entrance with the rounded crown of his cock. She was already spasming with need. "Say it."

"We're in a relationship." She whispered the words, and they were almost lost entirely when he drove into her.

He groaned in her ear as he muscled his way inside. She gasped, her fingers digging into his shoulders.

"You okay?" He breathed the words in her ear, ragged and harsh.

She was stretched wide to accommodate him, just on the safe side of her limits. "God, yes." Her voice was strained and breathy, and her body tensed with the decadent sliver of pain his invasion caused.

His dusting of chest hair teased her hardened nipples. Gannon's tattooed arm took just enough of his weight off her.

He wrapped her hair around his other fist and slowly, slowly eased out of her. She watched his eyes when he sank back into her and saw the fire there.

"Fuck. Honey, I can't stop."

"Don't you dare stop." Paige urged him on with her body. Jacking her hips up to meet his thrusts, she clung to his shoulders, nails digging in and scraping flesh. He pinned her with his body and his eyes. Those hazel orbs held her enthralled. She took and took as his hips slammed into her, the floor biting into her back, her ass. But he was inside her where she needed him the most, and nothing but the finish line mattered.

She saw the glaze come over his eyes. The sweat dotting his forehead and arms belayed his effort to hold back. There were no words now, only the soft grunts that escaped Gannon's throat, the cords of his neck standing out with the strain.

"Yes!" she begged. Paige hitched her legs up higher over his hips and felt her sex ripple around his shaft. "Gannon!"

He released her hair only to grip her breast, squeezing, plumping, and Paige flew over the edge at full speed. She felt herself close around him, and then he was driving into her, holding himself there, his feet digging into the floor so he could stay fully sheathed in her.

His shout of triumph as he came inside her ripped through the dim light. She quaked beneath him, feeling him temper the power of his thrusts to match the waves of her own release, his pleasure echoing hers.

CHAPTER 45

W hat are you doing?" Paige asked. Her head was pillowed on the arm he had tucked under his head. They were both staring up at the unfinished ceiling in the master bedroom.

"I'm composing a thank-you note to your mother in my head."

She laughed, rising up onto her elbow to study him and prod him in his ribs. "Very funny."

"Dear Leslie, I can't thank you enough for being a pompous ass and forcing your beautiful, stubborn daughter to get out of her own way," he recited.

"You're ridiculous."

"And you're thinking about pizza." Gannon screwed up his handsome face as if he was trying to read her mind. "And trying to figure out what this means."

Paige flopped back down on her back, breaking the eye contact. She'd been doing exactly that.

"I don't want to be in a relationship right now, Gannon."

"So you used me for sex?" he asked in mock horror.

"I forgot how hilarious you are after sex," Paige grumbled, stretching her arms over her head.

Gannon reached over, his large palm closing over her breast. "I'm hilarious all the time. You just have a terrible memory."

"Today's my birthday." She wasn't sure why she'd said it besides the fact that it had been poking at her in her head. She'd seen her mother on her birthday, and Leslie hadn't remembered. Paige had barely remembered. Her life was full steam ahead right now, and she didn't have time for things like relationships with sexy, smoldering men or birthdays. As rebellious as her mother considered Paige to be, it appeared as though she were following in the family's footsteps after all.

"Today's your *birthday*, and you let me fuck you on the floor of a *construction zone*?" Gannon was surprisingly pissed.

"Uh, thank you?" She wasn't sure what kind of answer he was expecting.

He propelled himself off the floor, dragging on his jeans. "Get up." When she didn't move fast enough for his liking, Gannon hauled her to her feet.

"Geez, is this a wham-bam-thank-you-ma'am?"

"Put your clothes on, Paige. We're having a birthday."

"Don't be ridiculous. I don't want a birthday."

"I don't want a birthday, Gannon. I don't want a relationship, Gannon." He was misquoting her in an obnoxious falsetto. "Sometimes you're really infuriating, you know that?"

"You were a lot nicer to me when you didn't know it was my birthday."

But he was too busy looking at his watch and muttering to himself. The shine of sex was rapidly wearing off, and Paige wished that she had kept her big, fat mouth shut.

"Let's go!" The order was given over his shoulder as he trundled down the stairs to the main level.

Paige tugged her sweater back in place, zipped her jeans, and shuffled down after him. "Yeah, yeah. We're going."

———

Darkness had fallen on Brooklyn, at least as dark as the borough could get with its army of LED streetlights. They drove for a few blocks before Gannon cut the wheel and expertly worked the oversize pickup into a parking space on the street in front of a closed fish market.

"Stay here."

Before she could even come up with a smart comeback, he was slamming the door and stalking down the block. Paige rested her head against the seat and sighed. She'd chucked her will out the window today and embraced the bad decision that was Gannon King. *Again.*

Paige frowned through the windshield. She didn't feel like she'd let herself down. She felt...satisfied, smug even. There was no doubt that time spent in bed—or on the floor—with Gannon was never time wasted. The man made pleasure an Olympic sport. But she'd expected to feel guilty for letting herself down, for caving. She didn't have time for a man as demanding as Gannon. She didn't need any distractions at this point in her life.

But as she ticked off the reasons for keeping her distance, none of them held the weight against the argument her postorgasmic body was making. She *liked* him. Even when he was being a temperamental ass. He pushed her outside her comfort zone, challenging her at all turns. And she was stronger because of it.

Paige blinked, convinced the spectacle approaching the truck was a postorgasmic hallucination. Gannon was loaded down with shopping bags. Clipped to his jeans was a bouquet of balloons proclaiming birthday sentiments. Flowers peeked out of one of the bags.

He opened his door and started shoving bags and balloons into the back seat. "Don't look at this stuff," he ordered, pointing a finger at her. "You just turn your pretty little self around and ignore everything back here."

She turned around, shaking her head. "You're ridiculous."

"*You're* ridiculous," he countered.

They drove the half dozen blocks to his apartment, and when Paige tried to help unload, he slapped her hands away.

"Go upstairs and unlock the door," he said, tossing his keys at her.

Relieved that she didn't have to be part of the attention-calling birthday parade, Paige jogged up the three flights of stairs and let herself into the apartment. Not much had changed since her last visit this summer. The couch was still leather and battered, the kitchen was still tiny, and the bedroom still reminded her of long, late hours of pleasure.

She did find something new here. The shelf next to the TV held a framed picture that hadn't been there before. She picked it up to examine it. It was one of the candid shots from the set of *Kings of Construction*. Paige was standing hands on hips in a tank top and shorts, giving orders and grinning. They were at the Russes', midshoot.

She heard the commotion in the hallway and put the frame down just as Gannon stormed in with his haul. He kicked the door closed behind him and dumped the lot on the kitchen counter. Without bothering to unclip the balloons from his belt, he yanked a bottle of wine out of the cabinet and opened it.

He poured a glass and handed it to her, the balloons buffeting against each other over his head. She couldn't not laugh. A scowling birthday fairy delivering wine? No one could keep a straight face.

"Take your wine and go take a shower." He started unloading items from the bags. She spotted a giant box of condoms and raised her eyebrows.

"That should get us through the night," she quipped.

He held out a shopping bag to her. "Shower," he insisted. The giant smiley-face balloon with hearts for eyes peeking over his head ruined the effect.

She sidled up to him. "What are you going to be doing while I'm naked and soapy in your shower?" Now that she'd had him again, she wasn't even close to done with him for the night.

He leaned down, kissing her hard and then nipping her lower lip. "Taking care of dinner."

"I'm not that hungry." She rose up on her toes to press a soft, suggestive kiss to his mouth. He deepened the kiss, his hands settling on her hips. She let him take the lead as he walked her backward. Her body was humming to life again, a slow burn that began to build in her belly and lower.

She felt cold tile under her feet and Gannon's heat at her front. He pulled back, and she stared up into his lust-glazed eyes.

"We have all night," he promised as if he was reminding himself as much as her. "Shower, dinner, dessert."

The way he said *dessert* gave Paige a delicious shiver up her spine.

"Sure you don't want to skip straight to dessert?" she offered.

"If you keep looking at me like that, it'll be more like breakfast." He closed the door harder than necessary.

Paige caught her reflection in the mirror over his vanity. She saw flushed cheeks, bright eyes, and a kind of excitement that glowed from within. That was what Gannon did to her. She felt loose, relaxed, *good*.

Maybe a shower wasn't a bad idea, she decided. She poked through the grocery bag he'd shoved at her and was delighted to find her favorite shampoo, conditioner, body wash, even moisturizer. He'd thrown in a few impulse items too, she noted with amusement. There were two tubes of ChapStick, a stick of deodorant, and a new toothbrush.

It looked like she'd been invited to spend the night. And with an early shoot start tomorrow, she certainly wouldn't complain about the shorter commute from Gannon's apartment. Not that a night in Gannon's bed left much to complain about.

She cranked on the hot water in the shower stall and stripped. Looking at her wine, she shrugged. *What the hell?* It was her birthday after all. She took the glass with her into the steam.

———

Hair still damp and body now clean, Paige padded into the kitchen in one of Gannon's T-shirts and her own underwear. She wasn't sure which of them was more startled by the other. Gannon raised his head and promptly dropped the spoon he was using to abuse a bowl of something dark and chocolaty.

He'd lost his shirt, splattered with the same dark chocolaty substance from the bowl, while she was in the shower and replaced it with a Kiss the Cook grilling apron. He stood eyeing her, bare feet braced, jeans low on his hips, and a sexy-as-sin half grin on his face.

"You look good in my shirt."

"You look good in your apron."

There were two large grilled chicken salads still in their plastic containers on the counter. He picked up the spoon and rinsed it in the sink before returning to the bowl.

"Whatcha making there, Chef King?" Paige asked, topping off her wineglass and sneaking behind him to fetch a beer for him from the fridge. She twisted the top and set the bottle on the skinny scrap of counter next to him.

"Do me a favor and peel the stickers off those things," he said, jerking his chin toward the muffin tins peeking out of their own grocery bag.

"You can't be serious," Paige demanded, her brain refusing to make sense of what was happening.

"They're stickers," he insisted, missing the point. "It's not that complicated. Get a grip, princess."

"You're baking me cupcakes."

"Yeah, well, if you would have bothered to share anything personal at all, like the fact that it was your birthday, it would have been a really nice Death by Chocolate cake from the bakery around the corner. But you didn't, so you have to deal with these. Peel."

Words failed her. Gannon King was baking her cupcakes on her birthday and yelling at her about it.

She slipped her arms around his waist from behind and laid her forehead against his muscled back.

"You're not going to cry, are you?" he asked gruffly.

Her lips curved. "No."

"Good. Save it for when they're done and burnt and you still have to eat them or you'll hurt my feelings."

The cupcakes were only a little burnt. But Gannon made up for it with the yellow crown candle he lit and stuck in the chocolate frosting of one. He didn't sing her "Happy Birthday," which would have only embarrassed them both, but he did demand she make a wish.

And when the second can of chocolate frosting was put to even more decadent use a little later, Paige felt like her wish had come true.

CHAPTER
46

The next morning, Paige woke up wrapped in the sanctuary of Gannon's inked arms to good news.

"What's that?" Gannon grumbled, squinting at her phone over her shoulder.

Paige held up the phone. "That's Malia and her doctor. She's wrapping up her treatments this week. Carina says she's cautiously optimistic…and she thinks Malia's doctor is a hottie."

"Replacing me so soon?" Gannon sighed, burying his face in her neck.

"You're still the king of hotness," Paige promised. She wiggled her butt against him and was rewarded with the prod of his erection.

"Don't you forget it," he said, his voice muffled by her hair. "Do you keep in touch with a lot of the families from the show?"

"Just a few each season." Paige sent Carina a reply with several exclamation points. "The Dufours and the Ledlers."

"From the last show?" Gannon latched on to that. He rolled her onto her back and busied himself raining kisses over her chest and shoulders.

She hissed in a breath when he lazily ran the rough of his tongue over her nipple. "I felt…bad. About leaving before the reveal." She arched against him, her body awake enough to demand more of the pleasures of the night. "I flew back out in September to see them and got to meet their new daughters."

Gannon lifted his head. "No shit? Really?"

"Huh?" Paige's brain was clouded with the heavy fog of lust.

"The adoption? It was finalized?" he prompted. Gannon accented his question with a bite on her shoulder. "Are they using the cribs?"

"Ouch! Yes. I have pictures." Gannon had designed and built two cribs for the twin girls. Cribs that were at the heart of a happy family. "What time is it?" She frowned.

He picked up her phone and looked at the clock.

"We either have time for showers and breakfast here, but I make shitty eggs and burnt toast, or we can see just how efficient we are between the sheets and grab coffee and breakfast sandwiches to go."

They were very efficient, it turned out. Efficient enough that Gannon felt like his taste of Paige was more an appetizer than a meal. He'd remedy that tonight after shooting wrapped. He followed Paige into the bathroom and watched her frowning at her tangle of hair.

"I should have dried it last night. It looks like a rat's nest condominium."

340

He reached behind the bathroom door, yanked a Kings Construction hat off the hook, and settled it over her dark curls. "There. Problem solved."

She tugged the brim lower, tucked her hair behind her ears, and managed to look adorable. He reached over and adjusted the fit.

Paige grinned at him. And not just the work smile but the full-on blinding wattage that punched him in the chest every damn time. Her blue eyes were warm beneath the bill of his hat, her face bare and unbelievably pretty. His heart took that stumbling stutter.

"What?" she asked, cocking her head.

He wasn't going to blow it all now by professing his undying love to her. Again. He had a plan and he needed to stick to it.

He shrugged and reached for his toothbrush. "Nothing. I'm just liking how this day started."

Paige pulled her toothbrush out of the holder and rinsed it under the water. "Listen," she began, reaching for the toothpaste. "To avoid repeating any past mistakes, I want to be clear about something."

Gannon snatched it away from her and squirted some on his toothbrush. She swiped it back and spread some neatly on her brush.

"Why do I have the feeling that you're about to piss me off?" he asked, brushing vigorously.

"I'm not trying to piss you off," Paige insisted. "I just want to make sure you understand that I'm not looking for a relationship right now."

He stopped brushing and stared her down in the mirror. "Sure know how to make a guy feel special, Paige."

She wrinkled her nose at him and bent to spit. "You know what I mean. I like you, Gannon. I like being with you. But I don't have the time to devote to a relationship."

He turned on the water in the sink, spat, and rinsed. "But you want to continue to have sex?"

She looked guilty. "Well, yeah."

"And you're not having it with anyone else?"

"Of course not! And neither are you, by the way." She rinsed and caught the towel he threw at her.

"So we're having monogamous sex. What about dinner? Do I get to have meals with you?"

"I know what you're doing," she warned him. She pointed her toothbrush at him.

"Meals, sex, probably some sleepovers." He ticked the items off. "But not a relationship."

"I just don't want you to expect things from me like…"

"Like what? What does a relationship mean to you, Paige?"

"I haven't given it much thought."

"Yet you're positive you don't want to make time for one?"

"Look, I just want to be straight with you. Okay? I don't want to be thinking about next steps and questioning what we are and aren't. I want to focus on work."

"So no relationship," Gannon clarified.

Paige looked relieved. "Yes. No relationship."

"Agree to disagree." He pressed a kiss to the top of her head. "Hurry up, princess. I need coffee." He sauntered out of the bathroom, leaving her glaring after him.

"So glad that's settled," she said and scowled.

———

When they got to the brownstone, Paige was happy to realize both crews were already assembled. A jump on the schedule never hurt any TV show. However, her dreams of being ahead of schedule were dashed when she pushed open the front door.

"Surprise!"

She would have turned around and run, but Gannon and his chest were blocking her. Felicia had her hands full of a tray towering with doughnuts and bagels. Cat, in skinny jeans and an azure off-the-shoulder sweater, skipped over, a chintzy dollar-store tiara in her hands.

"You didn't think you could sneak your birthday past us, did you?" she teased, settling the tiara on top of Paige's hat.

"Technically I did, and this is the day after," Paige muttered, shooting Gannon a dirty look over her shoulder.

He winked and shoved her forward into the melee. There was coffee, every breakfast carb known to man, and then quite possibly the worst rendition of "Happy Birthday" ever performed in the history of the song.

Bradley pocketed his phone after the singing came to an end. "This is going to be gold for the blog," he said, cheerfully biting into an everything bagel slathered with sour cream and chive cream cheese.

Flynn, to Paige's eternal embarrassment, presented her with a gift bag containing a new tank top proclaiming her to be El Jefe and a peck on the cheek, which earned him a shove from Gannon.

They dined on doughnuts, bagels, Danish, and coffee, and Gannon announced the celebration could continue after work with pizza and beer. Paige finally convinced them all the party was over and that there wouldn't be any pizza and beer unless they actually completed shooting for the day. As everyone scattered, she took a doughnut and a moment.

In less than twelve hours, he'd baked her cupcakes, thrown her an impromptu surprise party, and given her four body-shattering orgasms. It wasn't going to end well, of that she was certain. Their feelings for each other were too volatile to have a polite going of the separate ways. No, it would be messy and painful, and even without the inevitable breakup, the demand on her time that a relationship with him would require would be astronomical.

But he'd gotten her balloons and remembered what brand of shampoo she used. He'd given her this job, this show, this opportunity. And what she felt for him, it didn't fit so neatly in the like or lust boxes. It was something deeper. Something she wasn't ready to name yet. She kicked at the metal leg of the worktable that was buckling under the weight of tools and miscellaneous construction supplies.

And she'd be an asshole if she didn't at least give this a shot.

Nail guns echoed from upstairs, and somewhere two circular saws were making quick work of studs. She found Gannon in the kitchen, checking measurements for the new back door onto the deck.

"Fine. We're dating," she announced, crossing her arms and glaring at him. "Happy?"

He looked up at her from where he kneeled on the floor. "Ecstatic."

"If I screw this relationship up by not spending enough time with you or not meeting your needs or being too selfish, you have no one to blame but yourself," Paige insisted.

"Consider me warned." He climbed to his feet and swiped his palms on his jeans before grabbing for her. She was fast, but he was faster, and he was wrapping his arms around her in a tight hug.

"We're at work," she reminded him, shooting nervous looks over his shoulder.

"Well, honey, that's one of my needs. I'm not hiding this from my guys. They're practically family. You can pretend to be whatever you need to be in front of your crew, but my guys would take it personally if I lied to them."

"Damn it, Gannon."

"We're doing it right this time, and you've got to be ready to deal with the consequences. I'm not going to be your dirty little secret. Stop pouting."

She felt the lines forming on her forehead. "I'm not pouting! I'm thinking. I've never announced a relationship before."

"You're putting too much thought into this," he insisted.

Felicia wandered in, munching on a chocolate éclair. "Hey, Paige. How many mics you think we'll need today? I had two conk out on me. Pieces of shit."

Gannon looked at Paige, nodded toward Felicia, and prodded her in the back.

"Uh, Felicia. I wanted to tell you…something."

"You're not shitcanning me, are you?"

"Geez! No!"

"Well, you kind of had that nauseous 'I have to fire you' face."

Gannon chuckled behind her. Paige shot him a dirty look over her shoulder. "No, it's just I… Gannon and I are… We just started dating. And I wanted you to…you know…know." Paige limped through her explanation.

"Okay, so I'm not fired, and you two are together?" Felicia clarified.

"Yeah, that's the gist."

Felicia whooped and picked up the mic of the headset she was wearing around her neck. "Bust open the kitty, boys. Gaige is in the building!"

There were corresponded whoops and cheers from all floors of the house.

"You had money on this?" Paige covered her face with her hands.

Felicia shot her an incredulous look. "No one was going to bet against Gannon," Felicia said. "I mean, look at him. Who says no to that?"

Gannon preened like a peacock.

"So what's the money from?"

"We each threw twenty bucks into the pot to go out and celebrate when y'all started bumping uglies. Got quite the stash just waiting on you two."

Paige decided her hands were just fine where they were and kept them over her eyes.

"Just so you know, Felicia," Gannon said, coming up behind Paige and sliding an arm around her shoulders. "We're pretty serious."

"Well, well." Felicia's eyebrows winged up her forehead. "Personally, I'd like to say about friggin' time."

"My sentiments exactly," Gannon agreed.

"I'm gonna go spread the word. You two'll come out with us tonight, right? Celebrate?"

Gannon squeezed Paige's shoulder. "Sure." It came out as a croak, but hey, it was an affirmative.

Felicia bebopped out of the room whistling "Happy Birthday."

"See, princess? That wasn't so hard, was it?"

WINTER

CHAPTER

47

The house was taking shape, Gannon noted with pride as he nudged an open box of tile out of his way with the toe of his boot. It was slowly morphing from hellhole into blank canvas. Sunlight streamed through new replacement windows onto freshly sanded hardwood. The musty smell of stale air had been replaced with the fresh scents of sawdust and sweat. And progress was happening everywhere.

The framing on the upper floors for bedrooms, sitting rooms, and bathrooms was finished, and they would have Gannon's office and small workshop on the lower level framed in by midmorning. Then they'd let the drywallers loose on all four floors.

Drywall was always the turning point. They'd gutted the old plumbing, wiring, and HVAC, lugged out radiators, patched the floors that could be salvaged, and tamed the exterior. The roof was new. The landscaping was looking more like overgrown yard and less like an untouched jungle.

The irony was that between demo and drywall, very little of the renovation process was interesting to viewers.

Footage of his team running new electric or building HVAC ducts rarely ever made it to the screen. Audiences loved demo day and seeing new walls go up to define reimagined spaces, but they had no interest in what lay within those walls. The innards, as he liked to think of them, were the meat of any project. It wouldn't matter if you had shiny tile on your backsplash if your fifty-year-old plumbing was dumping water everywhere. But viewers generally didn't hold his views.

He ran his hand over the new studs that framed out his master bedroom.

The shooting schedule that had remained fairly light was ramping up to the long days that came with the design process.

But it was symbolic of a vision becoming reality. This was the point in the process when his crew stopped thinking he was insane and started seeing the potential.

Potential and vision were two things he was rarely wrong on. And that was what he saw in his relationship with Paige. He may have had to drag her into it kicking and screaming, but they worked better than either of them had anticipated. And he'd had rather high expectations there.

He'd gotten used to waking up to her, to finding her wrapped around him or vice versa. When they were awake and working, she kept him grounded, and he pushed her to stretch. She'd stretched into the role of director and surprised no one but herself when she rocked it. She'd worked behind the camera long enough that she was able to start crafting the stories in real time, making it easier for the editors in postproduction to flesh them out.

She'd impressed him with what she'd absorbed about the construction process and scheduled shoots with sensitivity to his crew that Gannon and the rest of his guys appreciated.

And on their off time, they'd built a tentative personal routine too, something he took as part and parcel of being in a relationship. They spent the dark of the night tangled up with each other, playing as hard as they worked. On their occasional days off, they'd fix a lazy brunch at his place, experimenting with simple recipes that they could handle, and spend the afternoons tag-teaming projects. When Becca was out of town, which was most of the time, Gannon lent Paige a hand with whatever tasks she trusted him with.

Her copious amount of research was being refined down and organized into a useable storyboard for the film. Her list of interview commitments was growing. And he liked being part of it all.

He'd come home after a beer with Flynn the other night only to be accosted at the front door by a bouncing Paige. She'd landed a commitment from a highly respected women's rights activist she'd thought was out of their league. And Gannon, with his newfound knowledge of women's rights pioneers, recognized not only the woman's name but also several of her more notable accomplishments.

They'd celebrated with pizza and wine and Cat at Nonni's. And as they laughed around the dining room table, Gannon realized he had everything he'd ever wanted. A brainy, sexy, stubborn woman who made him want to be a better man, one his grandmother and sister adored. A home designed to be the springboard into the beginning of the rest of his life. He had a thriving business that kept him engaged and interested and a fledgling furniture venture on the side. He worked with his hands, made things that became a part of family histories.

He had everything.

He just needed to freaking lock that shit down.

And besides Paige herself, there was only one other complication he could see fucking everything up.

The season finale of *Kings of Construction* was airing tomorrow night, which meant a viewing party with cast, crew, and suits at some swanky hotel bar. The event was casual—no cameras, no Meeghan Fucking Traxx ambushes. But there would be plenty of shoptalk and ass-kissing and other bullshit. Postproduction had run with the love triangle story line, which unfortunately played great with viewers. Attention on social media had ramped up steadily as the season progressed, and Gannon was predicting it would get even worse with the finale.

As far as he knew, Paige had been so buried in the new show and her documentary planning that she hadn't noticed the attention.

But there'd be no protecting her from it tomorrow when they aired the footage of Meeghan crashing the set. And that pissed him off.

He wasn't sure how Paige would play it. She'd managed to run this new show without too much interference from the production company that had screwed her over for entertainment. But going face-to-face with the shot callers tomorrow night felt like it was just asking for a fucking disaster.

His first instinct was to charge in there and threaten the shit out of everyone. It seemed to have finally worked with Meeghan. But as gratifying as that would be, it would create more issues for Paige than it would solve. Paige needed to stand on her own two feet and flash her own two middle fingers. But that didn't mean he wouldn't be standing right behind her, ready to kick ass should she ask him to.

Gannon hoped to God she would stand up for herself and take a few swings while she was up there.

He had to have faith, be patient. Two things that weren't anywhere near the top of his list of strengths. He shook his head, standing in the doorway of the master bedroom. He'd taken her here for their second first time. They'd christened nearly every room in the house since then. But he had more plans for her. Bigger ones. They just had to get through tomorrow night.

———

Paige steeled herself when the car rolled up to the hotel on West Forty-Sixth Street. She wiped her palms on the skinny slate-gray trousers she'd decided on. She would know everyone in the room, yet she couldn't shake the feeling that she was wandering into a lion's den.

The men who had pulled her strings all season long were behind the towering glass doors, probably swilling sixty-dollar glasses of scotch at the bar and patting themselves on the back for another hit season.

But they weren't expecting the new Paige. And that would play to her advantage. The new Paige had made her first appearance last month at the St. James Thanksgiving, an intimate, catered affair at her mother's house. In no uncertain terms, Paige had told both her mother and sister that she was dating Gannon and would be launching her new career as a documentary filmmaker. They were welcomed to agree or disagree with her choices because their opinions carried no weight. Her mother had icily changed the subject, but her sister had subtly raised her wineglass to Paige.

Paige considered tonight just another battle in the war.

She was meeting Gannon here, a tactical choice. She wasn't here to look like arm candy. She was here to kick ass. She hadn't yet told the brass that she wasn't coming back next season and why. The pay and experience from Gannon's new show gave her enough security that she could afford to walk away from *Kings of Construction* rather than sticking it out another season. She was done being pushed around, and they were about to find that out.

She stepped out onto the sidewalk and tied the belt of her wool trench tighter, warding off the December chill that was determined to settle into bones. Her red Mary Jane stilettos made a confident click as she approached the doors. The doorman, his cheeks rosy from the brisk air, let her in with a wink and a smile.

Fortified by the friendliness of a stranger, her choice of outfit, and her own inner rage, Paige was more than ready to face the enemy.

She strolled into the back bar, which Summit-Wingenroth had reserved, and ordered herself a bourbon. Glass in hand, she slipped out of her coat and joined the party, heading straight for her crew clustered around two high-top tables near the other end of the bar.

It was like old home week, catching up with Louis and Rico. Louis had just found out he was going to be a grandpa for the first time and was flashing the sonogram like it was an Oscar for cinematography. Rico had returned, relaxed and ready for a new project, after two weeks bumming around Cancun's hotel zone.

Mel and Sam regaled Paige with behind-the-scenes stories from their respective new projects and fished for details on her love life until Cat rescued her.

Ever fashionable in black leather leggings and a body-hugging sweater in a shade of burnt orange that no other human being could pull off, Cat dragged her back to the bar for another drink.

"Holding up?" Cat asked, waving her empty glass at one of the bartenders.

"So far so good. Haven't screamed 'I quit' or kicked anyone in the face yet."

354

Cat glanced down at Paige's shoes. "Ooh, good choice."

Within seconds, a fresh drink was placed in front of Cat despite the fact that her drink order fell behind several others. Paige grinned. "You ever get tired of being adored by millions?" she asked.

The flippant response she expected from her friend didn't come. Cat looked over both shoulders and then pulled her into a corner away from the rest of the party.

"Did you kill someone?" Paige demanded.

"No! Where do you get these ideas?" Cat rolled her eyes.

"With you, anything is possible."

"Well, let's see if you can predict this. Gannon's been talking about your documentary a lot, and I think you should interview me."

"Uh, what?" Cat was one of the highest paid new talents on the network, and with endorsement deals, she was sitting pretty.

"When Gannon and I were in talks with the network, they offered me half of what they offered Gannon."

"Are you kidding me?"

"I wish," Cat confessed. "They lowballed me, believing that either I'd feel so grateful just to be included that I'd accept or that Gannon wouldn't tell me what his deal was."

"That is crap," Paige hissed.

"Yeah, well, Gannon of course went to bat for me, and we ended up with equal deals. But then they tried it again at the beginning of this season. We were offered raises, but Gannon's was significantly higher. We threw down with the production company. Both equal or neither one of us would do the show."

"Cat, I'm so sorry. That's horrible."

Cat rolled her shoulders back. "I took Cindy, one of the VPs from Sumshit-Wingendick, out for drinks one night. Got her shit-faced."

Paige snorted at Cat's nickname for their production company. "What did she tell you?"

"That it wasn't a 'sexism' thing. It was just that production companies know from experience that women are usually willing to work for less, so it's standard operating procedure to lowball them. In cases when their male counterparts don't share their cashola info, most women don't even know to ask for more."

"You'd be willing to talk about this?" Paige asked. "You could get into serious trouble with the network."

"More than willing. If no one talks about this garbage, it's just going to keep happening. Just because I've got great tits and a vagina doesn't mean I'm worth less money or respect."

"Preach, sister!" Paige gave Cat a quick hug. "I'd love it if you'd be part of it. And we can talk to a lawyer beforehand to make sure you won't get into too much trouble. One of Becca's college roommates went to law school."

"Good. We can consult about Cindy too. We stay in touch, and she left the company midseason. She's interested in talking to you."

An insider with personal knowledge of industry discrimination against women? "I could freaking kiss you right now," Paige told Cat.

"Yes! Lesbians!" Cat punched her fist into the air in victory. "I knew you'd get sick of my brother eventually."

Paige laughed even as she felt the air in the room electrify. She didn't even bother questioning it anymore. It was just what Gannon did when he walked into a room. "Speak of the handsome devil," she breathed.

They studied each other from across the room, the air thick between them.

"I think he's waiting for you to make a move," Cat

whispered. "He doesn't want to force you into going public if you're not ready."

He'd do that for her. It would piss him off, but he'd play pretend if that was what he thought she wanted.

"I guess I'd better go give him a professional, cordial greeting then," Paige told Cat.

Cat grinned. "I guess you'd better. Oh, and, Paige?" Cat stopped her with a hand on her arm. "I'm proud of you."

"You know something, Cat? I'm proud of me too. Also, I love the crap out of you." She gave Cat a smacking kiss on her cheek and made the long walk across the bar to where Gannon waited for his beer, hands in the pockets of his very sexy leather jacket.

He didn't say anything when she stopped in front of him, but his eyes were far from quiet. She hadn't seen him since this morning, yet it felt like longer. She'd missed him, and she very well could have missed out on him.

If she'd learned anything this year, it was that Gannon was worth more than a job.

She stepped between his feet, looping her hands behind his neck and kissing him softly.

"Get a room," Felicia snorted good-naturedly.

Whistles sounded around them.

"Guess we know how the season ends," someone quipped.

Paige grinned up at Gannon. He settled his hands on her hips. "Hi, princess."

"Hi, Gannon."

"There you two are!" One of the suits who sat in on the preseason meetings bustled over, giving Gannon a hearty handshake. The man had stood next to her at the bar when she'd ordered a drink, but she'd been invisible until Gannon had laid lips on her.

Reading her like a book, Gannon squeezed her shoulder. "Good to see you, Raymond."

"Let's find that pretty sister of yours, and I'll buy my two stars a drink," Raymond suggested, patting the tiny beads of sweat off his forehead with a cocktail napkin.

"Paige!" Andy, casual as always in jeans and a flannel, wandered up.

"Andy! It's so good to see you." Paige slipped out of Gannon's grip for a hug. She'd grown quite fond of Andy over the season, and "fond of" had ratcheted up to indebted thanks to him giving her that out on the last day of filming.

"Do you have a minute?" he asked.

Paige glanced over her shoulder at Gannon, who was being dragged away by Raymond. He rolled his eyes at her and shrugged.

"Sure," she told Andy.

He guided her into the same corner Cat had, and Paige wondered what sort of confession she'd hear now.

"I'm glad to see you two patched things up," Andy said, tilting his beer in Gannon's direction.

"Me too," Paige agreed. She might be acknowledging the relationship, but she certainly wasn't ready to start spilling details.

"I heard you're doing a great job directing his new show," Andy continued, no more interested in hearing personal details than she was in spilling them.

"It's going well. I'm enjoying it."

He took a breath. "So I'm leaving the show. I'll be directing Drake Mackenrowe's new series starting this spring."

"Wow, congratulations. Drake's a great guy. I'm sure you'll enjoy working with him."

Andy nodded. "Thanks. Moving up the food chain, so to speak. Anyway, I gave them your name. For director for *Kings*."

Paige blinked. "You did?"

"We both know it should have been yours this season. But they've got plans for me and needed to season me up a bit. Anyway, I gave them your name, but…"

"But they weren't really interested," she guessed.

"I think they're more interested in continuing your on-screen story line. That's my guess. Ratings were huge this season. But yeah, they kind of gave me the pat on the head and shoved the suggestion under the rug."

"Well, thanks for letting me know. And thanks for putting in a good word for me."

Andy looked at her. "For what it's worth, it should be you."

"Yeah, it should be," Paige agreed.

———

They all crowded around the bar as the *Kings of Construction* theme song spilled forth from the TVs mounted over the bar. Paige hadn't watched any of the shows this season personally. She couldn't stomach the idea of watching herself on-screen in some highly edited, salacious storyline.

Instead, she'd made Becca watch each episode and give her the play-by-play.

Tonight would be the first episode she watched. And it was going to suck. Watching Meeghan strut out on set and lay those duck-billed lips on Gannon like he was her property? Paige could think of several things she'd rather be doing right now. The list included getting a root canal and Pap smear or having lunch at "the club" with her painfully conservative, half-deaf great-aunt Wilda who complained about the "disgraceful service" at full volume.

But she had Gannon at her back, Cat at her side, and a fresh bourbon in her hand. She could get through anything.

Watching episodes with the cast, crew, and postproduction was more entertaining than alone at home. Jokes and ribbing flew fast and furious. Even seeing her on-camera interviews wasn't too horrific. And when Meeghan Traxx slid out of her SUV, there were more than a few boos thrown out around the bar.

It was a relief when it was over. Viewing it wasn't quite as painful as living it, and Gannon's firm grip on her hips kept her from running screaming.

Cheers went up around the bar when the final credits rolled. One of the production company honchos got up and made a toast thanking them all for their commitment and how they were all part of the same team. No one was buying it, but it was par for the course.

Gannon's biggest fan, Raymond, caught up with her when she was putting her coat on.

"A really stellar season, sweetie," he said, gripping one of her hands between his two bear-claw palms.

It was now or never. "I hear Andy is moving on to another show," she said.

Raymond dropped her hand. "We're hoping you'll play a valuable part in the hiring process," he said, cheerfully spouting words that they both knew had no meaning here.

"Let's cut to the chase, Raymond. I'd like to be considered for director." Trigger pulled.

Raymond looked at her like she was a little kid who had just announced she wanted to be a hot dog when she grew up. He screwed up his lined face in a mask of sympathy. "Well, the thing is, we need someone we can count on as a director."

"What have I ever done that led you to believe I couldn't be counted on? I was on set the day after the accident," she reminded him.

"Well, now. I don't want to embarrass you, but a little birdy told me you had to leave the set because of Meeghan."

Paige took a cleansing breath in through her nose and out through her teeth, gritted in a smile. "You did your best to humiliate me on camera all season long for ratings, and I stayed and did my job because I'm invested in the show, in the families we serve, and in the Kings."

"That's another consideration. I understand that you and Gannon have a relationship. But that doesn't entitle you to director."

"Just like it doesn't entitle your college dropout nephew to a VP position in marketing?" Raymond sputtered and blustered, but Paige plowed on. "Listen, Ray. Me not having a penis doesn't hinder me from doing that job. Though the fact that Summit-Wingenroth has never hired a female director for any of its regular shows does make me wonder if you believe that genitalia is a requirement. I love working on this show, and I'll be the best damned director you've seen on it yet if you give me the chance."

"I really think we'd be more comfortable if you'd spend another year or two as field producer."

"I wouldn't be. It's taking a step backward from where I am now, and you've been pleased with my work on *King's Castle*. So really what you have to decide is whether you want to look for a field producer *and* a director for next season or just a field producer."

Raymond harrumphed, his cheeks flushed.

"Look, Raymond. I'm not trying to be a hard-ass here. I'm just telling you that I'm your best choice. You know it, I know it, and everyone in this room who I've worked with for two years knows it too. Think about it."

She patted him on the arm and strutted away.

CHAPTER
48

The chilled bottle of champagne was a spontaneous purchase, as were the mouth-watering brownies she'd found in the tiny scrap of bakery the market offered. After all, they were celebrating. Tomorrow was reveal day. Gannon would have his new home all to himself once the crews packed up and went their separate ways.

Paige had volunteered to pick up dinner and enhanced her salad choices with a hearty beef stew and fresh rosemary rolls while trying not to think about the "separate ways" thing too much.

Things were moving fast. Gannon's publicist had dropped the bomb that Meeghan and he had "parted ways several months ago"—a move that the production company had insisted waited until after the season finale aired—and that he and Paige were happily dating. Once the triangle was down to just two people, interest had cooled considerably. It was just days later that Summit-Wingenroth offered Paige director for season three of *Kings*. That news was followed immediately by the Welcome Home Network that Meeghan Traxx's show was not being renewed for another season.

Paige tucked everything into her market bags and sent a wave to the clerk on her way out the door. It was a friendly shop in a cute neighborhood walking distance to Gannon's apartment. The new house too, she supposed. Just in the opposite direction.

She started down the block, deciding she could pack mule everything back to the apartment without calling for a Lyft. The night was cold. Autumn had slipped away when they weren't looking and left the icy bloom of winter in its place. Christmas was in less than two weeks, and Paige had maintained her tradition of ordering all her shopping online and having gifts shipped directly to the recipients.

Well, except for Gannon. She'd picked up a few items here and there for him. And then felt silly about it. They hadn't discussed Christmas. She didn't even know if she'd see him on the day. They'd been so busy, so…committed. She'd spent more time with Gannon in the past weeks than she had any other person in her adult life. They worked side by side together all day into the night and then hurried back to his apartment for supper, showers, and sex.

Shooting on *King's Castle* wrapped tomorrow with the reveal. It would take most of the day to shoot, but it was all coming to an end. And Paige was going to miss it. The house, the crew, seeing Gannon every day. That was the part she was dreading the most.

Sure, as director of the new season of *Kings of Construction*, she'd have the pleasure of working with him every day again, but that wouldn't be until April. Late April. Between now and then, she and Becca would be crisscrossing the country and burying themselves in hundreds of hours of interview footage.

Would he wait for her while she lived her dream?

She was finally doing it. All those years paying her dues were going to pay off, and she would lead a project that she could be proud of regardless of how it was received. She was both excited and terrified.

Her phone vibrated against her hip, and she shuffled bags to dig it out. It was a text from Gannon.

Gannon: Meet me at the house. Need to show you something.

She frowned. That sounded like a problem to her. Were they missing furniture? Did something get damaged with the load-in? *Crap.* She hoped it was something they could at least shoot around.

Paige: I'm a couple blocks away. Be there in ten.

She looked at the time. If there was some kind of cosmetic issue, hardware stores would only be open for another hour or so, she gauged. She hauled bags and ass around the corner and down the street.

On the bright side, she wouldn't have to wait until tomorrow to see the finished product. She'd missed the entire afternoon of load-in today to shoot with Gannon on location at a thrift shop. They shot a cute bit with him shopping with Cat and Nonni for decor. The world didn't know it yet, but it was going to fall in love with a seventy-two-year-old.

Paige had been planning on sneaking out of Gannon's bed and into the house obscenely early in the morning just to get her own personal tour of the space to make sure nothing essential was missing on the call sheet.

But she could scratch the early call from her list now as the house loomed in front of her. On her approach, it looked as though every light in the house was on, making the entire place seem warm, inviting. Gannon might regret that, she laughed to herself. After having so many people in and out of the house for the past four months, he would probably prefer to throw the dead bolts and enjoy the solitude for a few weeks.

The lights they'd chosen in the courtyard, the ones that perfectly complemented the black iron lanterns on either side of the front door, cast a gold glow over the brick and beckoned her inside. She trudged up the front steps under the weight of the bags and was thankful when the doorknob turned easily in her hand. She deposited the bags inside the door and sighed.

It was perfection. The long, low leather couch faced the fireplace with its brick surround and rough-cut oak mantel. The cheery gas fire chased the chill from the room. The flat-screen TV—not nearly as colossal as the one he'd chosen for the second-floor sitting room—was on and showing the *King's Castle* logo.

The coffee table, which looked suspiciously like her own, stood between two overstuffed armchairs in a soft oatmeal fabric. The floors, oh the floors. The original hardwoods had been unsalvageable on this level, and Gannon had gone with a nearly gray random-width plank to lighten the space. It flowed from the front door all the way back into the kitchen.

He'd added just a bit of drama by painting the walls on this floor a shade of sea blue. It played against the gray of the flooring just as she'd thought when he'd shown her the samples. Rich, masculine, and peaceful. Gannon could come home and breathe easy here, shutting out the rest of the world on the other side of the front door.

She moved into the dining space, which was now open to the living room and kitchen. Between each room, he'd done casement openings with grand pieces of trim stained to match the original woodwork of the rest of the house.

The dining table and benches he'd built were here as well as the buffet and finished shelves. He'd been right about the metal shelf supports. Again, masculine and contemporary, playing off the historical building. On the wall opposite the buffet was a gallery wall of family photos.

Paige frowned, stepping closer. There was one of her here. The one he'd had in his apartment. And another. This one snapped from behind while she helped Francesca with the dishes after their pizza celebration. There were others—Cat and Gannon growing up, their parents mugging for the camera on the hood of a station wagon, and a large framed black-and-white photo of Francesca and her groom on their wedding day. Pop, she presumed. Paige pressed her fingertips to the frame. With Gannon, family would always be front and center where they deserved to be.

In her mother's dining room was a lovely Kara Walker original in black-and-white.

The realization, swift and hot, caught Paige unaware.

Her mother hadn't let anything stand between her and success. Not her daughters and certainly not her relationship. She'd known what was important to her, what would get her there, and what would take her further away from it.

But was Leslie St. James happy? A loud voice inside Paige asked the question. Was happiness the same as success?

The answer inside her was a resounding no. Success wasn't the same as happiness. Neither was satisfaction, and that was where her mother had made her fatal mistake.

Paige stared at Gannon's wall and felt her heart turn over.

There was a shot of the two of them standing on the front steps of this very house grinning at each other. The doors were open, and she could just make out the chaos of a filming day within. He'd put her on his wall, pulled her into his family, and made her fall in love with him.

She'd had no intention of letting any of it happen, yet here she was with a full heart and a need to tell him, tell the world!

Paige pressed a hand to her chest. Instead of an ache, there was a glow as warm and true as the rising sun. She *loved* him, and this was how it felt. Knees weak, she sank down on the bench at the dining table and tried to catch her breath.

She could do this. She could love him and film her documentary and make a difference. She could do it all. Somehow. It didn't have to be one or the other. She would find a way to make it work.

There was so much they needed to talk about. Living arrangements, for instance. There was no way in hell she could go back to her teeny apartment knowing Gannon was rattling around here with four gorgeous floors all to himself.

Gannon.

He was here somewhere. She started for the stairs and called his name.

But her phone dinged in her hand, drawing her attention to the screen.

Gannon: TV in the living room. Push Play.

"Gannon, I need to talk to you!" she yelled up the stairs. His text reply was succinct.

Gannon: Just shut up and push Play.

"It's not like me being in love with you is important or anything," she muttered under her breath. Resigned to whatever game he was playing, Paige returned to the living room and snatched up the remote she found on the couch.

She pushed Play, and the *King's Castle* logo disappeared. In its place rolled raw footage from *Kings of Construction* season one, episode one. Gannon was standing under an oak tree, arms crossed, giving a one-on-one to the camera, when he got distracted by something off-screen and lost his train of thought.

"I've loved you since this exact moment," Gannon's gravelly voice announced in a voiceover. "You were just off camera, and something Lou said made you laugh. The sunlight was hitting you like you were in a spotlight. You had this ratty hoodie on and gym shorts that showed off about a mile of those gorgeous legs, and then you turned around and yelled at me to hurry it up. I didn't know at the time that it was love, but my feelings for you haven't changed since that day."

For the second time that night, Paige went weak in the knees. She sank down onto the cool leather of the couch and tried to comprehend. The screen switched to Gannon sitting exactly where Paige was now.

"So that's how long I've loved you. Twenty-one months, twelve days, and"—he checked his watch—"ten hours." He gave her that arrogant grin from on-screen. "I didn't want to love you, so I did my best to get under your skin like you were under mine."

Clips began to roll of their arguments, including one of Gannon grinning as she stalked off camera away from him. The video continued with Gannon on set wearing a different tool belt than his usual one.

"This was the day it was two hundred degrees in the shade, and you showed up on set in those short cutoffs and a tank. I had a hard-on all day and had to hide it. I don't think I was fooling anyone. Not where you were concerned."

Paige pressed her fingers to her lips and watched as she came on-screen. It was her first one-on-one, and she was fussing with the body mic. "I don't want to do this," TV Paige muttered. Another few seconds of fidgeting, and then she gave an eye roll and a heavy sigh before slapping on her camera smile and delivering the necessary monologue.

She could hear the smile in Gannon's voice. "I love how you can be so pissed off and still function like an adult. I've learned a lot from you, and maybe I haven't told you that enough. But I have, and I hope you know that."

Her smile was watery now, and she swiped at a tear with the back of her hand. The next scene faded in. It was Gannon on the screen in a large workshop somewhere, talking to a welder behind a computer. The camera bobbled, and Mel, face pale and hands shaking, stepped on-screen holding a cell phone.

"What? What is it?"

Mel took a shaky breath. "There was an accident on set. Paige—"

He grabbed Mel by the shoulders, and Paige saw the panic in those hazel eyes. "Is she okay?"

"I don't know." Mel shook her head. "Andy texted, and he's not answering his phone. 'It's bad' is all he said."

"Keys!" Gannon yelled.

Lou panned to Gannon running out the door, and a moment later, tires squealed in the parking lot.

"That was the night I told you I loved you for the first time. I'd finally figured it out by then. You were sound asleep, drooling on my chest. And I told you. I should have told you every day since then, and I'm sorry I didn't, but if you'll let me, I'd like to make up for it," Gannon said from the screen.

Paige's tears were flowing freely now.

The scene changed again. This time it was Gannon ordering an injured Paige into her chair behind the camera. And then another of Gannon standing guard during Paige's one-on-one talking to the camera about the accident. He stood like a bodyguard just off camera, arms crossed, chewing on his thumbnail until he'd decided Eddie was done.

"Okay, that's enough," he interjected briskly. "Come on, Paige. I'll take you back to the hotel."

She remembered it even as she watched it. She argued with him, but Gannon won. While Cat and Rico were packing her into the truck, Lou caught Gannon taking a phone call on camera.

"No. I'm taking her back," he said, his tone leaving no room for argument for whoever was on the other end. "She needs her rest. You find me anyone on this show or on your damn network who works harder than her. She gave you face time. You got the gory details. Leave it alone, or I'll make it an issue. You're not going to exploit her pain for ratings."

He hung up, looking like he wanted to crush the phone with his bare hands. But Paige saw him catch a glimpse of her waving from the passenger seat, and his expression softened.

"Let's go, princess." They'd fooled no one, Paige realized. Looking at the footage after the fact, they couldn't have hidden their feelings from a blind man. There was too much there, and that was worth hanging on to.

When the scene changed again, Paige flinched. She knew exactly what day it was when she saw herself watching the SUV roll up to the curb. The camera captured Paige's ashen face when Meeghan strutted up to Gannon and laid one on him.

"You might wonder why I'm showing you this when you already witnessed it firsthand. What I wanted you to see was this…"

Meeghan had sauntered over to look at the footage, Paige had taken off, and Gannon had unfrozen. Swiping a hand over his mouth, he wiped the layers of gloss away and stormed over to her.

"Aren't you happy to see me, sexy?"

"What the hell are you doing here?" he demanded. But Gannon wasn't looking at her. He was looking for someone else. "What part of 'stay the hell away from me' don't you understand?" he demanded.

Meeghan sidled up to him again. "Don't tell me you don't want to play," she purred.

Gannon's face was a mask of anger and revulsion. "I told you before, I want nothing to do with you, so you'd better get used to that fact."

The voiceover began again. "Paige, I know we talked it through, but I needed you to see, really see that there hasn't been room in my life for anyone but you since the day I met you. And that's why I did this house for you."

Paige brought her hands to her mouth, shaking her head.

"I saw it, and I knew it was yours." He gave a little half grin. "Ours."

"Oh my God." It all made sense now. He'd asked her opinion on every room. She'd chosen half the finishes in the house and had zero suspicions. How had she not seen it?

"I know it's a lot to take in," the Gannon in the video said. "But the first few times I told you I loved you didn't go well. So I wanted to make sure that I got it right this time."

Paige's tears weren't silent anymore.

"Paige?"

She turned at her name and saw Gannon, in the flesh, standing behind the couch. She swiped at the tears that just wouldn't seem to stop falling.

"I love you, Gannon." She blurted out the words with no preamble, no buildup. But there was no keeping them locked in anymore. "I'm in love with you, and I didn't realize it until I saw your dining room wall."

"*Our* dining room wall." He smiled and strolled around the couch, his hands in his pockets.

"You're insane. This can't be happening." Paige shivered, wanting to reach out and melt into his arms.

"Here. Catch," he said. He slipped one hand from his pocket and threw something to her.

She caught it out of midair and held it up. It was a key chain with keys on it. "For the house?"

He nodded, silent and waiting.

She could barely see through her tears. The keys were warm in her hand. She brushed her thumb over them and felt something other than a key. Holding the key chain up again, Paige gasped.

The diamond was a fat solitaire with a halo of smaller diamonds on a simple band. She bent at the waist, desperate for breath and not believing her reality.

"I'll get down on one knee if you want me to," Gannon offered. "But we both know it's not my style. So how about I tell you what I want, and you tell me if it's something that fits."

She nodded, not trusting her voice.

"I want you to be my wife. I want us to work really fucking hard. I want to have kids with you. I don't know how many, but they'll probably be loud and stubborn like us. I want to call you first whenever I have news. I want to spend the rest of my life just trying to keep up with you." He shoved a hand through his short hair. He was nervous. Gannon King was shaking in his boots. "You're the best person I've ever known in my life, and if you tell Nonni that, I'll call you a dirty liar. But you *are* the best, Paige. You're smart and driven and so damn sexy and strong. You put up with me without crying all the time—except for right now. And I can't think of anyone in the world I'd rather share my life and this house with."

Paige tried to mop at the tears with the sleeve of her sweater, still clutching the ring in her hand.

"And just so you know," Gannon said, "the house is yours. Even if you say no. But I hope the memories of sex on the kitchen counter would haunt you forever if you go that route. So what do you say?"

"You propose to me by showing me footage of another woman kissing you, and then you call me a dirty liar and threaten to haunt me if I say no."

"Well, if you're gonna overlook all the good stuff, then yeah."

The smile felt like it would split her face. "I was just making sure before I said yes."

"Yes? You're saying yes?" Gannon stared hard at her.

"I'm saying hell yes." She threw herself into his arms, and he caught her, swinging her around.

"Thank fucking god. I thought I was going to throw up."

She cupped his face in her hands and kissed him. "Please tell me the bedroom is finished."

His gaze warmed. "Let's go look," Gannon said, carrying her toward the stairs.

"Wait! I want the ring on."

"I'll put it on when you're not wearing anything else," he promised, jogging up the stairs with her in his arms.

"Gannon? Thank you for not putting this on camera."

He squeezed her a little tighter. "They've had enough pieces of us. This is just for you and me, princess."

EPILOGUE

I hate wearing these things." Gannon scowled at his reflection in the hotel mirror as if he was in pain. His fingers were trying to loosen the tie he'd just tightened.

"But you look so good in them." Paige stroked her hands over the broad shoulders under his black suit jacket.

He snagged her wrist and pulled her around to face the mirror in front of him. "Speaking of looking good." He nibbled at her neck.

"Do *not* leave a mark," she ordered. "We're not going to a wedding with me sporting a hickey."

"What if it's in a place that no one else will see?" Gannon asked, his fingers edging the wide strap of her blush-pink dress off her shoulder. "Why are we going to a wedding again when we could be spending the afternoon in bed?" he asked, tasting her skin and drawing a crop of goose bumps to the surface.

Paige dropped her head back against his shoulder and smiled. "Not everyone wants to elope like we did, Mr. King."

"Mmm. Mrs. King. I still like the sound of that," he murmured, slipping one hand into the deep V at the front of her dress.

"You should be getting used to it by now," Paige teased, spinning in his arms to wrap hers around his neck. "It's been ten months. I think we can spare a few hours outside the bedroom."

"You're not going to make me feel guilty about wanting to spend as much time with you as I can before you have to take off on your screening tour."

Her documentary, shot over an intense three-month period, was finally wrapping up in postproduction and due to debut in a month's time. Her baby was being brought to life, and it was better than she'd ever dreamed. And her directorial debut season of *Kings of Construction* had the highest ratings so far that the show had ever seen.

"It was my understanding that you'd be accompanying me on my tour," Paige said, biting at his bottom lip.

"Of course I'm going. But it's going to be like shooting *Kings* all over again. I'll never have you all to myself."

She laughed and pulled him closer. "We made do then. We'll make do again." She felt his fingers at the zipper of her dress. "Don't even think about it," Paige warned. "We're already late."

"Where are you going?" he demanded when she made a dash for the door.

"I just want to call and check in with Becca at the office before we go."

Gannon had outfitted one of the bedrooms on the fourth floor into a state-of-the-art office for her and Becca. They'd nicknamed it "heaven" and had spent hours and hours up there filming interviews and reviewing footage.

"Don't even think about it," Gannon teased. "We're already late."

They arrived just before the glossy white doors to the Portland Unitarian Church closed and scooted into a pew next to her sister. "It's about time," the ever-punctual Dr. Lisa St. James said pointedly.

"Good to see you too, Lis," Gannon said, pressing a peck to his sister-in-law's cheek before slinging his arm around Paige's shoulders.

"He looks happy," Paige said, nodding at the groom, who beamed like a beacon at the front of the sanctuary.

"He's got a lot to be happy about," Lisa said and nodded.

Paige dug into her clutch for her tissue stash and offered one to her sister. Lisa shook her head.

"Softy," Gannon whispered in Paige's ear, his thumb caressing the bare flesh of her shoulder.

"Weddings always get me. And if memory serves, you got a little misty-eyed at ours," she pointed out.

"Allergies," he claimed.

The music rose and the doors to the back of the church opened. Malia, in a flouncy pink dress and a tiara that sat on her fuzzy new growth of hair, strutted down the aisle. Her pink high-tops were visible under the miles of tulle in her skirt. She skipped and then ran, jumping into the arms of the man at the end of the aisle.

Gannon cleared his throat, and Paige elbowed him in the gut. "Yeah, try not to tear up, tough guy."

"Crap." Lisa snatched one of the tissues from Paige and dabbed at the corners of her eyes.

"Just think, Lis. This wedding wouldn't be happening if it weren't for you," Gannon whispered.

"All I did was match a patient to a trial." But there was a slight curve to her lips.

The church doors opened again, and this time they all rose as Carina, resplendent in yards of ivory, floated down the aisle. The designer gown was fitted to her lean frame as if it had been sewed onto her body. Miles of veil trailed behind her. She was a breathtaking bride with eyes only for her daughter and soon-to-be husband, the man who had saved Malia's life.

She was so happy. There wasn't a person in the building who couldn't sense the radiating joy.

Paige didn't even bother trying to stem the happy tears.

———

"Gannon! Paige!" Malia barreled across the dance floor and jumped into Gannon's waiting arms.

"Hey there, pipsqueak." He spun her around, lifting her toward the tulle- and light-draped beams above their heads, and she squealed.

"I'm so glad you guys are here. Did you see my shoes? Aren't they awesome?"

"They are awesome," Paige said, returning Malia's one-armed hug. "How's school going?"

"Good! I'm playing baseball! I'm *really* good," she announced.

"I bet you are," Gannon said, setting her back down. "So what do you think of your new stepdad?"

Malia looked over her shoulder to where her parents were posing in front of the bar. "He's kind of the best. And he's super smart. He says I can be a doctor like him if I want to but that I shouldn't make up my mind too early."

Paige laughed. "He sounds like the best."

Carina and Dr. Singh waved in their direction.

"I'd better go," Malia said. "I want to make sure I get a good piece of cake." She dashed off, her pink sneakers squeaking cheerfully on the wood floor.

Gannon took Paige in his arms again, moving to the music. "God, I love that kid."

"You'd be a horrible human being if you didn't," Paige pointed out.

"Maybe we should have some," he said, his face serious but eyes dancing.

"Kids?" Paige clarified.

"Yeah," he said, guiding her in a slow spin. "Maybe three?"

Paige grinned, her heart swelling in her chest. "Three kids. That's a lot."

"Well, we've got all those bedrooms at home," he teased.

He leaned her back for a dip.

"It's a good thing, because I found out this morning that we're going to need one of those bedrooms."

She saw it, the question followed immediately by the spark of joy. He pulled her upright faster than necessary, and she fell against him laughing.

"You're not fucking with me?"

Paige shook her head, more happy tears clouding her eyes. "Nope. You're going to be a daddy."

He hugged her to his chest and then cupped her face in his hands. The music and lights and laughter faded into the background.

"God, I hope it's a girl," he said, sealing his wish with a kiss.

THE CHRISTMAS FIX

Cat stabbed the Answer button on her phone's screen while the makeup artist filled in her right eyebrow. "Hey, Laur. Tell me we're a go for shooting," Cat demanded.

"Put your eyebrow down, or I'm going to make you look like you have caterpillars crawling across your forehead," Archie warned her.

Cat wrinkled her nose at the makeup artist and smoothed the muscles of her forehead.

"Yeah, about that," Lauren began. "I don't think you're going to like this."

"They said *no*? Who in their right minds would say no to having their destroyed town rebuilt in time for Christmas for a network special?"

"I know," Lauren replied.

But Cat was on a righteous roll. "They don't have to wait for FEMA money, and we can guaran-damn-tee that their

Christmas Festival will happen *and* be bigger than ever. That's even more revenue for the town." Cat's voice echoed around the white walls of the hair and makeup room.

"I know. I know. Preaching to the choir, my friend," Lauren said.

"I shouldn't have gone straight to the network with this one. But who knew the town was run by a dumbass?" Cat lamented without moving her lips as Archie slathered gloss over them.

"Well, you see, Cat. I think it's a dumbass with a grudge. Apparently when you were in Merry for that episode of *Kings of Construction*, you ruffled some feathers."

"What exactly does that mean?" Cat demanded, drumming her freshly painted nails on the arm of the makeup chair.

"The city manager felt that the show turned his town into a circus."

Cat snorted. "We renovated the home of one of the town's most beloved families after they were hit by a drunk driver and nearly lost everything. That same house has two feet of standing water in it! I'm not going to just stand by and do nothing!"

"You sound mad."

"We saw the town. We were there. Half of Merry, Connecticut, was underwater two days ago," Cat argued.

"I know. I know. I was right there."

"Why in the hell would some city suit decide they don't need this?"

"Well, among a few other comments, the city manager's main refrain was he didn't want some network profiting off the trauma of his neighbors."

"As if I would let that happen!"

Archie poked Cat in the forehead with a makeup brush. "Stop it with the expressions until I get this shit on your face."

Cat stuck her tongue out at him but continued more calmly. "I want his phone number," she told Lauren.

"Are you sure that's a good idea? I mean, the guy still seems pissed about you and that bar fight when you were in town."

"*Bar fight?*" Cat's voice hit a high note that had Archie bobbling his makeup palette. "He's going to hold *that* against me? Obviously, he's never seen a bar fight before, or he doesn't believe a woman has the right to defend herself. Either way, I'm going to have to educate him."

"I don't know, Cat. He seems to think you're basically an Antichrist TV star who wants to swoop in and exploit his town's disaster for ratings."

"I hope you're paraphrasing."

Lauren laughed nervously. "To be fair, I think the guy is stressed to the breaking point. I mean, you saw how bad the damage was."

"Your pregnancy hormones are making you soft," Cat sighed. "Text me his number."

"Okay, but—"

"I'll handle this with tact," Cat promised. "I'm getting all the 'you're a big, stupid idiot' insults out now. Just don't say anything to the network yet about this city manager guy's refusal. We're doing a Christmas special, and it's going to be in Merry."

"Good luck. Please don't make him cry."

Cat disconnected and leaned back in her chair.

"You shouldn't yell at pregnant ladies," Archie commented, holding Cat's jaw in his hand as he swooped in with fake lashes. "Do not move a muscle."

"I wasn't yelling at Lauren. She allows me to freely express my displeasure at things that are stupid, like a city manager refusing what could be a golden ticket to saving his town's entire tourism income for the year."

"Uh-huh." His fingers deftly pressed the lashes in place.

"The town is devastated. Their huge moneymaker is the Christmas Festival every year, and government money isn't going to get them back on their feet by December."

"Mmm," Archie said, sweeping a bronzer into the hollows of her cheeks.

Cat's phone buzzed in her lap with a text from Lauren.

Lauren: "Here's his number. Noah Yates. Be nice!"

"Be nice," Cat mumbled.

"Stop pouting," Archie insisted. He swept the cape off her and angled her toward the mirror. "You're too gorgeous to be grumpy."

She eyed his handiwork in the mirror. She'd trudged into the studio still half-asleep with yesterday's hair spray wreaking havoc on her hastily tied ponytail, and now she looked like a cover-worthy model. Or at least a promo-worthy TV star.

"You're a freaking genius, Archie. You and your godlike hands and your magical potions."

"Nothing a gay man and his abiding love of Sephora can't fix." Archie checked his watch. "You've got five before they come pounding on the door demanding your hotness in front of the camera. Go make your call and eviscerate your city manager."

Cat blew him a kiss, careful not to smudge the violet lip gloss he'd so expertly applied to her mouth. "Will do."

She ducked out of the room into the hallway. They were shooting promos for her solo show's second season to run in magazines. Apparently, hosting a home renovation show when you were a woman called for her to be decked out in four-inch Jimmy Choos and a gorgeous, fitted dress the color of cranberries. She didn't mind it. If some designer duds—that she was totally keeping after the shoot—caught the eye of an audience and made even one little girl think that maybe she could wield a sledgehammer or a circular saw, then Cat considered her work done.

If people wanted to keep putting her in the pretty Barbie box, she was just going to keep cutting and smashing her way out over and over again until they learned their lesson. She may be pretty, but that didn't mean she was stupid or incapable or the slightest bit dependent on anyone. Catalina King had clawed her way up the ranks of reality TV to not just star in her own show but produce it as well.

And there was nothing she loved more than a chance to use her face to make a difference. Sure, it opened her up to public scrutiny. Two weeks ago, on a whim, she'd dyed her platinum locks a sexy caramel color with highlights. Twitter had lost its damn mind. People were still debating whether blond was better.

Cat took the attention in stride. Her life was perfect. A challenging job, a jet-setting lifestyle, a never-ending parade of new, interesting men available for casual consumption, and a project in the new year that would take her beyond TV stardom into something that really mattered.

But between now and then stood Merry.

She dialed Yates and tapped out an impatient beat with the toe of her shoe as the phone rang. After a handful of rings, it went to voicemail. She disconnected and called back.

"This is Noah," the man on the other end barked.

"Mr. Yates," Cat began. "This is Catalina King."

She heard an honest-to-God growl from the other end of the call. "I don't have time for this," he snapped.

"Frankly, Mr. Yates, your town doesn't have time."

Cat heard conversation happening in the background.

"Listen, whoever the hell you are," Noah snapped. "I'm trying to dry out an entire town here and figure out exactly how extensive the damage is. I've got people who might not be able to return to their homes for months and a town that is losing hope. We don't need some TV show coming in and churning out some sob story for ratings and advertising."

"What *do* you need?" Cat asked coolly.

"I need you to take no for an answer so I can get back to work. You're taking up time that I need to dedicate to more important things."

"Then maybe next time, don't answer the phone," she suggested sarcastically.

"Great idea," he snapped back.

"Before you continue your tirade, think about what you're turning down here. We're offering you a chance to rebuild quickly. The chance to get Merry back on its feet in time for Christmas. I know how much money comes into your town between Thanksgiving and New Year's Eve. We can help make sure that the park is up and running—"

"We don't need your bullshit pity, and I sure as hell don't need some reality TV star prancing around breaking her nails and punching my residents in the face while turning my town into some sideshow. We're good. We don't need you." And with, that he disconnected the call.

Cat took a deep breath and glared down at her phone. Noah Yates had no idea who he just pissed off. But he sure as hell was going to find out. She was going to save Merry's Christmas whether Noah wanted her to or not.

"Cat?" A production assistant poked her head out of a doorway. "The photographer's ready for you."

The real question was: Was Noah Yates ready for her?

Author's Note

Dear Reader,

OMG, let me tell you, that shower scene from this book has been in my head forever, haunting me! Not just the sexiness part but the whole vulnerability thing. I *love* writing couples who push each other's buttons so when they do finally let down their guards, it's even more intense.

I also loved how Paige and Gannon helped each other grow in necessary and interesting ways. That to me is the definition of a solid couple.

And of course, there's the proposal. He *bought and designed* an entire house just for her? Yeah, that's hotness.

Paige's work issues were partly inspired by Jennifer Lawrence's essay on *LennyLetter* about her male costars making a buttload more money than she was and the responsibility she felt for not fighting harder for herself. I think it's an issue that many of us can relate to (not negotiating for millions but being afraid to tell the world what we want because of the labels we'll face).

Anyway, thanks for picking up *Mr. Fixer Upper*! It's my tenth book. Can you believe that? ME NEITHER. If you loved it, please feel free to leave a review. Think I'm a fiction-writing genius? Sign up for my newsletter and stay up to date on all new releases. And I love talking to readers on Facebook and Instagram, so find me and we'll chat!

Thank you again, amazing reader, for spending your time on a book I wrote!

Xoxo,

Lucy

Acknowledgments

Mr. Lucy for your tireless dedication to details that would annoy, bore, and distract me.

Dawn Harer and Amanda Edens for their ability to know what I meant to type.

Inspiration, that fickle bitch, for bringing Gannon King to life on the page, already full formed.

Netflix for *House of Cards*, *The Unbreakable Kimmy Schmidt*, and *Arrested Development*.

Taco Bell for the Cheesy Gordita Crunch.

My readers for always being enthusiastic cheerleaders.

About the Author

Lucy Score is a #1 *New York Times*, *USA Today*, and *Wall Street Journal* bestselling author. She grew up in a literary family who insisted that the dinner table was for reading and earned a degree in journalism. She writes full-time from the Pennsylvania home she and Mr. Lucy share with their obnoxious cat, Cleo. When not spending hours crafting heartbreaker heroes and kick-ass heroines, Lucy can be found on the couch, in the kitchen, or at the gym. She hopes to someday write from a sailboat, ocean-front condo, or tropical island with reliable Wi-Fi.

Sign up for her newsletter and stay up on all the latest Lucy book news.
And follow her on:
Website: Lucyscore.com
Facebook at: lucyscorewrites
Instagram at: scorelucy
TikTok: @lucyferscore
Readers Group at: Lucy Score's Binge Readers Anonymous
Newsletter signup: